BORN TO FLY

Hawk Hunter scanned the F-16's instrument panel, took a deep breath, and waited.

Then it came to him. *The Feeling.* It was there every time he took off.

Other pilots strap in, do the checklist, prepare to take off. Fight the nervous energy that always creeps in.

Hunter would melt into the machinery. His brain linked with the on-board computer. His hands and feet became extensions of the flaps and stabilizers. His eyes became the radar; his ears the radio. He *was* the plane.

The radio crackled and a voice gave him the go-ahead to take off. Instantly, Hunter lifted the air brakes and was moving forward, gathering speed. 100 knots, 120, 150. His heart was pounding—a promise he had made to himself was coming true.

He pulled back on the control stick and the F-16 streaked off the ground and up into the cloudless sky.

**TOP-FLIGHT AERIAL ADVENTURE
FROM ZEBRA BOOKS!**

WINGMAN (2015, $3.95)
by Mack Maloney
From the radioactive ruins of a nuclear-devastated U.S. emerges a hero for the ages. A brilliant ace fighter pilot, he takes to the skies to help free his once-great homeland from the brutal heel of the evil Soviet warlords. He is the last hope of a ravaged land. He is Hawk Hunter . . . Wingman!

WINGMAN #2: THE CIRCLE WAR (2120, $3.95)
by Mack Maloney
A second explosive showdown with the Russian overlords and their armies of destruction is in the wind. Only the deadly aerial ace Hawk Hunter can rally the forces of freedom and strike one last blow for a forgotten dream called "America"!

WINGMAN #3: THE LUCIFER CRUSADE (2232, $3.95)
by Mack Maloney
Viktor, the depraved international terrorist who orchestrated the bloody war for America's West, has escaped. Ace pilot Hawk Hunter takes off for a deadly confrontation in the skies above the Middle East, determined to bring the maniac to justice or die in the attempt!

GHOST PILOT (2207, $3.95)
by Anton Emmerton
Flyer Ian Lamont is driven by bizarre unseen forces to relive the last days in the life of his late father, an RAF pilot killed during World War II. But history is about to repeat itself as a sinister secret from beyond the grave transforms Lamont's worst nightmares of fiery aerial death into terrifying reality!

Available wherever paperbacks are sold, or order direct from the Publisher. Send cover price plus 50¢ per copy for mailing and handling to Zebra Books, Dept. 2015, 475 Park Avenue South, New York, N.Y. 10016. Residents of New York, New Jersey and Pennsylvania must include sales tax. DO NOT SEND CASH.

WINGMAN

BY MACK MALONEY

ZEBRA BOOKS
KENSINGTON PUBLISHING CORP.

ZEBRA BOOKS

are published by

Kensington Publishing Corp.
475 Park Avenue South
New York, NY 10016

Fourth printing: June, 1988

Printed in the United States of America

PROLOGUE

He knew the airplane was coming.

It was an early spring day. The sun was shining. The whole mountain was melting, coming to life again after the long, cold winter.

The airplane was still some distance away, but the sound was unmistakable. He closed his eyes and saw it. Small engine, no more than 200 horse. It was a Piper Cub—10, maybe 15 miles to the southeast. One of the airplane's pistons was misfiring slightly.

He waited.

For two years, one month and six days he had lived on the top of the New Hampshire mountain. The camp—nothing more than a shack with a bed and a wood stove—had belonged to his family years before. He had visited there many times while growing up, so he knew the isolated mountain area well. But two years of trapping rabbits, opening cans and drinking nothing but stream water or melted snow was no life for a fighter pilot. He hadn't seen or talked to a soul in all that time. And until he had heard this airplane approaching, he wasn't sure that there was anything flying anywhere. He wasn't even sure if there were any people left.

Two years—a long time to be alone. When he first climbed the mountain, he was convinced it was to escape the chaos he envisioned would sweep the country. Did it ever happen? Did America commit national suicide after it lost World War III? Lost, not on the battlefield, but by the actions of a Russian mole who waited until America and its allies were victorious before he showed his true colors? Would he have felt differently if the traitor had been someone other than the Vice President?

He waited another hour before the airplane came into view. It was at the other end of the valley, flying slowly, being buffeted by the mountain cross winds. As it flew closer, he saw it was towing something—a sign like those once used to carry advertisements. Even with his extraordinary vision, it was still too far away for him to read. How strange it would be, he thought, if the first plane he had seen since the end of the war was pulling a sign for suntan oil.

Two years—it was a long time to think. That Christmas Eve. He had just arrived at Cape Canaveral to begin pilot training for the Space Shuttle. It was then he had heard of the Russian attack on Western Europe. SCUD missiles. Tens of thousands of them. Millions of Europeans dead—not by nuclear holocaust, but by nerve gas. A massive invasion of Western Europe had followed. Then China had been nuked. The Free World had struck back. He had been ordered to rejoin his unit, the 16th Tactical Fighter Wing, known in peacetime as the famous Thunderbirds aerobatic demonstration team. A day later they had been in Rota, Spain, bombing up for their first mission against the invading Red armies. War had broken out all around the world. Any country who'd had a dispute with its neighbor had decided to have it out now. Great battles raged; the earth was in flame. But nowhere had the horror compared with the Battle for Western Europe. There had been everything from hand-to-hand combat on the ground to killer laser satellites duelling high above in deep space. His squadron had been in the middle, flying above the killing fields, battling anything and everything that the Russians put into the air. For two months it had gone on relentlessly. But finally, it had been in the air that the battle had been won. The final push. Two straight days. Thirty-seven straight sorties for him. No sleep. No food. Living only on the adrenaline rush one gets when his country is at stake. It had been the largest air battle ever fought. More than 4000 aircraft, jammed into less than 200 square miles of airspace. It had been incredible. Even the soldiers on the ground stopped fighting to watch. And in the end, it had been the air forces of the Free World, led by the Americans, which won the battle. But America had still lost the war . . .

As the Piper flew even closer, he saw the tow sign's

words were made up of letters of different styles and uneven shapes. It was apparently cut from several different types of airborne ads. The thing looked like a flying ransom note.

Two years—it was a long time to spend on theories. When did the Vice President decide it was time to turn? Was it after the ceasefire had been agreed to? Or after the armistice had been signed? Or had it been after his henchmen assassinated the President and his cabinet? No matter. When the battles were over and America wasn't looking, he had turned off the Star Wars defense just long enough for 150 Russian nuclear missiles to obliterate America's MX and Titan ICBMs while they sat in their silos. The surprise attack had blown away most of the country's mid-section along with the nuclear deterrent. Another sneak attack on America. Had it been the only way the enemies of freedom could defeat her?

The Piper was now right in front of him, slow enough so he could read the sign: HUNTER—REPORT TO OTIS—JONES

It sounded crazy. Was the message for someone who was out shooting deer and for some reason had to report back to a guy named Otis at the request of Mr. Jones? Who were they? Game wardens?

Then, as the plane flew on past, it hit him. Could *he* be the "Hunter" they were looking for? Had he been up on the mountain so long that he didn't even recognize his own name? Otis *had* to mean Otis Air

Force Base, out on Cape Cod. And that meant there was only one Jones it could be—*General* Seth Jones, hero of the European Theater. The man the allies had followed into battle against the Russian Air Force. The man who had almost single-handedly won the war. The man on whose wing he had flown for two years in peacetime with the Thunderbirds and two months in wartime with the 16th. Jones was the man who had nominated him for the space program. The man who flew with his father in Viet Nam. The man who had watched over him since the day his parents' plane crashed. The man who had named him his own wingman the very first day he had climbed into his F-16. And now Jones wanted him to report to Otis.

He was packed and gone by noon.

CHAPTER ONE

It took almost three weeks, but he finally reached Otis. The cold morning fog was just lifting off the cranberry bogs, but the warmth of the growing spring would soon be evident. The sun was coming up. The base was starting to come alive. Smoke was pouring out of what had to be the mess hall. He could see lights in the barracks, smell the exhausts from trucks being started, even hear an occasional voice.

But he hadn't yet heard that one sound he was waiting for . . .

What was the general doing here? Could it be that people finally came to their senses and realized that the U.S. really *did* win the war? If not, what was the state of the country these days? What country *was* it these days? He had no idea . . .

He approached the base cautiously. He had spent the night in the woods nearby, the last time he'd have to sleep in a battered makeshift lean-to—or so he hoped. Standing at the very edge of the base perimeter, he pressed against the chain link fence and peered in. For all he knew, this could be a Russian base, or that of some kind of Russian client's occupying army.

Or was this a base camp of the army of The New Order? What was The New Order? Hunter could never really figure it out. Even before the dust had settled from the Russian sneak attack on the American ICBM sites, the Vice President was issuing orders to all military personnel still in the country to start enforcing The New Order. Laws that said there would no longer be 50 states, that America would be broken up into a dozen small countries and a patchwork of free territories. The traitor had said this was the settlement he had reached with the Russian Peace Committee to end the war—the war that everyone conveniently forgot American forces had won. But the swiftness that the new ruling came down smacked of years of pre-planning. (God only knew how long ago the Russian moles had infiltrated the American government!) There were so many questions: Why had some in-country National Guard units immediately started doing the Vice President's bidding—destroying military equipment, burning state capitol buildings, universities and libraries, blowing up TV and radio transmitters? How long had these units been compromised? The idea had been to complete the isolation of the American citizen. Not to let the ordinary Joe catch on that the Soviet Armed Forces were lying in cinders scattered all over Europe and Asia, decisively beaten by the Free World. It was the Big Lie. Win the battle, lose the war.

Hunter cautiously made his way along the base perimeter. Had the sign-towing Piper been just a ruse? Was the great General Seth Jones really dead, buried on the European battlefield? Was Hunter being set up? Logic again intervened. Crucial questions needed crucial answers. He needed proof.

He stayed close to the fence, passing through deep woods until he saw the main gate. He stayed hidden. The gate was manned by a single sentry. One look at the soldier and he knew things had changed.

The man was not standard military. His uniform was a bright green and he was wearing a chrome helmet, a headpiece usually reserved for parades and ceremonies. Nor was the sentry carrying a standard military firearm. Instead, he was armed with a cowboy-style pistol and holster, and a double-barrel, sawed-off shotgun.

A bizarre flag was flying above the guardhouse. It was a mishmash of green, blue and white, jumbled up in a field of uneven stars, stripes and what looked like dollar signs. Below the flag, attached to the roof of the guard house was a sign that read: Flight Operations Center—Armed Forces of the Northeast Economic Zone. Well, at least it didn't *sound* communist. More mysteries. More questions to be answered.

Then Hunter heard the sound he was waiting for. Off in the distance, probably at the far reaches of the base, came the distinctive rumble of a jet engine warming up. The noise filled him. For the first time in more than two years, he felt warm. He was ready for anything now. "Just get me airborne again . . ."

He emerged from the woods. The chrome-helmeted cowboy saw him coming and had his gun at the ready. Hunter had forgotten that his appearance wasn't exactly—well, friendly-looking. His hair was beyond shoulder-length and his beard covered nearly half his chest. His clothes were threadbare. He was carrying his meager belongings in an old laundry bag and he had the M-16 and ammunition belt in full view.

Just as he was about to speak to the guard, he heard a roar and instinctively looked in its direction. There was a trail of smoke and an orange spit of light, burning through the morning mist, but the outline was unmistakable. He felt a surge run through him— it was *that* feeling again. He watched as the fighter jet quickly disappeared into the low clouds.

The sentry raised his gun and cocked it.

Hunter smiled and raised his hand in the universal sign of peace. "Major Hawker Hunter to see General Jones," he said.

Five minutes later, the sentry led him into a small office. Sitting behind a dilapidated desk was a man he thought he'd never see again: General Seth Jones.

Hunter couldn't believe it. Jones actually looked *younger*. He was trimmer, leaner and meaner looking. His hair had grown out of its trademark military whiffle, and the resulting locks with a tinge of gray gave him a kind of professorial look.

The last time Hunter had seen him was at the NATO base in Rota. The squadron had just got word of the destruction of the American nuclear ICBM arsenal and that their forces were to be disarmed. Finnish Peace troops, the enforcers of the bogus armistice, had arrived and started systematically de-

14

stroying the 16th TFW aircraft, while the Americans stood by helplessly, under orders from the Vice President. It was only later—when the VP started broadcasting the Rules of the New Order from Moscow—did they realize he was a traitor. When the horrible destruction of the Wing's F-16s was completed, the Finns handcuffed Jones and drove him away. Hunter was convinced he'd never see him again.

But here he was. And the general proved to be still all-Jones Boy.

"What's this, corporal?" Jones said, putting on his sternest military face. "Another veteran looking for a handout?" Despite Hunter's long hair and beard, Jones could still see his handsome, oddly hawk-like features. Sloppy appearance or not, he knew the young man was still the best fighter pilot in the world.

Hunter snapped to a mock attention.

"Major Hunter, reporting for duty, suh!"

"You're out of uniform, Major," the general said.

"So are you, sir," Hunter replied, eyeing the senior officer's bright green, rather garish uniform. If the sentry wasn't still present, Hunter thought he would have probably embraced his old friend.

The general fingered his loud green coverall and said, "Do I detect insolence in your voice, Major? I'll have you know this is the standard uniform of the Armed Forces of the Northeast Economic Zone Air Patrol. I wear it proudly."

Hunter looked around the spare office, trying not to laugh out loud. A desk, a chair, a lamp and a coffee machine in the corner, and that was it. It was a far cry from Jones's surroundings back in the Thunderbirds days when his office was jammed with hundreds of mementos, including photos of just about every fighter plane ever made, plus several computers, a bank of telephones and telecommunications gear and a well-stocked, top-shelf, wet bar.

"Where have you been, Major? Hibernating?"

"Worse than that, sir," Hunter replied, still standing ramrod straight at attention. "I've been contemplating my existence."

"Obviously, you're suffering from post-World War III syndrome," the general said. "It's been going around."

Hunter continued. "Got a bunch of books, went up to a mountain and tried to find the meaning of life, sir."

"Jesus, not that!"

" 'Fraid so, sir."

"And what conclusions did you reach, Major?"

Hunter paused a moment for effect, then replied, "Well, sir, I discovered that every man has to believe in something."

"And . . . ?"

"And," Hunter said, looking around the general's empty office. "And, I believe I'll have a drink, sir."

"Scotch?"

"Neat, sir."

With the wave of his hand, Jones dismissed the properly impressed, if slightly confused sentry. He walked around the desk and hugged Hunter.

"Good to see you, Hawk," he said.

"Same here, sir."

Jones locked the office door and broke out his

emergency bottle.

"Had breakfast yet?" he asked.

Despite the early morning hour, they sat and ate stale doughnuts, while mixing the no-brand whiskey in with cups of steaming coffee. Then they talked.

"Well, Hawk," Jones said, swigging his laced coffee. "What the hell happened to you after Rota?"

"You really want to know?"

"Sure as hell," Jones said, smiling. "You tell me your story and I'll tell you mine."

Hunter took a deep breath. It seemed like so long ago. "Okay," he said. "Hang onto your hat."

Hunter began his story. After Jones had been led away, everyone took for granted he was heading for a firing squad. The members of the 16th scattered. But Hunter was determined to get back to America, or what was left of it. He knew there was an American sub base up in Loch Lomond, Scotland, and figured it was the only place where ships might be trying to get back home. So he walked. Right through Spain, through France and, after bribing a Frenchman to take him across the Channel, right up through England. It took him more than two months to reach Loch Lomond only to find the place filled with ex-GIs who had had the same idea as he. There were at least 10,000 men trying to get on no more than a half dozen Navy warships docked in the harbor. No one was in charge. The base was in a state of utter chaos.

Then he got lucky. At one corner of the sprawling base he found a battalion of Marines. They had set up an orderly camp on a hill inside the base and were grimly going about the task of staying civilized in the middle of all the disorder. Hunter fell in with them after pulling rank on a couple of the camp's guards and demanding to be taken to their commanding officer. His name was Captain John "Bull" Dozer and after a brief talk, he offered Hunter some grub and a place to sleep.

Dozer's outfit was going by the curious name of the 7th Cavalry—odd because the Marine Corps had no cavalry, per se. Over a pot of coffee, Dozer explained to Hunter that his unit had been fighting in Turkey when the last great battles of the war were raging. At one point they were surrounded by four Soviet army regiments near Ankara. Yet his Marines fought ferociously, and, unlike Custer's 7th Cavalry, caused the enemy to back off the siege and rethink the situation. By the time Dozer got his troops to more defensible ground, the war in Europe had been won and the Russians had agreed to the ceasefire.

Dozer promised his men that if they stuck together, he would get them home. He commandeered two Turkish airliners at gunpoint and forced the pilots to fly his 900 soldiers to England. His goal too was Loch Lomond and they had arrived two weeks before. When Hunter told him America was his goal too, they shook hands and agreed to work toward it together.

By the second afternoon, the six ships in port were overflowing with the survivors. One by one, they disappeared over the horizon. Hunter knew their chances of making it to America were nil.

Two days later the enormous outline of an aircraft carrier appeared off to the south. It was the *John F. Kennedy*. The captain came ashore and word quickly spread through the 5,000 remaining ex-GIs that they could hitch a ride to America as long as it was an orderly evacuation. The 7th Cavalry saddled up, and with Hunter tagging along, were among the first group to be taken aboard the great ship.

The voyage west took ten days, and as the faint outline of Manhattan appeared on the horizon, questions ran through the minds of the men on board. What was the country like now? Was there any country left to come home to?

They got their answers soon enough. As the ship neared the harbor they could see that what looked to be a mist enveloped the city. The mist was actually smoke. The city was burning. A collective shudder went through the men on the ship when they got a look at the Statue of Liberty. It was headless. The top had been blown off by some unknown catastrophe. As the *JFK* neared a docking point just off the southern tip of Manhattan, sounds of gunfire could be heard coming from the city streets. Welcome to New Order America, was all that Hunter could think of.

The ship docked and the passengers began filing off. Some stayed in groups, others just disappeared into the streets alone. Not many of them had any destination planned. Hunter gladly joined the Marines as they smartly formed up and marched down the gangplank.

Dozer told him that the 7th had decided to stay together no matter what. Technically, they were no longer Marines and Dozer was no longer their commanding officer. But they agreed to stay with him and try to reach Fort Meade, Maryland. The Marine captain asked Hunter to go with them, but Hunter had made up his mind that if New York City was an indication of the state of the country—and he was certain it was—then he wanted no part of it. He had already set his sights on getting to the mountain in New Hampshire. Still he knew it would be wise to stay with the Marines until they were out of the horrible Beirut-like Manhattan.

Dozer formed his troops into one main column and gave them the order to march. Their destination was the George Washington Bridge. The sound of gunfire was everywhere. No one had a clue as to who was fighting whom, but most of the destroyed equipment they came across bore the markings of the National Guards of New York and New Jersey. Were the two states battling it out for possession of the island?

They were nearing Central Park East when they ran into trouble. Scouts stationed ahead of the column got word back to Dozer that a small group of armed men were holding two women at gunpoint three blocks away. Using hand signals, Dozer instructed his men to surround the gunmen. When one of the gang members raised his rifle the armed men were cut down in a volley of murderous gunfire.

And then a strange thing happened. One by one, civilians started to appear. They had been hiding in doorways, alleys and in buildings. Shyly, cautiously at first, they began to emerge from their hiding places. Soon, there were a couple of hundred of them—old men, women, children. Some of them were wounded;

all of them were caught in the terrifying madness of the anarchy in New York City.

One man was particularly happy. He was running up and down the street, waving a small American flag and yelling "The Marines are here!" Just as he was running up to Hunter and Dozer, a shot rang out. The man's chest exploded from the sniper's bullet. He fell right into Hunter's arms. He gasped and tried to speak, but all that came out was ". . . Why . . . shoot . . . me?"

Then he died.

Hunter laid the man's body down on the street. He was about 65 years old, Hunter figured, just one of millions of New Yorkers. He located the man's wallet and looked inside. His driver's license said he was Saul Wackerman. A photo showed him, his white-haired wife and two daughters. Another photo showed his son—apparently an Israeli soldier—in full uniform.

Hunter looked back at the man. He was still gripping the American flag, so much so that Hunter had some difficulty prying it from his fingers. He folded the flag and put it in his own pocket. The look on Saul Wackerman's face would haunt the pilot for many years to come.

Then Dozer showed Hunter something which would also haunt him: one of the gunmen had been carrying a AK-47 Kalishnikov assault rifle. Obviously, there were plenty of guns in New York City these days. What was startling was the AK-47 was the standard issue rifle for the Soviet Army.

Several hours later they reached the George Washington Bridge. The Marines were heading south. Hunter was going north, determined to get to the mountain in New Hampshire before the whole world came crashing down. He thanked Dozer and bid him and his troops farewell, knowing he'd never see any of them again.

The general listened to it all, quietly sipping his morning brew and at one point, breaking out a box of Havana cigars.

Hunter reached into his pocket and produced a piece of cloth. He unfolded it. It was the flag he took from Saul Wackerman.

"We could both be shot just for your having that," Jones said nonchalantly.

"So that's what it's come to," Hunter said defiantly. He felt the flag for a moment, fingering the blood-stains that dotted one edge of it. He always carried it with him so he would never forget what it was like . . . before. He folded it carefully and returned it to his pocket. "They'll have to pry it from *my* fingers, before they take it away from me."

"They probably will," Jones said smiling grimly.

There was silence between them for a few moments. Then Jones clapped his hands together and reached for the bottle.

"Well, shit, Hawk," he said, freshening his coffee. "That's one hell of a story. No wonder you headed for the hills."

Hunter had to laugh. It must have sounded like an incredible adventure. And he didn't even tell him the part about how he had met and bedded down with a beautiful girl along the way in France.

"So what happened to you?" he asked Jones, reaching for the whiskey bottle himself. "We thought we'd seen the last of you when the Finns drove you away."

Jones let out a loud laugh and clapped his hands again. "I was in Paris, Hawk, old buddy. And did you miss some party, boy!"

CHAPTER TWO

When the New Order came down and the general was led away by the Finns, Hunter had assumed that the old man would be thrown in prison at best, or worse, executed. Actually, the officer had a free ride to the French capital where his handlers inexplicably set him free. Once there, he met many other ex-military officers who were of the same mind as he: We won the war and we still got screwed. With nothing else to do, they proceeded to drink the Paris nightclubs dry.

"It was great," Jones testified. "More booze than I've ever seen."

Paris was one of the major cities Hunter thought he was prudent in avoiding during his odyssey to Scotland. He had visions of deserted streets filled only with rotting corpses, its beautiful buildings in ruins, the curtains drawn on the proud French republic, finally defeated.

"You'd be surprised how good a shape the city was in," Jones told him. "Of course, considering that the largest battle ever fought in the history of mankind took place about 30 clicks aways, and that half the people had either been gassed or had *vamoosed* before the first shot was even fired, the ones who stayed were great. Writers, politicians, musicians, artists, old bucks who had fought the Nazis. These people just kept on celebrating. They didn't give a shit who won. They didn't give a shit that the Russians—or what was left of them—were just over the next hill. They just wanted to get back to their food, booze and getting laid. Everything else was secondary to them.

"I was traveling around with a bunch of crazy Brits. RAF guys. We busted up the town pretty good. But after a few weeks, we realized that the city was getting real hot—real fast. We knew Ivan was just over the hill, licking his wounds and getting ready to play the conquering heroes." He spat in disgust. "The filthy swine! We kicked their asses and they made like they just took over the world."

"They did," Hunter reminded him.

The general went on. A bunch of senators and government bozos were stuck in Paris after the armistice was signed. They had the Concorde—the famous SST—waiting at Orly Airport. Jones said a seat on that plane couldn't have been bought for a million dollars. The politicos were getting itchy to get out of Europe before it went Red. Trouble was, the pilot never showed up. Now they needed someone to fly it. Somehow, they knew Jones was in town.

"They got word to me while I was shitfaced, sleeping under a table in a bar on the Left Bank. Or was it the Right Bank? Anyway, they sobered me up and fed me. Then, we loaded the sucker up with French wines and chow, and it was *oeuvre*!"

He clapped his hands in joy, just thinking about it. "You should have come to Paris, Hawk, my boy. We had a hell of the time there!"

He got up and started another pot of coffee brewing. Hunter was astounded at the general's ability to land on his feet. There he was, crossing the Atlantic lashed to a bulkhead on the *JFK* in the middle of a hurricane, and Jones made the trip supersonically, in three hours, drinking the best wine and eating the best food in the process.

"It was the last congressional boondoggle flight in history," the general continued. "We put down in Washington, because New York City looked too hot to handle. These guys didn't want any part of it. Half of them were on their way to Weather Mountain. You know, that place near DC where they have a fully stocked city right inside the mountain and all the big shots are supposed to go when the bomb was dropped?"

Hunter had heard of the place.

"Well, I don't know how many of them made it past the door, but they were telling me about the place. They had enough stuff hidden away to last them for years. The place is so big inside they even have a lake there. These guys claimed you could water ski on it. One senator said there was even a plan to round up all the best call girls in Washington right before the shit hit the fan and get them down there too. You know, just to give them all something to do while they waited for the dust to settle? Yeah, we had our share of great leaders, huh? They needed women to continue the human race with. Let their descendants crawl out of the cave and run things. You know, keep it in the family. But can you imagine what kind of a bastard is produced when a politician knocks up a hooker?"

The thought of it sent a shiver down Hunter's spine. He took a slug of his whiskey-laced coffee.

Jones did the same, lit up a cigar and went on with his story. Once he touched down at Andrews Air Force Base outside of Washington, the politicians bolted off the plane and were gone without so much as a thank you. Except for one of them.

"One guy did give me a bag of French francs," Jones said, blowing smoke rings. "Big deal, I thought at the time. They were probably worth all of twenty-five bucks, and that was in France! He thought he was doing me this big favor and all he cared about was that his ass was home, so he was in a generous mood. Typical politician. Well, I hung onto them Frenchies, a wise move, I found out later.

"Andrews was pretty much abandoned. There were a few creeps around. Left behind GIs, MPs. These screwball National Guard guys. People like that. All of them were armed to the teeth and looking for trouble. I ignored them, but they had their eye on the plane. I saw a bunch of aircraft that had been blown up by some good little soldiers. Some assholes following the New Order to the letter, I suppose. Air Force One was there, or what was left of it. Lot of F-15s, gone. Pieces of them, scattered everywhere. It made me sick to look at them."

Jones became quiet for a moment. Hunter knew the general was thinking of the wasted, destroyed jets.

"I was beat and I had nowhere to go, so I slept for about two days right in the Concorde. Finished off the food and booze, then I realized that I could be sleeping in a real bed somewhere. I found some LC's office with a hideaway bed. I stayed there for two days, and you know, during the night some assholes sneaked down to the runway and blew up the SST? God, I'd heard of following orders, but some of these people carried it a bit too far."

Hunter nodded. Another example of a waste of technology. When would anyone get around to building a supersonic airliner again?

"I bummed around DC for a while," Jones said, stirring his coffee. "There were some people still left. All the restaurants were open. It was nearly business as usual, except they were practically giving the food away. Dollars were as valuable as used toilet paper, but I found out that people would take coins, including my francs. It didn't matter that quarters, dimes and nickels were all clad coins with not enough silver to fill a tooth. These people treated them like they were pure through and through. There were even people running around with *real* silver and gold coins. So they loved to see me and my francs."

Jones soon took residence in an abandoned swank Georgetown townhouse. It was his home for three months.

"It was party time there too," he said. "All over DC. Food, booze and broads. I was out in a bar every night. It's great when you don't have to go to work. Met a lot of funny people. But unfortunately, I also met a lot of people carrying guns, and not just .32 caliber water pistols either. It started getting tense. Pretty soon there were shootouts every night. It was Dodge City. I figured it was just a matter of time before a stray bullet would catch my ass, so I started thinking about getting out.

"Then I heard some of these new little countries were starting navies, armies, militias, things like that and they needed military people to help. I talked to a guy, who knew another guy who had a friend who knew about this job. Commander of the Northwest Economic Zone's Air Patrol—'ZAP,' for short. A little bulky, but it sounded good to me. They had a little money to spend and they were lucky. Most of their National Guard units were never turned on by the disarmament weirdos, so there were still a few guys around who knew how to take an order. I tell you, troops like that are a rare commodity these days."

Jones had traveled to Boston and met with the leaders of the Northeast Economic Zone. They promised him almost complete freedom. Just as long as he paid lip service to the New Order rules.

"You know, no radios, no TV, no old uniforms, no Stars and Stripes." Jones's voice cracked slightly when he mentioned the ban on the American flag. "That's why we have these stupid pansy color uniforms on, and that's why that candyass, three-dollar-bill flag is flying over this place.

"But I've always liked the Cape, and they let me fly, so here I came. Been here about a year and a half."

But Hunter was confused. Fly? The last time he'd heard, one of the New Order's rules—the most important one in his eyes—was that all military aircraft had to be dismantled as part of the demilitarization agreement. But he had heard jets at the base. Then, as if on cue, the sound of a jet taking off filled the office, shaking the coffee pot slightly.

Jones read his mind.

"We have a few planes here, Hawk," the general said, his smile looking like the cat that ate the canary.

"So I can hear," Hunter said. "But how'd you get around the demilitarization order?"

The general gave out a loud "Ha!" and waved his hand. "We were lucky, Hawk. And the traitors—our so-called Vice President and the rest of them—were stupid. Their New Order said 'dismantle all the combat aircraft' when it should have said 'destroy all combat aircraft.' so what do you think the smart people in Europe did? They just started taking the planes apart, cataloging the numbers and packing them away. And who the hell was going to stop them? The UN? The Finns? The Russians? No way. So these enterprising sorts packed all the pieces away, put it on ships and sent the ships everywhere and anywhere, just before the commies moved in."

"Every war has its profiteers,' Hunter said.

"You get the idea," the general said, pouring him another cup of coffee and adding a dash of booze. "Now, don't get me wrong. A lot of planes were destroyed. I mean, look what happened to us."

Hunter well remembered the day when the Finnish observers arrived and systematically blew up the spuadron's 12 remaining F-16s.

"Yeah, nice guys, those Finns," the general said, digressing for a moment. "They live in the armpit country of Europe and spend most of their time sucking up to the Russians."

Hunter felt a surge of rage flow through him. What a waste of money and technology?

"Anyway," Jones continued, lighting up a massive

cigar. "The New Order boys also screwed up by not including other military aircraft like cargo planes and tankers. Copters. And they didn't mention anything about de-commissioned aircraft either."

Hunter's vision of a flightless world was happily coming to an end.

"You've been to Wright-Patterson," Jones said in a puff of smoke. "You know how many planes were in mothballs there?"

"Hundreds, I would imagine," Hunter said, adding some hooch to his own coffee. Wright-Patterson Field in Ohio, Hunter knew, was the location of the Air Force's surplus aircraft storage area. It was like an elephant's graveyard for old planes; especially the sophisticated ones that had some years behind them but were too damned expensive to send to the scrap heap. So instead of shit-canning them, the Air Force just plugged all the holes, drained the tanks and had them sit out at Wright-Patterson to use in case of an emergency.

"Thousands," Jones corrected him. "And most of them just needed the screws tightened and the oil changed and they were ready to fly."

A tinge of panic took a swipe at him. "But, *what* is Ohio these days? Who's running things there?"

"No one, which is fine with us," Jones hauled out a map that was so new, it looked as if the ink still wasn't dry. It was the first time Hunter had seen the new countries and territories of America. "Ohio is now a Free State. In other words, it's an open area. No government. At least for the time being. A couple of guys out there realized they were sitting on a bonanza and opened up shop. All these little countries or

31

regions or states—or whatever they are—came running because everyone wanted to start their own air force. It's an airplane supermarket. We've got a couple of guys out there right now, bidding on some planes."

Hunter instantly wanted to see the place.

"What are you shopping for?" he asked.

"Mostly small stuff, fighters, attack craft. They've got everything. A lot of heavy bomber merchandise. B-58s, B-47s, even a couple B-36s." The general rose and poured himself a third cup of joe and added the mandatory splash of whiskey. "But we can't fool around with the heavies. We can't afford them and the runway here won't take a lot of it. Way too short. And where would we put them?"

"And what would you do with them?"

"Exactly," Jones replied with satisfaction. "The people running all these little air forces think the bigger the better. Now, I'm sure a lot of them are thinking of converting their B-47 into a cargo plane and, in some cases it will work.

"But you can be sure that some of these clowns are thinking differently. Some of these states are being run by the typical crooked and/or stupid politician who suddenly woke up and found he was a king. Hell, this so-called Vice President—what's his name again, Benedict Arnold?—appointed half of them. God knows what deals he made before he traded in his stars and bars for a hammer and sickle.

"Well, what happens when someone in the country next door doesn't want to pay a flyover tax? Or money at the tolls? Or starts fishing in the other guy's river? How much will it take before one of these pisspots in control gets mad enough and orders his B-36s to go and flatten the other guy's capital? It's already happening! They've been having a hell of a misunderstanding down near Florida and Alabama. Blowing the shit out of each other. Using gasoline bombs, napalm, terrible stuff."

"Napalm?" Hunter said, stirring his coffee with a pencil. "You can get napalm these days?"

"Oh yeah," Jones said, relighting his stogie. "Anyone who wants it can get 'palm from the Mid-Aks."

"Mid-who?"

"Mid-Aks. The Middle Atlantic Conference States. Everything from Delaware and Pennsylvania down to Georgia. New Jersey doesn't count. The 'Aks. They're real dangerous, Hawk. They were sitting on a lot of military hardware when the balloon went up and they must have either hid ninety percent of the shit when the New Order came in, or made a deal to keep it all because they still have a lot of it. I mean these guys are armed to the teeth and then some with tanks, PCs, howitzers. And they have a lot of men in uniform too. Lot of scumbags living down there even before the war. Now, at least, they're employed."

He let out a snort and took a healthy swig from his coffee mug.

"We'll be fighting them here next," he said, a touch of nervous caution in his voice. "They're already making noise. They took over several little territories around Kentucky and Tennessee. Just rolled over them. Sherman-to-the-sea type stuff. They have Fort Knox and made themselves rich. Now they want to talk to my bosses about 'Mutual Defense Treaties' and all this happy horseshit. It's a joke! They have a

33

bunch of crooks running the show and they can use a whole army as enforcers. I'd like to kick their asses."

"How are your . . . bosses?" Hunter asked.

"Ah, they're okay," Jones said. "They were smart enough to know that if you can't have a big army, you'd better have a good air force. Especially with all the coastline they have to protect. From old New Hampshire, to Boston Harbor, the whole Cape out here, right down to Long Island. They'll probably get Maine someday, too. Right now, that's a no-man's-land.

"They pretty much leave us alone down there. They give me money and I pay everyone and what's ever left over, I invest in spare parts and start saving for some more airplanes. We fly up to Boston every few days, buzz the city, just to let them know we're around. The people up there like it. They like to think someone's watching over them."

Jones returned to the map again. "We fly out to the Berkshires, go up around Mt. Washington, skirt down around Connecticut. That's about the range of our patrols. We could fly right over New York City if we wanted to, but the place is so heavy, you never know what they'll shoot up at you. You think it was bad when you were there? It's incredible down there now. Everyone has a gun, a missile, or a tank. And all they do is fight each other for the right to call this block or that apartment house 'their turf.' They enjoy it. Every man's a king and the fighting never stops. And it's a great cover for what really goes on down there, and I mean all kinds of smuggling. Guns, drugs, women, missiles, explosives, gasoline, booze—you name it. Enough parts to build your own goddamn B-52, if you have the gold or the silver or whatever to pay for it. And I know for a fact the Mid-Aks run most of the guns into New York City and trade them for protection—a free rein in smuggling stuff in and out."

Hunter's thoughts suddenly flashed back to Dozer and the heroic 7th Cavalry. Who knows what ever happened to them?

"We've seen a little action, mostly pirate ships and stuff," Jones said, helping himself to his fourth pick-me-up of the morning. "We've had some strange doings lately though."

He drained his mug and stood up.

"Come on," he said, pulling on his jacket. "I'll show you what we're flying these days."

Hunter thought he'd never ask.

CHAPTER THREE

Walking out into the brisk morning air, Jones began to show Hunter around the base.

The place was more runway than anything else. There were three of them to be exact, two which ran parallel to the ocean nearby, the third intersecting them at a 70-degree angle. The entire base was probably a square mile in size. There were six lonely buildings scattered about—two of them big, quonset-hut style hangars, two others served as housing for the base's occupants. The flight ops building had the base's control tower sitting beside it. The sixth building was next door, a catch-all mess hall, which he would soon find out, served as the well-patronized base saloon.

The base was surrounded by a chain link fence and guard towers every 500 yards or so. Soldiers walked the perimeter in pairs. He could see some rudimentary 20mm anti-aircraft gun positions ringing the perimeter, with a few mobile SAM launchers and even a couple of old Hawk anti-aircraft systems thrown in.

But the only aircraft sitting on the flight line was the Piper Cub that Hunter had seen towing the sign a few weeks before.

"I knew you were probably alive," Jones said matter-of-factly. "And, if you had made it back from Europe, that you were probably hiding out somewhere, waiting for the fall of civilization."

"I'm still waiting," Hunter said with a laugh.

"Me, too," Jones replied. "But I figured you would return to where your roots were. The mountains in New Hampshire seemed like a good bet, although I had that Cub flying all over the state before you spotted it."

They walked right over one of the runways. Hunter could see that although there were weeds popping up through the asphalt, there were also some tire skid marks, indicating that something besides a Piper Cub had landed there recently. Where were the other planes?

"Don't ask just yet," Jones told him, reading his thoughts again.

They walked in silence for a few moments, over the second runway and approached the beach.

"We lost twenty million people, Hawk," the general said, the bitterness evident in his voice. "When the double-cross went down and that Quisling left a hole in the Star Wars shield, the Russian ICBMs just kept on coming, all of them landing on or around our silos. Talk about overkill! They just about blew the country into two parts. From North Dakota on down, it looks like the moon. Craters as big as cities, forest fires that will take years to burn out. Even some of the rivers are on fire, who knows why."

"What about radiation?" Hunter asked, sniffing the air for effect. "Nothing seems to be glowing."

"Most of the bombs that fell were 'clean,' " Jones said with noticeable relief. "Thank God for that. There is some low-level radiation, not much though. But those bastards also sent over nerve gas, germ bombs, even some hallucinogetic stuff. It's scattered everywhere. They must have launched everything but the kitchen sink at us, and we didn't so much as fire a popgun at them."

"So much for nuclear deterrence," Hunter said.

"It used to be beautiful country out there, Hawk," Jones continued. "The Dakotas. Nebraska. Kansas. I was raised out there. I know. Now it looks like another planet. It's a no-man's-land out there. I've flown over it. It gave me the creeps. It's downright spooky and it's going to stay like that for a long time."

Hunter nodded, then said: "I know it sounds terrible, but twenty million dead isn't so bad, considering what could have happened if they had nuked our big cities," Hunter said.

"You're right," Jones said, stopping to light his cigar in the brisk, ocean breeze. "But they wanted something left for them to take over. This 'No Occupation' section of the treaty is a bunch of yabanza. You know and I know that as soon as those ugly, crude bastards get their hammers and sickles straight, they'll be over here, eating our food, fishing our rivers, screwing our women. They'll be able to take the *Queen Mary* over here, who the hell's going to stop them?"

Hawk felt the bulge of the folded American flag in his back pocket. "We'll stop them," he said, matter-of-factly.

Jones looked at him and laughed, but didn't say

anything for a couple of moments. "You could . . ." the general said, finally, thinking of Hunter's expertise in the air. He was widely known as the best fighter pilot ever. "You could probably shoot 'em all down singlehandedly."

Hunter steered clear of the subject.

"What's with this 'New Order' business," he asked. "Do people really give a damn?"

"No, not really," Jones answered. "It's a case of malignant neglect. That traitor Vice President set himself up as the New Order Commissioner, or some such thing, and then took his entourage of faggots and weirdos and Russians and went to Bermuda or Moscow or someplace to play house. Before he left, he set up a bunch of rules. All of them are designed to stop people from talking, or even thinking, about the old ways."

"I know it's 'illegal' to fly the Stars and Stripes," Hunter said. "What else did they come up with?"

"You can't even *say* the name of the country—the name before all this shit happened, that is," Jones said. "Not even the word, America. Now it's just The Continent. No more national anthem, no more newspapers, TV, radio. They even banned sporting events. But the Texans told them to go screw themselves on that one."

"And some people choose to follow these rules?"

"Well, yes and no. It's more like you can avoid a lot of trouble if you just keep your mouth shut."

"That was true in Germany in the 1930s," Hunter said.

"I know," Jones sighed. "But I look at it this way. If I start mouthing off, my bosses get upset. They get

39

upset because they have to deal with the New Order flunkies who are running around in Boston, looking over everyone's shoulder, collecting their 10-percent tax, off the top. I make too much noise, a New Order clown gets wind of it and tells my bosses to can me. They can my ass, I ain't got a job, money or a place to hang my helmet. What's worse, I can't fly. If I can't fly, I might as well die. You know that."

Hunter nodded again. "Me, too."

"So I play their little game. We've got a good thing going here. We can build it into a *really* good thing. The Northeast Economic Zone is just another word for 'We're making money.' They have good airport facilities in Boston. A lot of traffic goes through there. All the major convoys to the Coast go out of Boston and Montreal. It's big, big money. Real silver. Real gold. They pay a tax to that jerk-off in Bermuda. He keeps the Russians happy by sucking up to the Politburo. It all evens out. No one wants to jinx it by talk of the old days."

The general was quiet for a while.

"We're mercenaries here, Hawk," he said finally. "We're not soldiers fighting for a flag or a cause. We're fighting for a paycheck. We're guarding their investment. They're getting rich and putting people to work. People work, have food, they stay happy and quiet. Look, I have permission to raise an army here, train 'em, make a special forces unit out of them. The Leaders Council in Boston—they're my bosses—will give me just about what I need. In return, I protect their asses. I watch over their convoy routes. I make sure there ain't no pirates in their airspace. But if something big broke out, I mean like a war between the Zone and the 'Aks, I'm gone. And my people are gone too. It ain't like the old days. It ain't worth losing your life over."

Hunter let it all sink in.

"What's it like in the big cities these days?" he asked as they approached the beach on the other side of the runway. "I mean, I know New York City is like Beirut. But how about LA? Chicago?"

"Well, they're empty, most of them," Jones answered. "They figure that more than half—that's *half*—the Americans moved out of the country in the past two years. Didn't want to live here, simple as that. Of the one hundred million that left, most went north to Canada, and some went south to Mexico. There are huge resettlement camps up around Toronto, Quebec, Montreal, places like that. The Canucks were good enough to take our people in. They didn't get burnt so bad in the rumble. Mexico is another story, from what I hear. Lots of trouble down there. The Mex still remember we kicked their asses back in 1836. Lot of those people have moved back into the ROT."

"ROT?" Hunter asked.

Jones laughed. "Shouldn't call it that I guess. 'Republic of Texas.' Those crazy bastards finally got their wish. They are their own country now. Got a hell of an army, too, so I hear."

Hunter wasn't too surprised to hear the Texans were adapting.

"Shit, you don't think a little thing like World War III would stop those people, do you?" Jones said. "Let me tell you something: after the armistice was signed, the Texans took about a day and a half off to

41

change the colors on their flag and adjust their college football schedule. Then they went back to work.

"They knew that no matter what happened, people would always need three things: heating oil, gasoline and jet fuel. So they fired up their refineries and concentrated on just those three products. Since then, the world—such as it is—has beat a path to their door. Of course, the stuff goes at premium prices. Gasoline is worth about twenty-five old dollars a gallon these days. I forget how much that is in real silver. But that's why everyone just about stays put these days. No more jumping in the car to see Grandma. And there aren't that many cars working anyway.

"The heating oil is cheaper and a little easier to get. But still, these days you have two, three, maybe four families sharing what used to be one-family houses. That's how people are surviving. It's the buddy system. It's a lucky man who has a job—and he gets paid whatever is available. Food, clothes, heating oil, sometimes money, I guess. There's no such thing as a regular paycheck out there anymore. It's catch as catch can. That's why so many people are joining the army. Pretty soon, I think, everyone will be in the army in some capacity. For many of the little countries, it's the only secure job there is. Now, like I said, people here in the Northeast have it better than most. That's what we are protecting. The 'Aks cream their jeans thinking about what we have going here."

He relit his cigar.

"Of course, it's the jet fuel I'm most concerned about. We are worthless if we don't have the juice to fly. I can deal with Texans, or I can deal with some of the Arabs that are still alive and pumping crude. It's way cheaper with the Texans and more reliable, too. You can imagine what is going down in the Arab World these days! But with the Texans, they insist on a fighter escort for the ship, round-trip, no less. There are a lot of people out there who haven't the sweet deal we have here and who'd love to get their hands on a tanker filled with JP-8 fuel. And they wouldn't mind slitting your throat to get it."

"Things are that bad?" Hunter asked, feeling he'd missed a chapter of history during his exile on the mountain.

"They're worse," Jones said with a grim laugh. "Besides here and out on the Coast, and maybe in Texas, it's as if all the rest of the decent people were either killed in the war or are in hiding. Out there, only the scum survived. The seas are filled with pirates—and so are the skies."

"Air pirates?"

"They're everywhere, Hawk," Jones said, waving his hand at the sky.

They had reached the beach by this time. Hunter looked at the waves, crashing on the shore a few hundred feet away. Cape Cod, he thought. No place like it. A bunch of seabirds scattered as they approached a beat-up picnic table. Jones produced a small flask and with a mock toast, took a healthy slug. Passing the container to Hunter, the general pulled the table around to face the ocean, then sat down and closed his eyes, letting the early spring sunshine soak through his body. Hunter took a swig— it was ginger brandy—and sat down beside him.

"Well," Jones said, looking out on the shoreline,

"at least I have myself some beachfront property."

They both took another belt. Then the general continued his story:

"The West Coast was lucky. They didn't get screwed up too much, so they got their act together real early in the game. Now, we here on the East Coast are in almost the same position. Besides the airport, we still have some kind of industrial base, plus our ports can handle anything coming across the Atlantic—oil from the Arabs, food from Africa and so on. The West Coasters know this, so we do a lot of trading with them. They have stuff we want and vice versa.

"The problem is getting the goods back and forth. The Panama Canal went blooey in the first wave the Red slime sent over. The trip around South America takes way too long, although a lot of ships are doing it. And there's no way you can drive through what's left of the middle of the country."

"How come?" Hunter asked. "Highway system destroyed?"

Jones nodded. "Not only are there no reliable roads, but like I said, there are some really bad characters living out in the middle of the country— and there are more than a few of them."

There was a distinct chill in the general's voice.

"They're all crazy, Hawk," the senior officer said. "They'll blow your head off just as soon as look at you. They live in filth and squalor. They steal everything they can get and get it any way they can."

It sounded to Hunter like New York City. "Who are these people? Why did they turn so—anti-social, so quickly?" he asked.

Jones removed his baseball hat and ran his hands through his hair. "Who knows? ICBM shell-shock? Or exposure to nerve gas? Or maybe this hallucinogen gas the Reds sent over. Maybe this is what a man becomes when there is anarchy, I don't know. A guy in Boston told me there were a couple big prisons in Kansas that were busted open when the bombs started falling. He said it was done on purpose, by persons unknown, just to disrupt the recovery. Other people say that the wardens were just giving the prisoners a chance to save themselves. Whatever, a lot of them survived and some banded together and decided that the best way to make it in this brave, new world was to take what you want and kill if you had to get it.

"It's a treacherous place, these days, Hawk, my boy. That's why they call it the Badlands."

The Badlands. Hunter filed the term away in his memory, to be recalled many, many times.

"You mentioned 'air pirates,'" he said.

"Can you believe it?" the general said, taking a belt from the flask. "They're everywhere! That's what makes me believe that these people in the Badlands aren't just escaped cons or shell-shocked victims. The pirates got air bases out there! They are at least peacefully co-existing with the creeps. They have aircraft and they have to be getting fuel to be flying the stuff. That shows there's some kind of intelligence working. I mean, it takes more than a driveling idiot to fly a plane."

"Or fix one," Hunter added.

"Right," Jones nodded. "Well, however they're doing it, the skies are very dangerous. And not just over the Badlands, either, although that's where it's the worst. These guys are flying all over the continent and out at sea."

"What are they flying?" Hunter wanted to know.

Jones had to laugh. "Anything and everything, Hawk. You wouldn't believe what's still around. First, the pirates started showing up in old shitkicker jets like F-80s, F-84s, even a few F-94s, from what I hear."

Hunter immediately recognized the planes. They were Korean War vintage and early 1950's models. Sub-sonic stuff.

"And that's just the beginning," Jones continued. "Lately the bastards have been seen flying more advanced stuff—F-101s, F-104s, F-106s, lots of F-100s."

"Interceptors!"

"Right, they must have gotten into some Air National Guard bases, or something. Maybe even Wright-Patterson sold them the hardware. Who knows? That stuff might be old, but it's still very effective."

Hunter thought for a moment. F-80s, '84s, 94s, really anything in the double digits was slow, built before the sound barrier was broken. The F-100 Super Sabre was the first mass-produced jet to do it. Then anything made after that—the F-101 "Voodoo," the F-102 "Delta Dagger," the F-104 "Starfighter," the F-105 "Thunderchief," the F-106 "Delta Dart"—were all supersonic fighters. The Thunderchief, which pilots in 'Nam called "Thud," was one tough fighter-bomber. The others were quick, rocket-firing planes built when the threat from Russia was thought to be through a bomber attack, air raid sirens, the whole

46

bit. Before ICBMs became the rage. And the Navy had a whole different family of planes, carrier attack craft like A-4s. Most of these jets had made their mark in Southeast Asia. American ingenuity had turned planes originally built to protect the North American skies and seas into camouflaged birds of death, a horror in the skies above the rice paddies.

"But," Hunter said, "if the pirates have some Air National Guard bases, they must also have some later stuff. A-10s and the like."

"They probably do, Hawk," Jones confirmed. "But as you know, those planes are for ground-support. Tank busting, that sort of thing. The pirates are more interested in catching you in the air. They jump you and either you land where they say, or they shoot you down. You can try and get away, but they fly in wolfpacks, just like the Luftwaffe did. It's hard to outrun a dozen or so fighters. That's why it's so hard to move materiel back and forth to the Coasts."

"So, how do you do it?" Hunter asked. "You said something about 'convoys?' "

"Yep. Convoys." Jones answered. "The Northeast is the major trading partner with the Coasters. We both assembled a lot of airliners. Boeing 707s, DC-10s, DC-9s, 727s. Anything big and airworthy. They ripped out the seats where they had to and made cargo carriers out of them. That's how ninety percent of the goods get delivered. We have a big convoy that leaves Logan Airport in Boston every three days. The time changes for security reasons, but anyone hanging around can tell when a convoy is getting ready to leave. I mean, it's hard to hide getting forty, fifty airliners getting ready to fly."

47

"And the pirates have spies, I assume," Hunter said.

"You assume right there, Major," Jones said. "They know when we're coming and they attack just about every convoy we send out. They get a few planes every time. Mostly, they shoot them down. But sometimes they can place a rocket or a cannon burst in just the right spot, enough to disable it. If the pilot brings the plane down relatively softly, there may be something left over for the pirates to take as booty. So if a plane is disabled, or if they catch a plane trying to make it alone, the pilot knows they'd just as soon shoot him down, so he is more inclined to land the thing and take his chances."

"And you have to fly over their territory to save fuel?"

"Right again. We can't waste a drop, even at the expense of losing a few birds."

"Well, I know it's hard in a plane like an airliner," Hunter said. "But why don't the pilots just bail out?"

"Because they'll shoot you anyway. Always remember that. They've shot at parachutes. Christ! That's child play for them. They hijacked a plane about a year ago. This was when people actually flew from coast to coast. The pirates forced the pilot to land at one of their bases, the airport in Tulsa. They put a gun to his head and told him they just wanted the plane and that they would let the people go. He really had no choice but to believe them, and as it turned out, he was the first one to get it. Then they lined up the men and shot 'em all, right on the runway. They killed off all the old women, and the young ones they could screw, they did. It was a massacre. That ended regular passenger service for a while."

"That's just plain terrorism," Hunter said. "What's the point of it?"

"That's just it, Hawk," Jones said, anger creeping into his voice. "There is no point, other than to destabilize the country, which, if you haven't noticed, is already pretty unstable.

"Some people say 'It's their turf.' It gets into that old territorial thing. But I don't buy it. There's something behind it. Something—or someone—is controlling it. It's too coordinated to be so random, but they try like hell to make it appear that way."

"Who would be behind it?" Hunter asked. "These Mid-Aks?"

Jones was silent for a moment. He looked out to sea. "Maybe," he said finally. "They *are* crazy. They're worse than the pirates in a lot of ways. I have no doubt that the pirates get fuel and stuff from them. But airplanes? I just don't know. The Mid-Aks aren't big on air power. They're more concerned with who's got the biggest army. In fact, they've *got* the biggest goddamn army on the continent already."

"Who else could it be?"

"Well, there are some screwballs running things in Chicago," Jones said, shaking the flask and taking a drink. "The Family, they call themselves."

"Religious zealots?" Hunter asked, taking the flask from the general.

Jones laughed. "No, although we've too many of those running around too. The Family is nothing more than the crooks who were running things in Chicago behind the scenes when the war started, come out in the open. They didn't miss a beat. They

49

were out collecting 'taxes' the day the New Order came down. They've also built up a large army, some airpower, too."

The older man thought for a second, pulling on the end of his unlit cigar. "But Chi-town's pretty close to the Badlands, so I think they'd just as soon leave the pirates alone," he said.

They were both silent for a few moments. Hunter letting all the new information be absorbed; Jones trying to untangle all the seemingly loose ends of the destabilization that was sweeping the continent.

"I just don't know," Jones said finally. "The pirates, the goonies in Chicago, even the 'Aks are getting support and—I think guidance, if not direct orders—from somewhere. I just don't know where. I do know it's getting worse. A big convoy left Boston last week. More than seventy planes in all, including escorts. The pirates knew they were coming. Chopped them up something terrible. Shot down thirty big planes. What a horror show."

One word sparked in Hunter's mind. "Escorts?" he asked, looking out on the nearly empty base.

Jones immediately read his thoughts. "Patience, my boy," he said, taking the last swig from the flask. "No, we're not in the escort business. That's a job for free-lancers. And they can have it."

"Free-lancers?"

"That's right. Free-lance fighter pilots. It's the latest rage. Get yourself an airplane and get hired out to ride shotgun for the air convoys. Good money. Trouble is, you rarely live long enough to spend it."

"How come?" Hunter was fascinated.

"Because, you're the first one the pirates go for,"

Jones said coolly. "You can be flying an F-14 with Sparrow missiles up the ying-yang, but if twenty F-80s jump you, it's just a matter of time."

"Unless . . ." Hunter said slowly. "Unless you're good enough."

Jones looked at him. "That's right, Major," he said. "And you're the best pilot ever to sit behind the controls—better than anything I've ever seen or heard about. And there isn't a person left standing who knows airplanes who would disagree with me if I said you could probably be the richest man in this continent within a year. You'd be in demand. Leading convoys of seventy-five, shit—one hundred planes or just some rich cat who needs his diamonds moved via a Piper. You'd be the man they'd want riding shotgun.

"But I don't think you're that greedy. I don't think it's in your make-up. Free-lancers will shoot for anybody—for the highest bidder. Half of them would sell out to the pirates for the right price. And it's happened. A convoy flying along all of a sudden loses its escorts? Next thing you know, *boom*! jumped by the bad guys.

"No. Not you, Hawk. Maybe if you had to earn a quick buck someday, you would do it. But you're the type of man who has to fight for a flag. Fight for something to believe in. For a cause."

With that, the general lifted the rim of his cap and shielded his eyes against the morning sun. He was looking for something, far out on the ocean on the eastern horizon. It was nearly a cloudless day and the sun was bouncing off the sea, forming a huge field of sparkling, floating jewels.

The general was still, his eyes squinting. Suddenly, Hunter realized how quiet it was. There was no wind. The symphony of seagulls' squawks and other sea fowl squeals was silent. Even the waves seemed to have temporarily halted their relentless crashing against the shore.

Then he *felt* it.

He didn't close his eyes for this one. He wanted to see it first. An excitement started to shake him. Slowly, a distant roar, getting louder. More intense. Angry. Powerful. An almost heroic sound.

It was a sound he knew well . . .

Then he saw them. Five specks just above the horizon, each trailing a thin, gray, wisp of smoke. They were getting louder by the second. He knew it would soon be unbearably loud, but he waited for it with glee.

Closer and closer, the specks grew bigger, their forms taking shape. They were no more than 25 feet above the waves and flying in a perfect chevron formation. About a half mile out, Hunter began to recognize wings, and tail sections and air intakes and engine noise. He managed to steal a quick glance at Jones. The general had a smile a mile wide.

Instantly, the jets were right over them. Head up at a 90-degree angle, Hunter took a mental snapshot of the five fighters as they were right above him. They seemed to hang in the air. He felt a thrill shoot from his head to his heart down to his toes and up again. These *muthas* were *flying*!

The leader was flying an F-4 Phantom. A Viet Nam-era fighter-bomber, the F-4 looked like someone had shut the hangar doors on it before it made it all the way out. Its wings were cranked upward on their ends, while the rear stabilizers were bent downward. There were reasons for the bizarre shape: air downwash, lateral stability, dihedral angles. It was an ugliness that only a pilot could love. The plane, though decades old, had a lot of guts in its day—it could fly at 1450 mph—and was always a favorite of flyboys. It was the only thing the Air Force and the Navy ever agreed on. Both services flew them. Hunter could see a 20-mm cannon on each wing, with two Sidewinders and an old Bullpup missile hanging underneath. The Phantom was was loaded for bear.

The leader's wingman was flying an F-8E Crusader, a plane nearly 40 years old, yet still deadly looking. It was the first aircraft carrier-launched plane to break 1000 mph, and saw a lot of action in Viet Nam. Its entire wing could tilt upward by about seven degrees, giving it a humpbacked look, but making it easier to set the baby down on a bouncing carrier. The jet was armed with two 20-mm and what looked like about 2000 pounds of bombs. It had been ages since Hunter had seen one and he couldn't imagine where the general's people had found it.

On the leader's port wing there was an A-7 Corsair that looked to be carrying a Seapup missile as well as some anti-personnel bombs. Strangely, the smallish plane was just a more recent, down-sized version of the F-8 Crusader. The Navy used them during the early '80s and some of them saw action in Grenada and over Beirut. An odd little plane—this one was a two-seater and looked like a trainer—Hunter had never flown one, but knew there were a lot of them in Air National Guard units at the outbreak of the war.

The two remaining planes were T-38 trainers. A simplified, stripped-down version of the kick-ass F-20 Tigershark, it was the type of plane Hunter flew at NASA for training purposes. In fact, he was sure he recognized these two particular jets as NASA property. Each plane carried an Exocet missile, jury-rigged to its fuselage.

It was an odd menagerie of aircraft, representing different eras of flight, different services and different missions. Each one was painted in the same green color as the general's suit, and it looked like someone had done the job with a paintbrush.

The planes streaked overhead, and pulled up as one, staying in formation, and angling up 80-degrees. The after-noise hit as did the wash from the low-flying jets. Hunter felt the wind and the smoke and exhaust mixed with the spray kicked off the ocean from the powerful machines hit him right in the face. It felt beautiful.

He looked at Jones. The older man's smile hadn't dulled an iota. "Dawn flight," he said, producing a new cigar and ritually spitting off the end, "That was our Air Patrol."

The planes peeled off and, in sequence, began their landing approach. Five minutes later the fighters were taxiing up to a hangar where Hunter and the general were waiting.

The canopies opened, a ground crew appeared and placed a ladder beneath each cockpit of the still whining jets. The first three pilots to emerge Hunter had never seen before. And he didn't recognize the other two until they were down from their planes and had removed their flight helmets. Suddenly he realized he was looking at two smiling, familiar faces.

Captain J. T. Toomey. Lieutenant Ben Wa. Two pilots from the old Thunderbirds team.

It was good to see them. They had performed together for a year before the war and had been tight—just like all of the T-Bird teams over the years. Then they went to war together. Never did Hunter think he'd see them again. But here they were.

"Hey, flyboy," J. T. "Socket" Toomey started off. "What do you think, that the world stops turning because you go off and live on some mountain like a yogi?" Toomey was the designated Mister Cool of the group. He was ruggedly handsome, with a face that looked like an ad for an aftershave.

Ben Wa, the crazy hula-hula boy from Maui, gave a deep, solemn bow. When he was made a member of the team, people scoffed that the Air Force was including him as a token Oriental. That was before these people had seen him fly. Wa let his wings do the talking.

"Good to see you, Hawk," the diminutive Wa said, smiling. "Can't do any tricks without The Wingman."

"I only see five planes," Hunter countered, with a laugh. "What am I going to fly?"

At that moment, he would have flown the Piper Cub.

Toomey and Wa loooked at the general.

Jones only smiled. Relighting his cigar, he motioned to the group to grab Hunter and lead him toward the back of the hangar. Even members of the ground crew had stopped attending to the jets and followed the group of pilots to the last bay in the building.

It was covered floor to ceiling with a white drop cloth. The only thing Hunter could see inside the shroud was the glare of two powerful lights, throwing weird shadows around the inside of the structure.

Without fanfare or suspense, Jones drew the curtain back and revealed what was behind.

Hunter felt a lump immediately form in his throat.

Sitting before him was the most beautiful F-16 ever built.

CHAPTER FOUR

It was his old airplane—the F-16 he had flown when he was a member of the Air Force Aerial Demonstration Squadron, as the Thunderbirds were officially called. He had last seen it just before reporting for his NASA shuttle training.

It was painted in the traditional colors of the Thunderbirds. Its snout was wrapped in red, white and blue stripes, as were the tips of its wings. The tail section had a webbed design of blue bordering four large stars and eleven smaller ones on a field of white. Centered on the tail was the unit's symbol—an American Indian-style drawing of the mythical Thunderbird, a circle on its breast which contained a white star. Inside the white star were the silhouettes of four jets.

The jet looked to be in excellent condition—he could tell that it had just been recently overhauled, and given a fresh coat of paint. But for all its authenticity, the '16 still looked different to Hunter. Something was missing.

Then it hit him: All of the plane's Air Force markings had been removed.

"It's the 'law,' Hawk," Jones said, reading his thoughts again. "Like we were talking about, no references to the old days allowed."

"But I thought you said, no one cared about these bogus laws?" Hunter just felt the jet wasn't complete without its old markings.

"In this case, it can get mighty dangerous, real quick," Jones told him. "The New Order will pay any pilot one-hundred-thousand dollars in real silver for shooting down any plane flying with the old USAF markings. All they have to do is produce the evidence. That's a lot of money these days, and there are a lot of free-lancers out there who would gun you down for it. Christ, the New Order would even pay an air pirate."

"Screw the New Order," Hunter spat out.

"Think you can still handle her?" Jones asked him, knowing the reply.

"I suppose I could give it a try," Hunter said, at that moment, the happiest he'd been in nearly three years.

Ten minutes later, he was taxiing down the runway.

The F-16 was a pilot's dream come true.

It was built light—nearly 80-percent of its frame was aluminum, and only 11-percent was the heavier steel. The designers wanted it that way—the lighter the better. The reason? Because they outfitted the thing with a kick-ass GE turbofan engine that could boot 27,000 pounds of thrust on demand. The combination made for a highly aerodynamically superior thrust-to-weight ratio. In other words, the engine thrust power was nearly twice the weight of the entire airplane. Throw in the forebody strakes for vortex control; a wing blended to the body for greater overall lift; a variable wing camber for automatic leading edge steering flaps; one hundred and fifty more examples of state-of-the-art aerodynamics and a dash of American ingenuity and what came out was simply the best maneuvering fighter plane ever built.

The cockpit was a video game come to life. It was crammed with science fiction-type avionics: a "heads-up display" which projected up on an invisible TV screen right in front of the pilot all of the critical control data needed to fly the plane. The pilot could keep an eye on the controls, know where he was going, know what his weapons status was and who he was shooting at—all without ever looking down at the control boards.

But the HUD capability was just the beginning. The plane carried its own video recorder and playback for mission analysis—everything done during a sortie could be recorded and brought back ready for broadcast. The video capability also allowed the pilot to pre-record mission elements for playback during his flight. Seeing this in the cockpit, Hunter had to wonder whether anyone had TVs anymore.

The F-16 had an autopilot that could do just about everything an average human pilot could—some claimed more. But it took more than an average person to understand the alphabet soup of subsystems inside the plane's cockpit: INS, TACAN, TF, IFF/SIF, AAI, ILS, JMC, JVC, ADF UHF, BIT, DMT, ENG, PROG, TGT, HSI, and on and on. It was at once brilliant and bewildering. To the casual observer—and way back when to the uninformed Senate appropriations committee member—the cockpit looked impossibly confused, as if a mad scientist had had a hand in its design. Some pilots believed that was accurate.

The plane was completely "fly-by-wire;" its flight control system was fully electronic. Unlike other planes, the control stick was not between the pilot's legs. Rather it was off to his right side. By using the stick, the pilot had at his fingertips his weapon release, display control, engine trim switch and gun trigger.

The side-stick controller always gave Hunter the feeling that he was flying the plane from an armchair—in fact the F-16 had a recliner seat, tilted upward by 27 degrees. Both were essential to flying such an advanced supersonic fighter and that the F-16 was. Wide open—at "full military"—it could haul ass at nearly three times the speed of sound.

Of course, Hunter knew the reason to fly that fast and accurately was to get where you're going and shoot at something once you got there. Again, the F-16 came out on top. It was a technological schizo. Whether its mission was to dogfight an enemy—a match it almost always won, thanks to its M-16 20mm rapid fire cannon and four air-to-air missiles—or blast him on the ground, the plane could do both, no problem. It could maneuver like a fighter but carry enough ordnance—conventional free-fall bombs, dispenser weapons, napalm, you name it—to be a bomber. And with the fire control system up on the "heads up display," with everything else, the pilot never had to take his eyes off the target.

And with multiple accuracy, "track-while-scan"

high-velocity search, and quick-reaction, fingertip weapons firing additions, the plane was quick on the draw. If the pilot launched an air-to-air missile, the opponent usually had only seconds to live. It was that simple. Challenged to a duel, the F-16 was unquestionably the quickest gun in the West.

If the mission was to bomb—tanks, troops or other airfields—then all the pilot would do is switch on the Doppler beam, sharpen the baby to 64:1, add the ground target indication/tracker and push the button. Anything targeted, moving or not, was instantly blown to smithereens.

And it was good on gas . . .

The F-16 was just under 50 feet long; its wingspan just a hair under 33. The tail rose 17 feet from the ground. It was deceptively small—a direct contradiction to the idea "bigger is better." In the world of the jet fighter, small is better. It means you're hard to detect, either on a radar scope or to the eye. Hard to see means hard to hit. Hard to hit extended a pilot's expectancy by a few minutes, or hours or even years. No wonder they all loved the '16.

The plane could climb, dive and turn on a dime— and pull 9gs while it was doing it. Even better yet, it could do it on a full tank—other planes in its class had a hard time doing 7gs and that was only possible with less than a full fuel load.

But a plane is only as good as its pilot. And Hunter was unquestionably the best. So the F-16 fit him like a glove. A match made in heaven.

His favorite thing about the '16 was that no aircraft was quicker off the ground. Unlike other jets, which required a ground crew to get them cranked up, the F-

16 had an automatic starting system. Just like turning the key in a car, the engine would fire up and be capable of lifting off 51 seconds later. Also eliminated was the 20 minutes or more start-up time that pilots of other planes needed to program their on-board computer. The F-16's computers were churning in less than a minute. All the pilot had to do was pre-record the flight data onto a computer cartridge then load it into the aircraft's computer system. Jones, knowing his wingman would be anxious to get airborne, had already pre-recorded such a cartridge for Hunter.

So, because of the plane's quick reaction capability, Hunter was able to strap into the cockpit, have the plane towed out of the hangar and, just a few minutes later, be sitting at the end of the runway, giving his instruments the final check-over.

This would be a solo flight—like someone seeing an old lover for the first time in a while, Hunter wanted no company. It would be him and the bird alone. It was something his fellow Thunderbird pilots could understand.

He waited for clearance to take off. The base's control tower, in a far cry from its heyday, now only needed a single traffic controller, but he was still the only person who could give a pilot permission to take off. So Hunter waited.

His hands felt good on the controls again. The engine purred like a kitten. The plane had been obviously well-maintained. His thoughts went to the story Jones told him of how he managed to get it: The general had made a convoy run a year before and intentionally stopped at Nellis Air Force Base in Las Vegas on the way back east. The place, once the home base for the Thunderbirds, was now abandoned—and off limits—shut down by the New Order. Jones had set down there anyway, and saw nearly 100 planes lying destroyed on the runways, courtesy of the New Order fanatics. But this didn't prevent him from poking around. He happened upon one of the unit's old supply hangars, busted the lock off with a crowbar and when he swung the door open . . .

"There she was," he had said. "Sitting there like the day you left her. Why those clowns didn't bust her up like all the other planes on the base, we'll never know."

The next convoy west, Jones clandestinely hired a C-130 cargo plane out to Nellis, along with a ground crew, who, over the next several days, secretly took the plane apart, packed it and shipped it east. If they had been caught, it could have meant his losing his job at the least; execution by the New Order at the worst. But they didn't get caught. And once Jones had the F-16, he knew it was time to lure Hunter out of retirement.

Suddenly, the radio crackled and a voice gave him the go-ahead to take-off. He remembered Jones' only request. That was to stay away from the mainland. He didn't particularly want anyone—including his bosses—knowing that the unit had a sophisticated F-16 at the base, not right now anyway.

He scanned his instruments once more and took a deep breath and waited . . .

Then it came to him. *The Feeling.* It was always there every time he took off. He became disembodied. In a higher state of mind. The mechanics of flight became as simple as the wink of an eye. It was this—

this instantaneous osmosis—which set him apart from other stick jockeys. It was indescribable. Other pilots strap in, do the checklist, prepare to take off. Fight the nervous energy that always creeps in. Hunter would melt into the machinery. His brain linked with the on-board computer. His hands and feet became extensions of the flaps and stabilizers. His eyes became the radar; his ears the radio. Other pilots flew with their brains; Hunter flew with his heart. For him to fly an F-16—or any plane for that matter—was as easy and as natural as it was to walk. And that was what set him apart from the others. "The Feeling." It always came to him. It was there the first time his father let him take the controls of the Cessna when he was barely 11. He had never told a soul about it. He couldn't. It was beyond description. Yet, he always recognized it and let it wash through him. From that moment on, he *was* the plane.

Instantly, he lifted the air brakes and was moving forward, gathering speed. 100 knots, 120, 150. His heart was pounding—a promise he had made to himself was coming true. Up on the mountain he had vowed to fly again, somehow, some time. Now, he was doing it. He pulled back on the control stick and the F-16 lifted off the ground.

A tantalizing thrill ran through him. He was certain he could feel his heart pounding against his flight suit, the excitement was so intense. Like a fish back to water—or more accurately, a bird back to wing—he was again where he should be—flying.

His colleagues on the ground watched as the red,

white and blue fighter tore down the runway and lifted off in a flash, a bright cone of fire pouring from the tail. They followed the plane as Hunter stood the '16 straight up on its tail and climbed. And climbed. And climbed. The fighter went straight up into the cloudless sky until it was out of sight. The former Thunderbird pilots shook their heads.

"Two years away from it," Toomey observed. "And the boy is still the best since Orville and Wilbur."

Hunter let the g-force flow through him as the plane climbed higher. It was rejuvenating. The further he got from the ground, the better he felt. It was a classic battle between him and the law of gravity, and, when he was flying, he was winning. He never wanted to come down.

Still the F-16 climbed. 25,000 feet. 30,000. 35,000. Up to 40,000. He was in ecstasy. 45,000. 50,000! 60,000! He could see the dark edge of the stratosphere above him. Was it all worth it? The time spent on the mountain, in a cocoon, waiting. At 70,000 feet—14 miles high and nearing 1200 mph—he let out a whoop! Goddamn! It was worth it, he decided at that moment. He had been reborn.

He turned the plane over in a backward loop and started down. Straight down. The gs increasing, the engine roaring, the ground getting close, real fast. His colleagues on the ground saw him coming, fast and true, like an arrow shot from heaven. No one had the control, the coolness of their friend Hunter. They admired him and, not so secretly, envied him.

He pulled up smoothly, barely 100 feet above the runway. Jones had wisely ordered the airspace above the field to be cleared, a standard procedure when the team flew their exhibitions. Work had stopped completely at the base as word that Hunter, "the greatest pilot ever born," was putting on a show. When the Thunderbirds performed in the old days, Hunter would do a solo spot, and it was always the crowd pleaser. As the entire base—pilots to sentries—had their eyes upward, it was clear that nothing had changed.

He ran through all the old stunts like he'd never stopped performing. Loops. Eights. One point starburst. Upside down crossover. Controlled stall. Four point turns. Eight point turns. He ended the exhibition with a blistering low altitude buzz of the base. Even the seasoned pilots on hand had to let out gasps of admiration. The boy was born to fly.

Then, it was over. Time to come home. He set the plane down softly. The '16 had performed superbly. With a couple of squadrons of these, he thought, he and his friends could clear the skies of any opponent. He was itching for the chance. Hungry for action. He rolled the plane up to the hangar and shut it down. There, a ground crew appeared and helped him unstrap. He climbed down to the tarmac where Jones was waiting for him.

"Fair," the general said, coolly lighting a cigar to camouflage his smile. "Just keep your nose up and don't be so much of a hot dog and you'll make it."

"Yes, sir," Hunter replied, knowing he deserved some ribbing. "Thank you, sir. How many more of these you got?"

Jones suddenly turned serious. "That's the bad news, Hawk."

Hunter waited.

"We've looked all over, asked around, offered good money," Jones said slowly. "Couldn't find a single one, next to this one."

"You mean . . . ?" Hunter said, fearing the worst.

"You're right on top of it, Hawk," Jones said, looking at the F-16. "The New Order got to all of them. Pranged them. The incredible fools."

Hunter closed his eyes.

"As far as we know," Jones said, "this is the last F-16 left."

CHAPTER FIVE

Later on that night, after chow and before the bourbon was broken out, Hunter and Jones sat in the pilot's lounge smoking cigars. The room was small and cramped, but homey, thanks to the half dozen overstuffed chairs that were jammed into it. Its walls were covered with snapshots of the Thunderbirds in action in the old days. In the corner, a VCR—the only TV available these days—cranked away, displaying a porn movie on a jumpy black and white screen. Hunter avoided watching it for fear he'd burst a seam. He couldn't remember the last time he'd made love to a woman. Was it in France?

It had been one hell of a day for Hunter—his reunion with the general and the Thunderbirds, Jones' updating him on the radical changes across the continent, the exhilarating flight, the shock of knowing that there was probably but one F-16 left in the world. It was hard for Hunter to believe that less than 48 hours before, he was still cooped up in the cabin on the mountain.

"Well," Jones said, finishing off a cup of coffee. "Do you want a job or don't you?"

"Job?" Hunter asked.

"Yes, Major. That's what one gets when one has to earn a living. It's a totally alien subject to you?"

It was true, from his childhood, through M.I.T., through the Air Force Academy and into the service, he had never held a *regular* job.

"Look," Jones said, leaning forward in his chair. "It's not much pay. Just enough to keep some silver— some real stuff—jingling in your pocket. But these days, what's to buy? Booze. Women. Cheap cigars.

"But I'll guarantee you all the flying time we can manage to give you fuel for. And, it's your '16 if you want it."

"I accept," Hunter said quickly.

"Now wait a minute," Jones said, holding up his hand in caution. "Let me explain the job. We are talking about routine stuff. Escorting tanker deliveries, border patrol, training new guys if we get them planes to fly. Chasing pirates if they break our airspace is about the only action I can promise you. At least, for a while."

"I accept," Hunter said again.

"Will you wait a goddamn minute? You had better lay out your options, Hawk. Like I said, you could make a fortune as a free-lancer, doing trans-continentals. There's a company, right up in Boston. Headhunters, always looking for flyboys for convoy duty. They'll pay you more in a week than I can give you in a year."

"But I accept *your* offer," Hunter repeated.

"Will you cool your goddamn jets?"

"Look, will I be working with you and the guys?" Hunter asked.

"Yes," Jones said, with a wave of his cigar. "But . . ."

"And will I be flying that '16 out there?"

"Of course, but . . ."

"Then, I accept your offer," he said with a smile.

"All right, wise ass," Jones said in exasperation. "You're hired. Now, will you listen to me?"

"Go ahead. Boss."

"I'll kick your butt," Jones said, reaching for a label-less bottle of bourbon. "You listen to me you hot dog . . ."

The general stopped for a moment, looked around for a glass, settled on an old styrofoam coffee cup and poured himself a stiff double. Hunter realized that whatever Jones had to tell him wasn't a laughing matter.

Jones took a deep belt from the coffee cup. The stuff was rot-gut; but moonshine's biggest asset was that it was available. In the old days, you wouldn't give it to your worst enemy.

"There's going to be war," the older men said deliberately.

Hunter was puzzled. "There's already been a big one. I thought *it* was 'the war to end all wars.' "

Jones sighed and shook his head. "No, I mean right here, on the East Coast. With the Mid-Atlantic Division."

"The Mid-Aks?" Hunter asked, looking out for a cup for himself.

"You got it. Things started to smell a few months ago. Little things. Here and there. Nothing that could stand on its own. But when you add them up . . ."

"Things like what?" Hunter asked, after locating a

70

chipped and cloudy tea cup and pouring himself a drink.

"Well, the boys in Boston have never got along with Mid-Atlantic. They feel they're just a little too cute for them. I mean, seeing them raise an army that could kick-ass on half the continent, that's nothing to be taken lightly."

"Especially when you have them for neighbors," Hunter added.

"Check. There ain't nothing between us and them except what's left in New York City. Boston figured that if they wanted to put people to work, like a People's Army, building roads, repairing things, then, what the hell?"

"People's Army sounds a little too familiar," Hunter said.

"I agree. It's Russian to the gonads. But still, Boston didn't mind all that much. I mean, there are eleven other countries out there now, and several free zones and unclaimed territories . . ."

"And the Badlands. And the pirates."

"Right. Who can blame them for starting an army? There's a lot of kookaboos running loose."

Hunter nodded in agreement, refilled Jones's cup and put a head on his own.

The general took a swig. "But it started with this shit at Fort Knox. I mean, they killed some people down there. Locals. People who just happened to live near the place, and who had some guns and squatted on it, using a little of the gold at a time.

"But you see, it was the way the Mid-Aks did it. They didn't attack these folks right away. In fact, they did business with them. Then, they entered into a

71

'mutual cooperation pact' or something with these people, who were actually no more than four or five hundred, and calling themselves Kentucky Free State.

"Next thing you know, just when the Kentuckians thought they could do business with Mid-Atlantic— *boom!*—the Mid-Aks accuse them of some such nonsense, and they attack them. Wipe 'em out. It took all of an afternoon. Five hundred or more dead. The Mid-Aks sitting on top of a pile of gold. Who's going to say a thing?"

"Well, is it common knowledge about what happened?" Hunter wanted to know.

"Maybe," Jones replied. "There ain't no more newspapers, Hawker. We used to complain about the press doing this and that. You know how much I hated sucking up to those bastards during the Thunderbirds' days. Now that they're gone, no one knows what the hell is happening on the other side of the mountain or in the next town over. We have one hundred million people still living on this continent, but ninety-nine point nine million of them are woefully uninformed."

"What did the New Order Commissioner and his goons do?"

"Not a thing. And they knew about the Fort Knox thing. That I know for a fact. I've some good contacts up in Boston. Guys I've done favors for. They keep their ears to the ground and they keep me informed. The New Order heard about the Gold War within days of it happening. Did nothing."

"Go on," Hunter said.

"Well, the Mid-Aks used the gold to build an even bigger army and that's when they went after the

72

Florida-Alabama Union. But it was the same style. First, they played it cozy with them, opening up trading centers on their borders. Letting people travel back and forth without much hassle. Then again with this 'mutual pact' shit. Course, these Florida-'Bama Unionist guys didn't exactly know what went down in Kentucky. Then the 'Aks proposed that the two regions 'merge,' to use their term."

"Right," Hunter said. "Just like when Hitler 'merged' with Poland."

"You're catching on, Hawk. But this time, the Mid-Aks didn't even wait for an answer."

"You mean they just walked in and took over?" Hunter asked.

"Just about," Jones said. "But first they started a diversion. Now, remember, not many people know this is really what happened. It was real early one morning. A couple of ships sailed in from nowhere, anchored off Miami and opened up on the city with big guns. Then they started offloading troops! In landing craft, yet! These guys, armed to the teeth and all dressed in black, start splashing ashore. The Union guys don't know what the fungoo is going on. These troops could be from Cuba, for all they know. So they stop 'em on the beach. Cut them up bad and bloody. But while they're doing that, the 'Aks hit them from the north. Poured in like ants.

"It took a little longer this time. There are some tough sons of bitches down Florida and Alabama way. I mean, Roll, Tide. They weren't like a bunch of hillbillies sitting on six billion dollars in gold. They fought back. Man, they had tanks, howitzers, a few choppers.

"But they had no money. And no money meant no air cover. And no air cover meant it was just a matter of time before the bigger army won. The Mid-Aks finally squashed them. Took about a month. It was a bloodbath. And from what I hear, the Mid-Aks didn't take kindly to the conquered population. Killed kids, old women. Sold the good looking women. Shit like that."

"And, again, the brave New Order was on the sidelines?"

"With their fingers up their whatzis. I mean, this happened practically right next door to them. Florida's not that far from Bermuda. They're either scared shitless of Mid-Atlantic . . ."

"Or . . . ?" Hunter asked.

"Or they're in bed together," Jones said, worry crossing his face.

Hunter ran his fingers through his long hair. It sure didn't take the world very long to get screwed up.

"You said, you've smelled other things?" he asked Jones.

"Oh yes," the general replied. "You see, most of the people on the continent want nothing to do with Mid-Atlantic. I mean, we won't trade with them, and neither will the Coasters. The Texans demand real coin, up front from them, but that's not a problem, since they locked up the gold supply."

"Then the Mid-Aks are probably the richest of the countries," Hunter said. "But are they the strongest?"

"Not yet," Jones replied. "Right now, in the pecking order, with all things considered, we here in the Northwest are probably the strongest this side of the

Badlands, and that's in good part because we're lucky. We have some airplanes and pilots. The Boston Army is strictly paid soldiers, but they seem loyal. Small, but good. When I get through with the training of the Special Force here, we'll be better. The 'Aks don't go in for jets. Probably too stupid to fly them. They have some ships, and I hear they've been buying up helicopters. But they're *too* big, if anything, and they got a lot of territory to patrol and a lot of pissed off people under their control.

"On the other hand, we've got stable and easily patrolled borders to the west, thanks in part that New York State is now a Free Territory. The ocean covers our ass to the east and a friendly Canada sits over us.

"And the Coasters are the same way. No real enemies close by. They're the strongest west of the Badlands, with maybe the Texans a close third. The Mid-Aks are definitely fourth on the list, but they're trying like hell to be number one. God! I think I'd prefer those hoodlums in New Chicago than these bozos down in Mid-Atlantic."

"So, what 'smells?' " Hunter asked, draining his cup of hootch.

"Well, just this," Jones said. "I was up in Boston last week. Just making the rounds, seeing my contacts. They run everything out of a skyscraper now. The old Prudential Insurance building, I think it was called. It's one of the tallest things around."

Hunter knew the building.

"Anyway, suddenly, I start hearing things like: 'Maybe the Mid-Aks ain't that bad,' and 'They've changed their ways. They want to play it straight from now on.' "

75

"You're kidding?" Hunter was amazed.

"No shit. But you see, these guys in Boston didn't stop being politicians just because someone dropped the bomb. They're like the Texans. Texas didn't stop pumping oil, and the Boston politicians didn't stop making deals. I mean, these guys wrote the book on how to make a deal."

Hunter was familiar with it, having spent a lot of time in Boston when he attended Aeronautics School at M.I.T.

"What these Boston pols have their eyes on is a piece of that real gold," Jones continued. "I mean, forget the clad. The currency of choice now is silver. But that's only because there's so much of it still around. People settle for silver, but they do crazy things for gold.

"So now there's talk on the Leaders' Council about let's give the Mid-Aks a chance. Exchange ambassadors. Get to know them. This kind of happy horseshit. Meanwhile, they're building the biggest goddamn army since the Civil War!"

Jones was silent once again. He was plainly worried about dragging Hunter and the other pilots into what could be a deadly situation. Not that they couldn't fend for themselves. But who wants to risk getting his ass shot off for a country that hasn't been around long enough to feel any kind of loyalty to?

"Well, the long and short of it, Hawk, is that one of the last things I heard when I was up there was some asshole talking about a 'mutual cooperation pact' with Mid-Atlantic."

"Sounds like they're going down the primrose path," Hunter said, sensing Jones's rising alarm.

"Oh, some of them want to get screwed, do you see?" Jones said. "There's really nothing in the Northeast Economic Zone that's not worth selling out for. And, if the Mid-Aks can come in the back door, well, it sure would make it a lot easier on them."

"So you mentioned something about a war?" Hunter asked, getting the general back to his original statement.

"Oh yeah," Jones answered. "But not right away. Maybe a year. Maybe longer. But it's coming. I can feel it. My bosses—the good ones anyway—won't let this dirty dealing go on, if they can help it. They might not be full military guys, Hawk, but Jesus, they have a better perspective on right and wrong than most of these chowderheads in Boston do."

"And you'll fight?" Hunter asked him.

"I don't know," Jones said slowly. "I don't have any real loyalty to the Northeast, although it sure is better than a lot of the gabonzo that's going down for governments these days.

"I'd like to fight because the Mid-Aks are like the commies in my eyes. They're pigs. No respect for human life or rights. They rape. They sell young girls. They kill old people and kids. What the hell ever happened to live and let live? I refuse to traffic with sub-humans!"

He took a slug right from the hootch bottle for effect.

"But if they got into the pants of the crooked pols in Boston, we'd be overwhelmed, I think. They'd start cutting our fuel rations. They'd start yanking me around, so I'd be missing the details of running this place. Just when things would be at the worst, the

'Aks would come down on us like a ton of bricks. When that shit starts happening, I'll know it's just a matter of time. And we could fight. But I don't believe in killing a lot of good pilots just because a bunch of politicians get screwed and like it."

Hunter thought for a moment. Need to fight for a cause, the old man had told him earlier in the day. But he also wanted to serve the general.

"I'm with you all the way, sir," he said.

"Thanks, Hawk."

There was an awkward moment of silence between them. The general was like a father to him. He would go the extra mile and then some for the man.

"Just one more thing, Hawk?" Jones said.

"Name it, sir," he replied.

"Get a hair cut and a shave. You're a mess."

Just then, Ben Wa and Toomey burst in. They were obviously drunk, a state that Jones and Hunter were also reaching.

"Hawk, old buddy, your compadres have arrived!" Ben announced. "Girls?"

With that, four of the most beautiful girls in the world walked into the lounge. There was a blonde, two brunettes and a redhead, each one wearing a tight sweater and short skirt, each one made up to the hilt. Each one obviously looking for a good time. They had come to the right place. Hunter's eyes went wide and he felt a pulsating start up in his loins.

"Ladies?" J.T. announced. "Meet the famous Hawk Hunter, cover-boy, fighter pilot, whiz kid and astronaut-in-waiting."

There was a round of greetings and an orgy of eyelash fluttering, but he was oblivious to it all. His eyes were transfixed on the redhead's breasts.

Jones leaned over to him. "Go ahead boy," he said. "Get your pipes cleaned. Just leave one for this old man and make sure you're down on the flight line at eight tomorrow morning."

Hunter took the redhead by the hand and headed for the quarters Jones had issued him earlier.

It had been quite a day . . .

CHAPTER SIX

Hunter settled into the base. For the next six months he enjoyed the surprisingly pleasant routine of a fighter pilot in the New Order world. It was a life of daily patrols of the Northeast Economic Zone's outlying borders, keeping an eye on the nearby sea lanes, and an occasional tanker escort mission. Jones had decided long before to leave the air convoy protection business to the free-lancers. He needed live pilots—not dead mercenaries. Thanks to the growing power of the air pirates and the increasingly treacherous skies above the Badlands, the life expectancy of a free lancer was now measured in days.

Hunter was happy. He got all the flying time he wanted, a place to sleep, good chow, women. What more could he ask for? Except maybe a little combat action, now and then.

The continent was in a state of change, too. People were adapting, coming out of hiding. A regular little community—quickly nicknamed "Jonesville"—sprang up on the base. Tired of living in groups or in hiding, some civilians occupied the abandoned GI housing outside the base. Others started building anew. Within two months of Hunter's arrival, there were more than 5000 people in the neighborhood. They liked the security of having an army and air force nearby to protect them from the unknowns of the post-war world. Many worked at the base, and Jones, the true-blue capitalist who became an unofficial Big Daddy *cum*-governor for the area, allowed the citizens to set up shops inside the fence. They even started their own militia-style police force.

What was better was that eligible women began frequenting the base, mostly party girls who loved mixing it up with the soldiers, especially the flyboys. Some were even charging for it, an enterprise Jones wisely let continue unabated. Every pressure needs a release, he would say.

Training of the Zone Air Rangers continued. Jones was able to dig up some helicopters for them—eight big Chinooks, to be exact, dubbed "The Crazy Eights." The choppers were chock full of machine-guns, rocket launchers, cannons, anything that could shoot. Within a few months, the former undisciplined, shoot 'em up army was becoming the crack special forces unit Jones had wanted it to be. They trained in airborne assaults, coordinated attack with air support and guerrilla/night fighting.

The size of the ZAR increased to 500, enough for Jones to take 250 of them and establish a half dozen outposts on the Zone's western borders. The string of bases served as combination frontier posts and early warning system. Each place had a working, though rudimentary, radar system. If anything flying was seen approaching the Zone's airspace, the news was flashed by clandestine radio sets to Otis. If the sighting was deemed possibly hostile, two ZAP fighters would scramble. There were two fighters—usually the F-4 and another smaller plane—on alert at all times. The ZAP radar net was also good for keeping track of the air convoys that left Logan Airport on a more regular basis. Knowing where every plane was helped the 50 or so planes get properly grouped for the long voyage west. But the service was a luxury and the convoy pilots knew it. Once the air parade left the Zone's airspace they had to wing it—usually—until they were in range of similar radar stations run by the Coasters on the far side of the Rockies.

But despite troubles in the middle of the country, things seemed to stabilize—at least in the Northeast Economic Zone—now nearly three years into the New Order.

For the most part, all talk of alliances with the Mid-Atlantics died down. The Leaders Council silenced the troublemakers if temporarily and concentrated on making money. Jones had finally let his bosses know that he had hired Hunter *and* his F-16. They were delighted. And once they realized that Jones had assembled nearly the entire former Thunderbirds demonstration team, requests for aerobatic shows started pouring in.

The ZAP put on impressive shows for visiting government or trade officials. The other countries on the continent—with the exception of the Coasters and the Texans—barely had the equipment and manpower to put two or three jets into the air. And here was ZAP, flying modern fighters and performing precision team aerobatics high above Boston.

Hunter loved doing the shows, although others in the team came to view them as a pain. Jones knew better. There were spies everywhere these days; more than a few of them, he was sure, had taken up residence in Boston. Any potential adversary—Mid-Ak, Family, or even Russian—watching the expert flying of the demo team had a very clear message to send back to their bosses: Don't tangle with ZAP.

The air pirates learned that lesson the hard way.

Hunter had been at the base for about eight weeks when they first heard about a roving band of pirates operating on the edge of the Northeast's frontier. The area—once known as upstate New York—was now called the Free Territory of New York. Free Territory was just another way of saying, "every man for himself." There was no central government as there was in the Northeast Economic Zone. Most of the major cities were evacuated during the war, many of the residents fleeing to Quebec. The people who remained lived in the many small towns and villages that dotted the Territory. These people simply governed themselves. Most of the time, it worked.

Sometimes it didn't.

As reports of the air bandits became more frequent, it was soon obvious that they were preying on anything that flew around the Catskills and all the way up to the Adirondack Mountain Range. In two weeks' time several planes—stragglers, solo artists—had been shot down. Others were forced to land, their cargoes stolen, their crews killed. The area wasn't too far from the well-traveled convoy routes, but this band of pirates—touchingly known as the Cherry Busters—were avoiding the big stuff and going after the small potatoes. What was worse, this happened before the ZAP radar string was brought on line.

Because every airplane that flies needs people on the ground to keep it that way, roving pirate bands always carried a substantial ground maintenance entourage. These mechanics—prisoners and ex-gas station owners mostly—traveled with the bandits, servicing the planes and occasionally acting as ground troops. They were paid by sharing in the booty. Frequently these ground support crews were as dangerous, if not worse, than the pilots they served. The Cherry Busters were no different. While the pirates' terrorized the skies above, small villages and towns on the Zone-New York Territory border were attacked by the Buster's rampaging ground crews.

Jones had been watching the situation and had increased the air patrols in the area. He quietly dispatched a 100-man Ranger unit by helicopter to sit on the border in case it was needed. But there was little else he could do. The pirates were operating in an area that was out of his jurisdiction and Jones's bosses in Boston warned him strongly and repeatedly that they wanted no part of anyone else's problem. As long as the pirates didn't violate the Northeast Economic Zone's airspace, Jones and ZAP was powerless to stop them.

But then the Cherry Busters made a mistake. The bandits' ground crews blew into a town that straddled the border with the Northeast Economic Zone and held it for three days. By the time the Rangers heard about it and got there, the place—once a town of 600—was in ruins, burnt to the ground. The Rangers found evidence of mass executions, torture, looting. The bodies recovered were those of old people and men, some of whom had fought back. As always, anything young and pretty was gone—young girls were the pirates most sought-after booty. Other women, those not quite measuring up to the pirates' standards, were found dead also, but not before they had all been brutally raped.

Although the demolished town sat literally, right on the border, Jones had seen enough. Screw the orders from Boston. He had his own policy. It was called Hot Pursuit. He deployed ZAP's battle units into the area with orders to seek out and destroy the Cherry Busters. The same orders were given to the Rangers. The search for the pirates had begun.

ZAP recon flights had not yet pinpointed the airstrip the pirates were flying out from. Just about every known airfield in the region big enough to handle the Cherry Busters' hodge-podge of jet fighters was kept under surveillance. Yet the bandits couldn't be found.

Then ZAP got a break. Residents living near a remote section on the border told the Ranger unit that they heard engine noises every night nearby, although there wasn't an airport for miles. The Rangers radioed the information back to Otis, and Hunter fired up the F-16 and headed for the area. Flying high enough to evade any shitbox radar the pirates might have, it took Hunter only about 20 minutes to locate the pirate base. It turned out that ZAP was looking in the wrong place for the Cherry Busters all the time. The pirates weren't using an airfield at all—they were using a highway. The bandits had found a certain section of the abandoned New York State Thruway that was straight enough for the right distance to handle fighter take-offs and landings. They managed to hide all their support equipment in buildings nearby and parked their aircraft under the forest canopy at the side of the roadway.

Hunter spotted a series of tire marks on a section of the highway close to the border. The straight lines of black were the unmistakable result of jet landings. It was a subtle, but dead giveaway. After hearing Hunter's report, Jones ordered an immediate air strike on the pirates' base.

It was Hunter's first action in years, and it turned out to be surprisingly dull. Leading a flight of four—his F-16, the F-4 and two A-7s—Hunter caught the pirates on the ground just as the sun was coming up. Hunter and the two-seat F-4, piloted by Ben Wa with Toomey riding in the rear as the weapons officer, flew air cover as the A-7s delivered several tons of effective—and expensive—blockbuster bombs onto the makeshift runway. The pirates never got a plane into the air—their entire contingent of six jets was destroyed on the ground. Hunter's contribution to the raid was confined to two strafing runs to suppress some token groundfire that had been pestering the A-7s. It was over in a matter of 20 minutes. The Cherry Busters' base was destroyed. The gang was history, scattered. The Ranger unit, waiting nearby, managed

86

to rescue some of the pirates' hostages left behind as the bandits fled.

From then on, aside from a few scrambles, air pirates gave the area a wide berth. The brief campaign became known as the Thruway War, significant because it was the first time ZAP drew real blood. Jones was pleased the unit had acted and performed in a highly professional manner.

Trouble was, his bosses weren't . . .

Every month, the team was asked to perform on the so-called Profit Holidays, occasions decreed by the Northeast government to celebrate the financial successes of the region. On these occasions, businesses would shut down in the capital city and the citizens would line the banks of the Charles River and watch ZAP do its stuff.

There were many reasons to celebrate. Convoys were leaving Logan Airport every other day now and Boston Harbor was filled with ships carrying goods from what was left of the civilized world. As the number of declared Profit Holidays increased, so did the performances—and the popularity—of the ZAP team.

Some of the members of the team had trouble reconciling the government set-up in Boston. But to Hunter, it was simple enough. Everyone living in the Northeast Economic Zone worked for the government. The business of the region was commerce. And business was booming.

Logan Airport was the busiest trading center by far

on the East Coast. A convoy left the airport once every two days now, usually as many as 60 huge airliners with nearly half as many escort craft. The skies across the continent were still dangerous. But the attitude was similar to the days of the covered wagon pioneer. If 55 of 60 planes made it, it was a successful trip.

Boston's natural harbor called to many ships; lines that in the pre-war days would have stopped in New York City, now avoided the place with a passion, all for Boston's gain. So, the Profit Holidays were actually the holidays for a government in which everyone worked for—and benefitted from—the financial conquests of the state. Some called it Socialism for Profit but unlike past Marxist experiments, this one worked. The economic success of the Northeast Economic Zone grew by leaps and bounds.

And so did ZAP. The general continued to lobby the more rational minds in Boston that the tiny Air Patrol was important to the survival of the government in the turbulent times.

"They make a lot of money in import duties and trade taxes and for running one of the few operating airports on the continent," Jones would explain, endlessly over drinks at the base's heavily patronized pilot's club. "If they give me just one percent of what they are making, I can build them an air force that will kick the grease out of anybody."

Their victory in the Thruway War was seemingly the proof. For a while, the Leaders Council gave Jones all the money he asked for.

And someone had to spend it and that job fell to

88

Hunter. Jones made him the base procurement officer; the man in charge of buying new aircraft for ZAP. Armed with bagfuls of real silver, Hunter was able to cut deals with aircraft brokers from Texas to Canada. Word about ZAP was getting around the country—the air corps that kicked ass on the Cherry Busters, the air corps with all the money—and the dealers would gladly come to Otis to talk purchases. Within a few months, Hunter's acquisition had increased ZAP's inventory to 18 planes, a dozen of which were operational at any given moment. Most of the aircraft he bought were A-7s, the National Guard attack planes that were in abundance simply because they weren't rushed overseas when World War III broke out. They were hidden in great numbers when the New Order went down. Hunter was able to buy a six-pack from a dealer who had hidden them on an island in the Florida Keys just before the Mid-Ak occupation forces took over the state after their war against the Florida-Alabama Unionists. He spirited them away on a ship to Texas and let Hunter have the planes for a song; he was more interested in keeping them out of the hands of the Mid-Aks than making any kind of profit.

The little A-7s, while hardly glamorous, fit the bill in the post-war world—the new era of "anything will do."

Hunter was also able to buy two creaking F-106 Delta Darts, an arrow shaped plane that was at one time the mainstay of the interceptor force protecting North America. That was in the days before the ICBM. The jet fighter, which could still reach near

Mach 2, had had its last gasp in Viet Nam. But Hunter was able to find two of them hidden in a hangar at a small airport in what used to be the state of Maine.

In a few months, thanks to Hunter, ZAP had increased its inventory to two F-4s, the F-8, seven A-7s, the two F-106s, five T-38s and his F-16. He was able to recruit pilots—including a dozen former Massachusetts Air National Guard flyboys as well as a handful of semi-trustworthy free-lancers. The pilots-for-pay were either tired of the long, dangerous hours on convoy duty, or felt their number was coming up and decided to lay low for a while. Meanwhile the original members of ZAP—the former Thunderbirds pilots—took on added responsibilities as instructors and trainers. A firing range was set up in a desolate bog near the base, and anti-ship operations were practiced on a target ship that had been scuttled and in place off the coast of the Cape for years before the war.

Hunter was also able to hire on some cracker-jack mechanics to care for ZAP's air fleet. He knew, as every other pilot did, that a good "monkey" was worth his weight in real silver. In many cases, the monkey was the only thing that stood between a successful flight and the pilot impacting onto the side of a mountain somewhere. These days, good mechanics were in as big demand as good pilots, maybe more so.

Hunter was given a free rein—and bags of real silver, even a little bit of gold, courtesy of the Leaders Council—to buy as many aircraft as he wanted. There

90

seemed no shortage of equipment available—or salesmen. A representative of the enterprising owners of The Wright-Patterson Used Aircraft Company—a man known only as Roy From Troy—would turn up on Jonesville's radar like clockwork on the first day of every month. Always flying in some God-awful airplane that was usually almost too big to come in safely, Roy From Troy nevertheless would circle the base and schmooz with the air traffic controllers, who would usually relent and let him land. Once granted, he'd bounce in and emerge from his transportation, a case of scotch under one arm and one of his traveling bevy of blondes under the other.

Roy would corner Hunter every trip and display a battered photo album filled with pictures of his inventory of old U.S. military aircraft. "The best defense in an unpredictable world," so his company's motto went, "is a better offense." It was written on his business card, on the beat-up photo album cover and sometimes painted on the side of the plane he'd blow in on.

Roy From Troy would always be touting his monthly specials—"the last B-29s flying," or "Two F-94s for the price of one, July only." The hand of one of Roy's blonde sales assistants slowly moving its way up to the buyer's crotch was part of the standard operating procedure and led to more than a few sales. The story was told of a Texan air commander who woke up from a drunken stupor one morning and found two of Roy's blondes in his bed and a line of nearly useless B-57s out on his runway. Roy was long gone, but left a note thanking the commander for the real silver and telling him he could keep the blondes.

Despite all of the temptations, Roy couldn't hide the fact that his catalog consisted of heavy bombers mostly—old beasts like B-47 Stratojets and B-58 Hustlers—the kind of museum piece aircraft that the speedy ZAP wasn't interested in.

"No *probleemo*," the aircraft salesman, would say. "Catch you on the next trip." Then the ZAP pilots would drink the scotch and bed the blondes and Roy From Troy would move on the next morning, to other customers, some of which may someday turn out to be adversaries of ZAP. That is, if they weren't already. No matter. Everyone understood. It was the art of business. Capitalism, to the delight of all, wasn't missing-in-action.

Hunter *did* do business with Roy on occasion. He bought a pair of Huey H-1B helicopters from him to supplement the eight the ZAP already flew. He was also able to buy some spare parts for the F-106s. And he always had the salesman—as well as many others—on the lookout for another F-16.

But the biggest deal Hunter and Roy ever consummated was for the general's F-111.

The F-111 was a strange airplane. Designed in the mid-60s, the jet was built too big to be a combat fighter but too small to be a heavy bomber. Its most visible characteristic was its movable wings; it was the first of several flex-wing airplanes built by the airpowers in the 60s and 70s. With the push of a button, the wings could swing forward whenever the airplane was landing or on a slow, low-level bombing run and then be swept back for supersonic flight. In fact, the airplane's wings could be stopped at any point.

But it was what was on the inside of the airplane that intrigued Hunter. The jet was packed with sophisticated, if slightly outdated, navigational and auto-pilot gear. In fact, it could literally fly itself, carrying its two-man crew along simply for the ride. The airplane's computers, programmed before the flight, could start the engines, taxi the airplane, get it airborne, fly to the target, bomb the target and return to its airfield. The airplane also carried a super-radar system called Terrain Avoidance. This system would allow the pilot to set an altitude—usually something low like 200 feet off the deck—and lock it in. From then on the airplane would fly at precisely that altitude, raising and lowering automatically, whether it passed over a mountain or a pebble. The technique was very helpful for low-level attacks when the pilot—automatic or not—wanted to sneak in under the radar but didn't want to cope with the hairiness of flying that low at supersonic speeds.

The general had once told Hunter a chilling story about an F-111 he had seen in Viet Nam. The pilots in the aircraft had taken off from Da Nang. The airplane was serving as flight leader for three other F-111s to bomb the Na Trong Bridge, a hot target just outside of Hanoi. The bridge was ringed with anti-aircraft guns and SAM missiles, but the flyboys managed to blow up three of the four spans anyway. On their last pass though, the flight leader took a direct hit from an ack-ack position. Damaged, the airplane flew on. It returned to Da Nang, landed and taxied up to its station. The ground crew quickly blocked it off and scrambled up to the pilots. They pried the canopy open and found both men long dead. Each had had his head blown off over Na Trong. But the airplane came back.

Hunter knew the old man would love the airplane, and that it would beef up ZAP's capability, so he finally bought it from a very happy Roy From Troy. The salesman had been trying to unload it for some time. No other Air Patrol had the expertise to fly or maintain it. But then again, no other Air Patrol had pilots like Hunter and the Thunderbirds or mechanics like those at Jonesville.

As expected, the general took to the F-111 like a kid to his first Chevy. He spent many a night alone, tinkering with the airplane, giving it all kinds of weapons and snooping abilities. Despite his cowboy demeanor, the general was a whiz at aeromechanics— almost as good as Hunter himself. Whenever the old man had a spare moment, he took the F-111 for a cruise, usually a terrifying low-level flight, with the Terrain Avoidance gear kicked in and the airplane roller-coastering over mountains and buildings alike. Occasionally, Jones would invite one of the other pilots along—an invitation more and more of the flyboys politely declined in deference to their stomachs, if not their equilibrium.

Yet, despite the diversion of the F-111 and the growth in size and popularity of ZAP, Hunter noticed that the general's behavior had taken a strange turn. His flights in the F-111 became more frequent, but obviously less pleasant. He stopped logging in destination codes or filling out the necessary fuel-use forms. He also started committing the cardinal sin of flying: not filing a flight plan.

Jones seemed worse whenever he returned from his trips to Boston. The Leaders seemed to be making him jump through hoops, sometimes ordering him to report to them every day, then cancelling the meeting once Jones had arrived. Like any good soldier, Jones put up with it, for the sake of ZAP and his men.

But the old man's mysterious behavior was starting to be picked up by the other pilots. Rumors began flying around the base that he was sick, shell-shocked or just plain old. Hunter knew he would have to talk to him about it and was waiting for just such an opportunity, when one night in the base club, Jones spilled his gut to his wingman.

"It's just a matter of time now, Hawk," the senior officer said. "The Mid-Aks are really setting us up this time."

"Give me details," Hunter told him, ordering another round of drinks.

"You remember a while back when I told you I heard talk of kissing ass with the Mid-Atlantic?"

Hunter nodded. He remembered the conversation very well.

"Well, this time, it's more than talk. I've got proof there have been secret meetings between some of the Boston Leaders and the 'Aks."

"Proof? How so?"

Jones leaned in conspiratorially. "The Flight Operations Director up at Logan is a buddy of mine. It's a good job, but he always has the Leaders on his ass about something. Adding airplanes to a convoy at the last minute, getting rides for their wives and girlfriends. Shit like that.

"Well, he told me that for the past half year or so, four or five of the Leaders and a bunch of their flunkies were flying out of Logan almost every other weekend. No matter what the weather was, no matter what was happening in the capital at the time. And using the airport's Lear jet to boot!"

"So?" Hunter asked.

"So, they're not filing a flight plan and they're not entering anything on the airplane's log. This guy gets suspicious. These bozos are using up a lot of fuel that he's responsible for and he thinks they're just buzzing around, burning the stuff up for no reason. So what's he do but start checking the distance indicator and he finds the airplane is going the exact mileage every trip. And it's landing somewhere, because it's coming back with gas still in the tank. My buddy gets a map out and starts plotting possible destinations. After a little detective work he figures out that the only suitable landing field for a Lear within the mileage range was down in Baltimore."

"The capital of Mid-Atlantic," Hunter filled in.

"Right. These guys are meeting with them. They'd have to be! I asked this guy who the pols were and he gave me the names of the five slimiest whozits on the Leaders' Council. And one of them turns out to be the guy who I told you first started dropping hints that the Mid-Aks weren't all that bad."

The general seethed whenever he talked about the Mid-Atlantics. This time, a vein was bulging out of his forehead so prominently, Hunter thought it would burst.

"I hate those bastards," Jones said, finishing his beer in one gulp and calling for another in the same motion. "They're dirty. They're rapists. They're child murderers. I'd love to bomb the faggots back into the Stone Age."

"What do you think is up?" Hunter asked. "Some kind of a trade deal?"

"Shit, no," Jones said. "I'd bet a bag of real silver they're talking some kind of mutual-cooperation pact, again. Some of the good guys on the Council are gone. If five of the others are playing footsies with the scum—well, there are only eleven people on the Leaders Council. Lock up one more vote and they've got the God Almighty majority. Then we'll all be expected to suck up to the 'Aks."

The other pilots drinking nearby had overheard the conversation and drifted over to the table where Hunter and the general were drinking.

". . . And once they get in our pants like that," Jones continued, realizing he had the attention of every pilot in the bar, "We'll never get rid of them. They're like a bad case of the crabs. Then it's just a matter of time before they make their move."

The pilots started to shift uneasily. They knew the general wasn't prone to this kind of talk, even with a half dozen drinks in him. If anything, the normal Jones would be bragging about kicking ass on any potential enemy, in the air or on the ground. But Jones was clearly worried, and Hunter had to admit the old man was starting to give him the creeps.

"Look," Hunter said, sipping his fourth beer of the night. "We can get fifteen airplanes into the air at any given moment. We've got the Air Rangers. If the Mid-Atlantic ever made a move, we could nail them before they ever left their territory. They don't have an air patrol. We would have air superiority from the beginning. And I don't care how big an army they have."

"Right, Hawk," Jones said. "I agree. They've got about two divisions—forty thousand men under arms. But it would be hard for them to attack us directly. We could probably drop the Rangers right into Baltimore and have them clean house. But a state of war has exist for that to happen. And from what I hear, these guys are talking marriage, not war."

Hunter could only shake his head.

"Look what happened down South," Jones continued. "They were passing out candy to kids one day and slaughtering them the next. They don't fight fair. They're sneaky. They're as sneaky as the Russians. And because the Leaders Council is a 'democracy,' if that's the word for it, the Mid-Aks could be attacking downtown Boston and the Council would have to take a vote on whether they should spend the money to go to war or not."

There was a murmur of agreement from the other pilots who had had enough of the dour conversation. A fresh slew of bar girls had appeared at the front door and the flyboys turned their attention to more interesting subjects.

"Look, Hawk," Jones said, when the others were out of earshot. "It's worse than I'm letting on. I think we can be prepared up the yazoo, and we won't be able to fire a shot."

"What do you mean?" Hunter asked.

"I mean, I think they're planning on getting us from the inside."

"Spies?"

"Spies, saboteurs," Jones said, nodding. "A mole on the Leaders Council."

"A mole? You mean an 'Ak on the Council?"

"Well, maybe not an 'Ak." Jones replied. "But someone working for them. Letting them know every move the Council makes."

"Why?" Hunter had to ask. "How much could they pay him? And in what? Real quarters? Dimes?"

"Gold . . ." Jones said, reminding him the Mid-Aks first conquest involved the brutal takeover of Fort Knox.

"Well, that's true," Hunter had to agree. "They've got gold up the . . ."

"Booze. Broads. Drugs . . ." Jones continued, listing the various temptations at the Mid-Aks' disposal.

"Drugs?"

"Drugs," Jones said most definitely. "You know my buddy, the guy who's bitching about the Lear. He searched the plane one time. Found drugs in the ashtrays and in the can. All over the place. You know, just because we lost the war, it didn't mean the drug use—by bums and presidents alike—didn't just stop."

Hunter knew it was the truth. If anything, drug production—especially cocaine and marijuana—had increased. A lot of it was coming from Colombia, but most of South America was in on it too. It was their biggest export item. One of the greatest ironies of World War III was that of all the places on earth, the countries on the Southern American continent were the least affected. What was worse, since the war, many had become aligned with the Russians.

"Hawk," Jones said, making sure no one could overhear them. "If anything goes down, take whatever you can and head out West. Link up with my brother, Dave, out in LA. The Coasters would love to have you guys."

Hunter knew the officer's twin brother was the commander of a Southern California Air Patrol. Although, they hadn't seen each other in a while, the two brothers kept in touch.

Jones read his thoughts. "Look, Hawk, I know you'd be the last to bug out, but listen: This thing is bigger than just the Mid-Aks paying off a bunch of Boston pols with gold and drugs. There's something much more sinister behind it all."

"Like what?"

"I couldn't say exactly. And I wouldn't say unless I had proof, definite proof. But . . ."

"But . . ." Hunter said, urging Jones on.

"But I smell commies," he said finally.

Hunter's mind flashed to the flag that he still kept neatly folded in his back pocket. "Russians?"

"And . . ." Jones continued. "If there are Russians behind it all, then you'll be more valuable—to yourself and to this country—if you're alive. Same for the rest of those guys, our guys anyway. Those free-lancers.

Any of the people we have wandering in and out of the base. God knows what kind of informers we have here."

Paranoia, Hunter thought. But justifiable nevertheless.

"So, if—or I'll say when—the shit hits the fan, I'm ordering you and as many of the guys who can, to get your asses out of here and make tracks for Dave. He'll take care of you. Just let him know what the hell happened."

With that, Jones rose shakily from his seat and walked out of the bar. He had talked like the fan had already been hit. Hunter knew that when Jones talked like this, it was just a matter of time.

He downed his drink, and ordered another. He spotted a nice-looking woman, sitting alone at the bar, blowing smoke in his direction. Might as well get a piece, he thought, getting up to join her. Might not have much time left.

CHAPTER SEVEN

A week later, the real trouble began.

Hunter was called to the general's office one morning right after dawn patrol. He found the normally electric officer sitting nearly motionless behind his desk, staring out into space. He hardly acknowledged Hunter.

"It's happened, Hawk," the old man said wearily.

"What's happened?"

"I've been grounded," he said slowly, taking a measure of the words.

"Grounded?" Hunter asked, his voice going angry. "Grounded by whom?"

The general didn't answer. He just flipped a piece of paper Hunter's way. The airman picked it up and read it. It was filled with paragraph after paragraph of official gobbledegook, but the bottom line did read: "General Jones is hereby restricted to base for insubordination and disobeying direct orders. Effective immediately."

"What direct orders did you disobey," Hunter

asked, surprise joining his anger.

"Remember the Cherry Busters?" he asked. "Remember the goddamned Thruway War?"

"Of course I remember it," Hunter said. "We kicked their asses. They've never been heard from again."

"Boston said I overstepped my bounds going after them. They claim I was acting beyond my jurisdiction."

"That's absolute bullshit!"

"Sure," the old man said. "I know it. You know it. But they needed something to nail me on, and this is it."

"They may want you out of the way," Hunter said. "But that doesn't mean you have to go. Let them try and keep you grounded. Who's going to enforce this?" He hastily fashioned the document into a paper airplane and let it sail across the room. It landed perfectly in the office "round file."

"It's the beginning of the end, Hawk," Jones said, still staring straight ahead. "They're setting us up."

Hunter was fuming. He knew that Jones had more guts in his little finger than the whole Leaders Council ever dreamed of having.

"Look," he said, his confidence bolstered. "If the Mid-Aks make a move, we'd be on them in a second. They've got no air support or transport. They've got no air cover. What they've got is an army that's too big for its own good and no way to get them anywhere."

Jones reached into his desk and pulled out a photograph. It was a reconnaisance photo, the kind taken from an airplane camera, flying very high.

Hunter looked at it. It depicted an airport, easily identified by its criss-crossed runway lines. The runways were bare but alongside them were what looked like little dots, hundreds of them.

"I took that picture two days ago," Jones said, still staring blankly.

"Where is it?" Hunter asked.

"It's Baltimore Airport," he answered.

"Baltimore!" Hunter gasped. "The capital of Middle Atlantic?"

"Took that shot at 81,000 in the '111," Jones said, a hint of pride evident in the gloom of his voice. "Know what those dots are?"

"They're not airplanes," Hunter said, his trained eye studying the photo.

"You're right," Jones said. "They're helicopters."

"Choppers?" Hunter was really surprised. "Where the hell did they get them?"

"I'm not sure," Jones said. "Most of those copters are Hueys, old ones, just like we have. My guess is they're right out of the jungles of 'Nam, where they've been sitting with those little yellow bastards for years. With those choppers, the 'Aks can lift enough troops to take Boston, either by force or pretense. They could do it in less than a day's time. And we probably couldn't shoot 'em all down. We'd run out of ammo."

Hunter was just finishing counting the specks on the photo. There were 339 of them. "Lot of airlift," he whistled.

Hunter saw the general's spirits were sinking fast. "Fuck 'em," Hunter said. "We have the best guys. The best equipment. We'll still kick their ass!"

Jones looked up at him sadly. "You know, Hawk,"

he said, pulling out a cigar, "I believe you did lose your head sitting up on that mountain. You still think that having the best men, best equipment, best engine and best air-to-airs strapped to your wings is all it takes to win . . ."

"Well, isn't it?"

Jones slammed his fist down on the desk. "For Christ's sake, Hawk! It didn't help us the last time!"

With that, Jones stormed out of the office.

The last time. The words haunted Hunter for the rest of the day and the night. The last time. The Battle for Western Europe. The sneak attack on Christmas Eve. The first desperate days. The valiant allied effort. The turning of the tide. The mind-boggling battles of the Second Campaign, when men killed each other in hand-to-hand combat on the battlefield as satellites destroyed each other in space hundreds and thousands of miles above. In the middle of it all were the air battles, fought by men like Hunter, Jones, Toomey, Wa, and others—American soldiers of the air, fighting not because they like it or want it. But fighting because that was what they were trained to do. To protect their country. To insure that men could live in peace, and in freedom—no matter what the price or sacrifice. No matter what color, or race, or country. All men should be free. It was as simple as that.

And yet, they lost the war . . .

Not because of their heroics, but in spite of them. They had the best men and the best machines. Yet they lost the war.

The last time. The memories stung his brain. France, the Ruhr Valley, the battles in the skies over Western Europe. Living men against living machines. Quality against quantity. Human decency against human disgrace. They had won all the battles, fought harder and braver, sacrificed more in the name of their country than any American soldier had ever had—and for what? The proud but not idle boast. All the guns fired, bombs dropped, poison gas inhaled, cruise missiles fired and cities destroyed. And in the end, they had had the best—and still lost the thing with a simple stab in the back.

It seemed like such a long time ago . . .

And Jones, the man who led the final victorious charge only to have it all erased with the push of a button—acted as if it was all his fault. The weight of the world rode so heavily on his shoulders that Hunter sometimes wondered how the general ever even got airborne.

It rained hard and cold the next day. Everything was grounded as a damp fog shrouded the base. The weather only added to the gloom and isolation which was hanging over the Zone Air Patrol. Hunter sought refuge in the base bar. For hours, he sat alone at a table, staring at a half dozen used beer glasses. The place was nearly empty. Word of the general's grounding and its ramifications had carried instantly throughout the base and the club's usual party-party atmosphere was substantially subdued. Some of the free-lancers they had employed had already given their notice and left the base, sensing trouble was on the way. In the bar, only a handful of local people sat drinking. There wasn't a ZAP pilot or monkey to be seen. The atmosphere around Jonesville was heavy with uncertainty.

Something was coming . . .

Hunter was drunk when she walked in. At first, the dim light over the club's doorway cast a shadow across her face, managing to transform her hair color into dirty blond. But as soon as she stepped into the brighter light near the bar, her hair returned to its natural, brunette color.

She was small and sported a pert, nimble, curvy body. Her tiny, yet delicious looking breasts highlighted the blue, thin-strapped dress she wore beneath her raincoat. A slim figure and nicely rounded hips and rear added to the package. Her gorgeous legs completed the masterpiece. She was French. She was beautiful. And Hunter knew her.

When he had first looked up, after waiting several crucial seconds for his drunken eyes to focus, he was convinced that he was out on his feet and dreaming the whole thing. But then, after asking the bartender, who had pointed in Hunter's general direction, she saw him and waved, he knew it was her. The strange days after the war came back to him in a flash. The black and red sky. The dark days and darker nights. His long dangerous trek from Spain to Scotland. She was the girl he had met along the way. They had both sought refuge in the same abandoned farmhouse near the French coast. She had held a shotgun on him for more than an hour, until he convinced her he was not a rapist or a Russian sympathizer. Then they had talked. Later, by mutual consent, he had taken her—and let her take him. It had been brief; she was gone the next morning. But this girl had haunted his dreams—asleep and awake—since the last time he'd had seen her. And she had just walked in the door.

Dominique. He couldn't believe Dominique was standing in front of him, a mist welling in her eyes. He was on his feet, drunkenly trying to act like a sober gentleman, and failing miserably. It was surreal. This girl, the one who disappeared on that strange morning, was now here, in Jonesville smiling, if slightly taken aback at his boozy manner.

He tried to talk, but gave up and just listened. How did she get here? She had always wanted to come to America. Now, she had raised enough silver—he didn't ask how—to buy herself out of Occupied France and onto a boat to Iceland. From there she caught the once-a-month flight over to Montreal. How did she know he was here? She had heard of the famous ZAP while in Free Canada, and that a young, skillful pilot named Hunter was one of its leaders. So she made her way to Boston, and finally, bought a ride to Otis.

She got him to sit down and accepted his frantic offers to buy her a drink. They talked. She was thinking of staying in Free Canada or the Northeast Economic Zone as things were really getting out of hand in Occupied Europe. Terrorism, public executions, secret police, Russian soldiers on every corner, the every move of anyone the least suspect, monitored. Oddly, she told him just about the same things were happening in Boston.

She had also thought about him since they last met and shyly admitted that one of the reasons she came across was to try to find him. She just didn't expect it to happen so soon.

He asked her if she had a place to stay. She said no. He asked if she would stay with him. She said yes. She had to help him back to his quarters, where they collapsed into each other's arms. He retrieved her baggage the next morning and she moved in with him. It continued to rain for the next three days. He didn't notice. They didn't leave his room for all that time.

The weather cleared and winter settled in. The Cape was usually spared the harshness of the New England winter climate, though a few inches of snow fell occasionally. ZAP air activity was kept to a minimum, per Jones's orders. He thought it best to conserve all the fuel they had. Things continued to be tense between Jonesville and Boston. The Leaders' Council had sent down a dozen observers, patsies really, whose job was to make sure Jones obeyed his grounding orders. It was the ultimate insult. The observers were shunned by the rest of the base community as if they were carrying the plague. Wisely, Jones ordered a dozen Zone Rangers to discreetly keep tabs on the observers.

Most of this was played out at a distance from Hunter. With the slowdown in flying, Jones had told his hardest-working pilots to take some liberty. Hunter agreed with only a minimal protest and a promise from Jones to keep him informed daily of the deteriorating situation. "Enjoy yourself," Jones had told him, agreeing to send him a daily status report. "Enjoy that woman while you can."

Dominique was the first woman Hunter had ever lived with—the first he had ever *wanted* to live with. They talked, they ate, they took long walks together along the frozen Cape beaches. And they made love day and night. She cooked for him, cleaned his clothes, cleaned his quarters. She had developed the delightful habit of walking around the apartment clad only in a pair of black lace panties and a flimsy shirt. It was as if he had died and gone to heaven.

But just as his own life was starting to get good, things continued to plummet down the tubes in Jonesville. The observers had started talk of putting Jones on trial. A power struggle was going on in the Leaders' Council, and some of the Boston pols who considered Jones a threat were close to gaining the upper hand. This crooked, pro-Mid-Ak faction was determined to turn off the aid pipeline to ZAP. Routine requests, for fuel, ammo, food and clothing for the troops, were being held up, without explanation.

Things started going from bad to worse.

Little things. A half dozen false scramble calls over the course of two weeks—more false alarms than they had gotten in the past year. A pattern seemed to be forming. The ZAP radar net would spot something, but by the time the jet fighters got there, the bogies were gone.

Little things. The strange report the week before that a mystery ship was moving off the beach one night, running without lights or colors.

Little things. The fact that a Mid-Ak cargo ship—one of their very few—had managed to break down just a few miles off the coast of Boston, and asked for—and received—a tow into the Harbor. Such Good Samaritanism would have been unheard of barely two years before, when everyone in the Northeast was certain that their country was next on the Mid-Aks' list of conquests. How times had changed. It was just that fear that gave birth to the really powerful ZAP and ZAR, although in the ensuing years, it had been the air pirates who had caught most of the Zone Armed Forces' combined fury.

Little things. Like a tankerful of jet fuel, bound for Jonesville, suddenly delayed around the horn of Florida. The juice was now more precious than ever. Hunter was soon back working full-time, his two weeks in paradise over. He and Jones knew someone was probing their defenses and interdicting their supply lines. They were being set up. And there was little they could do about it.

It was having a devasteting effect on the general. Every day the lonely figure of the man would be seen, walking the perimeter of the base, checking the defense, checking the readiness of the Rangers. That done, he'd retire to the radio shack and call each of the outlying radar stations, checking on their status.

After consulting with key officers in ZAP and ZAR, Jones put the base on an unofficial war footing. This necessary measure spawned a barrage of rumors of an impending attack on Jonesville. The free-lance army in Boston—technically allies of ZAP and ZAR—seemed to be the leading candidate enemy,

111

although other variations had the Mid-Aks, the air pirates, even the Russians all named as the possible adversaries. Some of the civilians began reenforcing their dwellings with concrete, others simply left the area. The situation was so bad, Jones ordered the base blacked-out at sunset every night.

Hunter knew he had a tough decision coming up. He returned home one night after helping in the installation of several more coastal guns down near the beach. He hadn't flown in weeks and he was getting edgy. But sadness had overtaken that emotion.

Dominique had prepared a candlelight dinner for them, carefully making sure the windows in their apartment were properly covered. She knew the situation at the base was bad. But on this night, she could tell it was bothering Hunter more than usual. The look on his face scared her. He was so obviously wrestling inside himself. They ate quietly—he could barely look at her in the dim light of the candles. She tried to make small talk with him—her French accent giving a comically sweet turn to slang words she'd picked up from him. But it was useless. She knew bad news was coming.

They returned to the bedroom after the meal. She had opened a bottle of wine she had been saving for a special occasion. He didn't wait for a glass—he took two healthy swigs from the bottle, then kicked off his boots and lay back on the bed. He looked *so* weary to her. His handsome looks were turning old, his face becoming lined with worry. She tried soothing him by running her fingers through his long hair. He was quiet for a long time.

She removed her clothes, slowly, a single flickering candle casting erotic shadows all over the small bedroom. He couldn't help watching her through his barely-open eyes. Once she was naked, she slowly undid his shirt and pants. He didn't resist. Soon they were both naked. Finally, he opened his eyes and looked at her.

"Dominique, honey," he began slowly. "I'd love to ask you to stay with me. Forever."

A pang of surprise shot through her. Was this his way of proposing marriage?

"But," he continued sadly. "The world is so screwed up. The whole goddamned globe is shaking and it feels like it's going to collapse right here at Otis."

"Oh, Hawk . . ."

He held his hand up. "Bad things are coming, honey. We can get stomped out of here in a second's time."

"But you can fight them . . ."

"Sure, we can," he said, pulling her close to him. "If we decide to, we will. And it will be a hell of a fight. But we just don't have the numbers here. We're small, specialized. We can shoot anything down within a hundred miles. But this is different. This is a power play. It's politics all over again."

"Then, let's leave," she said. "You and me. We go. We can go up to Free Canada. None of this is happening up there. It's like a *real* world up there."

He was quiet once again. She was right. He was suffering from tunnel vision. There were places in the world—Free Canada, the best among them—where

113

the people were still civilized and the living relatively stable. Why not just pack up and leave America? What was keeping him here? Certainly not ZAP. Although he was proud of it and proud to serve with the men who comprised it, he was, in Jones's words, nothing more than a paycheck soldier. Then was it his loyalty to Jones that held him here? To a certain extent—but it was more for what Jones represented, than the man himself.

Hunter felt he and Jones were the last Americans. True Americans. Even his close friends like Ben Wa and Toomey seemed to be adapting to the Americanized New Order way of life. The kind of patriotism that he and Jones believed in was dying out.

"Hawk," Dominique continued. "We would be free of all of this. You could still fly. Fly for the Free Canadians. They need pilots as much as anybody. We could be so happy."

He closed his eyes and didn't speak for what seemed like an hour.

Finally he whispered to her. "I can't go. I have to stay. This is my country. I love you. Very much. But I love this country too. I have you now. I don't have it. I don't have the feeling I would need to leave it with a clear conscience . . ."

It was agonizing. He was torn like never before. He loved her so very much, he would probably consider even giving up flying for her. There had been girls and women before—but not like her. He wanted to be with her. But he couldn't give up his country—or what was left of it.

"Then I stay with you," she declared, her French stubbornness bubbling to the surface.

114

"No," he said. "No, I won't let you get caught up in this. This is my fight, not yours."

He pulled her up to him so that he was looking straight into her eyes. She was crying. She knew he wouldn't let her stay. Her eyes were so sad, so painful, he knew this was how he would remember her, always.

"I've already made the arrangements," he said firmly. "A Beechcraft is landing here tomorrow morning. Jones is moving some valuable documents to Montreal for safekeeping. Ben and Toomey are going to escort it up to the border. You're going to be on that airplane."

"No, Hawk . . ."

"Yes, Dominique." And that's all he had to say. She was crying openly now, her head buried in the hair on his chest.

They made love. Then they lay still and held each other for the remainder of the night, not speaking, not sleeping. This lasted about 50 years too soon, he thought. The sun came up. She quietly packed her things while he went out to meet the Beechcraft.

An hour later, she was gone . . .

Hunter went straight back to where it all started—the base bar. There he stayed, adding to his already exorbitant tab. He was devastated. He felt like an Exocet had homed in and exploded in his heart. Slowly but surely, he got drunk. The day passed, quiet, blurry but tense. He was the only one drinking in the bar most of the time. Everyone else was involved in the base's war preparations. Watching the activity through the window next to his seat at the rail, it seemed that every person he saw was armed and in battle dress.

Night came. But the war scare had also killed the normally after-hours festive atmosphere of the base's club. A few people wandered in. He retreated to a corner table, still sitting alone. Ben had come in earlier to tell him the Beechcraft made it to the border without trouble and that two Free Canadian jets had met them as planned and took up the escort from there. He thanked his friend and the Hawaiian left. After that no one bothered Hunter—no one dared even approach him.

The hours passed. His heart ached. Midnight passed into early morning. About 20 others had come in during the night to find refuge from the war jitters in the bottle. But it seemed like everyone was drinking alone. That was fine with Hunter. He was now at the point of drinking himself sober. Another day lost, he thought as the first rays of sunrise filtered through the bar's windows.

Suddenly, the whole world came crashing down on him.

There was a tremendous explosion. He knew right away the base's ammunition bunker had been hit. The bar lights blinked and a heartbeat later, the room was filled with flames. In another instant, a scatter-shot of flying shrapnel, red-hot and shrieking, perforated the walls of the bar.

Hunter was thrown 30 feet out of the structure. He remembered lying on his back, looking up at the early morning stars and hearing the air raid siren go off. Next, the mechanical thumping of the base perimeter guns started up. When he looked up, the barroom—

116

and the people that had been inside—were gone. The scramble Klaxon came on moments later. He slowly extracted himself from the smoking rubble and, without bothering to check for personal damage, he was up and racing across the tarmac toward his F-16.

CHAPTER EIGHT

The base was under attack. Two ships off the coast were pounding the area with their deck guns and missile launchers. There were soldiers firing mortars at them from the dunes on the beach. Apparently one of the ships had landed a contingent of commandos, some of the ghostlike figures were visible in the first streaks of daylight, others were illuminated by the ferocious fire that was blazing away at the bombed ammunition bunker at the edge of the base.

The runway lights were on, and Hunter could hear the familiar sound of the jets on the flight line winding up their engines. When he reached the line, his F-16 was already hot,—a quick-thinking monkey had turned the key and armed the weapons even as mortar shells were raining down around them. Looking around in the confusion and smoke, Hunter saw three other jets were hot, and a few in the process. He also saw several of their fighters had turned into burning wrecks. He felt a pang in his heart as he saw good aircraft go up in smoke.

He was the first one to taxi out onto the runway,

never pausing for anything as trivial as take-off clearance or wind direction. His only thoughts were on bombing the shit out of those ships off shore, then swinging around and tearing up the ghost troops on the beach. He would figure out who the hell his enemy was later.

As the jet moved forward, he felt the drag of a dozen all-purpose bombs hanging on his wings. No problem. They wouldn't be there long. His avionics were switching on. One-by-one indicator lights telling him his fuel load, weapons load and other sundry information flashed onto the HUD screen in front of him. It would still take his radar another minute or two to heat up. But he couldn't wait that long. He gunned his engine and started screeching down the runway.

The F-16 lifted off and he put the nose of the fighter right in the middle of the dull orange sun that was just peeking over the horizon. The enemy ships were about a mile offshore, their muzzle flashes giving away their positions in the ever-quickening daylight. A properly trained pilot would have gained more altitude, executed a bank to the right, swung around to his left and attacked the ships on a south-to-north heading, relying on the plane's computer to give him the correct direction and speed. But there wasn't time to do things by the book. These ships were bombing his home, his friends, his airplanes. Can't waste time. He flipped the fire control computer switch from automatic to manual. He'd do this all by himself.

His landing gear was barely up when he was screaming in on one of the ships, a craft that looked to be a light cruiser. It was painted in black camouflage and had about a dozen guns firing at the base. Hunter held the F-16 just 50 feet off the surface of the water, and was closing in fast. He pressed his cannon trigger. The familiar popping sound filled the cockpit as the powerful gun started to blaze away. The first shells sent up shots of spray as they hit the water and walked right up the broadside of the ship. Black uniformed sailors scattered as he bore down on them. They never expected to be attacked so quickly. He could actually see their horrified faces as he closed in, the 20 mm cannon pumping away. Just when it must have appeared to them like the crazy pilot was about to ram the ship, he eased up on the control stick and streaked up and over the craft, rocking it with an ear splitting scream and washing it with blazing jet exhaust. In a split-second, he was clear of the ship. Looking behind him, he saw several small explosions light up. Targets were hit. Fires began to burn.

The second ship lay just beyond the cruiser on almost the same heading. It appeared to be armed with a couple of dozen missile launchers, streaks of fire were bathing its decks as it launched missile after missile toward the beach. This ship was also serving as the enemy's troop carrier. Landing craft, filled with enemy troops, were still being loaded alongside.

Hunter never veered from his course. Still barely above the waves, but gaining speed all the time, he coolly flicked the Bomb-Safety switch on his control stick and line sighted the mast of the ship through the video projected target sight on the canopy in front of him. He started picking up some return fire, but it didn't concern him.

Like a torpedo-bomber pilot of World War II, he

released two bombs and yanked back on the control stick at the same time. The bombs seemed to hang suspended in the air before slamming into the side of the troop carrier. He pulled up and put the F-16 in a straight-up climb, the digitals on his altitude indicator flashing by in a blur. Soon he was out of sight of the ships, three miles above the action.

He gracefully started to roll the fighter plane over on its back. The last of the morning stars reflected off his helmet visor as he closed his eyes and relaxed, letting the G-force wash over him. The few seconds of intense action were now replaced with the serenity of flight. He was calmed. It felt good to be back in the saddle again.

The plane properly flipped over, his mind properly, if briefly rested, he began a wicked dive, anxious to return to the battle. His radar had just now switched on and the UHF radio began to crackle. In the wall of voices, he was able to discern Ben Wa and Toomey talking, exchanging heading information and target coordinates. He also heard another familiar voice— "We are under attack! Two enemy ships are firing on our position. Troops have been landed. Please relay instructions." It was Jones, calling Boston, reporting the attack. Technically, Jones had to get an okay from the Leaders' Council to take any armed action, but this procedure was lost in the burning rubble of Jonesville. Still, the general, a soldier to the end, was calling his commanders, asking them for permission to act.

As the earth rushed up to meet him, he saw the outline of the attacking ships against the vast ocean. Both were burning. He saw two A-7s—it had to be Wa

121

and Toomey—following his lead by streaking across the wavetops, attacking the ships side-by-side. He detected some spits of fire coming from the stricken craft, indicating that not all of the anti-aircraft fire was suppressed. Not yet, anyway.

He smiled. Pulling the F-16 out of its dive, he banked hard to the right and put the jet into a screaming 180-degree turn. He was sure the A-7s— and anything else that got off the ground—could handle the ships. It was time for him to visit the beach.

There were hundred of soldiers splashing ashore after being disgorged from one of dozens of World War II-style landing craft. It struck him that this was a fairly elaborate seaborne invasion. But who was the enemy? He pondered the question only for an instant. The answer would come later. Now, the first order of business was to destroy this mysterious invader.

He checked his bomb load and confirmed he had ten 500-pounders left. He put the jet into another 180 and lined up with the shoreline. He could see soldiers scampering as they heard him approach. He opened with the cannon and flipped the Bomb-Ready switch. Four pushes of the button and four bombs fell in a neatly timed sequence, one right after the other. The four explosions ripped through the groups of soldiers as they vainly tried to find cover. Soon, the frozen sands on the beach near Jonesville ran red with the blood of the unknown attackers.

He executed another loop and bore down on the beachhead again. He could see a T-38 and an F-106 strafing the beach ahead of him. He didn't even think to call them on the radio. The pilots and planes of

ZAP were just doing their thing. Quickly, but not quietly blowing the shit out of anything that moved.

Suddenly, an indicator light and buzzer told him a shoulder-launched missile, fired from a position hidden in the dunes, was homing in on him. He calmly dropped four more bombs in sequence, and then, using a maneuver from his Thunderbirds days, rolled the plane six times in quick succession. The trick baffled the anti-aircraft missile and it slammed into the side of a sand dune, exploding harmlessly.

He pointed the F-16 straight up, once again and flipped it over on its back. Only the F-16 could handle all this maneuvering while still carrying a full fuel and bomb load. "What a plane!" he yelled, banging the console with an appreciative fist. "What a fucking plane!"

He set his sights on two landing craft that were just reaching the beach. The soldiers on board never had a chance as Hunter placed a 500-pounder in each craft. The bomb, more suitable for taking out hardened gun positions and the like, simply obliterated the two small ships. Looking back, he saw bodies, and parts of bodies, flying wildly through the air. They looked like busted-up, blown-up dolls. Whoever they were, they, like the guys on the ships, just succeeded in getting themselves killed. Sorry guys, he thought. You just got yourselves hooked up with the wrong customer.

CHAPTER NINE

Hunter made two more passes over the beach, using up the rest of his cannon ammunition. The A-7s did the same. It didn't appear to make much difference—the beach and the shoreline were covered with the bodies of the black-uniformed attackers. He could see the Rangers, who had immediately met the invaders on the first line of sand dunes, now start to emerge from their positions and pick over the dead soldiers. The situation on the beach seemed to be in hand.

He rolled right, out to sea. Offshore, the two ships were burning fiercely. The secondary explosions that were continually rocking the vessels told him that there wouldn't be very many survivors left on board. The cruisers was going down bow first. The missile launcher/troop ship looked no better. He doubted it would stay afloat long enough for them to inspect it and look for evidence as to who had attacked them and why.

He streaked over the base and saw the destruction the attack had wrought. A half dozen airplanes were destroyed and several buildings—including the ammo bunker and the club—were in flames. All the while, he could still hear the base radio operator repeatedly trying to raise Boston to tell them of the attack.

As Hunter made his final turn for landing, he was filled with a strange mix of confusion and elation. ZAP and the Rangers had stopped the invaders before they even reached the high water line. And, in all, the action had lasted only a half hour. Yet, some valuable men and equipment were lost in the surprise attack. And for what? Mercenaries killing other mercenaries? But that seemed to be the accepted norm in these days of the New Order.

He brought the F-16 in right on the tail of the A-7s, rolled it up to its station point and leaped from the cockpit. Monkeys quickly surrounded the plane and started to re-arm it. There was no way to be sure whether this was just a first of several attacks on Otis. Hunter, like the rest of the pilots, wanted to be ready, just in case.

The base was a scene of controlled pandemonium. Several fires were burning out of control, and the ammo bunker was still exploding. Rescue vehicles were speeding about, sirens blaring, lights flashing. Rangers were double-timing it to the beach to set up a defense line. Several jets went hot and took off to provide the base with air cover, should another attack occur. Hunter could see that a couple of civilian houses had also taken hits, and the base fire crews were battling those blazes. Everywhere there was smoke and the smell of spent ammunition.

Hunter was in full sprint, heading for the communications shack. He knew he'd find the general there. In fact, when he reached the front door, Jones was running out.

"The beach is secure, Hawk," Jones, clad in a combat uniform and carrying an M-16, yelled back over his shoulder to Hunter. "Let's find out who these bastards are!"

The two men ran across the runway to the scene of the battles, neatly dodging the pieces of flaming debris and rescue vehicles that were speeding about. They passed the wreckage of two planes on the way: one of the F-106s had bought it. So had a T-38. While the damage would hurt, Hunter considered them "acceptable losses." "Unacceptable" would have been if the F-4 or the F-111 went up. The destroyed ammo dump would be another story.

They reached the beach just as the Rangers were through mopping up. Not one of the invaders survived. The Rangers counted about 350 on the beach in all, with many bodies floating offshore. Each corpse was dressed in the same black, overall-style uniform. The beach was awash in blood from the carnage. At least a dozen landing craft were burning in the water; many others had sunk beneath the waves, carrying their troops with them. It had been a massacre. The invading soldiers never had a chance.

A Ranger lieutenant told Jones and Hunter that none of the attackers carried identification—no dogtags or papers, just a variety of weapons. Many M-16s, a few Stens and even a dozen old BAR automatics were found among the bodies.

But the Jonesville defenders had had another ally in the action; the attackers had picked the very worst time to attempt an amphibious landing: high tide. The waves were three to four footers and the wind was coming in off the water.

Hunter walked down the water's edge with Jones and watched the waves roll the bodies of the attackers in and out at will. Even the ocean water was running red, as if some huge fish had just been gutted.

"This was insanity!" Jones said, looking at the hundreds of broken bodies. "What kind of a commander would order an attack like this? At high tide, on a cold day, with no air cover? They walked right into our fields of fire!"

Hunter could only shake his head.

"This looks like a bad version of what happened in Miami a while back," Jones said, spitting the bad taste out of his mouth.

"You never did raise Boston?" Hunter asked, reading the general's thoughts.

"No," Jones said, kicking over the body of one of the dead soldiers. The man's mouth was filled with sand and his body was already starting to bloat. "But I just assumed that it was because no one was awake this time of day."

Jones knelt beside the body and took a good look at his face. Everything about him—the uniform, his belt gear, his sunburned face—pointed to one thing. "This guy's either a Mid-Ak or someone they've bought to do this," Jones said. "Either way, I see the Mid-Atlantic's hand in this. I can smell them a mile away."

"A distraction," Hunter said.

"Or just a screw-up in timing," Jones said, wiping his brow. "These guys might have just arrived a little too early. The main attack might be on the way."

"Could be, but from where?"

"At this point, anywhere," Jones said. He looked out at the bodies, rolling in the red suds of the surf.

"This isn't war, Hawk. This is greed."

The general didn't wait to hear his reply; he was already running back toward the radio shack.

"Christ," Hunter whispered as he took off after the general.

They sprinted back across the runway, passing the obliterated ammo dump as they ran.

"What the hell do you think that was?" Jones yelled to him, "a lucky shot?"

Hunter looked at the smoking building as the base fire fighting unit poured water onto the already hopeless structure.

"Inside job?" Hunter yelled to Jones.

"You bet your ass!" Jones screamed back. "You think some gunboat deck jockey could shoot like that without help? I'll bet you a bag of real silver that none of those 'observers' are anywhere to be found."

The thought ran a chill up and down Hunter's spine. Even with all their precautions, there had still been spies in their midst.

They reached the radio shack just as Wa and Toomey were arriving from the other direction, after helping fight one of the runway fires.

Jones yelled inside the radio shack: "Sparky! Any answer yet?"

"No, sir!" a voice from within answered.

That was all Jones needed. He physically collared Toomey and said: "J.T. Get a warm jet and scoot up to Boston. Fly around. Check it out. Stay over the downtown. But be cool. Fly high or low, but don't slow down enough to be recognized unless I tell you to. We've been calling the bastards since the first blast and no one's picking up the phone. Maintain radio silence. I'll call you if I have to. Bring a wingman and make sure you're armed."

"Will do, General," Toomey said with a sharp salute. He turned on his heel and ran toward the line of the T-38s.

The general turned to Wa. "Ben. Get the Phantom. You zoom up to Logan. Tell me what's going on up there. Stay high and out of sight. Jam 'em if you have to. And stay off the radio unless it's big. Link up with J.T. later."

"You got it," Wa said, already running in the direction of the F-4's station point.

Jones and Hunter entered the communications control building. A harried Ranger communications specialist was repeatedly broadcasting the same message, over and over.

"Boston. Boston. This is Otis. We have been attacked by hostile force from the sea. Initial wave repulsed. Need instructions."

Each broadcast was followed by a second or two of silence before the operator would repeat the message.

Jones scribbled something on a piece of paper and handed it to the radio operator.

"Here," the general said, "Add this to the message."

The sparky looked at the scrawled sentence and hesitated a second, then began broadcasting the revised message.

"Boston. Boston," the radioman called, "This is Otis. We have been attacked by hostile force from the sea. Initial wave repulsed. Seek permission to carry out retaliatory air strike against Mid-Atlantic States military sites. Need instructions."

Jones looked at Hunter and gave him a grim wink. "That should get them off their asses," the old man said.

Sure enough, the radio crackled to life.

"Otis. Boston calling," a wavering, broken voice began. "Do not—Repeat—Do not launch any aircraft until you receive specific orders to do so. Otis. Please acknowledge."

Jones looked out of the single story building's only window, just as Toomey's two-ship flight was lifting off from the base's one remaining active runway.

"Acknowledge, my ass!" Jones said, grabbing the microphone. "This is General Seth Jones, Commander of the Northeast Economic Zone' Armed Forces and Air Patrol. To whom am I speaking?"

"This is Corporal Buford Smith . . ."

Neither Hunter or Jones recognized the name.

"Well, Corporal Smith," Jones said. "I suggest you put someone with some authority on . . . immediately! We've been attacked. We have positively identified who originated the attack. We are obligated to the people we lost and to the free people of the Economic Zone to retaliate. Against the Mid-Atlantic States, immediately and with as much force as we can muster."

There was the sound of microphone changing hands on the other end then a long silence.

"Otis," a different voice began. "This is a direct order. Do not engage in any reprisal strikes. Do not to launch any aircraft."

Hunter would have bet that Jones would blow his top. But he was surprised with the coolness the general displayed in taking the microphone in hand

and asking: "To whom am I speaking now?"

Another silence, followed by . . .

"Captain Bobby Joe Spencer," the voice said, with more than a trace of arrogance. "Communications brigade, Special Marine Battalion, Mid-Atlantic Forces."

The declaration stunned but didn't necessarily surprise Jones and Hunter. The radio operator finally managed to speak:

"Sir! A Mid-Ak at the phone in Boston?"

Jones took off his trademark baseball cap and ran his hand through his short cropped hair.

"I'm afraid so, son," Jones said. In the distance Hunter could hear Ben Wa firing up the F-4.

"Captain," Jones said, calmly into the microphone. "Am I to assume that your forces are now in control of the government for the Northeast?"

Again, a short silence.

"You assume correctly, General," Spencer declared over the crackling frequency. "There has been a coup d'etat. Our special forces were . . . requested . . . to help restore order and control the situation at the Government House."

"And who invited you, Captain?"

"Chairman Turkson," Spencer answered. "First Minister of the Revolutionary Council of the Northeast Economic Zone."

Hunter recognized the name in the middle of the mouthful. Turkson was the Council member whom Jones had tagged as most likely to set up a dictatorship and screw up a good thing. He above others was the one who at first tried to gain control of ZAP, then, failing that, tried to destroy it.

131

"But, Captain," Jones said, the anger beginning to betray his voice. "The Northeast Economic Zone is a democracy, a form of government that you are obviously not familiar with. There is no Chairman and there is no Revolutionary Council."

"Well," Spencer answered in a voice with a more evident Southern tone, "There is now."

Jones turned to Hunter. "Turkson has taken over," he said. "He was the one who was winging down to Baltimore playing footsies with the 'Aks."

The general turned his attention back to the microphone.

"Captain. Your 'special force.' Was it stationed on the disabled freighter which was given port in Boston a few days ago?"

"Listen, General," the Mid-Ak captain began. "Senator Turkson told us you were a pain in the ass. Fighting for democracy, people free to do what they want. All that bullshit. Well, now that's over, Jones.

"Your kind went out with World War III. Democracy? Ha! When will you and your flag-waving flyboys wake up? This is The New Order. Survival of the fittest. And to the highest bidder. Anyone who's eating, got clothes on his ass and a roof over his head had better thank the people in power, the people who are running things. Money is power, Jones. Because without it—or us—nine-tenths of the people wouldn't know where to take a leak!"

"And you sound quite qualified to teach them that, Captain," Jones said, not resisting a grim smile. He winked at Hunter, then half-whispered to the radio operator to raise Toomey in the T-38.

"Captain," Jones continued, "then can I assume

that your forces are now running things in the North-east?"

"That's affirmative, Jones," the arrogant reply came back. "And let me tell you something else. We're here to stay. This part of the country was making too much money to be handled—doled out—to the citizens. Now, it will be in the hands of people who know what to do with it."

"Captain," Jones said. "What's to prevent me from launching an air strike right now, against Government House, and putting an end to your little game?"

"Try it, Jones," Spencer answered. "And you'll kill hundreds of those citizens you find so precious. We thought you might pull something like that. So we've rounded up a bunch of the plebs. Women, Jones. And kids. And they're at the Government House right now. Under guard. So, c'mon up, Jones, you and your God-Almighty air force. Napalm the women and kids. Do us the favor. Then we won't have to freed them.

"And what about my hitting Logan?" Jones asked Spencer. Hunter could feel the general stalling for time.

There was a laugh at the other end of the line. "Do it Jones! Nuke the fucking place. And then you'll be cutting the throats of even more of your innocent civilians. Bomb the airport and you've got no air convoys. No convoys means no money, Jones. No money means no food. No food means no lousy citizens, 'cause when it gets tight, there won't be enough to go around."

They were over a barrel. Jones knew it. Hunter knew it. Suddenly, the control tower room felt very

133

small, as if it was closing in on them. Hunter wished he had the Mid-Ak—any Mid-Ak—in front of him. He would choke the life out of him. Next to him, the radio operator had been using a separate channel to contact Toomey's T-38s.

Jones kept his cool.

"Captain, maybe we can make a deal. I'm assuming that you are broadcasting from the Government House radio station."

"Right again, Jones." Spencer answered. "And it's a great view!"

Jones smiled. Caught. The fish took the bait. Hunter knew it. Jones knew it. Even the radio operator knew it.

"Let's talk, Captain," Jones said using all the false politeness he could muster. Quickly taking another microphone from the sparky, the general was soon talking to Toomey's two-ship of armed T-38s. They were streaking in low over the water, less than a minute flying time from downtown Boston.

"J. T.," Jones began. "Here it is in a nutshell. The government has been overthrown by the Mid-Aks. We'll soon have our asses to the wall. Do me a favor will you?"

"Name it, sir," Toomey answered, after an appropriate pause long enough to let the news sink in.

"You know the Government House, right downtown, the old Prudential Insurance Building?"

"Yes, sir," came Toomey's crisp reply.

"On top, there's a communications shack. You can tell it because of all the antennas sticking out of the roof."

"Yes sir?"

134

"Take it out," Jones ordered. "Just the shack. There are civilian hostages being held in the building itself."

"Roger . . ."

"Come in low, J. T.," Jones counseled. "And stay over the water as long as possible. The radar in that city is kid's stuff so you'll be able to get in okay. Ice the shack and then get the hell out of there. Code Red Two."

"Code Red Two, sir?" Toomey asked.

"That's a roger. Good luck, J. T."

Code Red Two. Hunter knew the term, but hoped he'd never hear it. It meant the shit had hit the fan. The unit was ordered to disperse.

"Thank you, sir . . ." Toomey's voice trailed off.

"Good luck, sir," said a transmission from Toomey's wingman.

Jones was silent for a moment, then said into the microphone: "Are you still there, Captain Spencer?"

"Yes, sir," came the reply.

"Not for long . . ." Jones said.

The radio speaker crackled as the sound of a jet engine became evident in the background. Thumping and bumping followed, then a few moments of confusion as the sound of the approaching jet got louder. Shouts were heard. Then, came a loud explosion and the speaker went dead.

"Goodbye 'Ak," Jones said.

"That's one," Hunter said. "But how many others are there?"

The answer came an instant later.

135

"Blue Leader to Otis Base," the radio crackled. It was Ben Wa.

"Go ahead, Blue Leader," the radio operator said, adjusting the radio's dials for better reception.

"General?" Wa asked.

"Here, Ben," Jones said again grabbing the mike.

"General, this is too big for me not to break radio silence. I am looking at an unbelievable sight, sir."

"Go ahead, Ben."

"There are hundreds of them . . ." a voice, probably Wa's weapons officer in the rear seat of the Phantom said. Their voices were fading in and out.

Jones gave Hunter a worried look.

"Go ahead, Ben," Jones urged. "What's going on?"

"Sir, I am observing a large airborne force, heading two-seven-niner, due south," Wa said, the normally ice-cool pilot's voice shaking.

"Airborne?" Jones asked, the crackling in the transmission becoming more irksome.

"Hundreds of them, sir!" Wa said, his voice sounding weak and far away. "Heading your way."

"Hundreds of what, Ben!?" Jones yelled into the mike.

"Helicopters!" Wa finally said.

"Christ!" Jones exclaimed. He turned to the radio operator and said: "Son, get to the ops building and tell the commander to get that air raid siren going. Tell him to expect an airborne attack at any minute. Tell him I said to evacuate any civilians left on base and to order a Class Red Alert. Then get your ass in a safe place."

The radio man, a young Ranger, snapped a salute

136

and hurried out. "Good luck, sir!" he said on leaving.

Jones turned to Hunter. "Well, they succeeded in moving all those choppers up to Boston. Now they're heading this way."

Hunter took the mike from Jones. "Ben," he said. "What kind of choppers?"

"Everything, Hawk," Wa reported, his voice sounding fainter by the moment. "Hueys, Chinooks, Cobras, Apaches. Most of them look to be carrying troops."

"What's your position, Ben?" Hunter asked, reaching for a map.

"I'm orbiting at twenty-four thousand," came the reply. "I'm about ten miles off Logan at three hundred knots."

"Can you slow 'em down, Ben?" Jones asked.

"I can sure try," Wa answered immediately.

"Okay, Ben." Jones said. "J.T. and his wingman are in your area. Get on his frequency and link up. Make a few passes, then Code Red it out of there."

"Code Red, sir?" Wa asked. "That's serious . . ."

"Ben," Jones said. "You know I've always said that we are just paycheck soldiers. This isn't our fight. The government of the Northeast Economic Zone has been overthrown. That means our paychecks have stopped coming. That means it's time for us to go. We're joining the ranks of the unemployed."

"Any suggestions, sir?" It was J.T., who had finished off the communications shack on top of the Government Tower and had been monitoring Jones' orders to Wa.

"Try to make Canada," Jones told them. "They're

137

the closest friendlies. Lay low and wait until things cool off. Remember, you guys are celebrities. The 'Aks might just put a price on your heads.

"Now, just mix it up with those guys a little, and buy us some time to get the civilians out of Otis."

"Roger, sir," Wa replied.

"See you soon," J.T. radioed, his two T-38s falling in behind Wa's F-4.

"Let's go for the Chinooks," Wa said as the three planes closed to within a mile of the massive helicopter formation. "They'll be carrying the grunts."

"That's a roger," Toomey answered.

The three ship formation rolled out one at a time and, with the sun at their backs, dove into the mass of helicopters.

Wa went in first. His back-seat weapons officer fired the first shot, unleashing two Sidewinder air-to-air missiles simultaneously. The heat-seeking rockets found a couple of heavy, troop-laden Chinook helicopters, flying side-by-side at the head of the formation and homed in on each craft's hot engine exhausts. The missiles hit instantaneously. Chopper number one got it in the mid-section, splitting it neatly in half. Wa could see troops falling from the Chinook and into the ocean more than a mile below. The other chopper, its main rotor destroyed, flipped over wildly, taking out a Huey gunship flying to its left. Together the two Mid-Ak craft plunged into the sea, as the rest of the chopper formation scattered.

Toomey went in next. Armed with dual M-61 cannons, he sought out another Chinook. He pulled his trigger and riddled the aircraft with a 100-shot blast that took less than two seconds. He pulled up

138

and through the choppers who were now wildly scattered across the sky. He found a Huey in his sights and squeezed off another 100 rounds. The enemy chopper exploded instantly. He rolled to avoid the flying debris and found a Cobra gunship at two o'clock. Another squeeze, another dead chopper.

With only another squeeze or two left, he climbed out and looped back into the maze of helicopters that were attempting to get back into a loose formation. The main chopper force was now completely spread out over the ocean. It was then he noticed that one of the helicopters bringing up the rear wasn't of a familiar design. He'd seen the type of craft before, but in the confusion of the battle, it didn't register.

He sighted the mystery chopper and let go his final rounds, hitting the craft's tail section and immediately igniting its fuel tanks. The helicopter fell out of the sky trailing a long stream of black smoke down to the water below. It would much later until Toomey would realize that he had fought a historic engagement— that he was the first pilot since the end of the war to down a *Soviet*-built Hind gunship.

Toomey's wingman, a free-lancer named Charlie Waters, was the last of the pilots to take on the wave of choppers. By this time, the helicopter pilots were starting to fire back. Gunners in the waists of the Hueys and the Chinooks were drawing a bead on Waters as he started his first pass. He was met with a wall of machinegun fire as he made his way through the wall of helicopters, hard as it was for a chopper gunner to follow the jet fighter in close quarters. Waters' first burst of cannon fire neatly took out a Huey, but his plane caught a few lucky slugs from a

139

retaliating Apache gunship.

Suddenly, the T-38 was spinning wildly. The bullets had ripped away his flaperon control and Waters realized he was disabled. Unable to steer the plane, he fired off one last long burst, wounding a couple of choppers in the process. That done, he hit the eject button, clearing the T-38 just as it slammed into yet another Chinook.

Waters floated down, but to his terror, saw an Apache double back and move in his direction. Dangling helpless beneath the parachute, Waters could only watch as the swift little chopper approached. About 100 yards out, it opened fire. The rounds from the copter riddled the helpless pilot shaking him like a out-of-control marionette. Waters' bleeding, battered body immediately went limp and floated down into the sea about two miles off Boston. There it was quickly fed on by bloodlusting sharks.

CHAPTER TEN

Back at Otis, the Code Red evacuation was already underway. It was what they had been expecting short of a direct attack. This way, they had a chance to get out in one piece.

"They used to call it a bug-out in the old days," Jones said, addressing the base over the field loud-speaker system. "These days it's called 'a turnover in employment.' In other words, we've gotten our pink slips. Good luck and we'll see you out on the West Coast!"

The remaining jets of ZAP were being hurriedly warmed up. The air patrol's C-130 Hercules was already out on the edge of the runway, its four big propellers whirling, its engines kicking up a lot of noise and dust. Already, 18 ZAP pilots—mostly the loyal Air National Guard flyboys and the trusted free-lancers who had remained but had no jets to fly—were aboard. The plane would wait until the monkeys finished getting the remaining jets in flying order. Then the mechanics would get on board and the big Hercules would fly all of them out of harm's way.

At the other end of the base, the 250 Zone Air

Rangers assigned to Otis were preparing to pull out. Their Crazy Eight Chinook helicopters were being loaded with only the barest necessities—and as much ammo and guns as they could carry. There was some grumbling among the tough, elite fighters that they should stay and fight the 'Aks. Other, cooler heads, knew this would be foolhardy.

Under Jones's evacuation plan, the ZAP planes would pair up into two plane flights and simply leave. They would initially scatter in four directions, get fuel wherever they could, then re-group out on the coast, maybe within two to three weeks. It was a simple, catch-as-catch-can plan, which relied more on the pilots' abilities and instincts to survive than any coordinated plan to deploy to the West Coast. But the evacuation would be more difficult for the Rangers.

Their transportation—the eight choppers—had limited range and fuel capacity. They had to pick up 250 more troopers stationed in the listening posts on the Zone's western borders. A direct trip to the coast was out of the question right away. Jones's plan called for the Rangers' choppers to head for one of those listening posts. From there, they would have to tra-vel—and maybe fight—their way across the continent, eventually reaching the West Coast. In drawing up the Code Red plans, Jones knew ZAR would have the toughest time of it. After all, their route could carry them right through the worst of the Badlands, should they not be able to divert to the friendlier skies of Canada. The general estimated that they would lose anywhere from a third to a half their number—either to fighting or other temptations they would encounter crossing the volatile land.

Jones had already made arrangements with the local militia to provide protection and transportation for the civilians living on and near Otis. They, too, would have to evacuate the area. It burned his ass that he had to leave the people behind. It was a no-win decision. There was an outside chance that the Mid-Aks would leave them be and it was for this reason that Jones had made an important decision. That was, not to leave the base's various defense systems— the Gatlings, the SAM sites—on automatic, programmed to hit anything flying once ZAP pulled out. Leaving boobytraps was also *verboten*. He didn't want to enrage the Mid-Aks any more than he had to because the civilians fleeing the area would be the only group the 'Aks could take revenge on. Visions of the Russians strafing helpless refugees in the last war had made a vivid impression in his mind.

But this didn't mean that the military equipment would be left behind intact. Instead, the plan was that everything would be destroyed . . .

Among the last to leave would be the base MPs who were given the duty of destroying everything and anything that might be of help to the Mid-Aks once they landed. "Scorched Earth" they called it in wars past; don't leave anything for your enemy that could be exploited by him. The "everything and anything" included the Gatlings, the SAMs, the radar system, the precious fuel supply and whatever was left of the ammunition. Even the base's three auxiliary runways would be purposely damaged. Then—and only then—would Hunter and Jones take-off, drop one blockbuster bomb apiece on the base's last usable runway, then quickly get the hell out of the area.

143

"I'd give anything to see the look on the 'Ak commander's face when he gets here and finds the place empty." Jones told Hunter as they approached the flight line.

"Empty and useless," Hunter added as he watched the MPs detonate explosives on one of the base's perimeter radar towers. He looked out to sea where the attackers' ship was still burning. Although it had only been a few hours ago that they had repulsed the amphibious assault, it seemed to him like years. So much had happened. Once again, his whole world was crashing down upon him. Time for change anyway, he kept telling himself.

Jones also turned his attention to the beach where the early morning battle—and slaughter—had occurred.

"What a bunch of suckers," he said, spitting on the runway for emphasis. "The 'Aks probably hired them—free-lance infantry—to stage the raid. Just like in Miami. Probably promised them air support, too."

"Either it was a diversion," Hunter surmised, "Or, they figured that while we were chopping them up on the beach, they'd hit us from the rear with a million chopper troops."

"Whatever, leave it to the Mid-Aks to screw up an invasion," Jones said with a rare laugh. "As we know, timing is everything."

"Yeah," Hunter agreed. "Someone's sundial was off."

They reached his F-16 just as a pair of A-7s were taking off. Overhead, the first of the Crazy Eight helicopters was up and turning toward the west. More explosions were heard as the MPs continued dynamit-

144

ing the base's defense system.

Hunter figured the Mid-Ak airborne force was probably 15 minutes away. He watched as the second to last paired planes—the surviving F-106 and one of the T-38s—pulled away from the flight line and headed for the runway. The plan called for these planes to escort the C-130 during the trip west. The attending monkeys quickly climbed aboard two jeeps and sped away toward the waiting evac plane. The local militia had arrived and were carrying the last civilians out in a fleet of ancient National Guard deuces. The base was shutting down like a plant in twilight, just as Jones had planned. Within 10 minutes, Hunter knew, there'd be no one left. Time for a change.

Hunter told his monkeys to beat it, and they gratefully bid him goodbye, climbed on a jeep and headed for the C-130. Hunter loved his ground crew—they were the best on the base and had always felt it a privilege to work on the Thunderbird-adorned plane. Now Hunter, like the other pilots flying the ZAP fighters, would have to either find competent and trustworthy free-lance monkeys across the country—or fix whatever ailed their fighters themselves.

He climbed into the F-16, inserted the program tape and brought the engine up to trim. He was loaded with four Sidewinders, the blockbuster bomb, and a full load of cannon ammunition. Fuel conservation prevented him from taking anything else. The only clothes he had were the ones on his back. He managed to jam his M-16 into the F-16's cockpit, along with some ammunition. The only other personal item he carried was the threadbare flag he'd

145

taken from the body of Saul Wackerman.

Beside him, the general was strapping into the F-111, his mechanics having already departed. Being a much larger plane, the F-111 could carry about three times the bomb load of Hunter's plane. The general had carefully hung straps of small bombs along the flexible wing, as well as the blockbuster scheduled for the base runway. The plane also had an internal bombbay, but Hunter was sure the general left it empty—so much better for the F-111 to conserve fuel.

A jeep full of MPs rolled up to the two planes and gave them the thumbs-up signal. Jones waved back and the jeep sped off. The C-130 was already moving slowly down the runway, the MPs being the last of the base personnel to jump on. Once they were on, the C-130 pilot gunned his engines and the flying workhorse rumbled down the runway and into the air. Immediately going into a steep climb, it was soon joined by its escort fighters and together, the three planes took off in a southwesterly direction.

Hunter and Jones taxied their jets to the end of the runway and began cross-checking their instruments. As with all of the evacuating ZAP aircraft, radio silence would be strictly maintained, as would a reluctance to use their onboard radar unless absolutely necessary. A hot radar provides an easy homing target for many surface-to-air or air-to-air missiles. The Mid-Aks, although not operating any jet fighters of their own, probably had a few free-lancers in their employ with standing orders to shoot down any Zone aircraft they encountered in return for a handsome bounty for confirmed kills. It was important to keep the movements of the ZAP aircraft as secret as possible for as long as possible.

Just as they started their take-off roll, they could hear the radio chatter of the approaching chopper force. Once airborne, they could see it. The hundreds of approaching helicopters had swung out over the ocean and now were coming in from the east. The assault force looked for all the world like a swarm of angry bees out on the horizon. Hunter felt a temptation rise up inside of him—a temptation to meet the approaching swarm, cannons blazing. But he knew it would serve no good purpose—not now anyway. He was convinced that he would meet up with the Mid-Aks again someday. Then he would have his revenge.

Jones expertly put his plane into a roll, pulled back on the throttle and streaked over the now-abandoned base. He deposited his blockbuster bomb smack center in the main runway, causing a miniature mushroom cloud to blanket the landing strip. As he pulled the F-111 up, Hunter put his F-16 into a dive. Screaming low over the base, he pulled his weapons release lever just at the end of the runway. The bomb hit perfectly, taking out the last quarter of the strip, thus preventing the 'Aks from landing anything big at the base any time soon. Turning in his cockpit, he had to smile as he saw another mini-mushroom cloud rise above the base.

He linked up with Jones who was loitering nearby and together they went full afterburner. Hunter took one last look back. The first Mid-Ak choppers were just appearing over the base, their pilots confused not so much by the smoke and explosions as by the lack of groundfire. It would take the 'Aks a little while to catch onto what was happening. Then, and only then,

147

would they realize they'd been hoodwinked by the last official act of ZAP. Time for a change, Hunter thought as he turned to the west.

And California, here I come.

They had been airborne only about 20 minutes when he lost sight of the general. As usual, he was riding on the general's right wing when they began to climb up to a safe altitude. At about 40,000, he followed Jones into a monstrous cumulous cloud. When he emerged, barely a half minute later, the general was nowhere to be seen.

At first, he was tempted to break radio silence, but he resisted. The day was otherwise very clear. He twisted in his seat looking out the bubble-top, searching the sky for the F-111. Nothing.

He climbed up to 45,000 feet—then 50,000. Still nothing. He dove down to 30,000, then 25,000 then 20,000. Still, there was no sign of Jones.

He took a chance and switched on his radar. Just as it went hot, he saw the barest of blips at the edge of his screen. The profile indicator read out that the blip was large enough to be an F-111, but the plane's direction was due south. He and Jones had been on a heading of due west.

He thought it out for an instant and decided to double back and follow the blip. It was so unlike Jones to deviate from an agreed-upon plan that he was worried enough to take the risk. Something peculiar was going on. He could feel it in his bones.

He booted the F-16 in an effort to catch up with the blip. Traveling at close to 1300 mph, he knew that by

148

the time he could make a visual sighting, he and the mystery plane would be close to crossing over into Mid-Ak airspace. Still, he pressed on.

He continued to track the blip and finally got a visual sighting a few minutes later. There was no doubt about it. It was Jones. He had dropped his plane down to barely 10,000 feet and was still dropping when Hunter caught up to within five miles of him. They passed into Mid-Ak territory seconds later.

Suddenly, Hunter saw two more blips appear on the screen. They were smaller, faster craft and both were heading directly at Jones. If the general had followed his own orders, Hunter thought, he'd have his radar off and would be unaware of the other two planes.

Hunter wasn't taking any chances. He immediately armed his Sidewinders and floored the plane to full military speed to intercept the two planes. They came within visual sighting in seconds. Two F-101 Voodoos, mean-looking supersonic fighters that were the favorite of free-lancers and pirates alike. Both planes were painted in an evil-looking black and red trim color scheme, indicating a fighter-for-hire team.

All the while, the F-111 had been losing altitude, and Hunter strained to keep it in sight while streaking to intercept the Voodoos. Jones had slowed considerably and Hunter could see he had his flex wings spread out as far as possible, almost perpendicular to the plane's body. It was the configuration for a low-level bombing attack. By the time Hunter was within a mile of him, he had figured out what the general was up to.

Jones was leading a one-man bombing mission against the Mid-Aks. Hunter couldn't believe it, especially after Jones had convinced them all that he was pure mercenary. But Hunter had no time to wonder about the senior officer's motives. He'd have the two Voodoos to deal with first.

He knew the two pilots didn't see him to the last second. Either they were flying without radars or didn't have them turned on. Either way, it was a fatal mistake for them. Just as the first one rolled out to pounce on Jones' plane far below, Hunter fired a Sidewinder. The Voodoo pilot never knew what hit him. The air-to-air missile went right where it should have gone: up the exhaust pipe of the F-101. The plane exploded in mid-air. When the smoke cleared, there was nothing left.

The second Voodoo pilot had already started his attack dive when he realized his partner was gone. He started to take evasive action, but again, Hunter was quicker to the draw. A second Sidewinder flashed from under his wing. It met the Voodoo at about 15,000 feet, just as the pilot had managed to pull up out of his attack dive. The missile clipped the F-101's wing, shearing it completely off from the jet's fuselage. Spinning wildly, the Voodoo continued to plunge. It impacted into the side of a mountain, a ball of flame instantly erupting from it.

Hunter rolled out and started to dive of his own to catch up with Jones. He had no idea where he was. He had passed over a city that may have been old Philadelphia, but the only thing he was sure about was that, by this time, they were deep in Mid-Ak territory. Breaking through some clouds at 10,000 feet, he picked up the F-111 again. It was streaking barely 150 feet off the ground, coming on under any radar that might be around and heading toward what looked like a major city. Hunter could see the outline of the coast and the bustling harbor. Only then did he realize that city was Baltimore. Jones had decided to attack the very heart of the Mid-Aks' evil empire.

He watched as Jones made his approach. Even though Hunter knew they were both in "deep sierra," he had to admire the general's coolness. He knew there was nothing he could do to stop Jones from carrying out his bombing run. He wasn't even sure if he wanted to. He decided the best he could do was help now, and hope they were both around to discuss the matter later.

About five miles out from the city's limits, Jones started to pick up groundfire. Hunter was right on his tail at the moment, and Jones wiggled his wings to acknowledge his wingman's presence. The F-111 sped on, dodging several small, shoulder-fired missiles launched by troops on the ground, the plane's outstanding terrain-hugging feature lifting it up and down as dictated by the contour of the ground below.

They started picking up some heavy flak about two miles out. Hunter could see hundreds of Mid-Ak troops scrambling below as the two jets passed over barely 100 feet above the deck. Hunter's target acquisition equipment picked up a couple of fortified gun posts ahead and he put several bursts from the M-61 into both of them. But there were more guns than he could shoot at, and he knew the F-111 wasn't equipped with a cannon or any kind of gun to shoot back with. Hunter knew he'd have to ride shotgun for Jones for the whole bombing run.

About a mile out, the air was filled with flak,

missiles, and bullets from rifles of the troops below. It seemed like everyone on the ground was armed and shooting at them. Hunter saw the F-111 shudder from taking a few hits, but it never wavered from its course. He kept his F-16 continually rolling from side to side, its cannon flashing, stirring up columns of earth as the M-61 shells hit the ground or human targets.

Then, a missile—it looked like a Stinger—hit the F-111 midship. The big plane shook violently and began to lose altitude. But just as quickly, it stabilized and regained its heading, though trailing some bad-looking black smoke.

Within seconds they were right on the city itself, the F-111 neatly lifting itself above the on-coming skyscrapers. Hunter saw the plane's bomb bay doors open and knew Jones was preparing to drop whatever he had concealed inside the body of his plane.

All the groundfire had stopped by this time as they were directly over the heart of the city. Hunter was going slowly enough to see people scattering on the streets below. Because the Mid-Aks had no fighter jets of their own, their citizens were unaccustomed to seeing such aircraft above their city. Hunter also imagined that the city's air raid siren was cranking full blast.

When he saw Jones wiggle his wings again, he knew the general was coming to the end of the bombing run. All the while the smoke from the F-111 was getting worse. They had passed over the city and were coming up on its airport, which was located a few miles outside its limits. The airport was now a bristling Mid-Ak military base and training center. Hugging the waters of Chesapeake Bay, it gave the

Middle Atlantic states an easily defended outlet to the sea, as well as a place to launch their seaborne invasions from. Jones was out to put an end to that.

They started picking up some more groundfire as they approached the airport, but it made no difference. Jones had wiggled his wings a third time then pulled back on his stick and put the F-111 into a screaming climb. Hunter followed suit, guessing that Jones must have planned to drop something big. They had climbed to 20,000 when he saw a single, chubby bomb drop from the smoking F-111. The plane then stood on its tail and with its wings swept back, was kicked into afterburner. Now Hunter knew why Jones was getting them high and out of there quick.

The bomb he dropped was a nuclear one . . .

They were at 40,000 when the blast went off. Hunter rolled to get a better look and was astonished to see a mushroom cloud—this one very authentic—rising up from the airport. The blast wave hit his plane a few seconds later, rocking it and causing his instruments to blink. He knew that whatever—and whoever—was on the base was now vaporized. When or how Jones had managed to get hold of a nuclear bomb, he couldn't imagine. He was still awestruck by the size of the blast and the growing mushroom cloud rising over the airport base.

He should have figured that Jones wouldn't have let the Mid-Aks off so easily. Nor would he have involved the rest of the squadron in nuking the Middle Atlantic's main base. It was technically a one-plane mission, and that's how Jones had planned it all along.

153

The paycheck soldier talk was a cover. His hate for the Mid-Aks—their murderous, barbaric ways—had become personal a long time ago. With the constraints of the ZAP out of the way, Jones decided the time was right to deliver his own personal message of protest to the Middle Atlantic States. It was his way of avenging all the deaths and human misery the 'Aks had caused.

Mesmerized by the ever-growing mushroom cloud, Hunter concluded that the Mid-Aks had made a mistake a long time ago by making General Seth Jones their number one enemy. "You don't fuck around with General Jones," the saying used to go, and once again, the adage was proved correct.

The general's smoking plane had leveled off at 55,000 and had made a wide turn out over the Bay and headed due north. Hunter, realizing that after the nuking of the airport, something like maintaining radio silence seemed unimportant. He attempted to raise the general.

But he got no reply . . .

He followed the disabled F-111 as it flew out over the Atlantic and steaked off to the north. Off the coast of the old state of Connecticut, the plane started to drift to a course back over the land. All the time, Hunter was trying to raise Jones on both his VHF and UHF frequencies, but still got no response.

He pulled up beside the fighter-bomber several times and used hand and wing signals, again to no response. The F-111's canopy windows were tinted in such a way as to make it hard to see the pilot inside. Hunter dropped back to survey the damage to the general's plane and noted that while the jet was still flying, the hole in its side would soon force it down.

He figured the plane's radio might have been knocked out by groundfire, but it was spooky that Jones would not acknowledge his wing or hand signals.

And why the hell was he heading north?

Soon they had passed over into the Zone's airspace and still the F-111 flew north. Hunter could tell the plane was slowing down, gradually losing altitude. He pulled up beside it again, trying to get some response to his hand and wing signals, but it was to no avail.

After flying this way for 20 minutes, the landing gear on the F-111 came down. This further slowed the jet. Hunter surveyed the ground below and quickly calculated that they were somewhere over the forests of the area once known as Vermont. When the F-111 wings swept out and it banked to the left, Hunter knew it would soon be landing somewhere. He felt he had no choice but to follow suit.

Sure enough, as they broke through the low mists of the Vermont Green Mountains, an airport, carved out of the woods, came into view. The F-111 dropped down even further and began a final turn for landing. Hunter could see that while the strip, would be able to handle the short-landing F-111 easily, it would be a squeeze for the F-16.

After watching the F-111 set down to a perfect, three-point landing, he slowed his F-16, and lowered its gear. The strip would prove a tricky landing for the average pilot, but tricky landings and take-offs were one of Hunter's specialties. He coolly set the F-16 down, and immediately reversed the engine for a quick, if bumpy stop.

He couldn't help but think of the amazing events that had transpired in this single day—the explosion at the base club, the attack from the sea, bugging out of Otis, nuking Baltimore's airport and now, with the sun finally setting, his landing somewhere in Vermont. He felt it was time for a change, but this was getting bizarre.

He climbed out from the F-16 and looked around. Except for the F-111, the place was deserted. The only building was a small hangar, which looked like it was sealed up and locked tight as a drum. The general's plane stood at the far end of the runway, slightly off-kilter, its exhaust and wounded side still smoking. Hunter ran to the airplane, hoping to see the canopy popped up and a tired but triumphant Jones sitting on its wing.

But it was not to be. He clambered up onto the wing and crawled along the top of the fuselage to reach the cockpit. It was closed. He reached down with his foot and was able to trip the release handle. The canopy hissed once, then slowly opened. Inside, still strapped down, helmet on and sitting perfectly rigid, was General Jones.

He was dead, of course. Shrapnel from the missile hit had punctured his chest and he had bled to death probably somewhere over the middle of Baltimore. The plane, with its famous sophisticated computer-controlled flight systems, had completed the mission Jones had programmed it to, then flew him to this remote base. The spookiness of it all made Hunter shudder. Suddenly, he was very cold.

He pulled the general out and lowered the body to the ground with the help of the parachute straps. He took one long last look. Here was a truly gallant man; hero in Viet Nam, leader of the Thunderbirds, the soldier, who probably more than any other, turned the tide in the Battle for Western Europe. An officer who respected his men as pilots and as human beings, who felt that to fight for a just cause was the ultimate human experience. Now to have that life end here, on a wind-swept and desolate airstrip in the middle of the mountains seemed not at all appropriate. The man should be written up in history books. If there were any history books. He should have been accorded a full military funeral—a horse-drawn caisson, a flag on his casket, a 21-gun salute. But it was not to be.

Hunter felt like a huge part of his life had just been cut out, destroyed, vanished. Gone. For the first time in a long time, he felt utterly alone. Not at all like the solitude of his mountain retreat of a few years back. This was the emptiness one felt upon losing a member of his family. The frank realization that a person you knew, spent part of your life with and loved, was gone. Forever.

He knew he would never be the same again.

CHAPTER ELEVEN

He didn't even have a shovel to dig a proper grave for Jones. He felt lost. And stranded. He had very little fuel left in the '16.

It was getting late and a light snow began to fall. He covered the general's body with the parachute and hoisted it back up onto the wing of the F-111 to keep it from any hungry animals. Hunter knew he would be spending the night at the airstrip and that he had to find shelter and damned quick. The airport's hangar seemed the likely place.

He tried to force the office door open, but it was nailed shut from the inside. The windows were bricked over—again from the inside. He hadn't expected it to be so difficult. Finally, taking a wrench from the F-111, he began to work on the lock that tightly held the building's large sliding doors.

He had no idea why Jones had programmed the F-111 to fly to this place. It looked to be an old remote strip, possibly used by the Vermont Air National Guard, or maybe an airborne forest fire fighting unit. It was in the damndest place. The area, while technically within the territory of the Northeast Economic

Zone, had been vacated long before, its residents among the first to flee to Canada when the New Order came down. It was on the side of a mountain that was surrounded by larger mountains, each covered with snow, despite the month being late April. It was utterly desolate; there probably wasn't a human around for 50 or even 100 miles in any direction. Yet, judging by the tire marks and fuel stains on the runway, it was apparent that the airstrip had been used frequently in the last few months.

He finally managed to bust open the lock and move the doors of the hangar. It was dark by this time, and his flashlight was in his Personal Survival Kit, back in the F-16. He got inside and, after wheeling the big doors closed, wandered around, looking for a light switch that he knew would probably never work. He finally found a bank of them, and started flipping. Nothing happened . . . until the 15th switch. Suddenly, there was a crackle of electricity and two dozen high powered arc lamps hanging from the ceiling burst into life.

Strangely, he had assumed all along that the hangar would be empty, but he was never so wrong in his life. His jaw nearly fell to his chest as he looked around the building. "Holy Christ!" was all he could say. Over and over. "Jesus H. Christ, I don't believe it . . . "

It was Jones's last card to play and it came up the ace of spades. The hangar was filled—literally to the rafter—with enough bombs, guns, missiles, fuel and spare parts to outfit a small air force.

It was all packed away in stacks of wooden crates marked in stencil with signs like "Dangerous—Explosives" and "Napalm—Handle With Care." He saw at

159

least 50 M-61 cannons, just like the one he carried in his F-16, plus miles of ammunition belts hanging from the main beam across the ceiling. Hundreds, maybe a couple of *thousand* bombs—clusters to big block-busters, frags to anti-personnel—were neatly stacked, in pyramids against one wall. There were probably a couple of hundred air-to-air missiles—Sidewinders mostly—each individually wrapped in a separate protective shroud, and carrying a tag for arming instructions.

At the rear of the building, there were hundreds of barrels of JP-8, the jet fuel that was the lifeblood of a pilot. He checked to make sure it wasn't contaminated—a touch to his tongue told him it wasn't. Neither were the barrels of lubricating oil stacked neatly beside the jet fuel.

He was glad he didn't smoke. One match in the wrong place in this building and the resulting explosion would make Mount St. Helen's look like a pesky landslide.

In another part of the hangar he found a treasure of spare parts—from extra tires to crucial nuts and bolts—all appropriately marked. Hanging on the wall near the parts was a clipboard holding receipts for all the merchandise. Each form held Jones's typically scrawled initials at the bottom and each form carried the name of the same company: "The Wright Patterson Used Aircraft Company, Parts and Ordnance Division." So Roy From Troy's employers had diversified. Big planes weren't enough for them; they had to start moving the small stuff. Well, he thought, it was probably easier these days to sell an anti-personnel bomb than a B-58 Hustler. Somehow, Jones had bought all the stuff, little-by-little, as the receipts told it, and established a healthy reserve. He had beaten their system after all. If it ever came to war—real war—with the 'Aks, or the pirates or anybody, Jones had guaranteed that he would be sitting on top of enough material to make it very difficult to defeat him. Or, very hard to be victorious. Hunter realized that Jones would have made a perfect air guerrilla—a Robin Hood of the skies.

On examining the parts, he found that although they were manufactured for use on many different aircraft, they all had one thing in common: They could be used on an F-16. One of the beauties of the plane was that nearly 75-percent of its parts were used on other jet aircraft. From that point on he knew that while he might have the last remaining F-16 in the world, he would never have to worry about spare parts for it. That was, if he could always get back to this place. He quickly began to appreciate the desolation of the airstrip.

He pored over the stuff for the next two hours, but finally he nearly collapsed of exhaustion. He shut off the lights—which were powered by a silver cadmium battery—and using a Sidewinder shroud as a blanket, lay on a crate of napalm bombs and immediately went to sleep.

The deadly material proved to be an apt resting place for his dreams to emerge from. In them, he replayed the action of the battles the strange day before. Fighting them over and over. And through it all, there was Jones, baseball hat in place, cigar firmly in teeth, laughing, joking, flying as usual.

He awoke in the middle of the night, a single moonbeam shining through the only crack in the hangar's ceiling. Outside the wind was howling loud enough to be a blizzard. It sounded like a bad night on top of another mountain. It seemed like centuries ago that he lived on top of the mountain in New Hampshire. He was so sure back then that something was coming that he had spent whole months, doing nothing, waiting for it. It had come. Now, it was gone. Over. Complete. It was the general's last hurrah. He was glad he was part of it. But now, what was left for him to do? All they had fought for—one of the last places on the continent or even on earth that a man could be relatively free—was gone. Eaten up by the gluttons.

He fell back into an uneasy sleep.

He woke up a second time—an instant, a minute, an hour, maybe two hours—after he had drifted off. The wind was still howling and the old building was rattling. Maybe it was time to climb up on top of another mountain and wait it out again, he thought. Perhaps this mountain. He could hunt for food and make clothes out of the Sidewinder shrouds. He could read all the technical manuals in the place and drink napalm juice for breakfast. He could wait for the world to get fucked up to the max once more, then get shaken out. Live up here and wait and watch the world go by. Maybe that's what was in the cards dealt when he followed Jones here. Led by a ghost, what more symbolism could a man want?

But this time, he was sure, he'd be ⟨...⟩
longer than two years before he came do⟨...⟩
summit. That is, if he ever came down. At⟨...⟩
he didn't care. Screw it. Let the world rot⟨...⟩
worth it. Everything was gone. Everyone—
eral, ZAP, Dominique—gone. He was gone.⟨...⟩
one cared. So why should he?

He decided. He *would* stay and live on the⟨...⟩
tain. Live there forever, if he had to. He was ⟨...⟩
He couldn't care less, he told himself, if he ne⟨...⟩
into an airplane again. This was his home no⟨...⟩
closed his eyes. Again, he thought of the ge⟨...⟩
Again, he fell off into a fitful sleep.

He woke a third time, and the first thing he ⟨...⟩
conscious of was the folded piece of cloth stuffed into
his back pocket. It was the flag, Saul Wackerman's
flag. He reached down and touched it . . . Suddenly
he was hit with an intense light. Not from the outside
but from within him. Everything instantly became
very clear. His muddled thoughts of living—*hiding
out* was more like it—on top of the mountain were
washed away. Now, only one thought was in his head:

Give up? No *fucking* way.

There were many reasons. The general's death
could not go without some small measure of revenge.
Some small reminder that you might be able to kill a
man's body, but it's hard to kill a man's soul or his
spirit. And, he—Hawk Hunter, the greatest fighter
pilot ever—could not just hang up the wings and hide.
That just wouldn't be the answer this time.

Now it was time to fight. Work and fight and fig⟨...⟩

more. If he was the last person on the continent
still believed in what was once called the Ameri-
Way, then screw 'em all, because he'd go down in
es defending it. Anywhere. Anytime. Anyplace.
d do it for the guys who died in Western Europe.
d do it for the guys at Otis. For Dominique,
erever she was. For Saul Wackerman. For Jones
.

Inside, he felt a part of Major Hawker Hunter die
d another part be born. He closed his eyes and
eamed he saw an immense "W" written across the
y. It was miles long and wide and as solid-looking
s a cloud. He didn't know what it meant, but he was
ure the answer would come to him soon. For the third
ime that night, he fell back to sleep.

It was a different man who awoke the next
morning . . .

The dawn was cold and clear. He found a shovel
and buried the general in an unmarked grave. That
done, he drained the F-111's fuel tanks into his own
then attached two full external tanks filled with fuel
from the hangar to his wings.

He still had two Sidewinders left, and he attached
two more from the hidden arms cache. His cannon
was nearly empty when he landed. Now he filled it
once more. He attached an anti-runway ordnance
dispenser to the '16's belly and filled it to capacity
with hundreds of deadly little globe-like bombs.

Using the F-16 like a tow truck, he pulled the F-111
the cliff at the edge of the runway and nudged it.
e plane pitched forward and tumbled off the moun-

tain into the deep valley below, exploding on impact. No one would see the wreckage until late spring—if at all. Anyone curious to take a second look would have to surmise the plane crashed and that would be the end of it. Thus, the last chapter of the general's life would die with him. Only Hunter would know what really happened.

Two hours later he was airborne again. He circled the mountainside base, watching. Waiting.

" . . . 3 . . . 2 . . . 1 . . . Now!"

Right on schedule, sixteen delayed reaction fuses ignited and exploded right down the center of the runway. Eight more bombs went off on the tree line next to the runway causing eight big oaks to crash down onto the strip. He had set the charges so they would destroy and cover the landing strip, but leave the hangar unscathed. He didn't want any curious flyboys or pirates landing at the base and stumbling over the technological treasure. Even a helicopter would have a hard time putting down on the cratered and blocked runway. As one last bit of insurance, he had hung a sign he'd found outside the hangar door. "Danger—Radioactivity" it read. In this day and age, people tended to take that kind of sign seriously.

Less than an hour later he was flying high over the recently occupied base once known as Jonesville. . . .

CHAPTER TWELVE

Using the F-16's ultra-sensitive High Resolution Radar, he was able to project a detailed, three-dimensional map showing the activity of the base on his cockpit video screen. It was like looking down an invisible scope extended 50,000 feet to the ground. He could "see" the Mid-Aks had taken full possession of the place. The hundred of helicopters that had carried out the assault on the base the day before were foolishly lined up in neat rows along the cratered runways. A few warships were close by offshore. Several buildings were still burning. He could even discern the Mid-Ak flag flying over the place.

He made a gruesome discovery in a cranberry bog next to the base. Bodies, hundreds of them, were scattered throughout the marsh. These had to be civilians, the former residents of Jonesville. The 'Aks had caught them and slaughtered them. But he could also see the executions were still going on. The radar showed figures, some moving, some standing in lines at the edge of the marsh. Trucks filled with more people waited nearby. The 'Aks were systematically killing anyone they could find who was remotely connected to the former Zone Armed Forces.

He wasn't surprised. Disgusted maybe, but not surprised. It was the Mid-Ak way of doing things. Kill whatever stands in the way. The barbaric policy served two purposes: it eliminated bothersome mouths to feed and it served as a fear factor which demoralized any civilian who came in contact with them. It's easier to bring someone under your heel if they are convinced that it is useless for them to fight back.

Hunter intended to change that . . .

He made two more passes, taking note of the half dozen anti-aircraft sites the 'Aks had already begun work on. These didn't bother him and he was pleased to see no sign of any workable radar systems installed. He peeled off and was soon out over the ocean. One last check of his weapons revealed everything was in perfect working order. Turning, he positioned the F-16 between the sun and the occupied base nearly eight miles below. It would be one, long, screaming dive. They would never know what hit them . . .

Two officers were overseeing the Mid-Ak firing squad. The execution, going on since early that morning, had become dull and routine. Using helicopters equipped with heat-sensitive tracking devices, coordinating with mobile units on the ground, their troops had been rounding up citizens since early the night before. The civilians would be captured, held for transport to the marsh, then lined up, 20 to 30 at a time, before the firing squad. Only the young girls would be spared. They were transported directly to the base commander, who would pass them out as

167

rewards to his best officers. The firing squad officers knew if they completed this job quickly and cleanly, they too would be in line to get a fuckable young girl.

One officer was wiping his brow in the unusually warm, winter morning, when he heard the strange noise above him. Like a whistle, getting louder, fiercer by the instant. He looked at his comrade, who had heard the noise too. Instinctively, they both turned in the direction of the sound, and found themselves shielding their eyes against the sun. It was getting louder and closer, an awesome noise, that was beginning to panic the hundred or so people in the bog— civilian prisoners and executioners alike.

Next thing they knew, the F-16 was right in front of them. It had arrived so quickly, they never had time to move. One officer could see the face of the man flying the jet. Even with a helmet on and an oxygen mask attached, the 'Ak could discern hate in the pilot's eyes. In the instant before death that seems to last an eternity, the Mid-Ak officer thought it was strange to see such an oddly painted jet fighter swooping down on him. It was red, white and blue and looked like it had a bird painted on its underbelly. A bird of death. One second later, a M-61 cannon round had taken off his head.

His companion was bewildered. He could clearly see his comrade's severed spinal column, brain stem and neck muscles as the corpse stood upright for a terrifying instant before tumbling back over. The man's head, still wearing the standard issue Mid-Ak helmet, was bouncing away like a child's toy. A moment later, the other officer felt something wet on his chest. The mysterious plane had already passed over and was streaking toward the base, barely 20 feet off the ground. The man looked down and discovered that he no longer had a stomach—it had been blown away by an invisible, seemingly painless entry of a cannon shell. He saw red, coughed up bloody vomit and died.

The Mid-Aks in the firing squad were frozen in place. The civilians, some of whom were lined up ready to be shot, needed no further prodding. They were splashing every which way through the bogs, intent on getting as much distance between them and their would-be executioners as possible. These people were no strangers to Hunter, Jones or the other pilots of ZAP. And they would never forget who it was who had saved them—the familiar Thunder F-16 had returned, just in the nick of time.

"It was Hunter who saved us," they would say when re-telling the story over and over for years to come. "The Wingman saved our lives."

The base's control tower was filled with Mid-Ak officers, enjoying a mid-morning meal of liquor, food and young girls. The confident conquerors had turned the tower into their private club. They had no sophisticated jet fighters to handle, so why the need for a working control center? The helicopters just landed themselves, no need to coordinate them. From the tower, the officers could keep an eye on the base below and celebrate their victory at the same time. Not even the fact that their main base down in Baltimore had been incinerated the day before could dim the party atmosphere.

The base's new commanding officer, taking his turn on a nubile 15-year-old blond girl, paused to take a

169

swig of champagne. He looked out of the tower window just in time to see the red, white and blue jet streak by. He swore the pilot was looking right at him. It was as if the plane was hanging out there, suspended in mid-air. The officer could see hate in the other man's eyes. Who the hell is that? he wondered. The noise of the jet passing arrived a second later. It was so loud and intense, it broke half the liquor bottles in the tower. Many of the dozen or so officers present instinctively ducked upon hearing the ear-shattering noise. When they finally managed to lift their heads up, the jet had traversed the field and was turning around.

"Is that one of our jets?" someone asked, his voice one octave away from panic. "Do we even have any goddamn jets?"

They would soon have *that* answer. By this time, the F-16 had turned 180-degrees and was heading back toward them, 100 feet above the helicopter-strewn runway. Directly under the jet's belly they saw a device which started to spew silverish globes the size of a man's hand. There were hundreds of the balls, each one sprouting a small parachute. The officers watched, mystified, as the parachutes made their way to the ground and the jet sped off and out of sight.

"What the hell is this?" one officer, slightly enraged, shouted. "Is this some kind of a joke?"

All the time, the parachutes were making their way to the ground. When the first one hit, they knew it wasn't any joke.

Like a farmer sowing seeds, Hunter had dropped 500 anti-runway/fragmentation bombs from an array dispenser he had attached to the bottom of the F-16.

Each globe had the explosive force of 100 hand grenades, and was designed in such a way as to fragment into thousands of pieces of high-flying shrapnel. The first globe hit and exploded, rocking a helicopter nearby. Then another hit, detonating close to a squad of Mid-Ak soldiers who were crossing the runway. It ripped the six men to shreds. Then another bomb landed. And another. And another.

Within seconds, the runway and the surrounding area was filled with hundreds of the deadly popping bombs. It was like a long, deadly string of firecrackers laid down and ignited. Everything and anyone within a 100 yards of the runway was perforated by shrapnel from the exploding projectiles. The fuel tanks in the hundreds of 'Ak helicopters began exploding, adding to the chain reaction of destruction. Bodies were being flung everywhere. Severed arms, legs, torsos flew through the air. A half a man's body was thrown upward and splattered against one of the control tower windows. The sudden, grisly sight made even the iron-stomached Mid-Ak officers retch. The four young girls in the tower at the time took advantage of the confusion and fled, naked.

Within 30 seconds the runway and the base itself was a mass of bloody, fiery confusion.

The F-16, its powerful engine screaming, turned once again and headed back . . .

Many of the Mid-Ak troops began to panic and flee. Some did report to their anti-aircraft positions and lamely returned the fire, but Hunter, on his next pass, took these soldiers out with one squeeze of the F-16's gun trigger.

He looped and made a hard peel to the left, finding

himself 20-feet above the water, and heading for the biggest of the Mid-Ak warships. It was like a replay of his attack the day before. Black-uniformed sailors frantically running to their positions as he approached. The jet, so low its exhaust was churning up the surface water, unfailingly staying on target until the last possible second. The weapon release button was pushed. A 500-pound bomb ripped into the side of the ship and exploded.

He managed to strafe the other two, smaller ships in the harbor then executed a climb and back roll, leveling out at the far end of the base's number one runway and back for another strafing pass. The Mid-Aks on the ground were amazed that an aircraft could perform the maneuvers, the F-16 was going through. It was turning, spinning, climbing, diving, strafing, bombing. Anyone brave enough to stick his head up and risk a shot at the plane found themselves shooting into thin air.

Hunter systematically went about destroying primary and secondary targets on the base. He put a Sidewinder into the only Mid-Ak helicopter that was able to get airborne during the attack. He left the crucial radio antenna in ruins. The two warehouses were in flames. A row of Mid-Ak trucks was reduced to smoking hulks. He bombed a nearby dike, which allowed the sea to pour into the far end of the place, putting half the major runway under water.

He was running low on ammunition and fuel and knew it was time to start thinking about making a grand exit. He was carrying one last bomb—a napalm cannister he'd purposely saved for last. He wheeled around and headed directly for the control tower.

There were two Mid-Aks foolishly firing at him from that position, with the majority of the 'Ak officers were still cowering inside.

He lowered his flaps and his landing gear to slow the jet down to almost a crawl. Lining up the control tower in his video display sight, he could see figures running inside panicking as he approached. At 200 yards out, he performed a perfect four-point turn—first on the right wing, then upside down, then on the left wing and back level again. At the end of the maneuver he was right on the control tower. A push of the weapons release and the napalm cannister splattered onto the side of the tower.

The building was instantly engulfed in flames. Streaking past, he could see fiery figures, diving or falling out of the building as the burning gelatin spread. For the coup de' grace, he squeezed off a cannon burst which riddled the Mid-Ak flag flying above one of the buildings splintering its flagpole in the process.

Then he was gone in a flash . . .

The survivors of the murderous one-man air strike finally started to emerge once they felt sure the jet was gone. Looking around the base they saw almost the entire Mid-Ak helicopter corps in flames, every major building was burning, the control tower simply ceased to exist, two ships were sinking offshore, and the sea was uncontrollably pouring into the far end of the base carrying with it the bodies of the Mid-Aks killed in the attack.

On a sand dune, about a mile away, some of the civilians who only minutes before were slated to go before the firing squad, were bayonetting the remains of their would-be executioners. They would never forget what the pilot in the red, white and blue jet had done. Stealing the dead Mid-Aks' weapons, they regrouped and prepared to evacuate the area, using the commandeered Mid-Aks trucks.

Something in the sky caught the eye of one of the survivors and he called to his comrades to look. Some of the few remaining Mid-Aks saw it too. Miles up, its tail exhaust leaving a contrail, the outline of the F-16 could be seen. The pilot was skywriting a huge letter 55,000 feet up and miles across. Then the F-16 was gone for good, leaving a sight both friend and foe would not soon forget—even as the huge "W" drifted and eventually faded away.

CHAPTER THIRTEEN

He only had enough fuel to fly another 500 miles, if he kept it high and steady and didn't have to go into the fuel-gulping afterburner. Steering west, he was intent on getting out of the Mid-Ak controlled air space of what used to be the Northeast Economic Zone. They would certainly be looking for him—his plane was undoubtedly identified at the nuking of Baltimore. Now he had to wonder what the bounty on his head would be worth once word of the bombing of Otis reached the Mid-Ak High Command.

He was high over what was once called western Massachusetts when he got his answer . . .

He was aware of the two bogies even before they showed up on his radar scope. His sixth sense—that mysterious, almost spooky ability which set him apart from any other pilot who ever flew—had warned him that they were in the area. The blips on the radar screen just confirmed what he already knew—two fighters were gaining on him fast.

He remained cool and slowly drifted down through

the cloud cover, emerging at 45,000 feet. They were coming out of the southwest, free-lancers, most likely, alerted by the Mid-Aks that a high-priced fugitive would be in their area. And the Mid-Aks would like him shot down for good.

Supersonic bounty hunters were one of the new breed of flyboy in the New Order world. They had a couple of ways to make their money and it was only their ability as pilots that determined how rich they could be.

Air bounties were paid in two ways. "Bring 'em back alive," and the pilot—or a team of pilots—received the full reward. Shoot the fugitive down—and return the tail section of his plane as proof—and the hunter received half the bounty. Either way, a successful air hunter—mostly free-lancers looking for a little excitement to spell them from the monotony of convoy duty—could wind up rich very quickly.

Just how rich depended on the flyer's skills. It took a special finesse of flying for a bounty hunter to stalk, locate and force a fugitive pilot to land—safely—to be brought back alive. This could be accomplished in a number of ways: Some air hunters could simply persuade a fugitive to give up without a fight and follow him back to the payer's airfield. This tactic usually worked if the air hunter was loaded with buckshot and the fugitive was unarmed. If words and threats didn't do it, a clip of the fugitive's wing with a well-placed cannon burst just might. A good air marksman could blind the runner by sending a single shot through his radar. Or the tried and true tactic was to just stay on the runner's ass until he ran out of fuel.

Still, the bounty hunter had to provide a living, breathing body to collect the big money. This is why many of them worked with accomplices on the ground—shady characters who could be radioed and told to speed to the site of a fugitive's landing, find him, and capture him.

And if all else failed, the stalker could always blast the runner out of the sky and settle for half the reward. Either way it was a complicated, fast-moving, treacherous but ultimately profitable business. No wonder it attracted some of the best stick jockeys left on the continent.

"Fast Eddy calling one-niner-five F-16. Do you read me?"

Hunter had been tracking the two fighters visually for five minutes before they called him. They were about a mile below him and two miles back. A pair of F-104 Starfighters, fast, pencil-thin, short-winged jets. Both were painted in gaudy, red and yellow circus colors. As usual, the pilots were known by their gimmicky call names.

Hunter adjusted his UHF band frequency. The game had begun.

"F-16 acknowledging. Read you five-by-five, Starfighter. What's your problem?"

"You've got the problem, Mac," came the static-filled reply. "You the one who busted up the air base down on old Cape Cod?"

"News travels fast," Hunter replied, checking his remaining armament. No cannon ammo. One Sidewinder. Two Starfighters. It could get interesting.

"You pissed some people off, '16," the other pilot, known as Rick the Stick, radioed in.

"Mid-Aks? People?" Hunter said, re-checking his fuel load. "I don't think they qualify."

"Being a wise-ass will only make it harder on you, '16," Fast Eddie said. "We know you're down on fuel. And you ain't got enough to take the both of us on . . ."

"And we only see one air-to-air . . ." Rick the Stick added.

"Right," Eddie continued. "So why not come quietly, '16? Follow us on a three-seven heading."

"I don't know, boys," Hunter replied. "What's in it for me?"

"What's in it for you, '16, is that we don't trash your pretty airplane," Eddie said, a touch of hostility in his voice.

"Okay, Starfighter," Hunter said, eyeing a bank of clouds ahead. "What's in it for *you*?"

"We take you alive," Fast Eddie replied. "Three bags of silver and quarter bag of gold. Real stuff."

Gold, Hunter thought. The Mid-Ak's favorite currency.

"Dead . . .?" Rick the Stick added, "You're worth a dime bag of gold and a few lousy quarters."

Hunter could see that while the bounty pilots were talking to him, they had slowly narrowed the gap between him and them. The large cloud bank was just ahead. The Starfighters were now just a half mile below and riding a quarter mile off his tail.

"Make it easy on us, '16," Fast Eddie said as he and the Stick moved up to within a quarter mile of Hunter's jet. "Just lower your flaps and gear and follow us. The 'Aks ain't that bad."

"Yeah," Rick the Stick added. "Just lose that

178

Sidewinder too."

At that moment all three jets entered the cloud bank simultaneously. When the Starfighters emerged a few seconds later, the F-16 was nowhere to be seen.

"Where did the son of a bitch go?" Rick the Stick exclaimed.

"Christ! Check radar, Stick!" Eddie said, panic rising in his voice.

"No need," a voice, popping on in their headsets, said. "Just check your tail."

The Stick looked back just in time to see the Sidewinder leave the wingtip of the F-16. The missile was swallowed up by the Starfighter's jet exhaust duct. An instant later, Rick the Stick and his Starfighter were blown into a million little pieces.

"Air pollution," Hunter muttered as he climbed slightly to avoid hitting the flying debris.

"Jeezus!" Eddie exclaimed as he watched his wingman become one with the clouds. "How did you do that?"

"Practice," Hunter said, smiling. The old 360 loop-dee-loop—a quick climb, roll back and level—had been in the fighter pilot's bag of tricks since World War I. The Thunderbirds perfected it. But no pilot did it quicker than Hunter.

Fast Eddie, a former Air National Guard pilot gone bad, knew there was only one pilot in the world who could loop that quickly without killing himself with gas.

"Hawk Hunter?" he asked almost meekly into his radio set.

"The one and only," Hunter replied.

"Oh, God! Those goddamn 'Aks," Eddie said,

179

nearly screaming. "They didn't tell us we was going up against you, Hunter."

"That's bad employee relations, Eddie."

"Jesus, I should have known by the F-16," the bounty pilot said, turning to see Hunter directly behind him.

"Not many of them left," Hunter said.

"And there'll be one less," Fast Eddie said, a light bulb going off in his head. " 'cause, you ain't got no more air-to-airs left. And if you had any ammo, you'd have blasted me by now." Just because Eddie was a pilot didn't mean he was extraordinarily bright.

"Maybe I just like talking," Hunter said as he watched Eddie peel off to the south.

"I got three Sidewinders, Hunter," Eddie said, a new confidence evident in his voice. "And one of them is for you. When I bring back the tail section of the great Hawk Hunter, the 'Aks will pay me double the live rate. And I'll be famous!"

More likely they'd feed you into a hot engine, Eddie, Hunter thought. But he had wasted enough time with the Starfighter already. He had places to go. With a touch of the F-16's side-stick controller, he put the jet into a screaming dive.

Fast Eddie was on his tail in a second, prematurely launching one of his Sidewinders. It streaked by off to Hunter's left, missing by an eighth of a mile.

"Where'd you learn to shoot like that, Eddie?" Hunter asked, as he passed 20,000 feet and still diving. "A video arcade?"

"I got two more, Hunter," Eddie replied, arming his second missile and lining up the F-16 on the Starfighter's relatively crude targeting acquisition sys-

180

tem. "Say your prayers . . ."

"In the name of the father. And of the son," Hunter began, "Out of the park. Home run."

Eddie's second missile missed by a full 100 yards.

"Now I know why your plane looks like it belongs in a carnival, Eddie," Hunter said, checking his altitude at 5000 feet and still dropping. "A loser every time."

"Fuck you, Hunter," Eddie said with a mouthful of frustration.

They were both closing in on 1000 feet when Eddie launched his last Sidewinder. A deft flick of Hunter's wrist on the side-stick and the '16 casually moved out of the way of the deadly missile. It shot straight past and exploded on the side of a mountain below.

They were flying through the heart of the Berkshires, close to where ZAP had battled the Cherry Busters in the Thruway War a year before. Hunter was now down to 500 feet, following the twists and turns of a river as it wound itself through the mountains. Eddie was close on his tail.

"Still got my cannon, Hunter," Eddie boasted. "And you ain't got yours."

Hunter saw a stream of shells pass him on the right. He zigged in that direction, just in time to see another burst shoot by on his left. A zag back to his left put him back on his original heading. When Fast Eddie tried to shoot low; Hunter would take the F-16 up a notch. He'd shoot high, Hunter would be scraping the treetops. Whatever the bounty pilot did, Hunter was a split-second ahead of him. While Eddie was spewing out every curseword in the book—and inventing new ones—Hunter was enjoying the view.

The high-speed cat-and-mouse game continued for miles as the F-16 twisted and turned through the river valley of the Berkshires, the F-104 in close pursuit.

Suddenly, the river disappeared and a mountain loomed straight ahead. Hunter saw it. Eddie didn't.

"Goodbye, Eddie," Hunter said as he pulled back on the stick and stood the F-16 on its tail. The Starfighter, notorious for its bad handling at low altitude, just kept right on going. It slammed into the side of the mountain, its fuel tanks exploding on impact, spreading burning jet fuel over a wide area and igniting a forest fire.

God help us, Hunter thought, looking back at the ball of flame rising from the side of the mountain, if the Mid-Aks ever get any real pilots.

Thirty minutes later, he saw his immediate destination appear on the western horizon. A cross-check of his instruments confirmed he had about 10 minutes of fuel left—just enough to get where he was going. He started monitoring all UHF frequencies, searching for the right one on which he could announce his arrival. He knew he had probably already been picked up on radar and that dozens of SAM crews were tracking him. He just hoped they kept their cool long enough.

Syracuse. The once-bustling city stuck in the middle of upstate New York had long ago been evacuated, its residents now either scattered or citizens of Canada. But a new smaller city had sprung up, not in the middle of town, but at its airport. The Aerodrome they called it, and the last Hunter knew, an old friend of his was running the place.

The Aerodrome was a true product of the New Order era. Because most of New York state was now the Free Territory of New York, it was anything-goes as far as governments went. Most of the state was made up of small hamlets, where like the few larger cities not completely evacuated, the people had reverted to a kind of benign anarchy. Most of the people, though monetarily poor, enjoyed the set-up. But there was still a price to pay for the no-government-at-any-cost approach. Bandits perpetually roamed the deserted highways, and every so often, a roving air pirate squadron might blow through and terrorize the skies above the rugged mountainous country.

In the middle of this sat The Aerodrome, a haven of profitability and capitalism. It was all a question of location. Syracuse sat at an important crossroads of the air convoy routes. Single aircraft—cargo planes to fighters—used the place as a refueling stop. In the past, many air trains leaving Boston would fly a heading straight to Syracuse, where, if an aircraft had trouble—either mechanical or from pirates—it could set down safely. Smaller convoys flying down from Canada or from other places, would drop off goods and supplies at The Aerodrome for pick-up by other planes heading west. The base also afforded a large and well-staffed aircraft maintenance service; a place where an airplane could be overhauled, its engines torn down and rebuilt, its body rewelded, its avionics replaced or updated.

In many ways, the place was a modern version of

the old-style truck-stop. Several eating establishments were located there, as were twice as many barrooms. Other enterprises—uniforms, used flying equipment, custom aircraft painting—thrived at the airbase. Many escort pilots and free-lancers called the place home. The currency ran from old silver coins to an occasional piece of gold or a diamond. And outright bartering—a short escort mission in exchange for a bellyfull of jet fuel, a paint job for a new landing gear assembly—was common.

So was the more deviant activity. While the half dozen large hotels surrounding the airport were converted into flophouses for weary pilots, the 20 or so smaller ones served as whorehouses. One of The Aerodrome's main attractions was its Sodom and Gomorrah atmosphere. And flesh was just one commodity available. A black market flourished at the base. Guns, ammo, missiles, bombs, anything that could be attached to the underside of a jet or to its wings could be bought at The Aerodrome in any and all quantities. It seemed like everything—legal, illegal or otherwise—could be had at the place.

Although The Aerodrome started out as a private enterprise, all the activity at the base attracted many people to settle around it. Soon a city had arisen. Though born from the same idea as Jonesville—people liked safety in numbers in the New Order world—the place made Otis look like a hick town. More than 30,000 lived in the general vicinity, and more than three thousand passed in and out each day. The crime rate was high, the quality of liquor was low with the availability of a nice-looking piece of ass falling somewhere in the middle.

There was no police force, but common sense dictated the need for a standing army. Supported by the landing tax imposed on everyone flying through, the Aerodrome Defense Force—the ADF—was well-known for its tough, no-nonsense approach to protecting the base. ADF crews manned the radar stations, the SAM sites, the control tower and patrolled the border of the ten-square mile area claimed by The Aerodrome's operators. A squadron of ADF fighters—flying vintage F-105 Thunderchiefs—kept a close eye on The Aerodrome's airspace. The bandits, the air pirates and other troublemakers usually gave the place a wide berth. Of if they did find themselves at The Aerodrome, more often than not they would behave themselves, lest they feel the wrath of the ADF.

Syracuse was known to every pilot flying as an exciting, sometimes dangerous place. And every fly-boy from the Coasters to Texas knew there were two things you didn't do at The Aerodrome: Arrive without filing a proper flight plan ahead of time and arrive without money.

Hunter was about to commit both sins at once . . .

"F-16, this is Aerodrome control." The words burst from Hunter's radio. "We are tracking you on an unauthorized approach. You have violated our airspace. Leave the area immediately."

"I copy you, Aerodrome," Hunter said, biting his lip. "I'm low on fuel. Just a minute or two left. Request permission to land."

"F-16," the tough-sounding voice of Aerodrome control replied. "You have violated our airspace. Leave the area immediately or you will be shot down.

185

This is your final warning."

Hunter didn't doubt for a minute that they would shoot. He could see at least a dozen SAM sites ringing the base and was sure many more lay hidden in the dense forests which surrounded the base on three sides. He knew The Aerodrome was a valuable entity that needed constant vigilance and protection from pirates and other flying hostiles. And that was how it was in the heart of a Free Territory—shoot first and ask questions later.

"Aerodrome tower, this is F-16," Hunter radioed, playing one of his two ace cards up front. "I am Major Hawker Hunter of the Northeast Economic Zone Air Patrol. I am unarmed. I am low on fuel. I am requesting permission to land."

" '16, Aerodrome Tower," the voice came back, a slight hint of hesitation in its tone. "Verbal identification no good. We are tracking you on our ground air defense system. You have less than minute before we launch. Leave the area, immediately."

Time to show his last ace.

"Aerodrome control. Is Captain Mike Fitzgerald still in command?" Hunter checked his fuel. One minute left, tops.

"Launch sequence has started, F-16."

"Tower, please inform Captain Fitzgerald that Hawker Hunter is requesting landing clearance."

"Twenty seconds to SAM launch . . ." the radio crackled.

Hunter knew he had enough fuel to dodge one SAM, maybe two. But then he'd have to bail out and lose the ship. That was, if another SAM didn't get him first.

186

"Ten seconds . . ."

He began to prepare for evasive action when a familiar voice sprang from the radio.

"How do I know it's you, Hawker?"

"Because I'm the guy who taught you how to fly, you goddamned rum-soaked Irishman!" Hunter radioed back, his infrared detecting system warning him a SAM was about to launch. "Call off the SAMs!"

"Where?" the voice with a brogue asked.

"Nellis, Nevada." Hunter said quickly.

"What did we do the night I got my wings?"

"I brought you out on the Las Vegas strip, got you shitfaced. Then you lost a month's pay at the blackjack table." Hunter said. "And if I have to ditch because of your fucking SAMs, I'll personally kick your ass back to Caesar's Palace . . ."

"Cancel SAM launch," he heard the Irishman say. "Come on in on runway Two Left, Hawk. Wind speed 10 knots, south. I think you owe me a hundred bucks from that night and I want to collect."

Hunter saw his infrared detector cool down, confirming the SAMs had halted their launch sequence.

"You'd better have a bottle of good stuff waiting, Fitzie," Hunter said as he began his final approach. "Or I'll turn out into a bag of shamrock fertilizer."

Ten minutes later, Hunter was taxiing up to a runway station, where 20 or so nervous-looking ADF troopers were waiting. He shut down the engine, popped the canopy, and climbed out, only to find himself on the wrong end of twenty M-16 muzzles. Jumping down to the tarmac, he saw a familiar face emerge from the crowd of rifles.

It was the one and only Mike Fitzgerald, the only pilot who could fly a supersonic jet fighter into combat drunk, and live to tell about it.

"Hawker, me boy!" the diminutive red-faced, curly-haired Irishman said, planting a bearhug on him. "Good to have the famous Wingman visit with us."

"I should kick your ass back to Dublin," Hunter said in mock anger. "If you had fired more than two of those SAMs, they'd be picking me up from here to Canada."

"We just had to be sure it was you, Hawker, my friend," Fitzgerald said with a classic grin. "Besides, if I'd shot off the missile, and you had lived, what then? I would have to charge you for it, now, wouldn't I?"

Hunter had to laugh at the little guy. Born in Ireland, he somehow became an American citizen and immediately joined the service. And it was true, Hunter had taught Fitzgerald how to fly. It was back when Hunter was part of the Thunderbirds. All the members of the team did double-duty at Nellis Air Force training new pilots fresh from OCS. Fitzie was one of the last bunch Hunter had trained before he was accepted for the shuttle program.

In the sea of conservative military types that flooded a base like Nellis, Fitzie had been a welcome addition. A real Mick in the middle of a bunch of Mormons. No one was quite sure how he made it through high school, never mind jet pilot training school. But the Irishman proved to be a whiz at engineering and an outstanding fighter pilot. Before leaving Nellis, Hunter recommended that Fitzie be considered for Thunderbird duty once he earned his full captain's wings.

But his talent in the air didn't keep him out of trouble on the ground, and therefore he was always a little too much for the T-birds. Nellis, being just a stone's throw from the old gambling mecca of Las Vegas, provided every kind of temptation a fighter pilot could face. And Fitzie took them all on: brawling in the best saloons, sleeping with show girls, buzzing a casino at seven o'clock on a Sunday morning after losing at the slot machines the night before. Witnesses to the buzzing incident swear when Fitzie's jet went by, every slot in the place paid out a full price.

"Electromagnetism," Fitz had explained at the time. "Serves the bastards right for taking a poor serviceman's money."

Fitz snapped his fingers and the ADF troopers disappeared. "Are yer thirsty?" he said, smacking his lips.

"Only if you're buying," Hunter replied.

They started walking to one of the bars located in the base's main terminal building. The place was strictly hustle and bustle, as busy as an airport terminal in the pre-war days. Everywhere, there were pilots, monkeys, soldiers, and women—lots of women. Just about everyone Hunter saw was carrying some kind of sidearm or rifle. Hunter instinctively put his hand to his belt, just to make sure his .45 was still there. It was.

"Been a long time, Hawker," Fitzgerald said as they walked. "Been hearing a lot about you. Running your own air force and making things hard for our

189

friends, the pirates."

"You're the one in the limelight," Hunter told him. "You're known as the Great Fitzgerald. The man who runs the famous Aerodrome."

Fitzgerald gave a slight heel click and smiled. "We try, Hawker," he said, watching two shapely female terminal workers walk by. "Oh, how we try."

Besides being the only person ever to call him "Hawker," Fitzie was one of his favorite people. They'd burned up more than a few bottles of scotch in their day. It was good to see his carousing buddy again.

"Sorry to hear about your base," Fitz said, as they turned the corner into the crowded bar.

"Christ," Hunter said. "News *does* travel fast. We were only thrown out yesterday morning."

"Oh, but we were hearing rumors about it for a long time, Hawker," he said. "We get a lot of scuttlebutt here. Usually, the lot of it is pure horseshit. But then again, sometimes it comes true."

They reached a couple of barstools and Hunter was about to curse the Mid-Aks when he looked up and saw three of them, sitting at the bar.

His first instinct was to start throwing punches. His second thought was to reach for his service revolver. Fitzgerald squeezed both actions and calmly, but firmly, grabbed hold of Hunter's arm.

"Be cool, Hawker," he said, motioning the bartender to set them up.

"Jesus Christ, Fitzie. Mid-Aks? Here?" Hunter said, barely containing his anger.

"You're in a Free Territory, now," Fitzgerald said, his powerful hand still gripping Hunter's arm, leading him to an isolated table. "They have as much right to be here as you. In fact, more so. They had the proper flight clearance."

Hunter could barely control the urge to spit on the three black-uniformed men. "These guys are murderers, Fitz. They killed Jones, for Christ's sake."

Fitzgerald paused for a second. He, too, was close to Jones, a fellow Irishman. "Jones is dead?"

"Killed. Yesterday." Hunter replied, the words coming out for the first time, hurting on every syllable.

"It was he who nuked Baltimore, then?" Fitz asked as the bartender brought a bottle of scotch and two glasses.

"Yeah, it was him," Hunter said, taking a long slug of the whiskey. It felt good going down. "There was a coup in Boston. We had no choice but to bug out. Jones didn't think it was worth it, to fight the 'Aks. At least, that's what he told us. Then the crazy old coot tries to ditch me in a cloud and heads for Mid-Akland."

"You were with him, then?" Fitz asked in a whisper.

"Yes," Hunter said, tasting his second shot. "Followed him in, got two Voodoos off his ass then rode his tail until he dropped it. Or his plane dropped it. He took a piece in the chest during the final approach."

Fitzgerald knocked his back and poured both of them another. "Well, it caused quite a stir around here, I tell you. First nuclear bombing since the war and all."

"Screw 'em," Hunter said, his words seething with hate. "I wished I had been carrying, too. I would

191

have dropped another right on their ass."

A third shot was followed by a fourth. He could feel the whiskey taking effect on him. With his stomach empty, the liquor was speeding through his veins and right to his head.

"Well, you did your part, riding in with him," Fitzgerald said with a wink. "If those 'Aks knew it was you who rode shotgun, they'd probably dynamite the whole frigging terminal just to get you."

Hunter was tempted to tell him of his one-man bombing raid at Otis earlier that day, but decided to let it rest for a while.

Fitzgerald poured out yet another two shots and raised his glass. "To Jonesie," he said, a touch of sadness in his voice. "The poor bastard probably thought he'd live to see the stars and stripes fly again one day."

They toasted the general. Hunter had only buried him that morning, but it seemed like an eternity ago.

"He will not be forgotten," Hunter said, raising his glass.

"Hear, hear," Fitzgerald agreed.

Meanwhile, the Mid-Aks at the bar finished their drinks and left. A noticeable sigh of relief came up from the other patrons. It was like a great weight had been lifted from everyone in the room.

"What the hell are they doing here, Mike?" Hunter asked.

"On my sweet mother's grave, Hawker, I can do nothing to prevent them from being here," Fitzgerald said, his voice ringing with sincerity. "No one likes them. But they're customers. And we set this place up to serve a customer. Anyone, as long as he pays, can

192

ay.

"Look, Hawker, there are a thousand little wars going on across the continent. We can't take sides in them, big or small. It's bad for business. We can't make any enemies. We have to stay neutral. That's the only way it can work. We just don't deal with pirates, but that's only because they never pay their bills."

"How the hell did you get involved here, anyway?" Hunter asked him.

Fitzgerald motioned the barkeep for another bottle.

"Right place. Right time," he said with a smile. "I was laid up when the war broke out. Pranged an F-15 at Griffith AFB not far from here and busted up my leg. The war was over before they took the cast off. I walked out of the hospital the day they closed it down. Per the New Order. Everyone else left. Went to Canada. They were convinced the Russians were coming."

"So I heard," Hunter said. "People told me they saw it on TV and in newspapers, saying the Russians were about to invade."

"Aye! I saw them too," Fitzgerald exclaimed. "Scared me shitless. We knew the Vice President was a Quisling. We knew he let the Red ICBMs through the shield. The early warning system was going off for a day and a half over the TV. I was convinced the Reds were going to march over the pole and come down through Quebec."

"But it didn't happen," Hunter said.

"Aye, it didn't happen. Things started to calm down. A few of us banded together at Griffith. I was really the only pilot around, and one of the senior officers. Everyone else had gone to war and never

came back.

"We had a few fights with these New Order fanatics who showed up to destroy all the airplanes. Ass disarmament freaks. We gave them trouble, but in end, they would have overwhelmed us, so we took of in an old C-47 Spooky. Only had enough juice to get us here. We landed. It was deserted, so we stayed. There were twenty of us. Sergeants, monkeys, a few lieutenants. They're looking to me like I'm the leader. You know?"

Hunter had to laugh at that notion. The only thing he'd ever seen Fitzie lead was a tipsy conga line of show girls through the lobby of the Tropicana one night.

"We stayed here," Fitzie continued. "There wasn't a soul around. No airplanes, but plenty of food and booze. It was half party, half figuring out what the hell we should be doing."

"One day, a plane lands. A Lear jet, mind yer. Its engine is coughing and spitting oil. The pilot climbs out and sees us. A bunch of servicemen with long hair and beards who haven't heard a bloody thing since the New Order went down.

"He says 'Can you fix the plane?' and we say 'Sure we can fix the plane. But what do we get from it?' He says 'A bag a silver apiece,' and shows us a bag of real silver. Silver quarters, Hawk!

"Then he explained how the silver was worth so much more now. And that the New Order Commissioner and his gang were nothing but a bunch of arseholes lying on the beach in Bermuda while the Mid-Aks go hogwild. So we fix his plane and he says he'll be back.

194

"Soon, he is, with three more planes behind him. They need fuel. We got fuel. One needs a turbofan part. We go to the airline shop and juryrig one for him. He pays us. And they're on their way. It was one of the first air convoys going across to the Coast and it landed here.

"And it never stopped. Today we've got ten runways operating. No waiting."

Hunter was fascinated. If these were normal times, Fitz would have been many times a millionaire by now. As it was, the little man was very rich and powerful.

Hunter quickly told him his story. The triumph and the tragedy in Western Europe, the horror on the streets of New York City, his life on the mountain and his days with ZAP.

Then Fitzgerald asked him a simple, yet baffling question: "What are you going to do now, Hawker?"

It was a question he had no answer to.

"Long range, I'm making my way to a Coaster air base," he told Fitzgerald. "Jones's brother runs an outfit out there. But the bird is starting to get cranky. I need an engine job, some avionics work, some drop tanks and fuel."

"Well, you've come to the right place, my friend," Fitzie said with a grin "We can do all that work right here and you can visit for a while. Relax. Meet some girls."

"Sounds good," Hunter said, downing his seventh—or was it his eighth—drink.

"Now, just permit me one moment of unpleasantness, Hawker," Fitzgerald said. "How can you pay me for the work? Silver? Gold? A few diamonds per-

195

haps?"

The question hit Hunter like a 500-pound bomb. "How much will it cost?"

"Oh, I should say, at least fifteen bags of real silver, or a bag and a half of gold."

Hunter felt his stomach turn. "I . . . I don't have that kind of money," he found himself saying. It was the first time in his life the problem had ever come up. He instantly realized that he'd always been taken care of—whether it was by his parents, or a scholarship or the military. He had never had to pay to fly before.

"Well, Hawker," Fitzgerald said in that tone one person always assumes when money is coming between friends. "I can give you a break on some of the prices. Cut a little here and a little there. But you must pay for the materials. It's the way we work here. I would like to give it all to you. But I can't."

"I understand, Fitz," Hunter said. "It's not your fault."

Fitzgerald thought for a moment, then said, "Look, I *can* arrange to have you work for it. Earn your keep."

Hunter's spirits perked up. "You need a pilot?"

Fitzgerald slowly shook his head. 'Well, not right away, Hawker. But we do need line mechanics. And you're the best in the business."

"Are you telling me I have to become a 'monkey?' ''

"It's just temporary. You can fill in when we need a pilot, and work the line when we don't." He paused for a moment. "It's really the only way that I can see."

Hunter thought it over. "Well, if that's what it

takes . . ."

Fitzgerald clapped his powerful hands once. "Then it's settled, then. You can stay in my quarters. I have the whole top floor of one of the hotels."

"Just you on an entire floor?" Hunter said, reaching once again for the bottle.

Fitzgerald smiled and gave him an impish wink. "Just me and the girls."

CHAPTER FOURTEEN

Hunter started his job two days later. Fitzgerald pulled some strings and installed him as a crew chief for one of The Aerodrome's busiest repair hangars. The work was routine. Stripping down engines from all types of aircraft. Checking the plane's structure, its electronics, landing gear, control devices. One of his crew's first projects was a complete overhaul of an aging Boeing 707. They had to convert the one-time airliner into a cargo plane for convoy duty. His twenty man crew, along with three other crews in the hangar, would have it working like new in a month's time.

Hands down, he was the best mechanic on the base, so his duties increased. He was the one they called on for the emergency repairs at The Aerodrome. He quickly became the trouble shooter extraordinaire for the base. If there was a problem no one else could figure out, the call went out for Hunter and he always came through with the needed remedy.

He couldn't complain much about the work. The hours were long, but it actually felt good to get his hands dirty every day. His only flying the first month was taking the planes his crew had repaired aloft for a test run. He found himself behind the controls of a bewildering string of airplanes, from airliners to Piper Cubs, helicopters to fighters. The time he spent aloft became very important to him, whether it was in a creaky Boeing 727 or one of the base's F-105s. He appreciated every second he was airborne. He had been denied flight once before—during his exile on the mountain—and he didn't want it to happen again.

Meanwhile, is F-16 sat in a little used hangar at the edge of the base. He worked on it as much as possible, using used parts, in some cases designing new ones. The plane needed a complete overhaul, he had decided, but such a job would be expensive. Very expensive. Pricing it out with Fitzie, they had determined that he'd have to work for at least four months to get the repairs done and buy drop tanks and enough fuel to get him across the Badlands and on his way to the West Coast. He didn't want to wait that long—he had never waited that long for anything, it seemed. But he had no choice.

Then he found out that he didn't need to be in such a hurry to get to the Coast.

He had just completed his first month of work. After a long day on the line, he was sitting in one of the huge tubs found in Fitzgerald's suite, soaking in the water's warmth and enjoying a backscrub from one of the 10 maids Fitzie employed.

Fitzie's maids were all young, beautiful, and willing to please. Fitzie had issued them uniforms that were part-bikini, part pub girl. He liked to boast that they were on call, around the clock, something Hunter could testify to. Every night since moving into Fitzie's luxury quarters, Hunter had found the comfort of one, sometimes two of the maids. It was one of the best parts of his experience at the Aerodrome.

Fitz walked in while Hunter was getting toweled dry by Hunter's favorite, an Oriental beauty named Aki.

"You need a drink, Hawker, me boy. We've got some bad news for yer."

"Aki immediately gave the towel to Hunter and walked to the huge, luxurious bathroom's wet bar.

"Did you tell me that when you left Otis, a lot of your people flew out on a C-130?" a worried-looking Fitzgerald asked him.

"That's right," Hunter said, taking a drink from Aki. "All of the monkeys, a bunch of pilots and the base MPs. We were all supposed to link up out on the coast. Why?"

"They never made it out of Zone airspace," Fitz told him.

"What?"

"A pilot just back from Boston said he saw a C-130 with ZAP markings sitting in a hangar there. He asked around, because he knew you'd want to know. They told him that the plane was jumped by six free-lancers flying for the 'Aks. Tangled with the plane's fighter escort, but the C-130 caught some bullets in the fight. It had one engine out and another burning when the free-lancers forced it to land at Logan. They got a hefty bounty price for it, too."

"Jesus Christ!" Hunter said. "That plane was carrying some of the best flyboys and mechanics of ZAP."

"I understand, Hawker," Fitz said. "It sounds as if you shouldn't be in such a hurry now. It would have been a small reunion out on the Coast."

"I guess so," Hunter said slowly. What's the point in getting to the Coaster base if there weren't more than a few of them out there? He had to wonder whether any of the others—the pilots who took off in the ZAP fighters or the Crazy Eights—even made it.

"So, what happened to the people on board the C-130?" he asked Fitzie.

"They're being held prisoner by the 'Aks. Got 'em all locked up—house arrest—in the old Government building in downtown Boston. Know where that is?"

"I sure do. When the 'Aks took over, they filled the place with women and kids, so we couldn't launch an air strike against them there."

"Aye, Fitzgerald said, sipping a drink. "The 'Aks are big on insurance."

"Fitz, do you realize that they are holding enough talent and experience to start an air force? And a damn good one?" Hunter said in frustration.

"I know, Hawker. But I can't imagine any of your boys turning, can you?"

"No, not many. We had a few free-lancers who might. In fact, Jones was convinced that at least one of them was an 'Ak spy."

"Sounds like the Mid-Atlantics. Fookin' backstabbers," Fitz spat out. "I hate them, too, Hawker. But I have no choice but to deal with them. If I don't they'll be on my ass, like they were on yours."

If he had learned anything in his month at The Aerodrome it was a sympathy for Fitzie's "If you pay, you stay" philosophy. It was business, not politics. In fact, since the Mid-Aks took over Logan, business had increased at The Aerodrome. The Free Canadians, many of which were actually ex-patriate Americans, shared the almost universal hate of the Mid-Atlantic. They refused to deal with them, so had been re-routing their convoys away from Boston and through Syracuse, adding more landing fee money to Fitzie's already burgeoning coffers.

"Look, Hawker, this means you can stay here longer." Fitzgerald said. "Enjoy yourself. Why go off fighting wars that don't mean a pig's ass? These days, it's hired gun versus hired gun. There *are* no more issues. There *are* no more causes or flags to rally around. Why get killed if you don't have to, just because you're on someone's payroll? It's a different world out there, since you and I flew for the Air Force."

Hunter had heard it all before. It was the essence of the reason Jones bugged out of Otis. It was a mercenary's world. They were pawns in the new era of warfare-as-chess game. It was a game of bluffs and counter-bluffs. We've got more than you. We want your land. We've got ten thousand guns. You've got only five thousand. We've got a squadron of jets. You've got only a handful. Please vacate the premises. Go quietly. Find new work. We're the new bosses. Our countries have merged and you're out of a job. Argue and you die. And only the stupid mercenaries wound up dead.

Of course, personal disputes were common. The general's retaliatory strike on Baltimore was personal. So was his own leveling of Otis. The streets of The Aerodrome—especially on drunken Saturday nights—were the scene of many a personal knife fight, gun fight, even an occasional bazooka fight. That's why everybody—pilots to bartenders, monkeys to hookers—was armed.

It was Dodge City revisited. And more and more, pilots were choosing to settle arguments over girls, guns or money, not in the main street, where dueling wasn't permitted, but in dogfights. These aerial duels were fought high above a relatively unpopulated part of the Aerodrome's territory, known by everyone as "the OK Corral." The battles were photographed by gun cameras on chase planes and on the combatant's planes themselves, making it all the easier for the betting people in the saloons below to wager on the outcome.

And countries carried vendettas against each other occasionally. But the day of massive armies facing each other were probably gone for a while. No one wanted it. No country could expect it of their soldiers-for-hire. Not when it was so easy just to move on and find another job. And it would be bad for business.

"Hawker, me friend," Fitzgerald started again. "You can make a healthy living here. With no worries. You'll be rich. You have a reputation, boy. You could hire yourself out as the best escort flyer around, once you get your bird back together. Fly for me. No one will ever want to tangle with you. You can make it on your name alone. You've earned it. We have the work. We have the booze. We have the girls! What more can you want, lad?"

Hunter could only shake his head. Who knows if *anyone* ever made it out to the Coast? Who cared if he made it out there or not? And what the hell were they going to do once they got out there? Fitzgerald's offer was tempting, to say the least.

"Think about it, boy," Fitzgerald said on leaving.

Aki appeared carrying a freshly pressed pair of his coveralls. She took the towel from him and smiled. Her hand found itself lingering between his legs.

"Dress now?" she asked.

He looked at her beautiful Oriental features. Almond shaped eyes. Long black hair. Beautiful brown skin. Her lithe figure accented by the Fitzie-designed revealing maid uniforms.

"Dress? Now?" she asked him again, her hand stroking his upper thighs and more.

He drained his drink. "Dress, later," he said, leading her to the bedroom. "Think, later," he said to himself.

Hunter decided to decide about his trip only when his F-16 was back flying. When in doubt, procrastinate, he thought. One thing seemed certain: there was no longer any hurry. He had all the time in the world.

Or, so he thought . . .

It was early one morning, a month and a half into his new job, when he was told to expect a big job to land within the hour. The plane would need a quick radar controls replacement. It was carrying valuables and was overdue at its destination.

Hunter looked at the repair order, radioed in from the plane minutes before, and was surprised at one of the entries. It read the flight had originated in eastern Europe, via Boston. This made him suspicious. Just like the Free Canadians who refused to do business with the Mid-Aks once they took over the Northeast Economic Zone, many of the companies flying in from Iceland had disdained landing at Logan, diverting to fields in Canada instead.

So it was a rare flight that came straight over from Europe to Boston. He checked its final destination and got another surprise: New Chicago. The city and territories controlled by the notorious organization known as The Family.

From what Hunter knew of The Family, he didn't like them. They sounded like a variation of the Mid-Aks; smaller, but just as treacherous; a good-sized army, but no air force that he knew of. The Family made its money on heavily taxing its citizens, gun sales, drug running and selling young girls on the black market. Another enterprise was selling protection to the smaller territories surrounding the city's borders. Their links to the air pirates were widely-suspected.

Now a cargo plane was flying from eastern Europe, stopping off in Mid-Ak territory and continuing on to New Chicago. Hunter was very anxious to get a look at this mysterious aircraft.

An hour later, right on schedule, the plane appeared high above the field, circling while it received landing clearance. Hunter made sure that he was out on the tarmac when the plane came in.

He began to smell a rat when he saw the plane was not of usual manufacture. It was a huge Antonev AN-12 cargo jet, one of the largest planes in the world. It was carrying Czechoslavakian markings, the sight of which started a slow burn inside Hunter's stomach. The Czechs were allies of the Soviets, partners in the crime of the century. He had fought them in the skies over Western Europe. He had no use for them here in

Syracuse.

The enormous airplane lumbered in, touched down and taxied to a deserted end of the runway. Its engines still turned but it was soon apparent that no one was getting off. Only a handful of ground service vehicles approached the plane.

Hunter intercepted his mechanics who were heading to fix the big plane's radar.

"You guys take ten," he told his monkeys. "I'll do this one myself."

They gratefully accepted and handed him the radar replacement parts. He jumped into a jeep and drove out to where the plane was parked.

The fuel truck was just pulling away when he arrived. The cargo bay door in the rear of the ship was open and a man in a brown uniform motioned for him to come aboard. This should be interesting, he thought.

And it was. He had to walk through the entire length of the aircraft, starting with its cargo hold. The plane was packed with crates clearly marked with illustrations as containing rifles, bombs and missiles. The officer, though terse and unfriendly, made no attempt to prevent him from taking it all in as he walked through the two-tiered plane.

They reached a ladder and he climbed up and into the plane's cockpit. The flight crew looked at him indifferently as he undid the broken-down radar control module and replaced it with the new part. They spoke sparingly, but when they did, it was in some East European dialect. For the most part, the crew sat quietly while he worked, smoking cigarettes and drinking coffee.

The door to the passenger hold remained closed most of the time. But just as he was about to leave, the plane's navigator opened the hatch, probably on his way to the can. It was then that Hunter was able to see the valuables the plane was carrying.

There were probably 200 passengers aboard and every last one of them was a Mid-Ak officer.

He turned to the pilot and indicated the radar would have to be tested. The pilot pushed the appropriate buttons and a display of digital lights came on and flashed. The radar was working. The pilot nodded his head and barked something to his crew. Hunter had an idea but he knew it would take quick action.

He turned to the returning navigator and made a motion to his lips.

"Smoke?" he asked. "Can I bum a butt?"

It took a little more prompting, but finally the navigator nodded his head with understanding. He dug down into his coveralls pocket and came out with a pack of cigarettes. Hunter took one, then indicated his need for a match. The navigator, wearing a slightly put-out look, produced a small box of wooden matches. Just then his pilot barked at him again, and in one of those strokes of luck that always seemed to bless Hunter, the man handed the entire box of matches to Hunter, then gave him the thumbs out signal. The pilot was already running up the engines from idle to taxi and it was evident that Hunter was the only one holding things up.

He gratefully accepted the matches and climbed down the ladder. No escort this time; he would have to see himself to the door. The crew would pay dearly for this impoliteness.

Lighting the cigarette, he stuck the unlit end into the box of matches and then placed it in the straw packing atop one of the crates he was sure carried ammunition. Then he hurriedly left the plane, jumped into the jeep and cleared the area. The big plane was already moving before he was more than 100 yards away.

He was back at the hangar just as the big plane started its take-off. The cigarette had been burning for five minutes just as the plane got off the ground. His training had taught him an unsmoked cigarette will burn for six to seven minutes—it was one way a downed pilot could tell time. This time, the cigarette served as a fuse for a do-it-yourself time bomb.

The huge jet gained altitude and began its turn west when there was an explosion in the rear of the aircraft. It was followed by several others in quick succession as the crates of bombs and missiles began to ignite. The big jet shuddered once and started to fall. With another, much greater explosion, the Antonev plunged into a hillside about five miles from the base.

The shock wave created by the crash rattled things at the base. Everyone stopped what they were doing and ran to see the source of the explosion. They stared and pointed at the hillside, some of them not knowing it was the big plane that was burning fiercely five miles away. Some shook their heads at the sight of the tragedy.

Hunter, however, spat in the general direction of the crash. His bomb had done its work. He didn't care what anyone had said, this was war. He had no use for either Mid-Aks or Russian puppets, nor The Family, whose arms and ammunition were still exploding at the crash site. Screw every last one of them.

The phone in his hangar rang several times before he answered it. He knew it was Fitzgerald. He knew that the base commander might take some flak from the 'Aks, or even The Family, for the crash, though he also knew no one could ever prove it wasn't an accident. He was expecting anything from Fitzgerald—even a dismissal. But he got a surprise.

"Hawker," the Irishman began. "Those bone-heads. Did they pay you for that replaced radar part?"

Hunter almost laughed. "No, Fitz, sorry," he said. "All they had were Russian rubles."

"Oh, that *is* a shame," Fitzgerald replied. "And judging by that fire out there, it's going to be *awfully* hard to collect."

"Take it out of my pay," Hunter told him, as another explosion ripped through the wreckage of the plane.

"I just might do that," Fitzgerald said hanging up.

The airport crash crew was just starting to react. Hunter had to laugh again as he saw the base fire trucks, sirens screaming, purposely driving toward the crash site with all the speed of a two-legged turtle. As one truck drove past him, one of the fire crew looked his way and gave him a mock yawn. Hunter gave him the thumbs up signal. At least Hunter knew he certainly wasn't alone in his dislike for Mid-Aks. Or their allies.

Over the next few weeks he often wondered what the mission of the crashed jet had been. East European arms and Mid-Aks advisors flying to New Chicago. It made for a dangerous, volatile combination. And at best, he knew his sabotage only delayed whatever the hell was in the works.

Strangely enough, Fitz never caught any grief from anyone concerning the crash. No one even bothered to contact him concerning recovering the bodies, not that there was much left. Hunter also found this to be suspicious. The plane's mission was obviously something that had started out as a well-kept secret—only to be done in by a busted radar control. And a saboteur disguised as a monkey.

Another month went by, and during that time, he knew of several other planes that passed through the base, filled with Mid-Aks heading for Chicago. There was nothing he could do about them as he never got close enough to take any action. Nor did he want to put too much heat on Fitzgerald.

But as the weeks went on, he found himself getting restless. The situation in New Chicago, whatever it was, was probably building toward a climax. God only knew what the Mid-Aks were planning. And the Russian connection, though hard to prove, particularly bothered him. Besides, he *did* promise Jones that should anything ever go wrong, that he should report to the general's twin brother out on the Coast.

But it was more than that. He was getting *too* comfortable. He was flying more and working on engines less. He had fine liquor, good food and beautiful women at his disposal. His jet's repairs and overhaul was almost paid for and ready for air trials.

He increasingly felt the urge to move on.

The F-16 he unveiled a few weeks later was a completely different airplane than the one he'd arrived in. He had modified the engines to carry even more weight, then attached a half dozen more ordnance points on the wings and belly. He installed five additional M-61 cannons, the plane now boasted three to a side. He rigged a system whereby he could carry the extra cartridge belts needed to feed the jet's six guns, and drop them once they were expended, just like a spare fuel drop tank. He disconnected his in-flight refueling capability—he doubted if he could find a KC-135 Air Force tanker flying around these days—and used the weight saved for more on-board fuel storage.

He personally went over the entire ship and tightened every bolt, nut and screw. He re-wired it and returned its avionics. He bought and repaired a discarded LANTIRN pod—the magic box of electronic wonder that gave any plane carrying it the ability to see, fly and fight on the darkest of nights or in the worst of weather.

He cleaned every nook and cranny on the plane, inside and out. He repainted it, keeping the old Thunderbird design, but adding a streaking white "W" on its tail section. He wanted everyone to know who he was. The Wingman. He carried with him a reputation—he couldn't deny it. That reputation, while possibly enticing foolish bounty hunters or young, brash pilots looking for a part in New Order history, would save him fuel and ammo wherever he went. Not many would want to mix it up with him. They would see the near-extinct F-16 and the "W," put two and two together and give him a wide berth. This way, he knew, his reputation was worth something and that he could use it to his advantage. He also knew it was something that needed protecting.

He rolled the plane out, to the oohs and ahhs of ground personnel and pilots alike. It looked sleeker, quicker, deadlier. He, too, had changed. He was heavier, more muscular, his hair once again had grown out long. His features had always been described, ironically, as handsomely hawk-like. Now he looked like an eagle.

He expressed his thoughts to Fitzgerald, who while saddened that his friend had decided to move on, was understanding as to his reasons why. They both knew he wouldn't be leaving just yet, however. Because, although the F-16 was back and flying, he still needed money—a good sum of money—to make his way across the continent. Fuel and ammo were expensive these days. So were landing rights. He couldn't go out wandering across the continent unarmed, whether it was in his gun barrels or his money bag.

He had asked Fitzie to look around for some more profitable jobs for him to do, and eventually, his friend got him working a few convoy missions. Hunter could make more in one day, riding shotgun on a convoy than he could working a week in the maintenance hangar. It also gave him a chance to put the F-16 through its air trials.

He flew five missions in all—each one escorting five-plane convoys up to the Canadian border, where they would rendezvous with fighters from the Free Canada Armed Forces. The Canadians would then escort the ships for the remainder of the journey to

Toronto. In all each mission would take under an hour. They didn't pay the big money that a cross-continent mission would, but he was happy just to be flying regularly again.

He had just returned from the fifth mission—which was, like the first four, pleasantly routine—when he got a message that Fitz wanted to meet him. He was curious about the site that Fitz selected, a little, dark hole of a barroom called The Broken Wing. Located out in a small hamlet on the very edge of The Aerodrome's territory, The Broken Wing was a place you would go when you didn't want to be seen or overheard.

A light, warm rain was falling when he arrived at the bar. It was in a fringe area, as out of the way as one could get from the bustling Aerodrome. It almost looked like an old western frontier town, and just as dangerous. He parked the jeep and walked across the street to the saloon. He could see a few figures hurry out of sight as he approached. Other eyes watched him from the shadows.

He walked in and found the place smoky but nearly empty. The bartender recognized him and pointed to a dark corner of the saloon. There, he found Fitz at a table sitting with a man he introduced only as Gus.

"It's my pleasure, Major Hunter," Gus said after shaking hands with him. "We . . . my employers . . . are great admirers of yours."

"Gus has a job you might be interested in," Fitz said, ordering a round of beer. Hunter detected a subtle nod from his friend, indicating that Gus could be trusted.

"Major Hunter, we have a shipment, an extremely

213

valuable shipment, that has to be picked up and delivered here at The Aerodrome," Gus said. "My employers, who are well aware of your talents, specifically requested that you be the man to do the job."

"What's the shipment?" Hunter asked, eyeing Fitzgerald. "Sidewinders? Real silver? Gold?"

Gus hesitated for a moment. He was a tall, thin, dark-skinned man, with quick darting eyes. He was the type of person who, possibly unwillingly, gave off a mysterious air. He looked at Fitz, who nodded again, then said, quietly: "Diamonds."

"Diamonds?" Hunter asked. "How many diamonds."

"A small bag, Major Hunter," Gus answered, keeping his hushed tone. "A little under two pounds."

"Two pounds is a lot of diamonds," Hunter said sipping his beer. "What's the shipment worth."

Again, Gus was silent for a moment, as if he were adding numbers up in his head. "In pre-war terms, about twenty million," he said, ratherly calmly.

"Twenty million?" Hunter asked, not hiding his surprise. "Twenty million *dollars*?"

The figure even made Fitzie let out a long, low whistle, and he was probably worth a couple of million himself.

"That's right," Gus answered.

"What's that worth these days?" Hunter asked, taking a larger swig of his beer.

"That's hard to say, Major," Gus said, his calculator mind turned on once again. "Especially in these times of fluctuating currencies. But if I had to guess, I'd say upward of two-hundred million."

Fitz and Hunter looked at each other in disbelief.

Two hundred million dollars could buy half the countries on the continent, lock, stock and barrel.

The bartender wandered over and collected their empties, stopping the discussion momentarily. Fitz signalled him to bring another round. Once he was out of earshot, the hushed conversation continued.

"My employers are willing to pay you quite handsomely, Major, if you successfully retrieve the parcel," Gus told him.

Hunter looked at Fitz. "How much?" he asked.

"One hundred thousand dollars in real silver," Gus said, matter-of-factly.

A lot of money, Hunter thought. More than enough to get him where he was going and then some.

"Where's the pick-up?" he asked, definitely interested.

For the first time, Gus looked nervous. He bit his lip, then said, slowly, "Pittsburgh."

Hunter saw his vision of $100,000 take on a pair of wings and fly away.

"Pittsburgh?" He said. "You're moving two hundred million dollars in diamonds through Pittsburgh?"

Gus nodded.

Pittsburgh was a tough enough place before the war—nowadays, it was worse. Most of the city had been evacuated, but, as in many cases, a community of sorts—bad sorts—had sprung up around the airport. The Pitts, as it was universally called now, was well-known as a haven for terrorists, murderers, drug dealers, slave traders and other assorted scum of the earth. The place was also roundly considered as the unofficial home of the eastern air pirates, only because the airport controllers—shady characters themselves—allowed the airborne criminals to land and refuel there. Some claimed even men from the Badlands were sometimes spotted there.

"Why The Pitts?" Hunter asked.

"The diamonds are payment of a debt to my bosses," Gus said. "The payer insists that it be done this way."

"He's probably setting you up," Hunter said.

"Possibly," Gus acknowledged. "But with that much money at stake, my employers feel they have to take the chance."

"Then why don't you just hire a squadron of fighters and some chopper troops and go down there and get it?" Hunter wanted to know.

"No," Gus said, emphatically. "This has to be done quietly. As quietly as possible. That's why we have contacted you, Major."

Hunter thought for a moment. He was ready, anxious, almost itching, for a change. But flying into The Pitts might be a little more excitement than he needed.

Gus could tell he was tossing the job offer around in his mind.

"One hundred fifty thousand dollars, Major," he said.

Hunter glanced at Fitz, who was nodding, urging him to take the offer.

"I just don't know," Hunter said. "Just who *are* your employers?"

"I can't tell you that, Major," Gus said. "Not until you return with the diamonds."

"Well," Hunter said. "Can you tell me who they

aren't? There are some people I just won't work for."

Gus nodded.

"Are they Mid-Aks?" Hunter asked.

"No."

"The Family?"

"Certainly not," Gus said, slightly upset.

Hunter thought for a moment. Who was left?

"The Russians?" he finally said.

For the first time, Gus stared him straight in the eye. He rolled up his shirt sleeve to reveal a familiar-looking tattoo.

"Major," he began slowly, pointing to the eagle and globe drawing on his arm. "I was in the Marine Corps in the last war. I fought the Russians on the Yugoslav border. Two straight weeks of combat. Night and day. Hand-to-hand. I saw brave men die, fighting for their country. Fighting those godless bastards and winning. Only to be stabbed in the back. The Russians, you ask? I would never traffic with those war criminals."

From then on, Hunter liked Gus.

"You've got yourself a pilot," Hunter said. "Now, what's the plan?"

CHAPTER FIFTEEN

Forty-eight hours later, Hunter was wrestling the controls of an ancient C-47 Spooky cargo plane. It was a moonless, clear night, and the plane was heading due south, in the direction of The Pitts.

With him were two ADF pilots—Al and Zal—serving as co-pilot and navigator.

The C-47 was a two-engined workhorse of a plane, built some twenty years before either of them were even born. It was like a bucking bronco to steer, and it was very noisy. But it was as inconspicuous as one could get. The plane, a puddle-jumper Fitzie used for short flights and training, had lost its in-flight radio intercom long ago. It was also unarmed.

"I was in The Pitts once," Al, the tall, skinny red-headed co-pilot yelled to him, trying to be heard above the constant rumble of the engines. "I was coming back from a cross continent convoy job, flying one of the F-105s.

"I hit a bad storm and had to put down in The Pitts. Believe me, I would have rather ditched the Thunderchief and bailed out, but I knew Fitz would go nuts. So I put down there."

Both Hunter and Zal had heard similar stories of pilots visiting The Pitts—all too unwillingly.

"What happened?" Hunter yelled back.

"Well, as soon as I set down," Al continued. "I'm surrounded by a dozen goons with shotguns. It's storming. Terrible, thick stuff. It's the middle of the night. The place is dark, spooky. But here are these guys, pointing their guns at me.

"I had to pay a landing tax, a taxiing tax and a parking tax. All before I even got out of the goddamn plane. Luckily Fitz gives us extra money for stuff like that, because I didn't have much money of my own."

Hunter reassuringly patted the bags of silver he had in the pockets of his flight jacket.

"I pay these guys and they disappear," Al said. "Of course, no monkeys are around, so I have to block off and shut down myself. I go into the terminal figuring I'd get a cup of joe and wait until the weather cleared. There's only one place open. They got no coffee, no food. Just beer. So I order a beer.

"The place is filled with creeps and the bartender is mean and the size of a B-52. But it was warm, so I figure, what the hell. I order another beer and drink it and start to get another when the bartender says I have to pay for the first two. I ask how much. He says ten bucks. I say, ten bucks for two beers. He says no, ten bucks apiece for the two beers. Twenty bucks!

"I start to tell him to go fuck himself, when I see two bouncers start circling me. They got guns, and my .45 is back in the aircraft. I figure, screw it, I'll pay it and get out. But I got my money in my sock. So I bend down, take off my boot, put it on the bar and get the coins out of my sock. When I come back up, my boot is gone. The bartender says 'What boot?' His six buddies at the bar say 'What boot?' The bouncers say 'What boot?'

"Well, I know when I'm not wanted, so I just pay him the money and leave there, one boot and all. I swear, one of those guys must have eaten it. I figured I'll just go back to the plane and sit in it until the weather got straight.

"I go back to the place where I parked the Thud. No plane. I stop a couple monkeys—scuzzy-looking guys—and they say, 'What plane?' I call the tower on the phone and they say, 'What plane?'

"Well, I know that Fitz is going to go apeshit that I lost one of his Thunderchiefs. But I have to call him and tell him, so I do. He goes nuts, but then he calms down and says to just find the right person, bribe him and get the plane back.

"I say, great idea but I'm broke. He goes nuts again, but then says for me to sit tight, that he'll send another Thud pilot down with some money to get me out. I call the tower and they say that if I pay a take-off tax, they'll try to find the plane. It's a game. They know it. I know it. But what can you do?"

Hunter and Zal were enjoying Al's story. Many a pilot had faced the same kind of thing in The Pitts.

"So," Al continued. "Now I've got to wait for a couple hours for a Thud to fly down. So I go into the main terminal building to get some shut-eye. There's more creeps there, sitting in the dark, playing with themselves. Terrible. But I stretch out and finally fall asleep.

"Next thing I know, the Thud pilot is shaking me awake. He's got the money and the plane is back

220

where it was. He says to me, 'Where's your shoes?' I look at my feet and I can't believe it. While I was asleep, sure as shit, someone stole my other boot!"

They all had a good laugh at Al's tale, the last they'd have in a while. Up ahead, Hunter could see the faint outline of The Pitts' landing lights. He nodded to Al.

"Pittsburgh," Al said into the microphone. "C-47 Spooky requesting permission to land."

There was a silence, then the radio crackled to life. "Whadda ya want?" came the reply.

Hunter and Al looked at each other and shrugged.

"Spooky requesting landing clearance," Al said. "We are at ten miles out. One hundred thirty knots. From the north. Need your wind and weather."

"Fuck your wind and weather," the voice came back. "You got landing money?"

"Landing money, tower?" Al said, with a wink.

"Fuck you, asshole," came the reply. "Half bag of silver when you touch down. Real stuff. If you ain't got it, then get the fuck out of the airspace before we knock you out."

"We got the money. Can we land?" Al asked.

"Sure," the voice said. "Give it a shot. And pay the man in the black hat when you get here."

They landed without incident although barely half the lights on the airport's only functioning runway were working. The sun was just coming up and in the early morning light they could see why every flyboy who could avoided The Pitts like the plague.

They had to wheel their way in and out of tons of junk that littered the airport's taxiing apron. There were pieces of tail sections, wings, landing gears

221

scattered everywhere. Tools lying rusted where they'd been dropped probably years before. Jet fighters set up on blocks just like a farmer's old Chevy set on milk crates. Everywhere, the place looked like a slum; a slum in a perpetual state of chaos.

The main terminal building, which was designed like a saucer, with a half dozen spoke-like passageways coming out of it, was dingy and rundown. Where huge plate-glass windows once stood, now there were makeshift barriers of plywood. The control tower, off to the left of the main terminal, was also in a state of decay. It was unpainted and sported more than a few boarded up windows. Several machine guns protruded from the deck surrounding the tower, though they were unmanned at the moment.

On the side of the tower, where there was once a sign reading, "Welcome to Pittsburgh International Airport," someone had appropriately scraped off most of the letters and now the sign just read: Pitts."

They rolled up to a station beside the saucer-shaped terminal building and cut the engines. So far, so good, Hunter thought. The two propellers on the C-47 had barely stopped turning when a man in a black hat drove up in a jeep and rapped on the side of the plane.

All three of them made their way back to the rear of the plane and Hunter popped the cargo door and threw out the step. The man in the black hat came aboard. Once Hunter got a good look at him, he realized he was looking at one of the ugliest individuals in the world.

The right side of the man's face looked as if someone had taken an acetylene torch to it. It was the color of boiling blood and it looked as if it was still cooking. His left side had seven long deep scars running from eye to chin. The latest one was still stitched up, but a green, pus-like substance was oozing from it. He had no teeth and what looked to be only patches of hair. The man smelled rancid and his clothes—the hat, a full-length black coat and black boots, even his black wraparound sunglasses—all looked as though they'd hadn't been washed in years.

The man didn't introduce himself. Instead, he just said: "Got the money?"

His voice was barely a croak. Hunter couldn't be sure if he was armed or not; underneath the coat would be a perfect hiding place for a shotgun. However, he was certain that more than a few guns were probably covering the man from the terminal building and the control tower.

"Got the money?" the man repeated, a green-oozy drool leaking out of the corners of his mouth.

Hunter produced a half bag of silver. The man took it and shook it once, as if he could tell it was real silver and the right amount just by listening to the coins jingle. He gave Hunter a curt nod and stuffed the bag of coins under his coat.

"What's your business here?" he croaked, more green drool coming from his mouth.

"We're nail drivers," Hunter told him. "Here to pick up a load of nails. That is, if someone hasn't stolen them yet."

Nail drivers were pilots who carried loads of used nails from one location to another. While there was a slight rebirth of manufacturing in the days of the New Order, for some reason, no one was making nails, thus they were valuable items.

The man spat a long, green line close to Hunter's boot.

"You calling us thieves?" he asked defiantly.

"Sure," Hunter said, coming within an inch of the man's deformed face. "Thieves like us . . ."

Hunter then produced another bag of coins, a quarter full this time. "No more questions?" he asked.

The man greedily accepted the bag and hastily stuck it under his coat, not wanting any of his counterparts to see him. He's mine now, Hunter thought. Phase One of his plan was under way.

"We need someone to find our shipment," he told the man. "You interested?"

The man looked around quickly, then said: "Got to know what I'm looking for."

"The crate came in from Florida, two days ago," Hunter told him. "It's marked destination is The Aerodrome. Find it."

"How much?" the man asked nervously.

Hunter produced another quarter bag. "You get this now, and another half when you deliver."

The man was salivating green at the prospect of all that money. Hunter was sure the typical bribe at The Pitts was half as much.

"Might take a while," the man said.

"Get it here by sunset," Hunter said in no uncertain terms. "Or we come and get you."

"If it's here," the man said, jingling the silver under his coat, "I'll find it."

He left the plane quickly, got in his jeep and drove away.

"Do we trust a guy like that?" Zal asked. He and

Al had been fingering their loaded .45s throughout the encounter.

"We really don't have a choice," Hunter said. "We're in his ballpark. We play by his rules. For now."

But Hunter had to laugh to himself. Entrusting a $200 million shipment of diamonds to a drooling idiot would have been unthinkable a few years ago. Now it served as a good example of how business was done these days. Welcome to the New Order.

They returned to the cabin where Al broke out a deck of cards. They knew it would be a long, anxious wait.

They sat and played cards and watched as a bewildering array of aircraft came and went.

One airliner, an old Boeing 707, landed. Its smoking engine completely ignored by its pilots and the ground crew, they unloaded hundreds of crates marked: RIFLES. Another plane, an old P-3 Orion Navy aircraft with its markings painted over, touched down and was emptied of thousands of small bales plainly marked: "Marijuana. Panama People's Republic." Another 707 was loaded with boxes marked: DANGER EXPLOSIVES—TNT. Hunter couldn't help but notice that half the ground crew servicing the jet was smoking either cigarettes or joints. If the crates contained TNT and a spark found its way inside, the name Pitts would take on a whole new meaning—that of a half-mile deep crater where an airfield used to be.

All the while, large and small planes—each painted in strange bright colors—landed, unloaded passengers, turned around and flew off again. No two planes looked alike, but all of those disembarking were of the same ilk: Dirty-looking, shady characters. Each one scurried off their plane and to the main terminal building as quickly as they could, as if they didn't want to present themselves as too good a target. Hunter kept a close watch on the arrivals. Everyone was armed. Everyone was watching everyone else.

Another airliner, a Boeing 727 that was painted a ghastly pink, arrived and unloaded human cargo. Pulling right up next to the C-47, the rear door of the plane was lowered. Emerging from the inside were about fifty young girls, each naked to the waist and manacled and tied together with a long white rope. Two mean-looking women herded the young girls out of the plane and into the terminal, laying a cat o' nine tails on the back of anyone who was not keeping up.

"A slave plane," Zal said, finally.

"That's a crime," Al said. "Tying up and selling young stuff like that."

"It's a business," Hunter said, his own distaste evident. "Everything nowadays is a goddamn business."

They went back to their card game but were disturbed once again, this time by the arrival of three fighter jets. They were ancient F-100 Super Sabres, each one painted a garish color or pattern. The jets taxied up to the terminal and the pilots climbed out, barking orders to obedient monkeys that were scurrying around the planes.

One jet, flown by the pilot who appeared to be the leader, was painted entirely in shiny black, with a hideous looking laughing shark's face on its snout.

The second jet sported a bright yellow and green camouflage scheme, though Hunter had to wonder what the pilot was thinking of when he painted it. The colors alone would make the plane stick out in a storm at night. The third jet was decorated in a white and red checkerboard pattern that covered the entire plane. All three planes were armed with cannons and Sidewinders.

Each of the pilots was dressed in leather from head to toe. Upon removing their flight helmets, they all revealed heads shaved bald. The insignia on the back of their coats read: "The Stukas."

Hunter realized that he was seeing, for the first time close up, some authentic air pirates. And these bandits were from The Stukas, a notorious pirate squadron that roamed the skies of western Pennsylvania and eastern Ohio.

The three men checked over their planes, then brazenly strolled into the terminal building and disappeared. Hunter noted that each one was carrying a sidearm and a rifle of some kind.

During the afternoon and on toward evening, more planes arrived, off-loading all kinds of deviant looking characters.

"There must be a party going on here tonight," Zal observed.

"Yeah," Hunter said. "And we're not invited."

But now, it was getting dark and there was still no sign of the man in the black hat. Hunter was getting more anxious by the minute. He had hoped to avoid going into the terminal and raising suspicions by looking for the nails himself. But he knew that it would be easier to look for the man in the black hat

227

than it would be to look for the right crate. He would give the man another two hours, then he would have to act.

Darkness fell and a few of the rundown airport's dingy lights flickered on. By peering into the main terminal with binoculars, Hunter could see an event of some kind was about to take place inside. All of the characters who had flown in were gathering in the saucer shaped building. Soon a makeshift stage was set up and a spotlight of some kind rigged up.

That's when the first of the young girls was brought in. The crowd, many with bags of money in their hands, started shouting and waving their hands, much in the direction of another man, standing on stage with the young girl.

"A slave auction," Hunter said to Al, handing him the spyglass. "That's what the party is about."

After Zal had taken a look, Hunter peered through the glasses once again. Another young girl—a redhead—was up on the stage. Her hands tied above her head, the auctioneer, a crude looking man in a bright red suit, turned her around like a piece of merchandise, poking his barker's cane into her ass, between her legs and between her breasts.

The redhead was quickly sold and another girl brought up on stage. This one, a blonde, was crying as the crowd yipped and yapped at her. Hunter could see the three pirates were as close to the stage as possible, bidding for the girl. The barker soon pointed to the pirates as the winners and the young girl was turned over to them. Laughing and guzzling liquor, they carried the weeping child off to the side of the auction stage where two held her and a third pro-

228

ceeded to rape her, much to the delight of the crowd.

The auction continued, each girl sold one after the other. The crowd was getting drunker and rowdier and a few disappointed bidders started trouble at one point. But it all calmed down and the bidding started once more.

Suddenly the dusky air was split by the noise of a jet landing. As it taxied close to them, Hunter could see in the twilight that it was a two-seat, F-101 Voodoo. It carried the markings of the Free Canadian Armed Forces. Maybe this was the break he was looking for.

No monkeys appeared, so the back-seat pilot had to leap from the wing and block the plane off himself. That done, both pilots were on the tarmac quickly checking the undercarriage of the jet fighter. Hunter could tell by their uniforms that these were Canadian Sky Marshals, airborne versions of the famous Royal Canadian Mounted Police. He could see they were intently studying the three pirate jets parked nearby.

Hunter told Al and Zal to stay alert, then he left the C-47 and went over to meet the Canadians. They eyed him suspiciously as he approached.

He was direct. "I'm Major Hawker Hunter," he told them. "Of ZAP."

They both shook their heads.

"You're *the* Hawker Hunter?" the pilot, a captain named Frost said, disbelievingly. "Of The Thunderbirds?"

"That's right," Hunter said, hoping they'd recognize his face.

The pilots looked around, as if searching for Hunter's F-16. He started throwing out a few names of higher ups he knew in the Free Canadian Air

Corps. They stared at him for a few more moments then, apparently convinced he was the authentic item, asked almost in unison: "What the hell are you doing here?"

He knew he could trust the Canadians. Their air force had been closely allied with ZAP and helped keep the northern border clean of pirates. They carried with them an unblemished reputation of integrity and honesty. Like their counterparts in another time, they *always* got their man.

He told them the whole story. The diamonds. The Aerodrome. The man in the black hat. "Dangerous mission, Hunter," Captain Frost told him after hearing it all.

They were in The Pitts looking for a particular air bandit.

"Yesterday morning, he shot down an airliner over Lake Erie," Frost said. "Killed one hundred thirty six people."

"It was a senseless act," the co-pilot, Lieutenant LaFleur said. "He used the airliner as target practice. Put a Sidewinder into the side and watched it go down."

The pilot of the doomed plane was able to radio a description of the attacker before the airliner hit the water. The Free Canadians matched the description with a known pirate by the name of Rocko. While they didn't expect the murderer to be in such a public place so soon, they did want to put the word out that they—and about a hundred air bounty hunters—were looking for him.

Hunter then made them a promise. If they covered his ass in getting out of The Pitts with the diamonds, he promised to keep an eye out for the pirate named Rocko. They agreed.

Much relieved, Hunter walked back to the C-47.

As soon as the Sky Marshals entered the terminal, the bidding on the girls stopped. The Canadians had no jurisdiction in The Pitts, and it was not their style to go looking for trouble. But they did want to question the Stukas as Rocko had been seen on previous occasions flying with that particularly notorious group.

Hunter saw this as his chance to sneak into the terminal and search for the man with the black hat. He told Al to warm up the engines and be ready for a quick getaway. Then he and Zal loaded up two M-16s, took two high-flash percussion grenades each and left the plane.

Hunter found an unlocked door on the side of one of the spokes and they entered the terminal. The noise knew the Canadians were questioning some of the low-lifes attending the flesh-peddling event. He and Zal headed in the opposite direction. Soon they were into the far reaches of the sprawling terminal building—a bizarre area lit only by constant flickering lights.

The place was a mess. Debris was strewn everywhere. Windows were smashed. Businesses, some of which appeared to have been opened even recently, were trashed. The walls were covered with vulgar graffiti and crude drawings. This part of the airport lived up to its nickname quite nicely.

They walked slowly, carefully searching each room, waiting area and corridor they came to. Sometimes

231

they could hear shouts and laughter in the distance. But the peculiar set up of the airport building made it difficult to determine—even for someone with acute senses like Hunter's—where the noise was coming from. It was eerie, and the further they walked into the building, the spookier it got. The only sound they heard, aside from the shouts, was the low, steady drone of the C-47's engines warming up in the distance.

Suddenly, the air was pierced by a long, high-pitched scream. Hunter and Zal froze in their tracks as the blood-curdling cry echoed through the empty passageways. Hunter was able to pick up a direction this time, and signalled Zal to check his weapon and follow him.

Ten minutes later, they found the man in the black hat . . .

His hands and feet were bound and he was left sitting in a chair of one of the _____ sitting on his lap. His throat was slashed, a pool of blood splattering on the floor beneath his seat.

Hunter gingerly felt the body. It was still warm and gurgling. He was sure it was the man's scream they'd heard. He frisked the body and found the bags of silver he had given the man. This told him two things: the man had found the diamonds. And that his killers had taken them, leaving the relatively p_____ sum of the coin bags behind and escaping with the jewe__.

But they had left a trail. One of the murderers had stepped in the blood of his victim, and had left a set of bloody footprints. Hunter and Zal followed the trail and were soon outside a door marked: CONTROL ROOM—DO NOT ENTER.

Hunter put his ear to the door and listened. He could pick up six distinct voices. Not flyboys either. Pilots had their own way of talking and this wasn't it. He could hear the words "diamonds" and "asshole" dominate the conversation.

He motioned Zal to get on the other side of the door. Then, he reached for the percussion grenade and pulled the pin . . .

CHAPTER SIXTEEN

Captain Frost heard the grenade go off. In an instant, he and LaFleur had their .45s drawn and were running toward the noise. The unsavory slave auction crowd obediently cleared a path for them, then laughed once the Sky Marshals were out of sight. Why get so excited over a little thing like a grenade going off? People yelled for the auction to resume. More young flesh was trotted out. More money changed hands. Just another day in The Pitts.

"Hunter said he expected trouble," Frost yelled to his lieutenant as the two Canadians sped through the empty, sometimes pitch black passageways. "Sounds like he found it."

He had . . .

The Sky Marshals turned left into a partially lit corridor only to see Hunter and Zal at the far end, running out of a darkened section of the hallway and toward them at full speed. Hunter was carrying a sack in one hand, and a hand grenade in the other. Zal had his M-16 cocked over his shoulder, firing blindly. The sound of many angry footsteps was right behind them in the darkness. Not missing a beat, Hunter pulled

the pin and tossed the live grenade over his shoulder. It bounced once then rolled back down into the dark part of the corridor . . .

4 . . . 3 . . . 2 . . . 1 . . . Boom!

The grenade went off with a flash. A blinding light, brighter than a hundred flares, filled the corridor. The explosion seemed to freeze everything and everyone in place. In that instant, Frost could see more than 50 gunmen were chasing the airmen. The illumination grenade stopped the pursuers in their tracks as they instinctively put their hands up to protect their eyes. Then his eyes too were blinded by the intense flash. By the time Frost could see again, Hunter and Zal were racing by him.

"I got the diamonds! Let's get the hell out of here!" Hunter yelled as he raced past.

As if to emphasize his point, the corridor was suddenly filled with automatic fire. Bullets were whistling past them, ricocheting everywhere. The gunmen had recovered and were charging again, firing their rifles as they ran.

Frost looked at La Fleur, shrugged once, then both Canadians joined Hunter and Zal in the strategic retreat.

Led by Hunter and firing their weapons behind them, the four men raced through the maze of corridors until finally spilling out into the main terminal building where the slave auction was continuing. They were ignored by the crowd as they ran through the terminal and toward the door which led out to the runway. Outside, the C-47 waited, its engines turning anxiously. Hunter was the first to reach the escape door and he hesitated as the three others ran out. At that moment, the slightly bewildered gunmen reached the terminal, causing a few heads to turn in the crowd.

Confusion. It's the best cover to use to get away. He took his two remaining grenades, pulled the pins and held the clips. Just as the first of the gunmen spotted him across the crowded room, he let the clip go, reeled back and threw the grenade up toward the high ceiling. *Boom!* It exploded as it reached the pinnacle of its flight, brightly illuminating the room, and showering it with a million sparks. Once again, the bright flash stunned the gunmen, most of whom by this time had two large blue spots hindering their vision. This time, the crowd scattered. The room became a pandemonium of fleeing slave buyers and screaming, naked young girls. Some people dove for cover as the gunmen began shooting randomly. For good measure, Hunter pulled the pin on his last grenade and rolled it toward the middle of the terminal.

It went off just as he turned and ran out the door. The C-47 was already rolling toward the runway. Searchlights were clicking on, targeting the escaping airplane. Somewhere, a siren was blowing. Shouts, screams, and gunfire could be heard all over. Suddenly, the dead, dingy airport was alive in light and noise. Zal had reached the taxiing C-47. The Canadians had climbed into their jet and were quick-starting the engine. A searchlight on top of the control tower had the Voodoo in its beam and gunners in the tower started raking the jet with gunfire.

Hunter stopped, aimed and fired at the tower searchlight, knocking it out with his second burst.

The gunners turned their attention to him, but he was already running again at full speed, managing to stay one step ahead of the bullets.

He could see Zal waiting at the open door of the C-47, reaching his hand out to help him on board. Just then, the gunmen burst out from the terminal building and onto the parking apron. He reached the rolling Spooky, bullets licking his bootheels as Zal hauled him aboard. The Canadians were just backing the Voodoo away from the terminal when the gang of gunmen started charging the slowly moving C-47. Its engine screaming, Frost swung the F-101 around, and aiming it toward the pursuers, squeezed off a burst of cannon fire. The deadly stream chopped up the gunmen, killing some and causing the rest to hit the deck. Still moving, the Voodoo swung around and was soon right behind the C-47.

Both planes reached the end of the runway just as Hunter was settling into the pilot's seat of the Spooky. Every searchlight in the airport was pointing at them, and several rocket propelled grenades were being shot at them. Luckily for them, no one in the control tower thought to turn off the runway beacons. The two long intermittent lines of blue lights showed the way out for the two airplanes. Under a hail of bullets and rockets, Hunter started his take-off roll.

By this time, some of the surviving gunmen had recovered. They had commandeered an airport fire truck and now were speeding toward the airstrip. Zal was at the open cargo door, shooting at the truck as it approached the rolling airplane. Out his window, Hunter could see the truck was quickly gaining on them and knew he'd have to improvise the take-off.

237

Guessing at the wind speed and direction, he gunned the old plane's twin engines and yanked the throttle back.

The truck was pulling just about even with the plane when Hunter suddenly hit 99 knots. He pulled up the gear and pulled back on the wheel. The C-47 leaped into the air, in about half the normal distance needed for a take-off.

Frost, behind him in the F-101 had to shake his head in admiration for Hunter. No other pilot that he knew of could get a ship like that airborne so quickly. The fire truck full of gunmen now turned its attention to the Voodoo, but it was fruitless. The jet fighter streaked by them before they could even pull their triggers, leaving them in a trail of hot jet exhaust fumes.

Once airborne, the two planes circled the field once then headed north. "Just another day in The Pitts," Hunter said to Al and Zal.

But the chase was just beginning.

The plane's clock had just struck midnight and they had just broken out of the perpetual cloud cover which always seemed to hang over The Pitts. The moon was full. Hunter could see the Voodoo behind him, bringing up the rear. A familiar feeling washed over him. He suddenly felt aware of the presence of other planes. Sure enough, the C-47's battered old radar scope showed three jets gaining on them

"We got company," he said, reaching for the microphone. "Voodoo, this is Spooky."

"Go Spooky," Frost replied.

238

"Bogies to your six o'clock."

"We see them, Spooky. Do you still want to stick to the plan?"

"Affirmative, Voodoo," Hunter replied.

"Roger, Spooky."

Hunter knew the blips that were getting larger on the radar screen were the three pirate Super Sabres they had seen at The Pitts. He was sure one word was on the lips of everyone at the terminal, especially after the spectacular getaway.

That word was "diamonds."

The man in the black hat had found their shipment all right, Hunter theorized, but he had gotten greedy and foolishly told his superiors, the gunmen who controlled the airport. Instead of cutting him in on the action, they had cut his throat instead, then attempted to split the jewels among themselves. Hunter and Zal had arrived outside the Control Room door just as a fight broke out among the top gunmen inside. One flash grenade later, everyone in the room had been blinded and the next thing the gunmen knew, the diamonds were gone. An alarm had sounded and the chase was on.

Now, Hunter was sure, a desperate deal had been struck between the airport gunmen and the pirates. Get the jewels. We'll split later, 50-50. If the gunmen were foolish enough to deal with their erstwhile allies the pirates, the pirates were smart enough to know that if the jewels were recaptured there would be no dividing of the spoils.

Hunter checked the blips and saw the F-100s were gaining fast. Like most of the pirates' planes, the Super Sabres were equipped with night fighting equipment. Telling Al and Zal to hold on tight, he started evasive maneuvers, in an attempt to throw off the pursuers. But the jets stuck right with him.

"Spooky, this is Voodoo," Frost called. "Bogies gaining on you. Are you still roger on the plan?"

"Affirmative, Voodoo," Hunter said.

With that, Frost kicked in the Voodoo's afterburner and the jet fighter streaked by the lumbering C-47. He peeled off, taking one of the F-100s with him. The Voodoo was quicker and more agile than the Super Sabre. Frost put this to his advantage, executing a quick loop which put the Voodoo on the Super Sabre's tail. LeFleur, the backseat weapons officer, pushed a button and a Sidewinder obliterated the F-100.

But the F-101 kept right on going. It headed north and soon it was little more than a faint red light on the horizon.

The two remaining Super Sabres were now right on the C-47. A voice crackled across the radio. "Okay, you piece of shit," the gruff voice said. "Your Canuck buddy has turned pussy. Follow us on a three-four heading, or we grease you right now."

Before Hunter could reply, one of the F-100s opened up, tearing his left wing with cannon fire and starting a major fuel leak.

"That's your warning shot," a voice on the radio laughed. "Now follow us while you're still breathing."

Hunter's left engine was now on fire, his fuel pouring out of the perforated left wing. One of the pirate jets pulled alongside him, the pilot dropping his flaps and landing gear to slow the supersonic airplane down to match the C-47's 150 knot speed.

"This is your last chance, Spooky," the pilot in the

jet beside him radioed. "Airfield is three-four, ten miles. You can't last much longer. Put it down there."

Hunter knew the pirate was right. Even an extraordinary pilot like Hunter couldn't keep the old bird together for more than another two minutes before it broke up. And it would be suicidal if they parachuted out—the pirates were well-known for strafing chutists. He would have to take his chances on the ground.

Now, all he had to do is find the pirates' air field . . .

They were somewhere high over western Pennsylvania. The terrain below him was black as coal and twice as rugged.

"There ain't nothing down there but trees and mountains," Al said, straining to look out the C-47's window at the ground below.

"Well, we'd better find something smooth real quick," Hunter said, eyeing his fuel indicator. It had already passed the empty mark.

The Spooky shuddered once, then started vibrating violently. The left wing was aflame, and would soon break off.

"Where the hell is their base?" Zal yelled, the anxiety evident in his voice.

"Maybe they're just trying to crash us, Major," Al said. "That's how they usually work."

"Hang on," Hunter coolly reminded them. "Those '100s have to land somewhere. As long as we're flying, we still have a chance."

Just then, the left side propeller broke off and let go, taking most of the engine with it. The C-47 yawed wildly to the left.

"Christ!" Al yelled as the plane almost flipped

over. Zal was tossed like a puppet around the cockpit. It was all Hunter could do to battle the controls and try bringing the old plane back to level. The Spooky was shuddering so badly, he thought every nut and bolt must be ready to come apart. He finally managed to get the airplane somewhat leveled off, but he knew they had about 30 seconds left, tops. They were simultaneously running out of fuel, altitude and time.

Suddenly, a mile up ahead, runway lights blinked on. An instant later, other lights—in buildings, hangars and anti-aircraft guns—came on. A control tower materialized out of nowhere. Searchlights went up. It was amazing. One moment he was looking out on a sea of darkness, and the next he was looking down at a good sized, one-runway airbase that just wasn't there moments before. The pirates had dug an airbase right out of the side of a mountain. It was perfectly camouflaged on three sides and almost impossible to see at night. He had to give them credit. If nothing else, the bandits were masters of disguise.

He had to fly straight in. The plane's controls were starting to fail. His left engine had completely broken away leaving the wing to flap away in the wind. The right engine was sputtering and choking out thick black smoke. A lesser plane would have disintegrated long ago. But Hunter knew the Spooky would stay together until the last possible moment.

The two remaining F-100s, streaked past and went around again in order to land behind them. Below, he could see crowds of pirates had appeared along one side of the runway. He would have an audience for the landing. Assuming that he and his crew survived the crash, he wondered if they would survive the welcoming committee.

He came in wheels up, flaps down, floating along at 50 knots. Ten feet above the landing strip he cut the engine. Then, as softly as possible, he eased the Spooky down.

The flaming plane screeched as it touched the ground. It slid along the full length of the runway, the disabled wing and belly scraping the asphalt and sending up a shower of sparks. The left wing snapped off making the plane turn two complete 360s while still barrelling along the runway. Finally, as it neared the end of the strip, the C-47 went nose down and ground to a halt.

They were down. Now they had to get out. He, Al and Zal quickly scrambled to the emergency hatch beneath the cockpit and squeezed through. Then they ran. Hunter could hear a distinctive hissing sound and knew an explosion was seconds away. Even the pirates nearby were hitting the deck.

"Down!" he yelled.

All three hit the hard surface and covered their heads. The plane blew up two seconds later, producing a fireball that leaped into the air and scattered pieces of debris all over them and the runway. The ground shook as two more explosions wracked the plane. Then there was only the crackling noise of fire.

The smoke cleared and the rain of sparkling debris stopped. They shook the pieces of airplane off their backs and tried to shake some sense back into their heads. Then they looked up. Standing around them were more than 100 men, all of them armed, all of them dressed in leather, all of them sporting shaved heads.

243

"You fucked up our runway, boys," one of them said. "That makes us mad."

Not as mad as you're going to be, Hunter thought.

Hunter didn't have the diamonds; Captain Frost did. As planned, he had passed them to the Sky Marshal during the hectic moments back at The Pitts. He knew the Canadian would deliver them safely to Fitz and Gus—in fact, the jewels were probably already in their possession. So, in essence, Hunter had completed the mission. Now, all he had to do was live long enough to collect the $150,000 from Gus.

They were hustled up and pushed at gunpoint by six pirate guards toward a building located at the far end of the base. As they walked along, Hunter could see that theirs was hardly the first plane to crash at the base. In fact, wreckage of other planes—dozens of them—littered the end and sides of the runway. Many a plane had been forced down at the hidden airfield, their cargoes looted, their crews done away with. Hunter knew the pirates planned to treat them no differently.

They were pushed into the small, one-room structure that served as the pirates' jail. It contained three chairs, a few empty oil drums, one window, and that was it. The pirate guards didn't speak a word as they roughly searched them, then tied them to the chairs. Hunter detected the smell of alcohol on them as they fastened him to the wooden chair.

Once all three of them were secured, the guards checked the rope knots and left. Outside, Hunter could hear the pirate ground crew using a tow vehicle to hastily drag what remained of the C-47 wreckage to one side of the runway. Once the strip was cleared, the two circling Super Sabres landed. Hunter heard one of them run out of fuel just as it touched down. He knew the pilot would be particularly pissed off at them.

A short time later, the door burst open and the two surviving pilots, followed by another phalanx of guards, trooped in.

"Where are the fucking diamonds!" the lead pirate screamed.

Hunter recognized him as the pirate flyer who had flown into The Pitts in the black F-100 sporting the laughing shark's mouth. He was a big, dirty, fat slob of a man; Hunter had a hard time believing the man could squeeze himself into the cockpit of a jet fighter. He could smell liquor on the man's breath; in fact, the whole group of pirates reeked of a boozy smell. They were far from a military unit, Hunter thought; these Stukas were little more than a band of two-bit murderers and thieves. And to think many of them were probably officers in the country's armed forces at one time made them more of a disgrace to Hunter's way of thinking.

"Diamonds?" Hunter said with a straight face. "What diamonds?"

Al almost burst out laughing. What boot? What plane? What diamonds? It all seemed to fit.

"Don't give me that shit, you lousy nail driver," the man screamed again. "I almost pranged my ass 'cause you fucked up the runway and now you're going to play wise-ass?"

They obviously didn't recognize Hunter.

"Slice 'em, Jaws," one of the pirates told the screaming man. "Let 'em bleed and maybe the others will talk."

"They don't know where the jewels are," Hunter said. "But I do."

"So where are they, pretty boy?" Jaws demanded.

"Where they should be," he answered. "At The Aerodrome."

"He's lying, Jaws," the other pirate flyer said.

"Believe it, boys," Hunter told them. "I passed them to the Canadians and they flew right to Syracuse. Why do you think he took off when you intercepted us? He could have probably knocked all three of you out of the sky if he and I didn't have an agreement beforehand."

The pirate named Jaws looked like he was about to blow a valve. A vein was bulging out of his head with such pressure, Hunter expected it to pop at any second.

"You son of a bitch," Jaws screamed. "You got a lot of balls, buddy. We know you had a deal to pick up that shipment. If you were stupid enough to send that pisshead tax collector looking for it, then you ain't smart enough to pass them to that Canuck do-gooder."

Hunter looked the man in the eye. "You're a stupid fuck, aren't you?" he told him. "Do you think diamonds would survive a crash like that?"

The pirate guards looked at Hunter in disbelief. Jaws was the top man at the pirate base, and no one—friend or enemy—talked to the top man like that—and lived very long.

Jaws glared at Hunter. Then, oddly, enough, smiled. "I know you're lying. Jewels don't burn. They're out in that wreckage somewhere. If we don't find them by sunrise, you guys will help us look. You'll eat that wreckage if you have to. And as soon as we get what we want, you're dead meat. I'm gonna slice you up in a hundred little pieces."

"No. Burn 'em!" the other pirate flyer said, producing a bottle of brown liquor.

The pirate named Jaws grabbed the bottle from him, "Gimme that, asshole," he said, taking a long, sloppy guzzle.

"Yeh, that's a good idea, Mouse," Jaws said, wiping his mouth with this dirty leather flight suit's sleeve. "If we don't find the ice, I'll tie you to the exhaust nozzle of my '100 and start the engine *real* slow. Know what it's like to get a face full of engine exhaust?"

Jaws reached into his pocket and came out with a handful of pills. Amphetamines, Hunter guessed. Taking a swig of the brown liquor, Jaws washed the drugs down, then passed some out to his men.

"It will be dark for another four hours, nail driver," Jaws said, his eyes turning to glass as he spoke. "We're gonna go through that wreck out there. You'd better pray that we find those diamonds. Because if you guys have to help us look, you'll be begging for us to kill you by the time you're through."

With that, the hopped-up pirates laughed and left the room, locking the big wooden door behind them. Hunter heard Jaws order two guards to stand outside.

He looked at Al and Zal, who were cool and calm. He would have been surprised if they hadn't been.

They were, after all, ADF fighter pilots, highly trained and disciplined.

"This guy isn't even making sense," Al whispered. "What's he think, we hid the jewels in a crash proof box?"

"He's got to talk like that in front of his men," Hunter said. "It's a tribal mentality. He's just missed taking in the biggest haul this outfit ever dreamed of. If he can't produce, then the number two man might get some ideas about taking over."

He was free of the bonds five minutes later. It was simple for someone who had been trained to eject from a jet fighter while flying at supersonic speed, usually in the middle of a dogfight, and battle with a tangled parachute and live to tell about it. Compared to that, a triple slip knot was no problem.

He freed Al and Zal and they carefully eased themselves up to the window. Outside, the far end of the runway was bathed in light. The pirates had brought up two searchlights and played them on the wreckage of the C-47. The pirate ground crews were sifting through the wreck as the ragtag crash crew nonchalantly doused the smoking metal with a fire-hose.

There were 11 jet fighters parked at the base, all F-100s and all painted in bizarre, swashbuckling colors. A flag bearing the Stukas emblem flew above the field. There was a barracks and three other hangars on the runway, as well as a number of smaller buildings. All of the structures were painted in pine green camouflaged patterns. The hangar closest to them houses a couple of two-engine cargo planes. Another hangar further down the line looked like a repair shop; a stripped down F-100 sat out front. Another building was at the far end of the base, partially hidden by the edge of the thick forest. It was painted black, covered with netting and appeared locked up tight. Beside it was tied, of all things, a hot air balloon.

"What's with the balloon, Major," Al asked.

"Beats me," Hunter said. "Look at the long rope beside it. Maybe they don't fly it, but just let it up when they want to take a look around. Like an early warning system. They could see someone coming on the ground for miles away."

"They have radar," Zal said, noting the dish on top of the three-story control tower.

"Yeah," Hunter said, straining to take in as much as he could. "But it isn't spinning. A few ack-acks. But no big SAMs." He filed the bit of information away in his memory.

"They have transport," Al whispered, pointing to the ten two-and-a-halfs parked next to the maintenance hangar.

"That means there must be a way out of here on the ground," Hunter said. "They probably double their monkeys as ground troops and go on raids, like when supplies get low. There must be more than a hundred of them here, counting their support people."

At the far end of the runway, they could see the skeletons of more planes, aircraft the pirates had forced to land at the base, then looted, stripped for parts and discarded. The crews were all dead, Hunter was sure. The pirates very rarely left any witnesses.

It was three hours past midnight, time for them to get to work. They systematically began a search over

249

the interior of the holding room looking for the jail's weak spot. A weak spot meant escape.

The small building was made of plywood and logs, lashed together with rope. Its floor was stained with oil, suggesting it was once used as a storage shed. The structure's wood was sturdy but its ropes were rotten. They immediately set to work quietly stripping away the hemp in the far corner of the hut.

It was a tedious job, but by working together, they were soon able to tear away enough of the rope to weaken the bond. Another hour passed, and they were able to wiggle some of the logs loose. This, in turn, loosened the plywood enough to allow them to sneak out the back of the hut.

Occasionally, Hunter would leave the work and press his ear to the door and listen to the guards left behind to watch them. He had heard them guzzling liquor earlier. Now he was sure they were passed out. And from what Hunter could see, the rest of the pirate contingent was on hand at the crash site.

They slipped out of the back of the hut and into the woods with ease.

With most all of the pirates at the far end of the runway, Hunter considered stealing one of the bandit's trucks, but he didn't have a clue where the access road was. Stealing one of the jets was out, too. He might be able to hot start one, and get it airborne quickly, but the fighters were all single-seaters. And the two-engine cargo planes would be harder to start, taxi and take off in.

That left only the hot air balloon. And why not? It was far enough away from where the pirates were going over the C-47's wreckage. It looked unguarded and would be a quiet means of escape. He could worry about which way the wind was blowing later.

They easily made their way toward this dark end of the base. The pirates were terrible at security—they had no sentries, only one watchtower at the far end of the runway and not even a fence around the base. Lulled into a false sense of security by being isolated for so long, the pirates assumed no one could get in or out of their hidden base. But Hunter had been through enough to know that the first rule of any good soldier was "never assume anything."

They reached the black hangar and made for the balloon. It was filled and suspended five feet off the ground, tugging at its rope; they wouldn't have to light its burner until they were airborne—if they got airborne. Al and Zal climbed in and made ready to lift-off. But Hunter held up his hand, telling them to hang on for a minute. He sensed something. It was coming from the mysterious hangar. He had to see what was inside.

He quickly picked the rudimentary padlock which held the doors closed and was soon inside the hangar. He felt a wave of deja vu wash over him. He flashed back to the time he was inside the hangar at the base in Vermont where the general had left behind the motherlode of materiel. He was surprised by what he found then.

This time would be no different.

It was pitch black inside the windowless building. But there were airplanes inside; he was sure of it. What kind of airplanes? Jet fighters. The smell of JP-8 jet fuel was strong. But he would have to actually touch one in order to identify it.

He walked with his hands blindly in front of him, hoping the first thing he touched wasn't a face or a rifle barrel. He finally reached the pointed end of a plane. Running his hand along the fuselage, he could feel the long snout, the short, low wing and swept in rear quarter. Two air intakes up front, two exhaust tubes in the back. A 110-degree tail. A T-38? Could be, but this plane felt shorter. An F-5 Freedom Fighter maybe? It was the sister plane to the T-38 so it would feel the same. But the F-5, besides being rare, was a single-engined, subsonic fighter.

Then it hit him—an F-20! It had to be. The F-20 Tigershark was a souped-up, bad-ass version of the F-5; the same design but years away in performance from the T-38. He felt a chill run through him. The F-20 was his second most favorite airplane—next to the F-16, of course. How in hell did the pirates come to get possession of one? They were rarer than the F-5, probably as hard to find as an F-16.

But he did know why the bandits weren't flying them. It was simple. They were too stupid. They didn't have the know how. The F-20 was built 30 years after the pirates' F-100s were rolled out. The advances in avionics, computers and aerodynamics incorporated into the F-20 made the F-100s seem like a kids' toy. To fly one took more than just strapping in and taking off.

He walked along the hangar touching each plane, counting 12 in all. God damn, with 12 of these F-20s in the air, the pirates could kick ass on anybody. Yet, he could tell these planes had never been flown. They still smelled of fresh grease and their tail exhausts were practically brand new. Each plane may have been started once or twice for an engine test, but the birds had never left the ground. How they got there, he could not figure out, unless they were hauled up in trucks and assembled in the hangar. The fact that the place was locked up indicated the pirates knew the value of their treasure. But they were grounded by their ignorance.

He had to leave. He briefly flirted with the idea of leaving a fire which would eventually destroy the hangar and the classic airplanes, but he couldn't bring himself to do it. If he had one weakness, it was a respect for the beauty of a flying machine. He'd do anything to avoid destroying one. And so it would be with the F-20s. He knew the pirates would never learn to fly them.

And maybe he'd be back . . .

CHAPTER SEVENTEEN

Hunter had never flown a balloon before, but got the hang of it very quickly. Flying was in his blood. It came to him as naturally as breathing.

Hunter and Zal cut the ropes and slowly—silently—the balloon ascended. Above the black hangar. Above the nearby trees. Rising, free—like escaping from hell. Climbing above the bandit's mountain base. Above the skeletons of the raped airplanes. They quietly passed over the remains of the C-47, looking down on the pirates who were still picking through the wreckage.

Hunter knew if they were spotted the pirates would try to pick them off with their anti-craft guns, or, failing that, scramble a couple jets to shoot them down. But he also knew it would be a while before their captors realized they were even gone. The bandits were too hopped up with drugs and jewel lust to worry about them. But eventually, the bandits would check in on them, and then the shit would hit the fan. The Stukas would discover there were no diamonds, no prisoners and that the hot air balloon was missing. He knew it would be the end of the line for Jaws.

They drifted for a while, not caring which direction they were going in, just as long as they were traveling away from the Stukas' base. Eventually, he and Al were able to get the burner going without much trouble. Then it became a matter of letting air in to climb higher, and letting it out to descend. Lucky again, the wind was moving the balloon on a rough north-by-northeasterly course.

Hunter's thoughts kept drifting back to the hangar filled with Tigersharks. How ironic that he had been able to touch the beautiful jets, yet not see them. It was like a dream. Suddenly, he wanted a woman. Any woman. Then he wanted a meal. Then he wanted to be behind the controls of his F-16 again.

He didn't even think about the $150,000 . . .

Glad to be free again, they spent their time hanging over the side of the balloon's basket, taking in the pre-dawn scenery below. The sun came up and the terrain beneath flattened out from mountains to plains and valleys. The balloon, obviously stolen from its original owners by the bandits, was a bright red with yellow stripes. They were flying low and sometimes, they could see people watching them pass over. Some of them even waved.

At one point, they saw above them a huge air convoy passing over at about 35,000 feet. None of them had ever seen a convoy from this perspective before and it was a magnificent sight. The big air-liners-turned-cargo planes—707s, 727s, DC-10s and even a couple of Jumbo Jets—flew in three-point formations. There must have been thirty of them leaving an awesome white contrail pattern across the blue sky. Mixed in amongst the big planes were the smaller jets—fighters—weaving in and out of the formations, escorting the convoy. The airplanes produced a tremendous rumbling roar as they flew over. This group had probably taken off from Montreal and was heading for the Coast. Hunter felt good to see the jets. Finally, some evidence of sanity after the insanity of his life in the past few days—The Pitts and the Stukas' base. Life—and commerce—goes on, he thought, despite the decadence that swirled around the continent. He wanted to be with them—flying as part of the convoy. Aiding the stability, keeping the contacts to the Coasters open. He reached into his back pocket and felt the reassuring folds of the flag he always kept there. Maybe, someday . . .

It was about two hours after sunrise when he knew other jets were approaching. About 10 miles out, coming at them from the north, there were three of them, trailing smoke and flying just barely above their present altitude of 2000 feet.

"I hope these guys are friendly," Zal said, watching the planes approach.

"They could use us for target practice if they're not," Al said.

"Don't worry," Hunter said closing his eyes and detecting the distinct sounds of an F-105 engine. It was the kind of plane the Aerodrome Defense Force flew. "They're good guys."

The three jets were on them in a matter of seconds, passing them about a quarter mile out.

"Hey!" Zal yelled after getting a good look at the Thunderchiefs with the ADF markings. "That's my plane!"

The jets made another pass, one closer in so the pilot could get a good look at the passengers in the balloon. Then all three jets wagged their wings and continued south.

"It'll be good to be home," Hunter said.

An hour later a crowd appeared on the tarmac at the Aerodrome to watch as the balloon descended from out of the clouds. The jets had radioed that Hunter, Al and Zal were safe and heading toward Syracuse and word had spread fast around the base. They had all but been given up for dead.

The balloon landed and the first person to reach them was Fitzgerald.

"Do you always have to make things difficult, Hawker?" he said shaking Hunter's hand and wearing a mile wide grin.

"Wouldn't have it any other way, Fitzie," Hunter laughed. "Frost get here okay?"

"Sure did," Fitz said, with relief in his voice. "A good guy, he is. Not many people you can expect to carry two hundred million in diamonds for you these days. He told us that the last he saw of you, you was going down in the Spooky all aflame."

"That was the easy part," Hunter said.

"He wanted to bomb up here and fly back to look for you," Fitz explained. "But we talked him out of it. We sent those three Thuds you saw out for you

257

instead. But we knew that if we put an air strike on the pirate base—if we could find it, that is—the bastards would probably have killed you on the spot."

"You are right there, my friend." Hunter agreed.

Al and Zal had climbed out of the balloon and crisply saluted Fitzgerald.

"I'm recommending these two for promotions," Hunter told him.

"Promotions?" Fitz said. "That will cost me money, Hawker."

"They're worth it," Hunter said. "I couldn't have done it without them."

Hunter turned to the two men and shook their hands. He felt very close to them now. "I mean it guys. Thanks."

"Anytime, Major," Zal said.

"Sure," Al added. "When you go back to get those F-20s, let me know."

"It's a deal," Hunter told him.

"F-20s?" Fitzgerald asked excitedly. "What F-20s?"

Hunter put his hand on his friend's shoulder. "It's a long story, Fitz. Buy me a drink and I'll tell you all about it."

They drank and ate and drank some more. Then Hunter retired to the penthouse for a bath and a change of clothes. Aki was there, waiting to wash his back. She stripped off his clothes and eased him into the large sunken tub. As always, she climbed in with him. He lay back and closed his eyes, letting the hot

258

water wash over him. He heard her clap her hands and was aware that another woman had joined them in the tub. He drifted off into a half-sleep, feeling the four hands work all over his body, soothing his wounds, both physical and mental. It seemed like he'd been gone for years, yet it had only been a couple of days. Like a lot of his adventures, the days seemed expanded—weeks of action compressed into a few hours. It was the way he had always been. It was the way he liked it.

Aki and her companion, another Oriental beauty named Mio, lifted him from the bath and led him to the bedroom. There, they made love to him and each other, then they stayed and watched over him as she slept for the next 24 hours.

He awoke from his deep sleep, well-rested and refreshed. Aki carried a message to him. It instructed him to meet Fitzie in his office as soon as he was able. Hunter dressed quickly, kissed Aki and Mio goodbye, then set out for the Irishman's luxurious control tower office.

When he got there, Fitz had the pile of diamonds spread out before him on his desk. Gus was with him.

"Good work, Major," Gus said, obviously pleased. "My employers are very grateful to you."

"That's right, Hawker," Fitz said, examining each diamond with careful interest. "You're in the chips now."

Gus produced a strongbox that was held tight by a pair of padlocks.

"Here you are, Major," Gus said beaming as he unlocked the box to reveal hundreds of bright silver coins. "Real silver, worth two hundred thousand dollars."

"Two hundred thousand dollars?" Hunter asked, staring at the coins. "I thought our agreement was for one hundred fifty?"

"I said my employers were grateful, Major," Gus said. "They suggested we sweeten the pot a little, as they say."

"Well," Hunter said, slightly embarrassed as he fingered the strongbox. "Please tell your employees that *I'm* the one who is grateful."

Gus looked at Fitz, then back at Hunter.

"Would you like to tell them yourself, Major?" Gus asked almost sheepishly. "They would like to discuss further employment with you."

Hunter was silent for a moment.

"Go ahead, Hawker, me boy," Fitz said, taking his attention away from the diamonds for a moment. "They are rich men who need your help. And they'll pay you for it. Go. Take your skills and let them make *you* a richer man."

Hunter looked at his friend, then back at the silver. "It looks as if I'm already rich," he said. "I've got enough here for fuel to fly the Coast and back ten times."

"I said 'richer,' Hawker," Fitz said, almost chastising him. "There's plenty of money to be made, lad. Go make it!"

"He's right," Gus interjected. "My employees *are* very wealthy men. But with wealth, Major, come

260

problems. Will you help us?"

Hunter thought for a moment. "Well, first of all, who the hell are your employers?"

"I can tell you now, of course," Gus said. "Have you ever heard of Football City, Major?"

"Football City?" he thought for a moment. "The big gambling city out in the Midwest?"

"St. Louis, Hawker." Fitz said, this time not bothering to look up from the gem he was examining.

"Formerly St. Louis," Gus said, correcting Fitzgerald. "Football City is the enterprise my employers operate. It is a free territory that encompasses all of the old city of St. Louis plus much more."

"But why 'Football' city?" Hunter was confused.

"Well, that is the major enterprise there, Major," Gus said. "Let me explain:

"We know you are familiar with Las Vegas, having been stationed there for two years. Well, Football City picked up where Las Vegas left off. You see, Major, people love to gamble. Gamble on anything. It's a relaxing yet exciting means of entertainment. In Football City, gambling is the way of life, just as it was in Las Vegas. But it is many times expanded. My employers actually bought all the working equipment left in Las Vegas after it was evacuated and shipped it east to St. Louis in the first year of the New Order.

"They started slowly, like any business. But they found out that just because the style of government here in the country had changed, people's tastes—for gambling and other things—were not diminished one iota. Soon, people were flocking to St. Louis. To live. My employers were able to give them work. To protect

261

them. We have a good sized army under contract and a small air force."

Hunter was still puzzled. "And you support all this through gambling on football?"

"That's correct, Major," Gus continued. "There is *so* much money around, these days. There is enough real silver on this continent to make a lot of people very rich. But because a lot of the former population now lives in Free Canada, and that other territories aren't as, shall we say, industrious, a lot of money that's around eventually comes to places like the Northeast Economic Zone, or to the Coasters or to Football City."

"But I've got enough money to last me a lifetime," Hunter said. "Why should I want more?"

"Because you never had money before," Fitz said to him, putting the diamonds aside and looking him straight in the eye. "So you've got yourself enough money to last a lifetime, have ya? Hah! You can never have enough money. Can't you see that? It's no longer like the old days, Hawker. This is a brave new world, my friend. My daddy, God rest his soul, used to tell me: 'Money talks and bullshit walks.' That's truer today than when he said it. And the sooner you realize it the better.

"You have to stop living in the past, man. You think you're up to date, but you're wrong. Dead wrong. You went and played war with ZAP, and a fine outfit they were too. But it was nothing more than you reliving your life before the New Order. It was like you were in the Thunderbirds and with your old squadron, too. Well, that's more like reliving your childhood.

262

And you were being taken care of, just like in the service.

"Aye. Some people don't need money—someone who's living on his own in a shack in Florida or in Maine, hunting his own food, clothing himself. What's he got to do with money? Nothing! What's he need money for? Nothing! Well, half the people left on this continent are living like that. And, I have to think, they enjoy it!

"But how long could we survive like that? We're men of technology, Hawk. We need it to survive. Or at least I do. And you do, too. We need the machines. They are our lives. We're specialists. The hunter, the survivor, he's a paleolithic. He's able to get by. But can you? And for how long?

"So I know what you're thinking. You lived up on that goddamn mountain for two years. Big deal, I say to that. Because you told me in the same breath that you were dying to get back. To come down off your fooking mountain. To fly again. Well, until you sprout wings, Major Hunter, you ain't flying anywhere unless you got an airplane. And an airplane is technology. And technology costs money. And you will, from this day on, need money. The more you get, the more you'll need. It's the curse of the 'Specialized Man,' Hawker. Like always, there are the 'haves' and the 'have-nots.' You just became a 'have.' "

Hunter was astonished at Fitz's speech. It was an admonishment only a good friend could give to another. Hunter knew it was true. He *was* behind the times. Like it or not, this was the New Order. He couldn't change that. At least not right away.

"Major Hunter," Gus said after a while. "Please. Come meet with my superiors. See Football City for yourself. It's a very worthwhile enterprise, and, as I said, my employers are very interested in seeking your advice, your help in matters of grave importance."

"Look at it this way, Hawk," Fitz said, returning his attention to the diamonds covering his desk. "They'll be able to pay you a lot more than I can."

"But there's much more at stake here, Major," Gus said. The tone of his voice was absolutely grim. Studying him, Hunter thought Gus looked like a man of 40 going on 62. Another veteran with the weight of the world on his shoulders. "We in Football City are being threatened. We are facing an enemy—dark forces, gentlemen—that, if successful, will wreak havoc across the continent and ruin what little bit of stability we have in America now."

Hunter and Fitzgerald were silent for a moment. Both were surprised that something like the stability of the continent would affect someone like Gus. He seemed like a 100-percent mercenary.

Fitz had to ask: "Are you serious?"

"Deadly serious," Gus said, his face going dark.

"Just who is this threat?" Hunter asked.

"I can't say at the time, Major," Gus said. "All I can say is that you will get all your answers from my employers in Football City."

"And if I don't go?"

"Then the continent will be in utter chaos in less than a year." Gus replied, his somber but urgent tone not letting up.

"I'd like to help you out," Hunter said. "But I've

264

got to have some kind of clue of who you are fighting here. I'm assuming that someone wants to take over Football City?"

Gus hesitated, then answered, "Yes, that's correct."

"But you've got yourself a nice big army there, no?" Fitz asked.

"That's also true," Gus replied.

"Then," Hunter pressed. "Why is it so serious? Who's controlling these 'dark forces?' "

Gus was silent for a long time. Then he looked up and choosing his words carefully, said: "My employers are convinced the orders to destroy Football City are coming . . . from Moscow."

CHAPTER EIGHTEEN

Two days later, Hunter was flying the F-16 past the old St. Louis "Gateway to the West" arch. The giant white arch was now decorated with tens of thousands of flashing neon lights—beacons that could be seen for miles, enticing people to come and spend their silver and gold in Football City.

It had taken him two days to say his goodbyes. He had arranged to have $50,000 of his $200,000 split between Al and Zal. Fitz gave him a bellyful of JP-8 fuel free, and bombed up the F-16 for half the normal price. The Irishman agreed to keep in touch by radio, just to see what was up, but also to keep Hunter apprised of the comings and goings of the Mid-Ak planes that still occasionally put down at the Aerodrome on their way to New Chicago.

He spent the good part of his last day with Aki and Mio. He would miss the two Oriental bisexual beauties. Their baths. Their comforts. Their entertaining nights. They cried when he told them he was leaving. He promised, perhaps too hastily, that he would return.

In the end, he had agreed to follow Gus on to Football City only as a stopover on his trip to the Coast. He felt an obligation to make it to old California, just in case some of the ZAP pilots and crew had made it there. Always in the back of his mind were thoughts of the general and the captured pilots and the others from Otis being held in Boston. He couldn't let them down.

The flight from Syracuse to Football City took less than two hours and gave Hunter a chance to road test the new, improved F-16. It was good to get back in the cockpit of the souped-up jet. He tested his unique, M-61 cannon six-pack along the way and it worked perfectly. The plane itself felt lighter, faster, stronger. He was glad he had taken the time in Syracuse to overhaul it himself. Now he knew that every nut, bolt and screw had been installed and tightened by only himself.

He landed at the former St. Louis airport. The place looked a little like The Aerodrome; SAM sites ringed its perimeter, a dozen or more ack-ack guns did too. Soldiers in brown camouflage uniforms were moving everywhere. The airport was busy. Cargo planes would take off here to link up with the big convoys heading west. Because the city was so close to the Badlands, the airfield was the last stop for any stragglers in the convoys to put down, and live to tell about it.

A welcoming committee was waiting for him. It included Gus and two men who were introduced to him as Max and Murray. They had a stretch limousine waiting to bring him first to his quarters, then to meet their boss. But Hunter insisted on shutting down the F-16 himself. He trusted Gus, and the man assured him that the jet would be well cared for and placed under heavy guard. Only then would Hunter agree to leave it in the care of the airfield's ground crew. All he took with him was a duffel bag containing a change of clothes, his M-16 and his bag of silver.

The limo ride through Football City was eye-popping. It was obvious why no one called it St. Louis anymore. The place no longer even faintly resembled that old city. A massive reconstruction project had been undertaken. Gone were the slums and the seedy downtown business district. In its place a city of gambling and entertainment establishments had been planted. Now the downtown contained block upon city block of casinos, night clubs, restaurants, barrooms, hotels and what he was sure were high class whorehouses. The new city stretched for a mile in every direction. The streets were so brightly lit from the establishments' marquees, that street lights weren't needed. There were people everywhere, walking, talking, drinking, eating, leaving one casino to duck into another.

There were all *kinds* of people. Soldiers, airmen, cowboys, Canadians, children, couples—some who could only be described as tourists—who looked as if the bomb had never been dropped. And there were women. All kinds of women. He saw showgirls walking down the street in their costumes. He saw hookers, fine looking mamas of all races. Young girls, older women, women dancing naked in the windows of casinos. Women dressed like men. Possibly some men dressed like women. He saw a lot of women wearing men's suitcoats, vests, ties, hats—and miniskirts. Others wore only bathing suits. Some were even topless. Everywhere he looked, he saw women.

"The woman to man ratio is 3-to-1," Gus told him.

"This places makes Las Vegas look like a crap game in the backroom," Hunter said, his eyes glued to the window of the limousine.

"That's right, Mr. Hunter," Murray said. "It's more like Disneyland. You do remember Disneyland, don't you?"

Murray was a small, balding man around 50 years old. Hunter wouldn't be surprised later when Gus told him that Murray took care of the books for the city. He may have been one of the few accountants to survive World War III. Max, a tall, thin, scholarly type around 40, was the city lawyer, a nearly ceremonial job in a place where just about everything—short of murder and rape—was legal.

Gus was the fix-it man. They all worked for a man they called The Boss. His real name, Hunter would find out later, was Louis St. Louis, or, bowing to the local dialect, Louie St. Louie. He was the kingpin of the whole operation; the person, according to Gus, who conceived of the city, designed it, financed it, built it, and now reaped the profits. It was hard to believe he'd done it all in less than five

269

years. But Hunter knew Louie St. Louie was now at least $200 million richer, and according to Gus, the man was very anxious to meet the pilot who had delivered his diamonds.

They turned a corner and ahead of them loomed a mammoth stadium. It covered more than 20 city blocks, and was magnificently lit by at least a hundred sky-high light towers. The outside walls of the stadium were made of marble, with authentic gold inlay. Thousands of flags and banners flew in the breeze above its walls. It had a retractable dome, many ramps and walkways leading in and out, plus two very tall needle-nose towers, one at each end, that afforded anyone sitting in them the best seat in the house. The whole thing was beautiful—a beautiful monstrosity.

They pulled up in front of the stadium so Hunter could get a good look at it.

"Major Hunter," Gus said. "You wanted to know why we call this place Football City. Well, this is why."

"You play football here?" Hunter said, looking at the awesome structure.

"Well, not just any football, Major," Gus said. "Professional football. Football people who can remember what the old NFL was like can enjoy."

"And let me guess," Hunter said. "Football everyone can bet on."

"That's correct, Major," Gus said. "The revenues we need to survive here in Football City come from betting The Game."

"*The* Game?" Hunter asked. "You make it sound

like there is only one game played here."

"That's quite correct, Major," Max told him. "There *is* only one game. A game that never ends."

"What?"

"It's true, almost," Gus continued. "It's just one long game of football. It doesn't end until the season ends and the season is three hundred days long. The Game goes on, day after day, twenty-four-hours a day. The teams—and there are only two—are made up of five hundred men each. They substitute constantly, man for man, and team for team. The game always goes on. The point spread is always changing as the players enter and leave. The betting always constant."

In the pre-war days, Hunter loved football as much as the next guy. But a perpetual game?

"People can bet by the periods, quarters we used to call them," Max explained. "Or by the halfs, or by a match, which is four quarters. Some high rollers will bet by the day, or the week, or the month."

"The diamonds you picked up for us?" Gus asked. "They were payment from a man who had bet the entire three-hundred-day season."

"And lost?" Hunter asked.

"And lost," Gus confirmed.

"Lost two-hundred-million," Murray the accountant interjected. "That's the kind of money we are dealing with here."

"The final score last year was seventy-six thousand, nine-hundred eighty-one to seventy-three thousand, four-hundred fifty-two," Gus said. "It was pretty close until the end when the Gold team suffered injuries to six of its quarterbacks in less than two weeks."

"The Gold team?" Hunter asked.

"Right," Gus answered. "The two teams that always play each other are the Gold and Silver. A lot of the players are actually NFL players who were on teams when the war broke out. We scoured both coasts for good players. A lot of them are from Texas too. They are terrific athletes, and they make good money. Trouble is, there are so many of them that a lot of the players don't even know the majority of their teammates."

"But the place is empty right now," Hunter said, noting the lack of hustle and bustle that he imagined would be associated with such an occasion.

"That's correct, Major," Max the lawyer said. "Our season will open again tomorrow. It's our biggest holiday of the year. Mister St. Louis will thrown out the first football and the game will be on again, for another three-hundred days."

Hunter was fascinated at the idea. Sports as a city life? A never-ending football game? Bets from a piece of silver worth a dollar to nearly a quarter of a billion dollars?

They drove on, soon arriving at a palatial estate containing a building that was a cross between a hotel and a cathedral. It was surrounded by a high wrought-iron fence that stretched for a mile square. Many soldiers were on guard outside the fence; many tanks and armored personnel carriers were in evidence. Several small SAM positions were also directly placed around the perimeter. Inside the fence there was an area the size of a small city park, complete with trees, brooks and rolling greens. It was a golf course at one time, Hunter realized and now the place was still well-kept—and well-guarded. Hunter estimated another 200 or so soldiers patrolled these interior grounds.

The building itself, tall and red, with a rotating red beacon on top, was surrounded by a wide functional moat. It was at one time an exclusive golf club-cum-hotel, maybe a Hyatt or a Sheraton, before someone came in and did some extensive renovations. The building was big enough to house hundreds if not thousands of people. But as he soon learned, now only one man lived there: Louie St. Louie.

A quarter mile long road wound through the pleasant grounds leading to the moat. Four checkpoints also marked the way. The soldiers checked the limo at each checkpoint, and carefully scrutinized Gus, Max and Murray. Although all three were well-known in these parts, the soldiers went about their job professionally. Something about them sparked in Hunter's memory, but he couldn't grab hold of it. The last checkpoint was at the bridge, which was lowered for the limo to cross the moat.

Five minutes later, after a tour of the ornate lobby, Hunter was ushered in, alone, to the lush living quarters of Louie St. Louie, the man who served as designer, bankroller and, for all practical purposes, king of Football City. The room was huge. One wall was taken up by a long, well-stocked bar. Another

273

looked like it doubled as a movie screen. An immense window faced the east and provided a view out over the grounds of the former golf course. The remaining wall was covered with pictures of football players and scenes from football games.

Sitting in a chair looking out the window was Louie St. Louie. He was a tall, white haired-man of about 60, dressed in an all-white, three-piece-suit. A dignified chin off-set his ruddy complexion and a quick, down-home smile. He rose immediately and greeted Hunter like a long-lost son, putting a bear hug on him that threatened the airman with suffocation. Hunter detected a distinct twang in his voice when he spoke.

"Major Hunter," Louie beamed. "This is certainly an honor to meet you, sir. I am grateful for that, shall we say, little favor you did for me."

"My pleasure," Hunter said. The twang registered: Louie St. Louie was definitely of Texas stock.

"Well," St. Louie said. "Come on in, boy, sit down and talk to an old flyboy, would you?"

"You're a pilot?"

"I was," Louie said, heading for the room's wet bar. "Scotch, Major? Made yesterday."

"Sounds good," Hunter said, settling in a chair near the large window. Out on the grounds he could see a couple of hundred of the estate's soldiers doing calisthenics. Others patrolled in and out of the dots of woods that marked the course.

St. Louie returned with two glasses and an unlabeled bottle of Scotch.

"I haven't flown in years," St. Louie said, picking

274

up the conversation. "Not real flying anyway. I have a T-38 at the airfield. Fly down to Texas every great while. But I'm too busy here."

"You flew before the war?" Hunter asked, taking a taste of the bitter, strong Scotch.

"Before and during," St. Louie laughed. "B-52s. Stationed in Guam, moved back to California, when the shit hit. Me and my squadron took out half the goddamn Russian Pacific fleet with cruise missiles before they made us stop having so much fun. Fired the little buggers right off our wings. Go up with eight of them at a time. We must have flown fifty missions during the three weeks, bombing those Commie bastards right across the Pacific, all the way back to Guam, for Christ's sake."

There were a few moments of silence as St. Louie's eyes wandered off into space. Hunter knew the man was thinking about the Great Betrayal, the stab in the back, brave men lost for no good reason.

St. Louie suddenly came back to the present with the clap of his hands and a great smile.

"But gosh darn it, Major, I sure admire your flying. I saw you guys perform once when I was up in Boston, before the Zone went Mid-Ak."

"That seems like a long time ago," Hunter said.

"That's how things are these days, Major. We remember what it used to be like. Before the war. Before the New Order. Ever since, things seem to take longer. You can't move like you used to. I miss it."

"So do I," Hunter agreed.

"You've seen our city?"

275

"It's quite a place."

"And it's good for the people, Major. We've brought back more than half the original population, and thousands of people visit us every day. It gives them some excitement in their lives. There's not much excitement any more if you ain't a pilot or a soldier. People spend most of their time cooped up in their homes or wherever they live. They don't want to take a chance being out at night with all the scum roaming around the continent. But there isn't a whole lot that you can do at home either. Ain't got TV like we used to. No radio really. No new books. Football City gives 'em someplace to go. Something to do. Some link with the past. It's safe. We got sports. We got eating places. Music. Entertainment . . ."

"Women . . ." Hunter interjected.

"Wooo-eee, do we ever!" St. Louie laughed, reaching for the bottle to refill his glass. "They just come from all over, Major. They like it here. They ain't bumping around some small town somewheres or getting raped or killed."

"Sounds like it's worthing fighting for," Hunter said, his eyes traveling back to the soldiers drilling out on the fairway.

"Now, Major, I must confess something," St. Louie said, draining his Scotch. "We have a surprise for you."

"Surprise?"

St. Louie laughed. "Yes," he said, getting up to push a button. "I want you to meet our commander of my private security forces."

276

The security forces, the soldiers patrolling St. Louie's mansion and grounds, and now visible out the window, drilling in the field below. They seemed familiar to him.

"Captain," St. Louie called into an intercom. "Would you come in here please? Major Hunter is waiting to meet you."

Hunter stood and saw St. Louie was wearing a look of undeniable delight on his face. The door beside him opened and a man in battle fatigues walked in. He, too, was smiling.

Hunter looked at the man. He was stocky, ruddy complexion and a mass of black hair.

Then the face registered.

It was Captain Bull Dozer . . .

CHAPTER NINETEEN

He put a bearhug on Dozer. It was so good to see the man again. It was as if everything had come full circle.

"I can't believe it," Hunter told him. "What the hell are you doing here?"

"Just trying to earn a living," Dozer said, smiling broadly.

St. Louie poured a drink for the Marine captain and the three of them sat down.

Well, Hawk," Dozer began. "We finally did make it to Fort Meade; problem was, the place was empty."

"So what did you do?" Hunter asked.

"Well, there wasn't a soul anywhere around the base, and it had plenty of food and provisions," Dozer continued. "So we left the citizens there with a few of our guys who wanted to stay put for a while. They stayed for about a year, but then had to leave before the territory went Mid-Ak."

Dozers' troops had voted to stay with him. They respected his intelligence and sought his guidance. He correctly surmised that in the anarchaic continent, an army for hire might be in need in some places. So the

7th Cavalry walked west. They set up camp here and there, sometimes occupying abandoned or near-abandoned towns when possible. Some of these occupations lasted several months or more. The local population—once they realized that Dozer's troops weren't rapists or New Order zealots—welcomed the well-armed, professional unit. The countryside was filled with gangs of gunmen and raiders during these early days. But none was so foolish to tackle an entire Marine battalion.

The 7th gradually worked by its way to the Mississippi, and would have probably walked right through the Badlands if they hadn't landed in Football City first. The city was just in its forming stages. St. Louie, knowing a ready-made security force when he saw it, offered to hire the whole battalion to help protect Football City and train its own fledgling army. The 7th voted to accept the offer and had been in the employ of St. Louie ever since.

"I knew you were coming, Hawk," Dozer said. "And, I'm glad you're here. You're not a minute too soon."

St. Louie started to say something, but caught himself at the last moment. "We'll talk business later, Major," he said, cryptically. "Have you seen our Grand Stadium?"

Hunter detected the cautious switch in St. Louie's voice.

"I was a big football fan before the war," he said, picking up on the subject. "I'm glad to see it didn't die out completely, like just about everything else."

"It didn't, Major," St. Louie said, back to his relaxed self. "And it won't either. I won't let it. It's

279

too . . . *too American.*"

He slapped his knee with a crack for emphasis.

"Well," Hunter said, feeling some of the excitement too. "I hope I can catch a part of a game while I'm here."

St. Louie looked at Dozer. "Why, didn't they tell you, Major?" St. Louie asked.

"Tell me what?"

"Major," St. Louie said with a smile. "Tomorrow, at Opening Day. You're going to be the guest of honor."

CHAPTER TWENTY

The next morning, Hunter was sitting in St. Louie's special box at the Grand Stadium. The grandstands were filling up with people—the place held more than 250,000 and every seat would soon be taken. More people gathered outside to watch the action on two big TV screens. Football City had the only working TV system on the continent and they put it to good use.

Hunter watched as a hundred players each from the Gold and Silver teams went through their pre-game warm-ups on the field. Bands were playing. People were cheering. Footballs flying through the air. A contagious excitement ran through the crowd. Hunter felt good inside as he took it all in. There was nothing on the continent to compare to this. Not in the old Northeast Economic Zone days of Boston, or Texas or out on the Coast. This was, for want of a better word—traditional. Traditional and civilized.

Hunter sipped on a gigantic Bloody Mary. The night before was a pleasant blur. More pilot talk with St. Louie during dinner, more reminiscing with Dozer.

This led to more drinking at St. Louie's estate. Then he was chauffeured to his suite of rooms at the city's finest hotel, followed by yet another tour of the town with Gus and the Marine captain as tour guides. Free drinks. Free gambling chips. A showgirl named Alicia. Her underpants were hanging on his bedpost when he woke up. It took him a while to realize it—but he decided that this must be a vacation, the first one he'd had since his college days.

St. Louie was in the box with a couple of dozen other guests. The man had promised to talk business with Hunter after the game, so the airmen decided there was nothing to do but sit back and relax. Dozer was out on the field, supervising the security effort, his men sprinkled throughout the crowd in addition to Football City's regular army troop. Back in the box, a squad of scantily-clad waitresses made sure everyone was well-cared for. At the stroke of noon, both teams—1000 players in all—took the field. The game was about to begin. Suddenly the stadium's PA system sprang to life:

"Ladies and gentlemen!" the speakers boomed with an anonymous announcer's voice. *"Welcome to Opening Day!"*

The crowd responded with a thunderous cheer. The vibrations shook the whole stadium including St. Louie's box. Hunter felt a jolt run through him. Just like the old days, he thought.

The announcer continued: *"Starting our program today will be the Football City Air Corps Aerobatic*

282

Team."

St. Louie had told Hunter about the air demonstration earlier. The Football City leader confessed that the city's air corps *was* the demonstration team; the city only had five jets, and they were rather harmless and antique T-33s. Despite the enormous wealth of the city, when it came to defense, the money was spent on hiring an army. The city's jets—slow and unarmed—were strictly for show.

The crowd turned its eyes skyward as the jets appeared over the stadium. Flying in a standard V-formation the team executed a rather lukewarm series of loops, break-ups and eights. Hunter gave them an A for effort. The crowd, on the other hand, loved it.

St. Louie leaned over to him and said: "Someday, Major, we'll have a real air force."

Hunter looked at him and nodded. But St. Louie wasn't smiling. He looked more like an old man than a dignified cowboy. "Some day, Major," he continued with an ominous tone in his voice. "We'll need it."

He went back to watching the air demo team perform their routine. The crowd cheered with each maneuver. Hunter added his applause, although he could have performed the team's aerobatics in his sleep.

Suddenly, he knew something was wrong. Other aircraft were in the area. He could *feel* it. Even above the roar of the crowd and the noise of the Football City jets, he could hear other engines, more powerful, more threatening, heading their way.

He turned toward the northeast. Here they come, he thought. Just then a siren went off. The band

283

stopped playing. The crowd let out a collective gasp. An instant later, five deadly-looking fighter planes streaked low over the stadium.

"Where did they come from?" someone in the box yelled.

The jets were unmarked and painted entirely in black. They were all carrying air-to-air missiles.

"Who the hell are they?" someone yelled as the jets streaked over and began to turn.

Hunter began to shake with anger. *He* knew what kind of jets they were. A rage began at his feet and traveled at the speed of light to his head. He watched in angry silence as the fighters flashed over the stadium again and started to climb.

"Are they friendly?" someone else asked. The crowd began to move uneasily.

The Football City air demo was in the middle of a flyby high above the stadium. Hunter doubted if the demo jets even had workable radar or radios. And he could tell the mystery jets were preparing to attack.

The intruder jets weren't F-4s, or F-8s or F-104s. Not Thunderchiefs or Voodoos or Super Sabres. Nor any other pre-New Order American design. That's what shook Hunter as he stared at the aircraft. His blood began to boil. He hadn't seen jets like these since the war. He didn't think he'd ever see jets like these again. But here they were, above Football City's Grand Stadium. In the middle of the continent. Ready to attack the unarmed performing jets . . .

"They're pirate jets!" someone yelled. Screams came from the crowd. The impending panic of a quarter of a million people rippled through the stadium.

"No, they're not!" Hunter yelled, bolting from the luxury box. "They're Russian MIG-21s! And they're going after the demos!"

Helplessness. It washed over the stadium crowd as the black MIG-21s attacked the unarmed Football City T-33 jets. Two of the demos were simply blown out of the sky by the black fighters' firing their air-to-airs. Two others twisted and turned as each was picked up by at least two of the mystery planes. The crowd seemed glued to its feet as the dogfight swirled above them. Another demo was hit. Its wing severed, it plunged toward the grandstand. The stricken plane wobbled as the pilot tried to steer it away from the crowd. But he couldn't. Too late the people in the stadium began to react. The jet slammed into stands at the far end of the stadium, killing hundreds instantly and spilling burning jet fuel over hundreds more nearby.

The horrible crash snapped the fans out of their stupor. Panic set in. In seconds the crowd was pouring out onto the playing field and rushing toward the exits. Now the screams and cries were as loud as the cheering that had filled the stadium just minutes before. People were crushed, trampled, suffocated beneath the on-rushing sea of bodies.

Another Football City jet was hit, right above one of the needle nose towers. It was as if the mystery jets were intentionally firing on the unarmed planes when and where a crash would do the most damage. Again, the pilot struggled to control the jet away from the stadium. Again, he failed.

He managed to miss most of the crowd, keeping the smoking jet level as it crossed across the length of the stadium barely 200 feet from the ground. But the valiant pilot could do no more. The T-33 crashed into the base of the needle tower at the far end of the stands. The structure shook once, teetered, then came tumbling down. A dozen or so technicians housed in the tower were trapped and crushed as the structure slammed into the fleeing crowd.

High above the stadium, the last demo plane was caught in the crossfire of two mystery jets and was hit simultaneously by two air-to-air missiles. It disintegrated in mid-air.

Then, as suddenly as they had appeared, the black MIG-21s were gone. The attack had lasted less than a minute. Thousands lay dead or dying. Two fires were raging in the stadium; one where the tower had fallen, another where the jet had crashed into the stands. Tens of thousands of fans were still scrambling toward the exits, many others just stood in numbed disbelief. No one quite knew what to do. No one except Hunter . . .

He was out the luxury box door before the first missile was even fired by the MIG-21s. He didn't have to see the dogfight. He could *hear* it and know what was going on. Knowing the exits would be soon filled with panicking fans, he opted for climbing out on one of the girders that supported the stadium stands. He shimmied down the beam and was soon out on the street beside the stadium. The noise of the crowd and the screams of the jets high above filled the air. He saw the first jet come crashing down. Quickly, he looked around, trying to get his bearings. *Which way was the fucking airport?* He had to get to his F-16 . . .

Frustration. It was no use. The streets were clogged within seconds. Injured people fell out of the stadium by the hundreds, burnt, crying, bleeding. It *was* utter chaos. Sirens were going off all around him. The smoke from the fires inside filled his nostrils. It smelled of burning flesh. The street was a mass of suffering humanity. People grabbed him, some with burning clothes, others with burning skin. Overhead, he caught a quick flash of the mystery jets—their ruthless work done—disappearing into the clouds. They would be far away before he could even get to the airport. He hated to give up so easily, but there was nothing he could do now. In desperation, he shook his fist at the sky.

Rescue vehicles were arriving. Soldiers appeared and started treating the victims. Hunter looked around and began to think more rationally. He was needed here on the ground right now. People were dying. They needed help. His heart burning with hate, heavy with rage, he joined the rescue crews and started administering first aid.

He stayed there the entire day and most of the night, helping the survivors, recovering the dead. The lights usually used for the football games were turned to the parts of the stadium where the jet and the tower crashed. Rescue workers sifted through the debris, looking for more victims. The remains of the crashed T-33 still smoldered in the rubble. The sirens kept blaring; no one had bothered to turn them off.

Meanwhile, people were packing up and fleeing Football City in droves. Rumors, fueled by the fires rising out of the rubble of the stadium, raced through the city. Another attack was coming. Get out while you can. Head for the hills. Once again, civilization came toppling down.

"Who were they?" Hunter asked Louie St. Louie. "Who would want to do this?"

They were in the cellar of St. Louie's estate, in a makeshift war room. Dozer and a half dozen other top officers of the Football City Army were there, trying to assess the situation. Despite his protests, St. Louie's security forces had hustled him away from the stadium as quickly as they could. The first thing he did was order his troops into the city to help the people who were left find bomb shelters. He redeployed the SAMs surrounding his estate to the downtown area, in case a second attack did come. His army was on full alert, but aside from a few anti-aircraft guns, he knew they would be helpless should the black fighters return.

After leaving the site of the attack, Hunter had caught a ride to the airport, checked to make sure his F-16 was safe, then rushed back to St. Louie's estate. It was early morning.

St. Louie called him to an isolated corner of the room.

He spoke in a hushed tone. "The Family did this."

"The Family?" Hunter asked with some surprise.

288

"How can you be sure?"

"They're the ones who have been threatening us for months," St. Louie said. "Goddamn criminals is what they are! They'd be in prison or deported if it were the old days."

"What do they want?"

" 'A piece of the action.' Protection money for not attacking us."

"That's blackmail!" Hunter said.

"Sure as shit," St. Louie replied, angrily. "They've been at me for months. First, they came down here to gamble in the early days. I told my guys to keep a close eye on them. I never liked them, but I couldn't start kicking every shady character out of the city. These guys spent money.

"Then, they started sending their cozy ass ambassadors down here with gifts. Booze, women, even drugs. Trying to get me to sign a 'mutual defense treaty' with them."

"Mutual defense treaties are an old Mid-Ak tactic," Hunter said.

"Well, I'm sure they got it from these crooks that are running New Chicago," St. Louie snorted. "They're goddamn *mafioso*, is what they are."

"I hope you didn't pay them off."

"No way. I kept telling them to go to hell with their protection money. They got mad. Sent more threats. I got mad. Locked up two of their ambassadors for a couple of nights, then threw their asses right out of the city. After that it was everything from death threats to warnings of all-out war. Luckily, I have some pretty good intelligence guys. I was able to send agents up there. They'd been warning that something like this might happen, but I didn't think it would be this soon."

"How would you match up against them in a war?" Hunter asked.

"We're good," St. Louie said. "Damn good. But they've got a hell of a big army. Free-lancers, mostly. At least sixty thousand standing. Who knows what they would call up in reserves. It's an army of thugs. Lots of tanks, APCs and trucks."

"And MIG-21s," Hunter added.

"That's just it," St. Louie said, his voice rising in anger. "They never had an air force before. That's why we never got one. We figured if they ever attacked us, it would be by land. We have a hell of a defense line out there called the Mississippi River. It practically surrounds the city. If you control the seven bridges crossing it, you can keep anyone out. But these MIG-21s change the balance of power. And . . ."

"And?"

"Well, there's more," St. Louie ran his hand through his white hair. "My spies tell me that they've spotted some Russians in New Chicago."

The Russians. Orders from Moscow. Hunter had to think for a moment. The late, great General Jones had always believed that the Russians were operating, in some form, on the continent. Their aim was to keep things destabilized. Keep things out of kilter. Keep the people on the continent in disarray, so they could not become cohesive once again.

Hunter never quite bought it; his complex logic

process prevented him from doing so, although, he too, had seen some evidence of it. The Russian rifles in New York City. The whispers of collusion between the Russians and the Mid-Aks. The East European cargo plane he had sabotaged at The Aerodrome. It was heading for New Chicago. Now the MIG-21s . . .

Things might seem to add up, but Hunter, as always, needed proof. The Russian army couldn't fire a popgun after the war in Europe. They had been decimated, wiped out. No command structure, no weapons, no nothing. They had had a hard time consolidating their gains in conquered Europe. They had to rely on collaborators—like the Finns—to do their dirty work after the great battle. So how could they be operating over here? Could they have recovered so quickly in three years? He'd have to meet a live Russian, nose-to-nose, to believe it.

"Major," St. Louie continued. "This was the reason I wanted to meet you. After you came through on the diamond shipment, I knew you were the man I needed."

"This is the 'business' you referred to earlier?"

"That's right. Major. Last week my agents told me that New Chicago could launch a ground attack against us within a few months. Now it looks like they are ahead of that schedule."

"What can I do? I'm just one pilot. One plane. You need a whole goddamned air force."

"That's it exactly, Major Hunter." St. Louie was speaking in all earnesty. "This city is a jewel. It's the closest thing there is to the old days. Sure, it's based on gambling. But men are free here, Major. There are very few places on this continent where anyone can make that claim. Those criminals want it. To ruin it. Rape it. Destroy it.

"We know this is not your fight, Major. But we also know that you are a patriot. And patriots are also in very short supply these days. We are hoping you will help us. Help us fight for this last bastion of freedom in this part of the country. If we go, all that's left would be Texas and the Coasters."

Hunter was quiet for a moment. His mind was flashing. Western Europe. New York City. The mountain. Otis. Baltimore. His rebirth in the hangar in Vermont. The Aerodrome. The Pitts. The Stukas' base. Now, Football City. His search, his quest, his goal. Continue the fight for freedom. Fight for it until the last ounce of strength in his body was gone. For the brave men who died in the war. For the people trapped in the horror of New York City. For Jones and all he stood for. St. Louie was preaching to the faithful.

"What do you want me to do?" Hunter asked.

A wave of relief came across the older man's face. He looked like a cowboy again. "I don't care how much it costs. I don't care what it takes. Get us some pilots. Get us some planes. Get us some ground personnel. Get us ammunition . . .

"Get us a goddamn air force!"

Hunter smiled. He was one step ahead of St. Louie. He knew where there were pilots and monkeys. Some were among the best in the world. And he knew where there were airplanes, also some of the best in the world. He also knew where there was a hangar full of bombs sitting on a mountain in Vermont. That would be a start. He loved a challenge. He loved the chance to strike a blow for freedom. Good or bad, Football City stood for freedom. It was worth fighting for. It was worth dying for.

"Mister St. Louie," Hunter said, extending his hand to shake on it. "You'll get your air force."

Hunter reached into his back pocket. The folded flag was still there.

CHAPTER TWENTY-ONE

The huge C-5 Galaxy cargo plane descended out of the sky above The Aerodrome, its engines whining, its landing gear kicking up a skid of smoke as they touched the runway. The C-5 was the largest airplane ever built. It was half again the size of a 747 Jumbo Jet and would dwarf a 707. It could carry close to 600 troops plus their equipment. Or move a half dozen tanks, APCs, trucks, jeeps, whatever. Few jobs were too big for the mighty aircraft.

The Galaxy was a rare sight these days. So a crowd made up of Aerodrome ground crews, was waiting when the big plane taxiied up to its station point, its four massive engines still screaming. Fitzgerald was at the head of the crowd, his cigar billowing smoke, checking his watch. The giant plane was right on time.

The jet came to a stop and its engines began to shut down. The pilot's hatch opened and Hunter climbed out. Those assembled gave him a spontaneous round of applause. He laughed and waved back. It had been a month since he'd left The Aerodrome and most everyone at the base knew he was helping Football

City prepare for the impending war with New Chicago.

"We just can't seem to lose you, Wingman," Fitzgerald said, warmly greeting his old friend.

I'm just a stick jockey trying to make a living," Hunter said. "You got my message. Is everything ready?"

"Everything's set," Fitz told him. "This is a bit risky Hawker, isn't it?"

"Life's a risk, these days," Hunter answered. "How's Aki? Mio?"

"Both well and waiting for you," Fitzgerald said with a wink.

"Let me show you something first," Hunter said, giving his co-pilot the thumbs up signal. Slowly, the entire blunt nose of the jet began to lift, like a giant fish opening its mouth. Fitzgerald could see the air crew was already preparing to unload the plane's cargo.

A ramp was lowered and the first materiel offloaded were two dozen crates of various bombs, missiles, RPGs, and rifles, courtesy of the Football City Army. Next off was the first of two small, Cobra attack helicopters. With their rotors folded back, the bright red, diminutive choppers had the appearance of some kind of huge, alien insects.

"Cobras!" Fitz said, with admiration in his voice. "I been looking for one of them for years. How'd you manage to get hold of two?"

"Ever hear of the Cobra Brothers?"

Fitzgerald had to think for a minute. "The Texans?"

"That's them," Hunter said. "They've been tearing

things up down on the Mexican border for the past year. Things were real hot down there until lately."

"Well, I heard a lot about them," Fitzie said. "They're the best in the business. You were lucky to get them."

"St. Louis arranged it," Hunter said, watching as the crews wheeled out the second Cobra. "He's a Texan and he put out a call to his relatives back home. That's where he got the C-5."

" 'Tis a fine airplane," Fitz said, looking at the behemoth aircraft, then at the second Cobra. Each chopper was armed with twin M-16 cannons, which were placed on a turret located on the sharp snout of the aircraft. In addition to the cannons, the helicopter had short, stubby wings for missile firings. The two Cobra Brothers, who weren't brothers at all, had also ripped out the second seat in each of the choppers and replaced it with firing control systems capable of handling everything from small anti-ship rockets to flame-throwing techniques.

Next to be rolled out was a larger, rather beat-up looking helicopter. Fitzgerald was surprised to see the battered old beast of a chopper wheeled out of the belly of the C-5.

"And what the hell is this, Hawker?" he asked, his brogue ringing.

Hunter only smiled. The large chopper sported a coat of chipped red and white paint, one cracked cockpit window and a piece of rope to hold the side hatch door closed.

"Well, I can see why you carried this monster in the Galaxy," Fitzgerald said, looking at the beat-up helicopter. "It cannot fly, can it?"

"Oh, it does more than that, Fitz," Hunter said as the crew finished wheeling the chopper off the C-5. "Come aboard. I'll show you."

"Just promise not to try to get the thing airborne," Fitz said, inspecting a faded sign painted on the side of the chopper. It read: MAINE LUMBER COMPANY. Fitzgerald could only shake his head.

Stepping inside, though, he got a surprise. The interior of the helicopter was one long bank of computers, dials, switches, lights, flashing red, green and blue, digital read-outs, computer keyboards and video screens. Eight crewmen scampered around the inside, all dressed in blue flight suits and fighter pilot helmets.

"Mother of God, Hawker," Fitzgerald said. "What's this? A spaceship?"

The interior of the chopper *did* resemble a spacecraft. Actually it was a highly sophisticated firing platform, convincingly disguised as a flying lumber truck.

"Take a look," Hunter told him. He pushed a control button and automatically a section of the helicopter's bottom lowered, revealing a steerable missile firing platform. Fitz could also see more than a half dozen gun ports with M61 machine guns stationed at them. Three windows on the port side served three GE Gatling guns, each capable of firing 6000 rounds a minute. The walls of the craft held miles of belts of ammunition plus a potpourri of hand weapons from shoulder-fired SAM launchers to dozens of M-16s and Browning automatic rifles.

"What kind of helicopter *is* this?" Fitzgerald said, nearly flabbergasted at the aircraft's potential destructive firepower.

"It's an old CH-53E 'Super Sea Stallion,'" Hunter told him. "The Texans found it in an abandoned Coast Guard station down on the Gulf. They gave it to St. Louie and he let me tinker with it a bit."

"I see more than a bit of your hand in this," Fitz said, gingerly touching the computer panels. "Who but the famous Hawker Hunter could make heads or tails of all this computer mumbo-jumbo?"

"Well," said Hunter. "We did soup it up a little. It's got three separate engines and we super-charged each one of them. We can lift ten tons for one hundred miles or five tons for two hundred miles. We have radar jamming equipment on board, stand-off missile firing capability, LANTERN night-fighting gizmos. Plus we can carry fifty-five people on board, maybe seventy if we squeeze them on."

Fitz smacked his lips. "I've changed my mind, Hawker," he said, only half-jokingly. "You have to take me for a ride in it some time. Show me what it can do."

"If it's still in one piece when we get back," Hunter told him. "You got yourself a deal."

Two hours later, a C-130 cargo plane landed at The Aerodrome. On board were Dozer, the two Cobra Brothers, plus a 25-man Special Operation unit, drawn exclusively from Dozer's 7th Cavalry. Each member had volunteered to accompany Hunter on his quest to find an air force for Football City. Dozer's commandos had trained day and night for the past month on air assaults, rescue techniques and special weapons handling. Dozer and Hunter worked with them separately, spending days on end, with no sleep, practicing, training, studying. In the end every last one of them knew there would be no time or leeway for screw-ups. Football City had become their home. Theirs would be the first step in what would prove to be a valiant defense of that city and its way of life.

Hunter spent the next two days at The Aerodrome going over the plan with the assault force and the next two nights, enjoying the erotic delights of Aki and Mio. They could feel a distance in him this time, though. His mind was a million miles away. Thinking about the mission. Fitzgerald noticed it too. The night before the assault team was to pull out, he split a bottle of bourbon with his friend.

"It's a dangerous one," the Irishman told him. "Are you sure about using minimum air support?"

Hunter nodded. "Can't muck it up with jets this time, Fitz. We got to go in, hit them, get what we went for and get the hell out of there. The Cobra Brothers will keep them busy while we're in and help us shoot our way out."

Hunter produced a map and read it over for the thousandth time. "The Cobra Brothers will take off tomorrow at dawn," he told Fitz, reviewing his scheme one last time. "They'll arrange the refueling stop in Quebec. Then they'll meet us here." He pointed to a small speck of land off the coast of what used to be the state of Maine.

"Then," he said, "We'll all head out for the final destination and hope we find a full house when we get there." Fitzgerald looked at the map and where Hunter's finger was pointing and then poured them both a drink.

"To success," Fitz said, lifting his glass to toast.

"I'll give your regards to the Mid-Aks," Hunter tapping the point on the map labeled: BOSTON.

"I'm lucky in two respects," he told Fitzgerald. "First of all, St. Louie has spies everywhere. Damn good ones too. Without good intelligence, we'd be flying by the seat of our pants.

"Second, I have one hell of a strike force. Jesus Christ, they're good, Mike!"

"Yer just lucky," Fitz said. "Makes me wish I could go with you."

"You could do me a big favor by staying here," Hunter told him earnestly.

"Will it be good or bad for my business, now?"

"I won't answer that," Hunter laughed. "What I need is someone to feed the intelligence I get from St. Louis to me while I'm out there. He has guys right in the city for Christ's sake, watching the 'Aks every move. I need that edge."

"Consider it done, Hawker," Fitz said. "I can still play 'neutral' and slip a radio message to you now and then."

"I knew I could count on you, buddy," Hunter said, draining his drink. "Well, time to go."

"Good luck, Hawker, my friend," Fitzgerald told him, clasping Hunter's hand with both of his.

"Thanks, Mike," Hunter said. "I'll see you when I get back."

Thirty-six hours later, Hunter was watching the sun rise out of the Atlantic Ocean, and start its climb across the sky. He looked around at the bivouac. It was a smoky collection of tents and sleeping bags, two campfires, a cauldron of hot, morning stew on one, a pot of boiling coffee on the other.

They were on an island just a stone's throw off the southern coast of the old state of Maine. Hunter knew the place from his childhood. It was well-forested and difficult to see from the air. There were fields large enough to handle the three choppers on the mission. It was barely more than an hour flying time to Boston. Here they would review the plan one last time. Here he would begin his war against the Mid-Aks in earnest.

Even though the Mid-Aks now controlled the Northeast Economic Zone, the invaders had been wise enough to leave the Down Mainers alone for the time being. The typical Mid-Ak arrogance didn't jell at all with the Mainers, who, on their best days were only downright ornery. The Mainers didn't blink when the coup went down in Boston. They just kept fishing and farming and cutting wood. The wood was turned into lumber and the lumber would be transported down to Boston in helicopters, and it would stay that way just as long as someone was on the other end to buy it. Boston politics was about the last thing to concern the people in Maine.

So he knew the assault force would be safe to hole up on the deserted island, and to use the place to launch the attack. There were 25 assault troops—each one part of Dozer's Battalion, all veterans of the New York City days and many battles since—the Cobra

Brothers, the Stallion crew of six, Dozer and himself. He was proud of them; proud to be serving with them. In one short month, they had squeezed in more training than a Green Beret would get in a year. Good teamwork usually was the most important factor of any military operation, and this bunch, he had to admit, knew about teamwork.

He hadn't slept the night before. Didn't need it. He spent the night spelling the guards and rechecking the weapons systems in the Sea Stallion. The last intelligence report he had received, sent by St. Louie, coded and forwarded to the Quebec fueling system by the "neutral" Fitzgerald, said that the captured ZAP pilots were still being held in the Government Building. The report also confirmed the prisoners were jailed on the floors near the top of the building and that the security on the building's top-floor helipad, was light.

He called the whole team together and briefed them once again. The Stallion would lift off first, exactly at noon, and, disguised as a lumber chopper, would fly right into the heart of the city. There, feigning engine problems if need be, it would wait, with the Strike Force hidden inside, until sunset when the Cobra Brothers would arrive and start their diversionary tactics.

Hunter had confidence in his plan. Surprise would be his major advantage, but he also knew that the Mid-Aks had rudimentary radar around the city, at best. And bad radar meant bad SAM capability. He was sure the diversionary action would catch someone's attention. The plan called for one of the Cobras to sneak into the harbor at wave-top height, and put two rockets into the side of a liquid natural gas holding tank near a docking facility that St. Louie's agents had pinpointed. The target was perfect. Not only were there no civilians around for miles, but the Mid-Aks had foolishly set up an army ammunition dump close by. If the Cobra made it—and its trip required a rather perilous journey into the harbor and up the Mystic River, Boston's main water flow that emptied into the ocean—a third of the city along with the Mid-Ak ammo dump would go up in smoke.

Hunter ordered the Stallion loaded up and soon the big chopper was lifting off from the island base. The Cobra Brothers waved as it ascended and turned south, toward the occupied Mid-Ak capital. He checked each detail of the plan once again with Dozer and the assault force's five officers, only then was he completely satisfied everyone was ready.

It didn't take a long convoluted explanation to the troopers as to why they were going to fight a thousand miles away from home. They knew what was at stake. Simply their way of life. Twenty-five had accompanied him on the rescue mission, but all 900 of Dozer's men had volunteered. When it came to fighting for freedom, one usually never had to look far for recruits.

The Stallion cruised down the rocky coast of the former state of Massachusetts, passing over many abandoned cities along the way. The true sinister nature of the Mid-Aks hit home as Hunter looked out of the chopper's window at the near-desolate landscape of Boston's North Shore. Even after the war, the area had been alive, vital, working for the good of the Northeast Economic Zone. Now, it was practically deserted. The 'Aks had made good on their promise to evacuate the populace from all the coastal cities near Boston, except for those unlucky souls who were slave laborers. The invaders' mentality dictated that all the coastal ports should be militarized to handle the seaborne trade. What they didn't count on—call it arrogance, call it stupidity—was that most civilized people were loathe to trade with the Middle Atlantic occupying force. It was like dealing with the devil. The Northeast Economic Zone was now the Northeast Depression Zone. Business was bad for the Mid-Aks and it showed.

Hunter could feel the slow burn again rise up within him as he looked at the empty cities below. The Mid-Aks can't even make a dictatorship work! Their problem was that they weren't geared toward holding and occupying territory. Their threat was based on military strength, with little or no regard for consolidating their gains, or for taking advantage of the spoils of war, no matter how ill-gotten they were. Even Ghengis Khan secured and kept alive the trade routes he conquered. The Mid-Aks didn't. They were in it simply for the blood-lust of war.

That's why Hunter planned to give them a dose of their own medicine . . .

The helicopter flew right by the once bustling, now almost abandoned Logan Airport, without so much as a call from the field's control tower. The Mid-Aks' lack of security was laughable. They passed right over SAM sites which appeared not to even be manned. Several jet fighters sat sleeping on the runway. The wreckage of a crashed airliner decorated one end of a landing strip—wreckage no one had bothered to clear away.

They approached the skyline of downtown Boston, then made a turn to the north. Below was a deserted shopping mall, its merchandise long ago stolen by the conquerors, its buildings reduced to burnt-out shells. Even its huge parking lot was cratered. But the Stallion pilots found a level space big enough to put the chopper down.

It was a clear late spring day, but no birds sang and the trees were blossoming only reluctantly. Even Nature hated the Mid-Aks, so it seemed. The once-colorful, *profitable* city was now covered in a dull, prevailing gray. It gave more than a few of the strike force the shivers, although it wasn't a cold day.

The troopers sat quietly inside the helicopter, each man going over the part he'd play once the mission got underway. Hunter sat in the cockpit with the pilots, simultaneously checking the time, the weather and the area around the shopping mall. As far as they could tell, there was no one around to see them land.

Suddenly, a Mid-Ak armored personnel carrier appeared in the little-used avenue next to the parking lot. It was speeding along as if on a routine patrol, when it slowed and then turned in their direction. There was a sharp, instantaneous crack as every trooper flicked the safeties off their guns all at once. No one spoke. Hunter used his hands to urge caution and calm, then pointed at two of the troopers who were given extra duties just in case this eventually rose.

The two Marines, named Russ and Stitch, were

natives of Maine. They looked like it, acted like it and, most important of all, spoke like it. Hunter had arranged for these two only to be dressed in typical down Mainer fashion—lumberjack boots, heavy jeans, plaid hunting shirts, baseball caps. They would serve as the first dodge for getting rid of the Mid-Aks. Should they fail, the Stallion's three GE Gatling guns would be sighted on the APC, a split-second push of the button away from spitting out deadly shells at the rate of 600 per second. A two second blast would evaporate the Mid-Ak vehicle and crew, but would also cause a commotion. Hunter knew the best tactic would be to talk their way out of it.

Russ and Stitch climbed out of the chopper, tool cases in hand, and pretended to head for the craft's tail section. They faked surprise when the APC pulled up.

Six Mid-Aks leaped out of the back. Another, this one an officer, appeared in the access hatch of the tank-like vehicle.

"What's going down here?" the officer said, as the Ak troops unshouldered their rifles and aimed them at Russ and Stitch.

"Chopper broke down," Russ said in a flawless Down Mainer accent. "Got to fix it."

"Why are you here?" the officer asked. "This is a restricted zone. You hillbillies could have been shot down by one of our SAM crews."

That's a laugh, thought Hunter as he watched the scene from the corner of one of the Stallion's smoked windows.

"Chopper broke down," Stitch chimed in, mimicking to the letter Russ's accent. "Didn't have no choice

306

where to land her."

"Well, looking at that piece of shit, it's a wonder you made it down here at all," the officer said, eyeing the seemingly bruised and battered flying beast. "Do you have your ID papers?"

"Papers?" Russ said, innocently. "Ain't got no papers. Don't need 'em at home."

"You goddamn lumber jockeys," the officer laughed. "When you gonna get civilized? Everyone needs ID papers to live in this region." He turned to his troops and said: "Search the helicopter."

Hunter bristled. He put his hand up, indicating to the gunner sitting at the Gatling guns' computer controls to stand by. "Don't screw it up boys," he whispered.

"Suit yourself," Stitch said, calmly stepping aside. "Nothing inside . . ."

"We'll see about that," the officer said.

". . . Except the barrels of pig grease," Russ said finishing his companion's sentence.

"Pig grease?" the officer asked, momentarily stopping his climb out of the vehicle.

"Innards," Stitch said. "Traded our lumber for twelve barrels. Strong stuff. Figure the smell might have clogged up the engine."

He and Russ broke into a perfectly spontaneous two second laugh, then returned the dour expressions to their faces. The officer turned slightly pale. These guys should get an Academy Award, Hunter thought.

The Mid-Aks troops looked to their leader for guidance. Search twelve barrels containing bloody pig muscle, marrow and intestines? Even the Mid-Ak officer couldn't order his men to do that.

307

"If there were some slaves around," the officer said, settling back down into his position, "I'd sure as shit have them search that craft."

He sniffed the air. "Christ! I can smell it already," he said, putting his hand up to his nose.

Talk about mind over matter, Hunter thought.

The Mid-Ak soldiers quickly did the same as their officer thumbed them back into the APC.

"Get that smelly piece of shit out of here, pronto!" he screamed at Russ and Stitch as the APC belched a cloud of black smoke and lurched away. "I don't want it here when I come back this way."

"Try our best," Russ said, with a smile and a wave.

Once the vehicle was out of sight, Russ and Stitch climbed back inside the Stallion to a muted round of applause from the strike force.

"Pig grease?" Hunter asked them, smiling. "What the hell *is* pig grease?"

"Beats the shit out of me," Russ shrugged, settling back down on his seat. "Closest I've ever been to a pig is eating bacon and eggs."

CHAPTER TWENTY-TWO

As the sun began to set, anticipation began to rise aboard the chopper. Each man checked his black combat jump suit for ammo, hand grenades and the other necessities of hand-to-hand combat. Hunter looked around the interior of the craft. The assault troops were ready, helmets on, faces blackened, guns loaded. The chopper crew was ready, the pilot rechecking his instruments, the co-pilot fine-tuning the radar, the gunners lovingly patting their muzzles and testing their computer terminals.

Hunter checked the sun, then gave a thumbs-up signal to the pilot. The mighty rotors on the chopper began to turn, slowly at first, then gaining momentum. Soon, they were a blur of speed. The helicopter started to shake slightly, then whine as the engine came up to speed.

Hunter shook each man's hand then nodded to the pilot. The chopper jerked once, then slowly ascended into the air.

Twenty miles off the coast of Boston, the two smaller Cobra gunships were streaking inland. They passed several ships who paid them no mind. Soon the outline of the city was visible. The sun was setting down in back of the skyscrapers which marked the downtown. At the entrance to the harbor proper. Cousin One waved to his partner and peeled off toward the skyscrapers. Cobra Two stayed over the water, soon picking up the twists and turns of the Mystic River tributary which connected the city to the Atlantic Ocean. Up ahead, using his infrared viewscope in the twinkling light of twilight, he could see his target—a large, orange fuel tank with the letters BOSTON GAS fading on its side. A ship was docked close by, its igloo-like compartments marking it as a LNG tanker. He thought he could make out an East European flag flying above it. "All the better," he smiled, as he pushed his MISSILE WAITING button on the fire control panel.

Meanwhile the other Cobra was up and over the city, heading for the Government Building. The square, 52-story bluish structure that still had the name of its former owners—Prudential—painted on its peak. Below, the Cobra Brother could see the streetlights of the city burning away, some traffic on the roads, mostly military, and a few people ambling down the main streets. There were SAM sites located throughout the area, as well as AA guns. But amazingly enough, no one paid any attention to his bright

310

red chopper as it made its way across the sky above the city.

He put the Cobra into a wide orbit high above the Government Building and waited. It didn't take long until he saw the familiar Sea Stallion heading toward him. A blink of the Stallion's landing lights was the signal he needed. He armed his TOW missiles and fired a short, test burst of his cannons. The waiting was over.

Hunter was squeezed into the cockpit of the big chopper as it approached the helipad atop the skyscraper. There was a token force of guards out on the roof. Hunter could see the charred remains of the rooftop communication shack that Jones had ordered destroyed the day the 'Aks first moved on Boston. Fifty-two stories below, he could see several Huey gunships, parked on the plaza next to the building. His memory of blasting the Mid-Aks' main helicopter force at Otis raced through his mind. "Must have missed a couple," he thought.

The Stallion was now hovering above the helipad, the Mid-Ak guards looking on impassively. Choppers probably touched down and took off from the building several times a day. There was no central flight control. Helicopters just came and went. The guards looked on the Stallion as just another visitor—although, as helicopters go, a fairly grubby one.

The Stallion brazenly set down. The assault troops were up and ready, fingers on triggers, eyes on the helipad door which they knew led down to the interior of the building. A Mid-Ak guard ducked as he ran over to the side of the chopper. Hunter slid the cargo door back. The soldier, expecting to see an interior as unkempt as the exterior of the craft, stood dumbfounded for an instant as he took in the banks of blinking computer lights, the three Gatling guns poised at the chopper windows and the 25 heavily armed troopers bracing to leap out of the aircraft.

"What the hell is going on here . . ." the guard said, reaching for his pistol. They were the last words he ever spoke. The nearest trooper pointed his M-16 at the man's forehead and squeezed off a shot. The guard's head exploded like a bloody egg.

"This is it!" Hunter said as he was the first to jump off the chopper. The other guards still looked confused as the assault troopers poured off the Stallion The 'Aks were cut down before they ever knew what was going on, the racket of the Stallion's blades and engine drowning out the noise of the assault team's rifles.

In a matter of seconds, the top of the roof was clear of Mid-Aks. The entire strike force was off the ship and most were gathered around the door which led down into the building. Others were at pre-determined station points around the roof, serving as lookouts. Off to the left, Hunter could see Cobra Brother II sweeping in to strafe the street below.

The strike force stood frozen, looking to him for the signal to move. He looked at his watch.

"5 . . . 4 . . . 3 . . . 2 . . . 1 . . . now!"

One second later, the sky to the north of them opened up. It appeared as if a geyser of bright red, fiery blood had suddenly boiled up from the nearby river and splattered to all sides. The sounds of the explosion came next, an incredible booming noise. A shock wave hit the building that very nearly knocked some of the troopers off their feet. Holding on in the hurricane-like wind, they strained to watch a huge mushroom of fire shoot straight up into the sky. The whole building shook as if it would crumble. The city was suddenly lit again as if it were high noon.

"Holy Christ!" Hunter whispered. Obviously, Cobra Brother II had fulfilled his mission.

"Go! Go! Go!" Hunter heard himself yelling and it was no sooner said than done. The helipad door was blown open and the strike force was pouring inside. Below, the Cobra I started his first strafing run. Hunter could hear the confusion begin in the street as he followed the troopers through the door.

Digger Foxx fell off his bed when the LNG tank six miles away went up. He was one of the captured ZAP pilots who had spent the last seven months locked in the same room, an office-like affair located on the 48th floor. He had heard the helicopter come in, but had paid it no mind. Choppers were constantly shuttling 'Ak officials on and off the top of the building. This one sounded no different. He had just pushed aside the evening's slop of a meal and was drifting off to sleep when the gas explosion occurred.

He quickly picked himself up off the floor and wiped a cut that had opened on his forehead. The building seemed to be swaying. He looked out the window only to see the blinding flash of the LNG going up. He was certain it was a nuclear bomb and he expected in the next moment to be swept away in the winds of the atomic blast. Good! he thought. At least I'll take all of these fucking 'Aks with me.

Suddenly, the door burst open. Digger expected either to see a Mid-Ak executioner or the Grim Reaper. Instead, the face in the door was familiar.

"Hunter!" Foxx yelled. "What the hell . . . ?"

"Digger, old boy," Hunter said, smiling. "We've come to spring you."

Then he was gone. Foxx could see the corridor was filled with heavily armed, black suited soldiers. He could hear gunfire further down the hall, and the noise of doors being broken down.

A trooper stopped at his door long enough to yell to him: "Get your ass up to the roof, pal!"

Foxx didn't have to be told twice. He was out the door and bounding up the steps in a matter of seconds.

On the street below, Mid-Ak functionaries and soldiers were hugging for cover as the bright red Cobra gunship turned to make another strafing pass. Cobra Brother I had already destroyed six troop trucks and one of the Huey gunships parked in the building's plaza. His missiles spent, he zoomed back down to street level and pulled a lever simply labeled FIRE. The front of the insect-like Cobra grew a long flickering tongue of flame. He slowed the ship up to a hover and, spinning in a tight, quick 360-degree

314

circle, he set everything and everyone in range on fire.

He lifted himself out of the circle of fire and roared off, turned and returned to puncture the street with cannon fire again.

The Cobra made six passes before anyone started shooting back.

Mid-Ak soldiers inside the Government Building recovered from the initial shock and started flooding up to the top floors. They were met by the assault force at the 47th floor lobby and a fierce gun battle broke out. Most of the pilots were released by this time—20 in all—plus some of the monkeys and MPs that were being held. The rescued were herded up to the helipad and packed aboard the waiting Sea Stallion.

Hunter was everywhere during the firefight. Shooting it out with the 'Aks in the 47th floor lobby, helping the wounded to the upper stories, even breaking out a window to shoot at a surprised 'Ak gun crew on the building next door.

By now Mid-Ak forces on the outside were starting to react. Anti-aircraft crews were unlocking their guns, thinking that with the intensity of the flame from the gas explosion and the strafing of the Cobra, that a full scale air raid was under way. The gun crews, two located on a skyscraper directly across the street from the Government House, began opening up at random, shooting at what they thought were aircraft passing over. When they realized they were shooting at ghosts they turned their attention to the hand-to-hand fighting that was raging on the top floors of the Government Building and clearly visible through the windows of the building.

The officer of one of the gun crews realized that the helicopter with its engine running on top of the building wasn't a Mid-Ak aircraft at all. He ordered his crew to turn the gun around and start blasting away. Other gunners were now also keying in on the top of the building. Two searchlights went up, their lazing beams highlighting the huge Sea Stallion chopper.

The gun crew officer was certain that his crew would zero in on the intruding chopper and blast it off the top of the building. But he heard a strange whirring noise behind him. When he turned to look, he was staring down the barrel of a flame tube on the nose of the Cobra gunship. He saw a spit of flame leap out of the muzzle then was aware that his clothes and those of his gun crew were suddenly engulfed in flames. He could clearly see the face of the helicopter pilot. It looked grim, fierce, determined. The next instant, he felt the sensation of his face melting away. There was no pain. He passed from life to death so quickly, his nerve endings were dispatched before the sensory messages reached the brain. A moment later he was little more than a pile of cinders blowing high above the streets of Boston.

The assault force located and freed the remaining ZAP monkeys and MPs. Then, their work done, the troopers started slowly moving back up toward the roof. Explosive experts left behind powerful delayed reaction bombs in their wake. All of the pilots and liberated prisoners were soon aboard the Stallion. Hunter would be glad later that he supercharged the engines, as there were nearly 80 people jammed into the Stallion's cabin.

Meanwhile, the Wingman and a force of six troopers were holding off a large force of Mid-Aks on the observation deck of the building. The deck was lit by ultra-violet light, giving a dark spooky feeling to the place. Tracer bullets flew back and forth as Hunter's small group pinned down the 'Aks with a continuous stream of fire. It was only when he was certain that all the prisoners were free and aboard the Stallion that he began moving up toward the roof himself.

The second Cobra had sped to the scene and was now adding fire to the conflagration that was the street below. Both small ships weaved back and forth, taking out AA guns that threatened the Sea Stallion, while continually strafing anything that moved near the Government Building.

Hunter finally reached the top floor, flipped his last grenade down the stairwell and bolted out onto the roof. The Sea Stallion was hovering by this time, troopers in the doorway were waving him along. The side gunners were blasting away with their M61 cannons at the Mid-Ak gun positions on the roofs around the Government Building. Bullets seemed to be flying everywhere as Hunter zigzagged across the helipad toward the chopper.

Suddenly, out of the night, yet another helicopter appeared. It was a Huey troop carrier, ferrying troops to the scene of the action. Its pilot, already committed to landing, was attempting to set the chopper down on the helipad just next to where the Sea Stallion hovered waiting to take off.

Someone aboard the Stallion pushed a button and all three of the GE Gatling guns locked onto the Mid-Ak chopper. Another button was pushed just as the first Mid-Ak troops were jumping off the Huey even as it was still five feet above the helipad. The Gatling guns opened up with their strange, buzzing sound and instantly cut the Huey into two sections. Half the ship came crashing down onto the helipad, its rotor spinning wildly, chopping up the troops that had just leaped from the stricken craft. The tail section of the Huey, its rear stabilizing propeller still twirling, went flying off the side of the building, plunging along its side and into a crowd of Mid-Ak troops below.

Hunter had to duck out the the way of the rotor pieces of the doomed helicopter, but now was up on his feet and running toward the Stallion once again. More Mid-Aks had reached the helipad door and were blasting away at the big chopper. The assault force gunners were returning the favor with a vicious stream of lead. Somewhere, someone had fired a shoulder-launched SAM and it streaked by, spraying the helipad with sparks and fuel exhaust and adding to the pandemonium on the roof of the building.

Hunter finally reached the door of the Stallion and the pilots prepared to lift off when something caught his eye. It was just a glint of light reflecting off a metal bar on the uniform of one of the building's defenders. It struck a note in his head, and he turned and stopped. Then, as the incredulous assault force looked on, Hunter dashed back across the helipad, dodging the flames of the burning Huey chopper and the blizzard of lead. He reached the man with the metal bar on his shoulder and started dragging him back across the pad toward the Sea Stallion.

The gunfire around them had increased twofold as more and more 'Ak gunners found the range. Finally, Hunter again reached the edge of the Stallion's door, and with the help of the troopers aboard, lifted the man's body onto the chopper. He then leaped just as the Stallion started to pull away, two troopers grabbing him by the seat of his pants in order to prevent him from falling to the streets below.

The ship was out away from the building and picking up speed as he was finally hauled aboard. Bullets were still zinging past them as the chopper's door was closed and secured. Only then did he stop to take a deep breath. It was the most intense combat he had ever experienced and it had seemed to have gone on for hours. Actually, the rescue mission had lasted less than 15 minutes.

The Cobras were now linked up and leading the way out of the burning city. The three choppers raced toward the open sea, reaching the harbor and lowering down to barely wave-top level. The harbor contained a number of Mid-Ak warships, targets of opportunity that Hunter just could not pass up. He ordered the Stallion's missile platform lowered, and the target acquisition system turned on. Instantly, bits of information started popping up on the video display terminals. Computer lock-on firing systems started firing the small, guided missiles at the anchored ships. Each missile packed a mighty wallop of HE3X explosive.

Targeted to hit each ship below the water line, a dozen missiles flew out independently and found their mark. Soon, after a dozen brilliant explosions, the bottom of Boston Harbor was home for a good part of the Mid-Ak occupying fleet.

The chopper force quickly left the land behind and were out in the safer confines of the Atlantic Ocean. Only then did Hunter turn his attention to the man he had dragged aboard. With a gang of troopers gathered around him, he turned the body over. The man was dead, a bullet had caught him in the throat. But it was his uniform that interested Hunter. It was green, not brown like the standard Mid-Ak soldier, and of a completely different texture.

Hunter began stripping the man's suitcoat off, then his shirt. The bars he wore on his collar indicated that the dead man was a captain. But a captain in what army? That's what Hunter wanted to know.

He ripped away the man's shirt collar and found a tag with the number 561 stitched in. He flipped the label over and then had his answer.

There was writing on the other side of the tag. Not English, as one might expect a Mid-Ak soldier's uniform to read.

"What the hell kind of writing is that?" one of the troopers asked. "Dixieland?"

"Nope," Hunter said, pushing the dead man away from him and concentrating on the writing on the collar. It wasn't any kind of language found on the continent, not naturally anyway. His mind went into its flashback mode. The Kalashnikov rifles they had found in New York City. The East European cargo

320

plane he'd sabotaged. The MIGs over Football City's Grand Stadium. None of that had convinced him before of Jones' grand conspiracy theory. But now he had the proof positive.

The label indicated the shirt had been sewn somewhere in the Ukraine. The man wearing it was a Russian.

CHAPTER TWENTY-THREE

They had pulled it off, with very little damage to
themselves. Three strike force members wounded was
the final toll, none of them seriously. They had
struck—hard—in the heart of the Mid-Ak empire and
left it burning. They had rescued a talented group of
pilots and ground personnel and taught the Middle-
Atlantics a lesson they wouldn't soon forget. There
was nothing more valuable than good security. It was
a blow that the 'Aks wouldn't recover from for some
time.

Hunter found himself thinking about Jones as the
helicopters raced north, back toward their hiding
place off the coast of Maine. The general would have
approved of the mission, especially its outcome. He
could almost hear the old man's voice, whispering in
his ear: "Good work, Major. Detonating that LNG
facility was the next best thing to nuking the goddamn
place." Looking back through the chopper's window
toward Boston, he could still see a glow over the
horizon as the city burned. "This one's for you,
General," he said quietly.

They made their way back to the small island where

they grudgingly gave the Russian a proper, if hasty, burial. Hunter was now convinced, beyond a shadow of a doubt, that the Soviets were involved in a destabilizing effort on the continent. He may have rationalized away the Kalashnikovs in New York City, the East European plane at the Aerodrome and the MIGs over Football City. But now he had solid proof. Logically, there could only be one reason a Russian soldier would be protecting the headquarters of the Mid-Ak occupying force—a deep concerted agreement between the two evil hierarchies so involved that lowly Russian troops were now guarding Middle-Atlantic installations. Was it any different in New Chicago? He thought of little else during the trip back to the Aerodrome.

He was glad to see the rescued pilots and monkeys, most of them close friends from his days with ZAP. He explained his plan to provide Football City with an air force to counter the threat from New Chicago. The Family, he told them, was closely, if secretly, allied with the Mid-Aks, and by implication, the Russians. With no prodding they unanimously agreed to join the fight. Nearly a year in Mid-Ak captivity had neither dulled their courage, enthusiasm or, on a deeper level, their patriotism. Most were former military anyway who yearned for the old days. A fight for freedom was just what they needed after being cooped up for so long.

The three helicopters touched down at the Aerodrome just before dawn. The strike force and the rescued pilots, monkeys and MPs were exhausted, but exhilarated. Fitzgerald was waiting for them, cigar in mouth, coffee cup in hand. He did a little jig when he heard the attackers had taken such painful toll on the Middle-Atlantic.

"Drinks are on me!" he yelled to the returning warriors as they emerged from the helicopters in the pre-dawn light. He had set up a victory banquet for them at one of The Aerodrome's swankiest clubs. Despite the early morning hour, he transported the strike force—still dressed in their black fatigues—and the rescued to the club where a full sized jazz band played and an army of cooks, bartenders and waitresses were standing by to serve the returning heroes and the freed prisoners.

Sitting with Hunter and Dozer, Fitzgerald urged them to give him every last detail of the mission, right down to the number of delayed-fuse bombs the strike force had left behind. The Irishman was clearly enjoying himself listening to the story of the stunning raid.

"You're not acting much like a neutral now," Hunter mockingly scolded him, as the early bird Welcome Back party got into full swing.

"In business, I'm neutral," Fitzgerald said, smiling. "In me heart, I'm with ya all the way."

"Well, I don't know how much business the 'Aks will be doing in the near future," Dozer said, draining a Bloody Mary and starting in on his second plate of scrambled eggs. "Not unless they plan to have a fire sale."

"We've heard from St. Louie, again," Fitzgerald said, pulling a yellow sheet of telex paper from his pocket and passing it to Hunter. "It came in around midnight."

Hunter read the message: FAMILY AIR RAID

EARLIER TONIGHT ON OUR AIRFIELD. HEAVY LOSSES. CHICAGO TROOP BUILD-UP REPORTED.

"Things are getting worse out there," he said, stuffing the message into his pocket.

"Well, you've accomplished almost half your objective," Fitzgerald said. "You've got yourself some fine pilots and ground people. Now all you have to do is get them some planes to fly."

"That's the hard part," Hunter nodded.

"Aye, there's not much on the open market any more," Fitz agreed. "Wright-Patterson is down to selling World War II and Korean War stuff. Those planes could probably fly one mission, maybe two, then they'd plow themselves into the earth and stay there."

"St. Louie has been trying to hire on free-lancers," Dozer said. "But no one wants the job. They're all convinced that The Family will win this one, and no free-lancer wants to be on the losing side."

"Yes," Fitz said. "It's *very* bad for business."

The three friends were silent for a moment, then Fitz perked up. "So what's your next step, Hawker? Mio and Aki are standing by."

Hunter finished off his breakfast and poured another drink. "Later," he said.

With that, the airman stood and, clinking his spoon against a glass, got the attention of everyone in the banquet hall.

"I'm glad to see we all made it," he told them. "Please enjoy yourselves for the next five days. That's how long we've got before the next mission. And this one will be more dangerous than our excursion to

Boston. And when it's over, we go to Football City and that will be the biggest, most dangerous battle of all."

The hall was completely silent. Every eye was on him, taking in every word he had to say.

"We have dangerous times ahead, but the important thing to remember is that we stick together. Together, we can do it. Together, we can put the hurt on the Family just like we did to the 'Aks. We can put the hurt on anyone, whether they're from this continent. Or any other. We can make sure that if anyone tries to deprive us or anyone else of their rights, their basic freedoms, then they will have to think twice. Because they won't know where we'll be, or when we'll strike. We proved it in Boston. We'll prove it again very soon. Word travels fast these days. People will know who we are.

"So, have a good time now. There are plenty of bars here at The Aerodrome. Eat up. Drink up," he paused and smiled toward Fitzgerald, ". . . and tell them to put it all on Fitzie's tab."

A look of mock horror came across the Irishman's face as the assembled men laughed and applauded.

"Now," Hunter said to Fitzgerald and Dozer, his speech over, "I have to go grow a beard."

With that, the airman drained his glass and disappeared from the hall.

"What the hell does he mean by that?" Fitzgerald asked the bewildered Marine captain.

No one saw Hunter for the next four days. He was holed up in the cheap hotel room located above the

Broken Wing bar, on the periphery of The Aero-drome's territory. He left orders that no one—not even Fitzgerald, or Dozer or Aki and Mio—should disturb him. He asked only that any reports from St. Louie should be delivered immediately to him care of the bartender downstairs.

Those messages started coming in at a rate of one every two hours. Fitzgerald promptly summoned one of his most trusted officers who shuttled the messages back and forth, leaving them with the seedy-looking barkeep at the saloon beneath Hunter's room.

The dispatches told a story of a deteriorating situa-tion for Football City. War with New Chicago was now inevitable. St. Louie's agents reported the Family was completely mobilized and had begun stationing its troops near the city's extensive railroad yards. The Family leaders, headquartered in the ultra skyscraper once known as the Sears Building, had been making huge purchases of oil lately. They were stocking up to feed an army that would move south to Football City by rail, river and road.

The MIG-21s had attacked the city twice more since the raid that destroyed a third of Football City's airfield. St. Louie was trying to purchase as much SAM equipment as possible, but he was certain that the Family was intimidating most of the war suppli-ers. His attempts to get free-lance fighter pilots was going no better. Convoy duty was paying even better than ever. No pilot wanted to lose his plane—or his life—in a war between two cities that in the grand scheme of things, apparently meant nothing.

Football City itself was all but closed down. The party-party atmosphere was put on hold as the army prepared the city for war. Most of the population left after the first attack on the Grand Stadium and never returned. Defensive emplacements were being erected along the western shore of the Mississippi River, the natural barrier between Football City and the invaders from the north.

One of the last reports sent to Hunter gave the Football City intelligence corps' estimate that the Family would attack across the Mississippi within the next three weeks.

Thus was the situation when Hunter emerged from his self-imposed exile . . .

On the fifth day, Fitzgerald and Dozer got a message to meet Hunter in the Broken Wing. The Irishman and the Marine immediately drove to the bar, taking the necessary precaution to go well-armed, and found Hunter sitting at the same table Fitz had used to discuss the mission to The Pitts. The rest of the bar was empty.

They were shocked at Hunter's appearance. He had shaved his head and was sporting a five-day-old scruffy beard. An earring dangled from his left lobe. His fingers were covered with gaudy rings. He was dressed completely in leather and wearing dark glasses.

They were at first almost reluctant to approach their friend. Hunter's boyishly handsome looks were long gone. The man who sat staring at him from the table looked cruel, mean, ruthless.

Of course, that was the whole idea.

"What's the matter, boys," Hunter said, the old

smile returning instantly. "Too good to drink with me?"

"Hawker," Fitzgerald cried, pulling up a chair. "What have you done to yourself?"

"All part of the plan, Fitz." Hunter said, motioning the bartender to bring them a bottle. "What's the latest from St. Louie?"

"Nothing," Dozer told him. "Not a word since last night."

Hunter looked plainly worried. "Things are getting worse, fast. We're going to have to move quickly."

Fitzgerald almost looked embarrassed. "You know I'll help as much as I can," he said. "But I have to at least do it behind the scenes. I can maybe lend you a few ground troops. But I can't send my Thuds to Football City as much as I'd like to."

"I understand, Fitz," Hunter said sincerely. "If capitalism doesn't survive, what good is it if anything else does?"

"Aye," Fitzgerald said, a little sadly.

"I would ask you to do me a couple of favors though."

"Ask away."

"Well, I'll need an old plane and a good pilot, one of your guys, to come with me tomorrow night," Hunter explained.

"You got it."

"Then, I'd like you to hire out a couple of good fighter-bombers. Free-lancers. Someone who specializes in ground support. Someone we can trust."

"Got just the team," Fitz said, smacking his lips. "The Ace Wrecking Company. Two F-4 Phantoms out of Buffalo. Flyboy that goes by the name of Captain

Crunch runs them. They've helped me out in the past. He won't chicken out like these other free-lancers."

"Trustworthy?" Dozer asked.

"*Very*," Fitz answered. "Crunch's real name is O'Malley. His mother and papa are from the Old Sod. He's a good egg and his guys are top-notch."

"Okay," Hunter agreed. "Contract him. Tell him he's working for me, with the promise of a lot of business down the road."

"You got it," Fitz said.

"What else?" Dozer asked.

"I'll need the strike force primed and ready to go in two days' time," Hunter said.

"They're already ready," the Marine said. "They've been itching for action for three days. Waiting on you, I might add."

"I'm glad to hear it," Hunter said. "Tell them to get the Stallion warmed up. Also Fritz, think a few of your boys might want to make some overtime?"

"I'll make sure they do. How many do you need?"

"Two dozen," Hunter replied. "Plus a couple of choppers, Hueys if you can spare them."

"Again, you got it," Fitz said, calling for more drinks.

Dozer smiled. "Now Hawk, are you going to let us in on your plan or not?"

Hunter smiled and put his glasses back on. "You guys got about a couple of hours to kill?"

The next night, Hunter and a pilot named Clyde were landing an old C-119 Flying Boxcar on an abandoned stretch of the Pennsylvania Turnpike.

From there, they had a two hour walk to the nearest town, appropriately called Ruff Creek. Sitting on a bend in the Ohio River, Ruff Creek was the point of civilization nearest to the Stukas' hidden pirate base. It was little more than a collection of food stores, a handful of crowded homes and one saloon. The town would be the first stop in Hunter's outlandish plan to get St. Louie his air force.

Clyde was a good guy and an able pilot. He fit the bill, appearance-wise. Hunter knew they couldn't walk into a place like Ruff Creek, looking or acting normal. Thus his exile to not only change over his appearance, but also his karma. He had to think like a pirate, or someone of their ilk, to pull this off. Clyde already looked that way. He was rotund for a stick jockey, too big to make the grade if he were in the old time military. But those kind of things were long forgotten these days. He too, was bald, although quite naturally. A short, black goatee gave him a sinister look—just the effect Hunter wanted.

They reached the edge of Ruff Creek just after dawn. There hidden in the trees, they waited, slapping bugs, as the sun climbed the sky. Sure enough, around noon, a half track roared across the small bridge leading into the tiny town and parked outside the only barroom. A half dozen Stukas climbed out and stormed inside the place.

"Here to drink their noontime meal," Hunter said to Clyde. "Just like I thought they would."

They waited another two hours. More people drifted in and out of the bar, but the pirates remained. When Hunter figured the bandits were well on their way to being greased, he and Clyde made their move.

Some of the biggest events in history were started in motion by the slightest of moves. A word dropped here, a shot fired there. Hunter, himself a creature of history, planned to set an event in motion that he hoped would roll all the way from Ruff Creek to Football City and beyond.

He and Clyde walked out of the woods, across the bridge and into the saloon. Clyde was packing a sawed-off shotgun slung casually over his shoulder, and Hunter displayed a borrowed Uzi. No one even turned to give them a second look as they ambled to a table and motioned the waitress. The six pirates sat at the bar, drinking up a storm and grunting to each other in typically angry tones. There were several other patrons in the place, each one giving the bandits a wide berth.

"What'll it be?" the sulking waitress asked.

"The day's stew and a bottle," Hunter said.

"New in town?" she asked.

"You might say that," Hunter answered. "Any more like you around?"

She eyed him suspiciously.

"Looking for trouble?" she asked.

"Not trouble. Action," Hunter said with emphasis. "We'll pay for it, too."

She looked at both of them. "I'll bring your stew," she said then retreated into a room in back of the bar that served as a kitchen.

She reappeared after a while and gave them a bottle of cheap whiskey, two bowls and a pot of stew. Hunter threw two silver coins on the table as pay. The food was the standard fare in this part of the country, Hunter surmised after one bite. A few pieces of meat

332

swimming around a heavy gravy with chunks of vegetables. Both he and Clyde were legitimately hungry, so they ate heartily. Two glasses of whiskey apiece put a glow into the otherwise dreary saloon.

Meanwhile the pirates continued drinking, barely speaking to each other by the time darkness fell. A few more people entered the bar—shady characters every one of them—and moved to its darkened corners. Dim red and yellow lights were switched on, flickering occasionally as the generator out back struggled to produce the needed electricity.

Finally, several women appeared from the kitchen, looking not in the world like waitresses. They were wearing hiked-up skirts and low-cut blouses. Their faces were painted with rouge and their hair dyed almost impossible colors.

"World's oldest profession," Hunter leaned over and said to Clyde.

"Amen, brother," Clyde replied.

Two of the women immediately homed in on the pirates, but two more broke off and approached Hunter and Clyde. One, a blonde, was extremely attractive, in a slutty kind of way. She spoke to Hunter.

"I hear you boys are new in town," she cooed. "Can we sit down?"

"Sure!" Clyde nearly burst out. He had his eye on her companion, a tall redhead.

"I'm Carla," the blonde said as the women joined them. "And this is Kitty."

"Ladies," Hunter said with a nod.

"Are you guys pilots?" Carla asked. Her hand was already resting on Hunter's knee.

"Up from Florida," he told her. "Had some engine trouble."

"Oh," Carla purred. "That's too bad. Staying a while?"

Hunter took this cue to pull out a thick bag of coins.

"Maybe," he said, looking into her green eyes. She *was* pretty. Her blond hair looked natural, her teeth crooked but not unattractively so. She had a fabulous if skinny shape and a lovingly wide mouth.

Her hand was slowly moving up to his crotch. "Can I have a drink?" she asked.

"Be my guest," he said.

A waitress cruised by with two extra glasses. Hunter noticed that one of the pirates was watching them out of the corner of his eye.

A few drinks and some small talk later, Carla's hand finally made it to between Hunter's legs.

He leaned over and whispered to her. "How much and where?"

"Five real silver pieces," she smiled. "Seven for the bigboy. We got a place upstairs. Interested?"

He was, and in more ways than one.

The room was small and cheap. Just outside the window, the dim neon sign for the bar was flashing on and off. They'd been horizontal for an hour. She was gasping with delight. "You've got great hands, fly-boy."

"Need them in my profession."

A look of interest flashed across her face. "What do you do, honey? What are you flying up from Florida?"

He looked at her in the dim, flickering light. She was too pretty for this line of work.

"You into *blow-zeen*?" he asked. "Like in cocaine?"

She stopped stroking his bald head. "You've got some?" she asked excitedly.

"Have I?" he laughed. "Got a whole plane filled with it!"

"You do?" she asked, eyes wide, licking her lips. "We can only get it around here when those asses Stukas decide to get laid for real. That's how they pay us."

Interesting, Hunter thought.

She snuggled closer to him. "I'm real good on coke," she whispered.

"Sorry," he said, "Coke's for my boss. I just got to figure a way to get it to him."

"I thought you said you were flying it up from Florida, honey."

"I was, until the radiator went on the old crate we were using," he said with conviction. "Now we can't fly it more than five miles before we have to take it down again and fill the water tanks. That's why we're sitting in a shitty burg like this. We're following the river as far as we can to New Chicago."

"You working for the Family?" she asked, a trace of amazement in her voice.

"You know too much already, babe."

She tried again to snuggle close. "Come on," she breathed in his ear. "Give Carla some coke and she'll send you to heaven."

An odd choice of words, he thought.

"Sorry. No way," he said, getting up and putting his shirt on. He took out a handful of coins and put them on the bed.

"See ya around," he said, walking out the door. "C'mon Clyde. Time to go."

He could hear Clyde huffing and puffing in the next room. The sound was followed by a few curses then the unmistakable sound of a belt buckle being done up.

"Pay her and let's split," he called.

Clyde opened the door and joined him in the hall. Hunter gave him the thumbs-up sign. Clyed winked and nodded.

"Mission accomplished," he said.

They were quickly down the back stairs of the building, across the bridge and into the woods. At just about the same time, Carla was whispering the word "Coke," into the ear of one of the Stukas sitting at the bar.

CHAPTER TWENTY-FOUR

The engines on the old C-119 spit once, coughed a cloud of black smoke then kicked to life. Clyde brought the engines to trim and wiggled his flaps. They groaned in response. Hunter couldn't have found a better crate to pass off as a drug-carrying flying shitbox, he thought.

It was the day after Hunter and Clyde had set the table at the saloon in Ruff Creek. Now, next to the Flying Boxcar sat the Sea Stallion, brought in under the cover of darkness to the stretch of Pennsylvania highway that was 20 miles south of Ruff Creek and now glistening in the pre-dawn light. The 7th Cavalry strike force, their breaths like smoke in the cool, spring morning air were dressed in clean, black fatigues. They sat around the big chopper cleaning their weapons and applying charcoal to their faces. To a man they were in high spirits, if anxious ones. Most of them wanted to get this phase of their mission over with so they could return to Football City, where many had families and loved ones, and fight a more tangible enemy. They had come a long way since riding the *JFK* over from Europe.

Two jet black Hueys waited next to the Sea Stallion. Two squads of Fitzgerald's best troops—Territorial Guardsmen—complemented by the original ZAP MPs, waited inside. The Guardsmen were dressed in their standard World War II-style uniforms, complete from their tin pot hats to their GI boots. Volunteers all, Fitzgerald promised his men an extra full month's pay and a bottle of Scotch for going on the mission. The MPs, just lately sprung from prison, were ready for anything. Hovering overhead nearby were the Cobra Brothers, on the lookout for any unwanted guest to the early morning confab.

Parked further down the long straight of highway were two identical-looking jet fighters. They were the F-4 Phantoms known as The Ace Wrecking Company. Commanded by Captain Crunch O'Malley, the two fighter-bombers and the four-man crew, had hired out for special missions—ground support, air superiority, convoy duty—almost since the dawning of the New Order. Both planes were decorated in lettering reminiscent of an oldtime circus train. "No Job's Too Small, We Bomb Them All," was the motto painted on the side of each, an impressive "1" and "2" designating the jets' tail fins.

Parked at the very end of the highway-turned-runway was Hunter's F-16. Red, white, blue and waiting, it was bombed up and ready to go. One of the Crunch pilots had flown it down for him, a favor he greatly appreciated. It was like seeing an old friend again—a friend that had been neglected for too long. He was soon to change that . . .

Hunter conferred with Captain Crunch, and, their plan straight, gave the signal for the strike force to get ready. He climbed into the C-119 beside Clyde and started to taxi. The F-4s followed close behind. The assault troopers gave him the thumbs-up sign as he passed the Stallion and started his take-off roll. Phase Two was well underway.

"The Stukas will probably need more than a hooker's word that a snowbird is coming through," he told Clyde once the Flying Boxcar was airborne. "That means it's up to us to convince them. Once we do, they'll be licking their noses trying to get us."

He checked behind him just in time to see the Crunch jets take off. They would immediately climb to 50,000 feet, high above the pirates' rinky-dink radar, and orbit there, providing air cover just in case a stray bandit jet detected the C-119—that was, before Hunter wanted them to.

He steered the old plane toward the north.

"So first we've got to rattle the town a little," he said, sighting the small village sitting on the bend in the Ohio. "Hand on . . . "

He put the old plane into a dive, pulling it up at barely treetop level. The C-119 engines, devoid of the luxury of mufflers, were screaming with a roar that would wake the dead—or the dead drunk.

Two of the town's seedier residents were sitting on the steps of the saloon, suffering from chronic hangovers and waiting for the bar to open so as to treat the condition properly. The sun was just peeking through

339

the pine trees in the east when they heard a low, dull drone. It got louder and closer with every second. The men had just enough time to cover their ears.

They looked up to see the big gray hulk of a plane pass wildly over the center of the town. It was so low, it clipped the top of a chimney on the building across the street, showering them with a load of red bricks and debris. Then, with a mighty roar that shattered many of the town's remaining windows, the plane disappeared over the trees to the northwest.

That done, Hunter steered the aircraft northeast. Within a minute he was looking down on starkly familiar terrain. Trees, hills and rock. That was it. They were over Stuka territory. Up ahead the hidden base lay. It was even hard to see in the daytime, the shadows of the pine forest surrounding it, bathing it in a protective shadow of darkness. It made no difference to Hunter; he could have flown back to the place blindfolded.

Again, he dropped down as low as possible and gunned the engines. Clyde was sitting with a firm grip on the suicide handle, a smile chiseled on his face. This Hunter was an incredible pilot, but also a crazy man, he was convinced. Buzzing a pirates' base like this was like kicking nestful of hornets.

Of course, in Hunter's mind, that was the idea.

A half dozen lowly Stuka sentries on guard duty were the first to see the Flying Boxcar heading toward their base. Huddled in the single watchtower, they had all just woken up. They knew the trick of being a guard for the Stukas was just to wake up before the pilots did. It was an easy life because, except for three prisoners who escaped a few weeks ago, nothing ever happened. Few people who crashed or were forced down at the base ever lived long enough to tell anyone. So it added up to endless days and cheap-whiskey nights.

But now something was on the horizon. The low drone of the approaching engines arrived a half minute before the airplane itself. When it came into view, they saw it was big and silver and flying low. It couldn't be just another captured airplane the pirates were herding home, because a quick count of the fighter jets on the runway revealed that all the Stukas were accounted for.

Yet this odd-looking plane was heading right for the base. The situation had never come up before; the guards really didn't know what the hell to do. Finally, when it looked like the plane wasn't going to swerve from its path, one of them pushed a button which set off an air raid siren.

Sluggo was the new pirate leader. He had just recently replaced the deposed and deceased Jaws as top man. He was in the middle of an opium-induced hangover when the siren went off. The sound echoes strangely about his filthy living quarters.

"Gawd damn guards," he muttered, lifting his soporific body off the cot and walking to the window. "I'll cut them up if they woke me up this early for nothing."

He looked out the window and immediately saw the C-119. It was coming in low, its engines sounded like they were straining and one of them was smoking slightly. Engine overheat was the first thing to pop into his mind. The next thing was a conversation he had had with one of his lieutenants some time in the drug-filled swirl of the night before. A whore, Carla, had told his boys that a snowbird was passing through the area, trying to make its way up to New Chicago. It was supposed to have had a broken radiator. Had to stay by the river. Carrying a half ton of cocaine.

"Bingo!" Sluggo laughed. He smacked his lips. The plane he saw pass over the pirate base with a roar was so wobbly, he knew it had about five more miles max before it would have to set down. The likeliest spot, probably in the valley on the other side of Stuka Mountain. If he could get his ground troops mobilized, they might be able to get it while it was still down.

The whole base was up and awake with the blaring of the klaxon. Sluggo, barely zipped into his pants, was shoving his men onto the big Deuces and pointing them toward the road leading to the valley.

"There's an old shitbox plane, down in the valley!" he was screaming at his underlings, "It's filled with blow. Get it! Get it!"

One pilot ran up to him a guy named Rat.

"I'll go up and shoot the mother down," he said, running toward one of the Stukas F-100 Super Sabres.

Sluggo just managed to grab him by the collar of his leather flight suit.

"What do you have?" Sluggo yelled at him. "Dog-shit for brains? You shoot that goddamn plane down and that blow is scattered to the winds! Those snowbird pilots will dump it before they let us get them in the air. You know that. Now get in the Gawd damn truck and play soldier!"

By this time a small caravan of pirates—guards, ground mechanics and pilots, a hundred in all—was wending its way down the road toward the valley. A skeleton force of 50 were left behind to watch the store.

Sluggo was in the lead truck and seven followed behind. They reached the bottom of the mountain and had a clear look into the valley. There, through spyglasses, Sluggo saw his prey. Sitting near a bend in the Ohio River about a mile away was the C-119, its two crew members feverishly trying to fill the radiator on its right engine.

The pirate convoy lurched forward and started to race toward the plane. But just as they were closing in on it, the pilot had its engines going and the silver beast began to taxi. By the time the bandits reached the bend in the river, the C-119 had taken off.

"Shit!" Sluggo yelled. "Someone get me a map!"

A map was instantly produced and Sluggo pored over it. The next likely landing spot for the plane was 12 miles to the north, on a stretch of highway that ran close to a tributary of the Ohio.

"Stay in your trucks!" Sluggo yelled to his troops. "Stay in your fucking trucks! We're moving! We're moving!"

The pirate column pushed on. They kept the Flying Boxcar in view most of the time. It was following the twists and turns of the river, flying low and slow and trying to preserve its coolant as long as possible.

343

"Ha!" Sluggo yelled, wishing he had a beer to drink for breakfast. "We got him next time!"

The plane was flying so slowly Sluggo's column could see the straight patch of highway just about the same time the pilots of the C-119 did.

"Yahoo!" Sluggo was yelling wildly, his head, neck and half body hanging out of the window of the truck. "We do some blow-zeen tonight!"

Sure enough the C-119 set down on the highway, two miles down the road from the advancing pirate convoy.

"Go! Go! Go!" Sluggo was yelling, the driver of his truck flooring the accelerator on the already speeding truck. The pirates in the back were being unmercifully bounced around as the Deuce careened down the long-deserted highway.

But again, Sluggo would be denied. Just as the pirates closed in, the pilot gunned his engines and the plane was airborne again.

"Jesus!" Sluggo yelled, shaking his fist at the sky. "You mother! I'll get you!"

"Hey, boss," Sluggo's driver had the guts to suggest. "Why don't we get back to the field and get a couple of planes up to follow him?"

If Sluggo was armed, he would have shot the man. "I'm surrounded by morons," he said. "How far away do you think he'd be by the time we turned around and went all the way back there? In another 50 clicks, he's over the Death Children's turf. And we've lost him. He knows we're after his ass, now. We got him next time he comes down!"

Sluggo studied his map again. There was an abandoned airfield 15 miles away, just off the highway. It would be a natural landing place for the snowbird, because it was next to a lake that was fed by the Ohio River.

"That's it!" Sluggo said. "We got him now. I can taste that blow right now!"

The column pressed on, breaking the old 55 miles per hour speed limit on the highway by plenty in an all-out effort to reach the next landing spot for the snowbird.

Twenty minutes later, the pirate convoy reached the old airfield. Sitting at the end of the runway was the elusive C-119, one of its engines smoking heavily.

"Up yer nose with a rubber hose!" Sluggo yelled upon seeing the apparently disabled plane. "He burnt the engine right off the old bird. Now it's ours for the picking."

He ordered his driver to floor the truck and soon the nine pirate vehicles were racing across the wide-open field in a helter-skelter motion, each one intent on getting to the plane first.

The bandits were too busy trying to feed their insatiable drug habits to notice the helicopter partially hidden in the woods on the other side of the lake . . .

Despite the breakneck race, Sluggo's truck was the first to reach the C-119. He held up his hand, and all the other pirate trucks reluctantly screeched to a halt about fifty yards from the plane.

"Now listen up, you boneheads!" he said, climbing on the hood of the Deuce. "Let's not forget who's the

345

top man around here. I say who gets dibs on the any blow inside that plane."

"What about us!?" a pirate named Zonk yelled. "We want some too!"

His comment was greeted with a chorus of "Me, too!" from the other pirates.

Sluggo looked out on the 100 or so bandits. "Hey!" he yelled. "When we iced old Jaws, you guys were sucking up to me like no one's business. Now, if anyone here wants to go where old Jaws went, then he can just step his ass forward right now!"

The pirates were silent—so silent, if they listened hard enough, they could have heard the sound of two jets approaching . . .

Sluggo knew no one would call his bluff. He looked out on the gang of pirates, ground crew guys mostly. It never failed to amaze him that guys so stupid knew how to fix a supersonic jet fighter. They were like mice. They liked to be led.

"Okay," he yelled, jumping down from the hood. "That's better. Now, me, Rat, Mal and Eddie are going inside the plane. The rest of you guys wait here."

Again, a sullen silence fell over the bandits. It was almost quiet enough to hear the two F-4s heading their way . . .

Sluggo climbed inside the plane, his .45 drawn. It was filled with large bales, 50 or more, all tied tightly with bale and heavy duct tape.

"No one home," he said, putting his gun back in his belt and drawing out a Bowie knife. "Those flyboys are long gone. They'll never be able to show their faces anywhere again after losing this much of the Family's blow."

"Quick, Sluggo, rip one open," Mal the pirate said after following the top pirate into the otherwise empty plane. "Let's see what we got."

"It's got to be pure," Rat said, actually salivating at the thought of all that cocaine. "The Family doesn't buy stuff that's been stepped on."

"I'll step on you, if you don't shut your mouth," Sluggo said, threatening to slap Rat on the side of the head.

Sluggo gently punctured one of the bales and a thin stream of white powder flowed out. He reached down with a cupped hand and captured a pile. Wearing a toothy grin, his eyes closed, he put the powder up to his mouth and tasted it.

A look of horror came across his face.

"What the fuck!" he screamed. "This is sugar!"

"What!" Rat screamed as he lunged at another bale, cutting it open and tasting it for himself. He immediately spit out the substance. "It *is* fucking sugar!"

"We've been screwed!" Sluggo screamed.

"Hey! Listen!" the pirate named Eddie said, cocking his ear toward the plane's door. "What's that noise?"

The four pirates froze. It was a high whining noise. Getting louder. They looked out at the rest of the pirates, who had also heard the sound.

As they watched, one of the pirates out in the field shouted something and pointed to the northeast. Instantly, the gang started to scatter.

Sluggo jumped from the plane just in time to see the two F-4s of The Ace Wrecking Company bearing down on the open field. Each plane dropped two cannisters. Sluggo knew they were filled with napalm. He also knew they were sitting ducks . . .

The four napalm bombs exploded simultaneously, dispersing a tidal wave of flaming gasoline jelly all over the field and the desperately fleeing pirates. More than half the bandits were incinerated where they stood. The flames engulfed the pirates' trucks and the C-119, trapping Sluggo and the other three bandits.

The F-4s climbed out and swung back around for another pass. This time they came in with cannons blazing, picking off the remnants of the pirate force, sometimes two or three at a clip. The two fighter-bombers went around for a third time, and managed to pick off several more pirates, before streaking off toward the south.

In the woods across from the small lake, a Huey helicopter started its engine and slowly began to climb.

"That's a doggone pity," Clyde said, looking at the aftermath of the sudden, deadly effective air strike. "I kind of liked that old Flying Boxcar."

"Yeah," Hunter, sitting beside him, said. "It's a real shame."

Most of the fifty pirates left behind at the Stuka base went back to sleep almost immediately after

Sluggo's ill-fated column left in search of the snow-bird. The day had dawned bright, hot and sunny, and outside was no place to be with a hangover, which the majority of the pirates were suffering from. Most just drifted off, with nothing much else to do, to wait for Sluggo to return and portion out the cocaine.

Back on the Pennsylvania Turnpike section turned runway, the F-4s of The Ace Wrecking Company were being re-armed. The Sea Stallion and one of the black Hueys were warming up, their complements of strike force ready and waiting inside. High above, the gigantic C-5A Galaxy orbited.

The second black Huey landed and Hunter and Clyde jumped out. They shook hands and headed for their assigned stations; Clyde to the Sea Stallion, Hunter to warm up the F-16.

His plane was ready to go in less than a minute. His six cannons were fully loaded. On his wings were four 500-pound iron bombs, plus four air-to-ground anti-personnel missiles. The F-4s carried similar loads. The Stallion's Gatling guns were twisting and turning as their operators put them through a last effectability check and the big chopper's loaded missile platform was lowered and raised once to make sure everything was in working order.

Hunter saw the strike force was ready. He ran through one last instrument check in his cockpit, then started the F-16 on its take-off roll. He lifted off smoothly, the same old excitement running through his body as the plane broke the bonds of earth. It was good to be flying the '16 again. He really felt nowhere as much at home as in the cockpit of the remarkable

349

fighter.

In quick succession, the rest of the strike aircraft took off. The F-4s were quickly airborne and riding in formation with the '16 in the lead. The Stallion lifted off, followed by the Hueys and the Cobra Brothers. The five choppers fell into formation, with the Cobras in front, the Stallion in the middle and the Hueys in the rear, and turned to follow the fighter jets heading north.

On the steps of the saloon in Ruff Creek, the two town drunks sat, still picking pieces of chimney brick out of their hair. The day was getting hot and they wished the bar owner would wake up and open for business.

They had all but forgotten about the crazy pilot who had severed the chimney across the street with his low flying antics. Probably the Stukas again, they had reasoned in their hungover minds, chasing some poor bastard out of the sky. Someone should stand up to those assholes some day, they had said. Put an end to the bandits' harassing of the Creekers and stealing of all the whores.

Suddenly, they heard another rumbling sound, this one ten times louder than the low flyer a couple of hours before. They looked up in amazement to see three jet fighters—not Stukas, either—flying in formation, passing directly over the town and heading north. The planes were followed by five helicopters, flying so low, the two drunks could see armed soldiers staring out the windows at them.

One of the drunks waved. One of the soldiers waved back. Little did the drunk know that he would never see a Stuka pirate in Ruff Creek again.

For the second time that day, the sentries in the watchtower at the Stuka base were rudely awakened. The rumbling of the approaching strike force was shaking the legs of the tower. Empty liquor bottles from the night before crashed to the wooden floor. One of the guards managed to reach the air raid siren button, and the wail warning signal started up again.

Hunter checked with the Phantoms and all three jets greened up. He did one last instrument check, then climbed to 13,000 for his pop. This air strike would be a pleasure.

Hunter went in first, dropping two of his 500-pounders and scoring a direct hit on the Stukas' maintenance hangar. The building disappeared in a cloud of smoke. Captain Crunch followed, putting two bombs right on the base's control tower. Crunch's second Phantom made it three-for-three burying one of the pirates' barracks and igniting a fuel tank nearby.

Hunter climbed, put the F-16 into a tight 360 and came back in, dropping a third 500-pounder on the storage facility where he, Al and Zal had once been held prisoner, and a fourth on the sentries' watchtower 100 yards away. Crunch took out another storage building and his partner added another load into the already burning fuel tank.

The target thus softened up, the assault choppers, on Hunter's orders, moved in.

"LZ is hot," Hunter radioed the Stallion pilots, as

he streaked in to strafe the runway. "Drop down quick and keep the props moving."

Some pirates were still running out on the runway, trying to get to their gun positions, or taking shots at the jets flying over. Others were firing rifles and machine guns at the descending troop helicopters.

"Cobras!" Hunter called into the radio. "Soften the LZ will you?"

The two Cobras seemed to appear form nowhere and strafe the bandits as they dove for cover. Cobra Brother One stayed on the tails of five bandits who ran into a concrete bunker next to the runway. Pausing to hover for a moment, the Cousin soaked the structure with his flamethrower. The five bandits emerged, completely engulfed, and ran wildly until they were mercifully shot down by Cobra Brother Two.

The Sea Stallion was the first to come in. The troopers, led by Dozer, leaped from the craft before it even touched down. They were met by a band of determined pirate guards firing a variety of weapons from behind the parked F-100s and from the ditches lining the runway. A sharp firefight immediately eruped. The assault team hit the pavement and started pumping lead into the pirates' positions. The battle was at such close quarters, the pirates were hurling hand grenades and the troopers were picking them up and throwing them back. The pirates fired shoulder-launche SAMs right into the assault team. The attackers returned the fire with their RPGs.

All the while, the Cobras were making breakneck strafing runs, using their flamethrowers and TOW missiles, flying so close to the defenders' lines, the pirates had to duck.

Hunter had lowered his flaps and landing gear and flew as slowly as possible over the battle. While most of the fighting was taking place on the Sea Stallion's port side, Hunter saw a group of 20 or so daring pirates, trying to sneak up on the chopper's starboard side, and attack it from the blindside. That was their mistake; the starboard side hid all three of the chopper's Gatling guns.

"Stallion," Hunter radioed. "Goofballs on your backdoor. Lock on."

"Roger, '16," the call came back. "We see them."

The bandits were detected on one of chopper's target acquisition video screens just as they started to charge. In less then a second, the chopper's shutters opened up to reveal the guns. Inside, the gunner pushed a button. In an instant, every pirate was severed at the waist by a one-second, computer-controlled burst from the chopper's Gatling guns.

"Hueys!" Hunter called, after twisting and flying back over the runway. The two Hueys came in, landing on either side of the Stallion. More of the strike force troopers jumped out and joined the fray. By this time, bullets were flying everywhere, as were RPGs and cannon shells. The airwash from the choppers gave the appearance that the battle was being fought in a windstorm. Hunter continually passed over the battle scene, adding cannon fire when and where it was needed.

Although they were outnumbered, the strike force quickly gained the upper hand on the runway. The pirate guard broke and started to retreat, half heading for the nearby woods, the other toward the graveyard of wrecked planes at the far end of the landing strip. Dozer and the Stallion troops pursued the bandits into the sea of twisted metal, smashed jet engines and burnt out fuselages. There were many places for the bandits to hide, and the assault team had to work each plane, one at a time, to flush out the defenders.

Meanwhile, the choppers themselves were catching fire from the bandits in the woods and from some of the perimeter AA guns. One of the bandit gun crews had leveled their guns and were blasting away at the choppers on the runway. Hunter quickly swooped in and put a air-to-surface missile right into the AA nest, silencing the gun.

The Ace Wrecking Company Phantoms reappeared and started buffeting the woods hiding the pirates with murderous cannon fire. At the battle of the airplane graveyard, Dozer called Hunter on the radio.

"'16? Dozer here. We got a nest of snipers. Can you put an arrow in that 707 wreck?"

"Roger, Captain," Hunter answered. "Heads up."

Hunter turned, and bore down on the target. He immediately began picking up anti-aircraft fire from all over the field. Below, he could see the group of pirates, hiding in the burnt out cockpit area of the wrecked convoy plane, training their machine guns on the assault troopers. Sighting through his HUD, he squeezed the firing button and felt the resulting kick as the air-to-surface missile left his wing and instantly impacted on the pirates' nest. He pulled up, turned left and looked back through the bubble canopy to see the missile had done its work.

"Thanks, '16," Dozer radioed. "We owe you a beer."

"No problem," Hunter called back. "I'm picking up the tab when this one's over."

The battle was slowly winding down as the attackers started to take control. Hunter made several more passes over the base, just to make sure. The place was almost totally aflame. The airplane graveyard was burning. A small forest fire had started. From the air, it appeared that every building was either raging out of control or smoking heavily—every building except one—the black building at the end of the landing strip and away from the fighting.

High above, the C-5 Galaxy circled the base, waiting for his call. Once he was sure the big plane could come in safely, Hunter radioed its pilots.

"Galaxy. '16 here," he said. "Runway clean. Join the party, will you?"

"Roger, '16," the C-5 pilot radioed back. "Looks like we've been missing all the fun."

"Heads up down there," Hunter called to the ground force commanders. "C-5 coming in, followed by the F-4s and the '16."

A chorus of 'Roger" echoed back through his earphone.

The huge silver Galaxy descended onto the runway like a giant, graceful bird. It touched down smoothly, kicking up a minimum of smoke and dirt as its dozens of wheels touched the runway. A small parachute on the plane's tail helped slow down the big craft with runway to spare.

The F-4s came in next, side-by-side, their wheels

touching the landing strip at precisely the same instant.

By the time he brought the F-16 in, the Galaxy's wide-flap mouth was open and Fitzie's monkeys, mixed with some from the old ZAP, were filing out and forming up outside the huge airplane. Also aboard were twelve of the rescued ZAP pilots. He knew they'd be itchy to get into the action. He taxied up to the staging area, shut the engine down and jumped out of the jet.

Dozer and the assault force officers were waiting for him. He shook hands with them, saying "Beautiful work. What about casualties?"

Two dead, six wounded, none seriously. The landing strip was littered with bodies of dead pirates. The surprise attack had decimated what was left of the Stukas.

"It's hard to believe that some of these guys are actually pilots and mechanics," Hunter said to Dozer, looking at the carnage on the tarmac. "Drugs. And greed. That's what killed them. What a waste."

Then he turned his attention to the matter at hand . . .

The black hangar was still locked up and apparently untouched. As before, Hunter quickly picked the lock on the doors and swung them open. To his great relief, he saw the twelve F-20s were still there.

"There they are, boys," he said to the army of monkeys standing around him. "Get 'em working. We have an hour, ninety minutes tops!"

With that, the mechanics methodically attacked the sophisticated jet fighters, removing the engine cowlings and lifting the engine access hoods. The ZAP pilots each staked a claim on one of the jets, admiring the beauty of the rare airplanes. For them, it was a dream come true. A week ago, they were languishing in the Mid-Ak's skyscraper prison. Now, they were about to pilot one of the most sophisticated jets ever made.

Outside, he could hear occasional gunfire. The Cobras were still airborned, supporting the attack troops as they chased the remaining pirates through the woods.

"Where the hell did they ever get these planes, Hawk?" Dozer asked.

"Beats me," Hunter said, running his hand over the fuselage of a F-20. "They're right from the factory, never been flown."

"I admit I don't know anything about airplanes," Dozer said. "But these look like beauties to me."

"Beauties is the word," Hunter agreed. "Long ago, the government didn't even want to buy these babies. Thought they would be too much plane for the pilots."

"Too much plane?"

"That's right," Hunter answered. "They can fly and turn faster than some pilots can handle it. The gs can be tremendous, even when the plane isn't kicked in all the way. The '16 is the same way. In many respects it's hotter than these planes, but I'm partial to it."

"Well, either way, St. Louie will be happy to see them, I'm sure."

Hunter nodded slowly. "Yeah," he said, moving to help one of the monkeys check an engine. "If we're not too late."

Within an hour, the first of the F-20s rolled out of the hangar. The pilot, the former ZAP flyboy named Digger Foxx, was in the cockpit. He gave the thumbs up signal, pushed his throttle and started the take-off roll. Every eye was on the F-20 Tigershark as the plane sped down the captured runway. Suddenly, it leaped into the air. A cheer went up. The pilot did a neat 180 and the brilliant red and white fighter came in low over the field, wagging its wings.

Dozer shook Hunter's hand. "Success!"

"Yep," he said. "One up, eleven to go."

They watched as the plane sped off toward the north for its first refueling stop at the Aerodrome.

In two hours' time, all of the F-20s were successfully launched. A special squad of explosive experts had blown up the pirates' F-100s after stripping the planes of any usable parts and munitions. The rest of the attacking force climbed into their aircraft and they too were soon airborne and heading for the Aerodrome. All the while, the pirate defenders in the woods, under the mistaken notion that the main pirate force would soon return, had continually peppered the assault team during the F-20 take-offs. Dozer's men had returned the fire, but stayed at their positions on the perimeter of the base.

Finally, everyone was gone. Hunter was the last to leave. As he started his takeoff roll, a few mortar rounds came crashing down onto the runway, coming close, but missing by enough so as not to cause any damage.

He yanked the throttle back, left the ground and put the F-16 into a tight turn. Streaking back low over the landing strip, he deposited four bombs in succession onto the runway. The bombs, specially made blockbusters, cratered the landing strip beyond repair. Then he put the F-16 into a screeching, steep climb. When he reached 40,000 feet, he leveled it out, knowing he was high enough for his jet engine to emit the water condensed contrails.

Far below, a few of the beraggled pirate defenders crawled out of the woods to claim what was left of their base. The place was a total wreck, the bodies of their dead comrades were everywhere. They were mostly in a state of shock, having no idea who the attackers were or how they came to know that the F-20s were hidden there. Only later would they discover that one of the three prisoners who had escaped in the hot air balloon weeks earlier had led the raid.

One of the pirates looked up and saw something moving high above the destroyed base. He told his comrades and together they watched as a huge "W" formed in the sky.

It was a sight they wouldn't soon forget . . .

CHAPTER TWENTY-FIVE

Two days later, the sun was shining over Football City. The city was under a complete war footing. Everywhere, tanks, APCs, howitzers, military trucks, moved through the streets. While St. Louie had found problems equipping his air force, buying land weapons was no problem at all. And, strangely enough, neither was manpower.

It was precisely at noon when they heard them coming. The low distant rumble, more akin to thunder than anything else. Getting louder, getting closer. The sound was deeper than the noise of the attacking MIG-21s. Soon, every eye in the city was looking upward, hand over brow to shut out the bright sun.

St. Louie was at the Grand Stadium when he heard the noise. The place had been turned into the main staging area for Football City's armed forces. All work at the stadium stopped as the soldiers looked up.

Then someone yelled: "There they are!"

St. Louie looked up. Sure enough, high up he could see six dots, flying in a chevron, emerging from a gigantic cumulus cloud. Right behind were six more. He felt an excitement run through him. Had Hunter really pulled it off?

He got his answer as the jets descended, and then flew in formation right over the stadium. They peeled off, one by one, with professional precision and made their landing approach to the battered, but still operating, Football City airport.

He immediately jumped into a jeep with three of his staff officers and was at the airport just as the third pair of F-20s were coming in.

"My God!" he exclaimed. "They're beautiful!"

Within minutes, all 12 were down and taxiing to their holding stations. Next the big C-5 landed, carrying the Sea Stallion inside, plus the Cobras. Two C-130s circled the field once, and set down, carrying Fitzie's army of "volunteer" monkeys, the ZAP mechanics plus Dozer's strike force.

"Look!" one of St. Louie's officers said. "They look like F-4s!"

It was true. Captain Crunch and his F-4 Ace Wrecking Company had decided to join the Football City forces—free of charge, St. Louie would find out later.

The final plane to land was the lone F-16. St. Louie made sure he was at the station point when the jet taxied up.

The canopy popped and Hunter jumped out. St. Louie, overjoyed that his city now had not just an air force, but probably *the* most sophisticated air force on the continent, couldn't resist putting an old Texas bear hug on Hunter.

"You did it!" St. Louie told him. "You just might have pulled our asses out of the fire!"

"Not yet," Hunter said, cautiously. "We still have a lot of work to do and a tough fight ahead of us."

"I know it," St. Louie said, his initial exuberance disappearing. "And things have gotten worse."

Hunter turned the plane over to the airport ground crew and sat down in a long abandoned airport coffee shop with St. Louie. A bottle appeared. Dozer joined them.

"What's the situation?" Hunter asked.

"Bad," St. Louie said, pouring out three drinks. "We've spotted advance elements of Family troops sitting right across the river from us. Our recon boys tell us their main columns are stretched on the road and the rails from here all the way back to New Chicago."

"Any tanks, howitzers?" Hunter asked.

"A few, not many," St. Louie said, a slight note of relief in his voice. "But they've got a lot of artillery, a few rocket launchers, and some heavy mortars. They have it all loaded up on tractor trailers, old semis, Diamond Reos, things like that. It appears like they're moving some of their troops by train and the rest plus the equipment by truck."

Hunter took another drink and thought for a moment. "Where are they getting all the fuel to move them? Those big rigs need diesel and I'm sure they've got gasoline-powered vehicles, too."

"You're right," St. Louie said. "Our spies have seen them hauling fuel in old gasoline trucks—Mobil, Exxon, Sunoco—you name it."

"But, where is all the petro coming from?"

"Well," St. Louie said. "It's coming from New Chicago. The Family has an oil storage area—a big one—right near the downtown. Ships come in off the lake and unload. Mostly under contract to East European concerns, I might add."

"And, what was this about some train yards up there?" Hunter asked, refilling his glass.

"That's right," St. Louie said. "Big marshalling yards right next to the oil storage farm. That's where they've been staging their troops."

Hunter was getting an idea.

"We'll need bombers," he said suddenly.

"Fighter-bombers?" Dozer asked, trying to read Hunter's mind.

"No, not just fighters," Hunter said. "I mean bombers, too. Big stuff. Nothing fancy, just good enough for one bombing mission."

"But where the hell are we going to find planes like that now, Hawk?"

"All we have to do," he said, "is find one man. If we do, we'll get our airplanes."

That man's name was Roy From Troy.

St. Louie's spies were good; they located the carnival-barker-turned-airplane salesman in two days. He had just returned from a selling trip to Canada when St. Louie's agents spirited him away, and with the help of one of the Cobra Brothers, got him to Football City in a matter of hours.

He nearly fainted when he saw Hunter.

"My God! I heard you were dead," he said to the airman. "They said the Mid-Aks got you over Baltimore. Or was it Otis?"

"Wishful thinking," Hunter told him. They were standing in St. Louie's command center in the basement of his mansion.

"Okay," Roy said, getting down to business as usual. "You guys got me here in the middle of the night, so I hope it's for doing a deal."

"We want bombers," Hunter told him simply.

"Bombers? I thought you were strictly fighters?"

"We need anything that will carry bombs a long way," Hunter said,

"Bombers are rare these days," Roy said. "Good ones anyway."

"I told you," Hunter said, already seeing dollar signs in Roy's eyes. Some things never change. "We don't need fancy. We just need something that's going to make one mission. That's all."

"Well, they are still in short supply," Roy said. "For some reason, bombers don't last as long as fighters."

"What have you got?" Hunter asked.

"Well, we'd be scraping the bottom of the barrel at Wright-Patterson."

"I said, 'Nothing fancy.' " Hunter reminded him.

"It's going to cost," Roy said, holding his hand up in mock caution.

"We don't give a bull's ass what it costs," St. Louie told him, the anger evident in his voice. "We're fighting for our lives here, mister."

"Okay," Roy said, dropping his huckster front for the first time that Hunter could remember. "I can see you guys are in a bad way here. Everyone on the continent knows you are. I got bombers. But I'm warning you. It's old stuff."

"How old?" Hunter wanted to know what he had to work with.

"Would you believe everything from a few B-24s up to a B-58 Hustler?" Roy said.

"B-24s?" Hunter said. "Liberators? They were retired at the end of World War II."

"Well, just about," Roy said. "But, you gotta remember, I'm in the airplane salvage business, too. We found a couple of B-24s that got stuck in the snow way up in Canada. Happened in 1943. They were heading over to Europe when they had to put down at an emergency strip because of weather. Well, the weather turned out to be a blizzard and it iced them right over. Preserved them perfectly. No one ever bothered to dig 'em out, until the Free Canadians let me do it. In fact, they paid me to get them out. I did and the boys at Wright-Patterson did them over real nice."

"But will they fly?" Hunter wanted to know.

"Shit, yes," Roy said. "Carry a shitload of bombs for you, too. Still got the Norden bombsights in them, for Christ's sake. They're collector's items, but you guys can get them for cheap."

Hunter looked at St. Louie, who shrugged.

"What else you got?" Hunter asked.

"I got four B-25 Mitchells. Got 'em from a flying club down south that didn't want the Mid-Aks to get them. They're also in good shape. These were ship busters from the South Pacific. Got double cannons in the nose, one on top, two on each side and one on the ass. Buy all four I'll give you a deal."

Hunter nodded. "Mitchells were a good plane. That's what Doolittle bombed Tokyo with. What else?"

"Got twelve B-29s," Roy continued. "Real good shape, only saw a little action at the end of World War II, and minimum stuff during Korea. I found them at an air museum out in California.

"I've got a lot of B-47s. Strange airplanes. No one wants them. They're stretched-out fighters. Long wings and bodies. Carry three guys, but two sit like they're in a fighter, one in back of the other. I'd hate to go a long way in one. They threw them together in the 50s, just so they'd have a jet that could make it to Russia carrying the Big One. You can get them for a song. I'm looking to get rid of them."

"You said you've still got a B-58?" Hunter was almost afraid to ask.

"The Hustler?" Roy said. "Yep. I got one. It's got to be the last one in existence. First big bomber to go supersonic, you know. And I don't mean one click over the line either. I talking about Mach 2-plus! Another stretched out fighter. Like a big F-106 Delta Dart. Fucking this is *too* big and it's got some mean engines. But I'll tell you something: it sucks up the J-P8 like crazy, but that shitbox can haul ass. Scares you to be moving that fast in something that big."

"What's left?" Hunter asked.

"I got a few C-130s," Roy said. "Just fixed them up. They could help you out. You can open the back and roll bombs out. Plus you put everything from a popgun to a howitzer in them. That's what they used 'em for 'Nam. Spectre gunships, they called them. Or Puff the Magic Dragons."

"C-130s are good stuff," Hunter agreed. "We can always use a few more. Is that it?"

"Just about," Roy said, trying to think. "Your boys kidnapped me before I could get my sales book. Or my girls."

"That's a pity," Hunter said.

"Yeah," Roy said, taking out a notebook. "So which ones do you want?"

Hunter looked again at St. Louie, who nodded.

"We want all of them," Hunter said.

Roy From Troy's notebook dropped at the same instant as his jaw. "All of them?"

"That's right," Hunter said. "We need them all."

"I'm talking about almost forty planes. What the hell are you guys gonna do? Fight World War II all over again?"

Hunter smiled. "Something like that," he said.

They cleaned Roy from Troy out of his stock and made him a rich man. It was by far the biggest deal of his life. The planes started arriving the next day, flying in from Wright-Patterson, carefully avoiding the Family's airspace during the trip. St. Louie used some of the diamonds that Hunter had delivered to him as payment for the bombers.

But more importantly, Hunter managed to hire most of Roy's pilots to fly the planes, just for the one time. The diamonds helped but, in most cases, once the pilots heard that they'd have a fleet of F-20s flying cover for them, plus Hawker Hunter in the lead, they knew the odds of their getting back were greatly increased.

The main target was the oil yards right in the heart of New Chicago. Hunter knew that an army moves on oil—more so than its stomach. Hitting the Family's fuel supply would hurt—hard. Maybe not right away. But some time, when the fighting reached the critical level, the enemy would turn and the oil wouldn't be there.

Trouble was, except for a few outdated and grainy photographs, Hunter had little information on the target area. He didn't want to risk sending a photo recon plane up now, for fear of tipping his hand to the Family. But there were crucial questions that would have to be answered right away. Oil facilities always proved to be tough targets. For instance, how much of the bomber force should concentrate on the oil tanks themselves? One or two bombs in the right place and the tanks will blow themselves up. Yet, as the Allies found during World War II, sometimes you can bomb the shit out of a refinery, and manage only a brush fire for your trouble. He wanted to hit the railroad marshalling yards at the same time, but the oil would have to have priority. That meant the very first plane in would have to score a direct hit on a large oil tank, hoping to set off a chain reaction that would destroy most of the oil farm and free up much of the bomber force to concentrate on the railroad yards and the city of New Chicago itself.

That's why he would be flying the lead plane . . .

For the next two days, he pored over maps and planned the approach of the mission. He knew he would have to fly the lead in one of the B-24s, because it was slow and yet could carry the good-sized bomb-load he'd need.

Problem number two was getting the bombs. Because of St. Louie's connection in Texas, he had a fairly stable access to guns and ammunition. The people in Texas, probably more than anyone else, knew what price freedom. They also realized that if the Family won this fight, they, the Texans, would probably be next. To those ends, they supported St. Louie as much as possible. Cargo planes from Texas arrived at Football City's airport every hour, carrying ammo, supplies and food. The material necessities of war.

But aerial bombs were a different story. And this was where Fitzie came through for Hunter again. While they were back at the Aerodrome, fueling the F-20s for the flight to Football City, Hunter drew Fitzie a map. It gave directions to a mountain way up in Vermont where a small airstrip was hidden. Fitz was able to rent two massive Sky Crane helicopters from a legitimate lumber company in Free Canada. Using the map, a highly-paid salvage crew made its way to the airstrip and dropped down running hooks to the cratered, debris strewn runway. It took them the better part of a day to clear enough area for the Sky Cranes to set down. Then, they broke the lock off the small hangar located at the edge of the field. Inside, just as Hunter said, was an eye-popping huge cache of bombs, air-to-air missiles and napalm. Using the Sky Crane's best-in-the-world lifting ability, the crew tied the bomb crates together and started lifting the ordnance out. It took them two days of working around the clock. Finally the entire motherlode was sitting in Syracuse, where it would take three trips by the C-5 to lug it to Football City. In a few days, Football City was well-stocked in aerial bombs. It was another legacy from General Seth Jones. It was almost as if he had foreseen the need for the ordnance some day and that's why he had led Hunter to the base that cold day.

But the recovery mission had a much more personal meaning for the Wingman. Using a smaller map, the salvage crew foreman located an unmarked grave near the edge of the strip. He was carrying a heavy bronze plaque made in one of Fitzie's machine shops. At Hunter's request, the man laid the plaque in the grave and ringed it with boulders.

It read simply:

General Seth Jones—Hero & Patriot

Thus, one more loop was closed in Hunter's mind.

Preparations continued. But a strange thing was happening. As Roy from Troy had told them, the impending war between Football City and the Family was on the lips of everyone across the continent, friend and foe alike. Word got around fast in these days. Suddenly, volunteers had begun to pour into the city. Many were Texans, but others were from all over—

Free Canadians, Coasters, exiled Zoners.

"Volunteers for freedom," Hunter commented to Dozer as they watched from a balcony of a building downtown the soldiers flood into the city. "People on this continent never forgot what it was like before the New Order. Before it was illegal to carry the flag, or mention the stars and stripes, or fly with it painted on your airplane. Before the New Order or the Mid-Aks, or the Family. Before the Russians stabbed us in the back. They may have forgotten about TV, and cars and paper money. But they never forget about freedom."

Dozer nodded in agreement, but Hunter knew he had to say more. He felt a fire start in his belly. He felt an anger build in his brain. He felt a lump form in his throat.

"They never forgot that they were . . ." he started to say, but, again, had to stop for a moment and regain his composure. Looking at the troops—*volunteers*—like the original Minutemen, walking past, heading to take up positions along Football City's defense line. He knew they would fight a battle that some—maybe most—wouldn't survive. But still they continued to come . . .

He felt something burst inside him. A flame ignited in his heart.

"God damn it!" he finally blurted out. "Look at them! *They never forgot they were once Americans!*"

The words stung in his ears. His mouth went dry. Fluid collected in the corners of his eyes. "God damn it!" he said. "I'm an American!"

He looked at Dozer. Tears were also forming in the

371

Marine's eyes. The tough leatherneck turned away and gazed out into space. "I'm an American, too, Hawk," he said quietly.

They stood in silence and watched the volunteers move through the city. Hunter knew this would be the biggest fight of his life. Bigger than over the Rhine, or anything with ZAP. This was against a very real enemy. One who, like the Mid-Aks, was in bed with the Russians. One who shared with the godless Soviets the same twisted ideal of government by slavery. Slavery of the mind *and* body.

Well, tomorrow, they would start to do something about that.

CHAPTER TWENTY-SIX

The next morning the strange armada of bombers began to form up on the Football City's airport runways. There were the two B-24s—Hunter in one of them—warming up next to the B-47s. The B-29s were already rolling, as were the C-130s. The cranky B-58 was sprouting black smoke and was, by far, the noisiest plane on the runway. The two-engined B-25 Mitchells looked small compared to the other flying brutes.

Bomb crews raced between the planes, loading a bizarre collection of ordnance aboard the planes. The napalm and high energy bombs from the Vermont hideaway were divided up equally among the bombers. After that, it was catch-as-catch-can. Everything from anti-personnel bombs in the B-29 Superfortresses to a pair of 18,000-pound blockbusters the B-58 was carrying. Hunter's B-24 was loaded with dozens of small incendiary bombs, 3,500 pounds in all. The B-47s were outfitted to drop napalm; some of the C-130s would drop delayed-fuse anti-personnel bombs while others would drop barrels filled with sticks of TNT. Hunter hoped it would all make for one hell of a fire.

Riding shotgun for the bomber force would be the F-20s. All 12 of them rolled off the runways first. The F-4s of The Ace Wrecking Company went next; they, too, would ride escort. St. Louie's spies told Hunter that bombers could expect MIGs to intercept them over the target area. If they did, they would have formidable opponents in the F-20s and the Phantoms. The spies also reported that the bombers would find the railroad yards and the oil facility ringed with hundreds of AA guns and SAM sites.

Hunter, as mission leader, radioed all the aircraft commanders in the force—38 in all. Each one checked off preliminaries leading up to their ready point. Hunter had held a briefing before the take-off, where last minute information on weather, fighter strengths and other details had been gone over. The mission had been planned and discussed and planned some more, but there was no getting around the fact that things tended to look a whole lot different up in the air than they did on a map.

Very few of the bombers had worthwhile targeting systems—the exotic equipment had been stripped from the planes long ago. Knowing this, Hunter had to plan the mission around providing the bomber pilots with targets they could visually acquire quickly. The groups would be flying in at one minute intervals, and he wanted to keep radio talk among them to a minimum so as not to help the AA crews home in on the radio frequencies.

Hunter checked his own plane, the antique B-24 Liberator, and found everything in working order. He looked at his navigator, Captain Dozer, specially trained for the flight, and gave him the thumbs up signal. Dozer returned the salute. Both men smiled. They had managed to find what had to be the last two girls in the city the night before and bedded them. It was better going into the jaws of death knowing that you had tasted life's one great pleasure at least one more time.

There were eight other men on board. A competent copilot named Ernie and seven of Dozer's marines. The 7th Cavalry, and some of the Football City special forces, had been pressed into service as gunners aboard the bombers. In fact, anyone who could point a gun was recruited. Like everything else in the daring bombing mission, the air crews had been improvised. It gave a whole new appreciation to the phrase "Flying by the seat of your pants."

Once he was certain every plane had checked out, Hunter rechecked the instruments in his own aircraft. Everything appeared A-OK. Time to go. He brought up the throttle and released the brakes. "Okay, everybody," Hunter said into his radio as the B-24 lurched forward. "Follow me."

The bomber force's flight path had them follow the Illinois River right up to New Chicago. They were flying high, at 40,000. Hunter's plan called for the planes to line up in pairs and triples, forming a train. The idea was to disguise the bomber force by making it look like a convoy to someone looking up from the ground. Though it would be unusual for a convoy to be passing through Family airspace, it was not unheard of one drifting off course and fighter strengths being what they were, no one bothered if a convoy passed overhead once in a while.

This cover gave the bomber crews a good look at the preparations being made on the ground by the Family. They were, in a word, extensive. By the time they flew over Peoria, they saw the roads approaching the capital were clogged with military traffic. The rails were the same way. Hunter, taking it all in from the lead plane in the force, wished he could unleash his bombs on these targets too. But he knew that every vehicle he saw moving down below had to run on fuel, and fuel was the major objective of the mission.

The flight lasted only a little over an hour before they were on the outskirts of New Chicago. They were still fifteen minutes away from their objective however, when their convoy cover was blown.

Hunter saw the MIGs first. They were still 20 miles away and a mile below them, too far for them to pick up the bomber force on the shitty MIG on-board radar system. But Hunter knew it was just a matter of time. There were two of them, possibly on a routine mission, possibly heading to bomb Football City. He was determined that they would never make it, no matter what their destination.

"Tigershark Leader," he radioed to the fighter escort commander, flying several thousand feet above the main bomber force. "Group Leader here. We've got company. Twenty-five clicks out. My five o'clock."

"Roger, Group Leader," the answer came back. "We see them."

"Okay, Tigershark," Hunter called. "Keep an eye

on them until we form up, then intercept."

"That's affirmative, Group Leader."

Hunter knew that the F-20s would handle the MIGs with no problem. But he also knew the MIG pilots would detect the bomber force and radio the information back to their base.

"Everyone else, get ready," he told the rest of the bomber pilots. "We're probably going to get a reception before we reach the target area."

Behind him, the bombers broke from the fake-convoy pattern and tightened up into boxes of fours and fives. There was strength in numbers, truer than ever in bombing missions. The combined number of guns aboard the bombers, plus the force's compacted flying area, would give attacking interceptors something to think about before they plunged in amongst the aircraft.

In less than a minute, the bombers were lined up in their proper attack formation. Some planes increased airspeed, while others dropped back. As planned, Hunter and the other B-24 were in the lead, followed by the four Mitchell B-25s. Behind them were the twelve B-47s, flying in three four-plane diamond formations. Coming next was the odd duck flight—the seven C-130s surrounding the B-58 Hustler, which had been bucking and shooting black smoke the entire way. The aging bomber had to make the trip flaps down and landing gear deployed just so it could reduce its airspeed to that of the propeller-driven C-130s. The dozen B-29 Superfortresses brought up the rear.

The two Family MIG pilots broke through a cloud bank and stumbled upon the bomber formation now about four thousand feet above them. Both pilots couldn't believe it at first. Neither could their flight controllers back in New Chicago.

"Chicago!" the first pilot radioed, a trace of panic in his voice. "Raghead Leader here. Do we have a convoy coming in?"

"Negative, Raghead Leader," came the reply.

"Well, we have visual with a large force approaching two-two-niner from southwest, heading your way."

"Raghead. Please resend. Flight ops says large force impossible."

"Chicago. Tell flight ops we're less than ten clicks from large force. Bombers. All types. Need instructions."

"Raghead. Need ID. What kind of bombers."

There was a pause in the transmission, then: "Chicago. Sounds crazy. We have visual on what looks to be old B-24s, Mitchells. A group of B-47s. At least seven C-130s. One plane that's smoking heavy. Maybe a dozen B-29s in the distance."

This time the silence was on the Chicago controller's end.

"Raghead Two," the controller radioed the flight leader's wingman. "Do you copy Raghead's sighting?"

"That's affirmative, Chicago," was the answer. "I count thirty-eight planes in all."

"Raghead Leader," the controller radioed. "Let me remind you of the disciplinary action for filing false reports . . ."

At that point, Raghead Leader snapped out. "Listen you assholes, I'm looking at the belly gunner of a B-24 Liberator. I know it sounds like a dream from

World War II, but these planes are real and they are heading your way. Now please give us instructions or we are going to vacate the sector."

All the while, Hunter was monitoring the radio transmissions. He had to chuckle at the MIG leader's plea to convince his controllers that he wasn't seeing things. But now, as those controllers decided what to do, he could detect another voice, in the background at Chicago flight control, barking orders. The voice was speaking in a heavy accent, and alternating between English and a foreign tongue. Hunter listened very closely. He needed to hear only three or four words of the foreign language until his suspicion was confirmed. Dozer was listening in and heard it too.

"That sounds like a Russian voice on Chicago control," Dozer called to him.

"It is," Hunter said coolly, though he was beginning to burn inside. "I'm not surprised. They're obviously controlling the MIGs, and probably a lot more in New Chicago."

"Looks like those East European planes you told me about were carrying more than Mid-Aks to Chicago," Dozer said.

"Just like those East European oil tankers on Lake Michigan," Hunter said. "Well, that's okay with me. It will only make this mission a little sweeter."

"Tigershark Leader," Hunter radioed. "Intercept."

"Roger, Leader," came the reply.

With that, four of the F-20s streaked past him, diving down on the MIGs. The Family jets never knew what hit them. One F-20 pilot locked on to Raghead Two in the dive itself and launched a Sidewinder. The missile dashed unerringly to its target, striking it almost head-on. The jet went up in a ball of flame and smoke. The pilot never had a chance, his flaming corpse was ejected by the explosion and was seen plummeting to earth along with the hundreds of pieces of wreckage.

"*We are under attack!*" the pilot in Raghead One screamed.

"ID attacking aircraft," Chicago tower radioed back.

"For Christ's sake!" the panicking pilot shot back. "They're F-20s!"

"F-20s?" the controller asked. Hunter, still listening in on the Chicago frequency, could hear a great amount of shouting and confusion coming from the New Chicago end.

"Raghead," the controller called. "Confirm F-20s." Silence.

"Raghead One, confirm F-20s."

Still silence.

"Raghead?"

Raghead wouldn't be answering anything except the doorbell in hell. The MIG-21 had taken two simultaneous Sidewinder hits and had simply disintegrated. No wreckage. No parachute. Just a puff of smoke.

"Target ahead!" Hunter called into the microphone. "Ten miles. Drop to assigned altitudes and let's get this party hopping."

With that, the two B-24s and the four B-25 Mitchells dropped down to barely 100 feet off the deck. Hunter had known all along that the only way they could successfully attack the oil tanks was to come in low, below the radar that controlled the Family's AA guns. He was bombing on sight. There were no video acquisition aids, no HUD screen, no fire-and-forget missiles. This one would be down and dirty.

Hunter could see the target off in the distance but straight ahead. Past the skyscrapers around New Chicago, there was the railroad yard and then the oil storage farm. There were easily 120 large round tanks. A couple of smokestacks were sticking out at each end of the facility, spouting flames of burnt off gas.

Hunter nosed the B-24 down even lower. That's when the flak started coming up. Puffs of harmless-looking but all too deadly smoke. He knew if one hits the wrong spot—like in the fuel-laden wing or the bomb bay—he and his crew would be one with the air in a matter of seconds. They started picking up small arms fire too. The plane was low enough that a well-placed bullet could also send them off packing to the Great Beyond.

The warning the MIGs had sent back had alerted the Family's defenses. As he passed the eight-mile-to-target mark, the air was suddenly filled with hundreds of flak explosions. St. Louie's agents were right again. The oil farm and the city were protected in depth by AA guns.

He ordered the gunners in the nose and in the tail of his ship to start firing back. He could see Family soldiers on the ground shooting at them with rifles and machine guns. Then the missiles started coming up.

"We're getting SAMs!" he radioed the rest of the bomber force. "Take evasive action."

There were hundreds of them. Big ones that looked

like flying telephone poles and other small ones that he knew where shoulder-launched. It was like the sky was filled with Fourth of July rockets. He weaved in and out, up and down in order to confuse the radar equipment in the AA guns and the SAM launchers. He could see the B-24 on his right was doing the same thing. The air actually became bumpy with flak and the wash from the SAMs' exhaust.

Six miles to target. He passed over the heart of the city and the air became even more intense with anti-aircraft fire. He could actually see gunmen in the windows of the buildings in the downtown section of the city firing at the bombers. It was incredible. He wouldn't be surprised to learn that just about everybody in New Chicago carried a gun, and they were all firing them at the attacking bomber force.

Three miles to target. Hunter's B-24 finally passed over the city and was above the huge railroad yards. Thousands of troops were scrambling below. If anything, the amount of anti-aircraft fire increased. He called for the Mitchells to move up alongside the B-24s. Strength in numbers. Together the six old airplanes, looking like a scene from a World War II movie, plunged on toward the target.

At two miles to target, they were aware of a new threat. There was a flak train moving alongside of them, firing away at the Liberators and the Mitchells. The gunners in all six planes returned the fire, at first aiming at the guns and then finally hitting the locomotive pulling the train. There were also towers scattered around the railroad yard, manned by troops with shoulder-launched SAMs. But the planes were so low, the soldiers had to shoot down at them as they streaked past.

Suddenly, one of the Mitchells got it. A SAM landed smack in the cockpit area, destroying it instantly. The B-25 flew on for a few ghostly seconds, then plunged into the railroad yard, hitting a fuel tank car and causing an explosion.

The five remaining planes pressed on. Hunter knew the bulk of the next flight of the bomber force—the B-47s—were right behind, but he could only guess how they were faring. He had an open line to them, and all of the planes in the strike, and could hear the usual calls between planes to start evasive actions, watch out for the flak towers and so on. But so far, he had heard of only three planes taking hits. One of them was the lead B-47. It had taken a SAM in one of its engines and had crashed into one of the taller skyscrapers in the city.

Meanwhile, high above them, the F-20s were tangling with two squadrons of Family MIG-21s. Even down 2-to-1, the Tigersharks were making mincemeat of the Russian-built fighters, as evidenced by a flaming MIG that had crashed off to Hunter's right. By switching back and forth to the enemy's frequency, he could clearly hear Russian voices intermixed with ones speaking English. Russian pilots flying the MIGs? No surprise. It was yet another suspicion of his confirmed. He was glad to hear, though, that most of the radio talk coming from the enemy pilots had to do with the fucking F-20s. "These planes are just too damned good," he heard one enemy pilot say. "What's next?" another pilot yelled. "F-16s?" That comment made him wish for an instant that he *was* in the '16, tangling with the MIGs. But now he was less than one mile from the oil farm. He returned his full attention to the matter at hand.

He gunned his engines and opened up a lead on the other planes in his flight. Thirty seconds later, he was right over the farm. He would head for the largest tank, the three other planes in his formation now following behind. He saw a large, silver colored tank with the word CHIGAS painted on its side, sitting smack in the middle of the complex. The tank, which was prominent in the old photos he had studied, would be his target. He pulled back on the old, steering wheel style controls and the B-24 rose slowly.

"Open bomb bay doors!" he called into the microphone to his bombardier, who was located in the forward compartment right below the B-24's flight deck.

100 feet . . . 50 . . . 25 . . .

"Now!" he yelled to his bombardier, who flipped a switch letting the hundreds of incendiary bombs tumble out. Simultaneously he yanked the controls back and put the big plane into a climb. He knew the Mitchells and the other B-24 would do the same maneuver. He pitched the plane to the left and looked back. The fire bombs had covered the oil tank and were burning like lights on a Christmas tree.

But nothing was happening . . .

It was like everything stood still. He knew he had to get lucky on this one. One of those bombs had to touch something off, or the party wasn't worth coming to.

"C'mon Jones," he implored to the spirits in himself. "Light the match."

Suddenly, one of the fires hit the right spot, probably a feeder line, and the tank exploded with a tremendous blast. The shock wave buffeted the B-24, so much so, he and Ernie the co-pilot had to work together to keep the plane level.

"Jesus!" Dozer yelled, nearly thrown from his seat by the blast. "What did you hit?"

"Probably a tank used to store jet fuel," Hunter said looking back at the conflagration he had caused. The Mitchells and the other B-24 had roared in and ignited smaller tanks nearby. Within 15 seconds of his drop, about a tenth of the huge oil facility was exploding and already burning.

He radioed back to the other bombers.

"This is Group Leader," he called. "B-47 flight. Go to Plan B. Drop early. Repeat. Drop early. We took the oil tanks. You take out the railroad yards."

"Roger, leader," came the replies.

He called back to the B-29's flying five minutes behind him and bringing up the rear. "B-29 flight leader, what's your ETA over the city?"

"One minute, Group Leader," the answer came back. "We hear you've caused an instant oil shortage in New Chicago."

"That's correct," Hunter confirmed. "Play Mrs. O'Leary's cow, will you? Drop your incendiaries over the city. Chicago's been long enough without a big fire."

"You got it, Group," the B-29 leader called back.

"You pulled the inside straight, Hawk," Dozer said, looking out the B-24's porthole at the flames below.

"It pays to be flexible, Captain," Hunter said with the smile of relief. "That tank farm is going to burn for days as it is. Wait until the C-130s drop their TNT into it."

"How about the Hustler?" Ernie asked.

"Those blockbusters would do the most damage at the airport, I say," Hunter said, calling the Odd Duck flight. "C-130s, this is Group Leader. You proceed on Plan A. Drop on the oil yards."

"Roger, Group Leader," the call came back.

"Roger, 130s," Hunter replied. "Hustler, you double back and unload on O'Hare. Wake 'em up. Repeat. Drop those big sons-of-bitches right down their throats."

"That's a roger, Group Leader," the B-58's pilot replied. "Then can I request permission to climb and kick this thing into afterburner?"

"That's affirmative, Hustler," Hunter radioed back. "You'll beat us all back. Put the beer on ice, will you?"

"That's also a roger, Group," came the reply.

By this time, Hunter had swung the B-24 in a high 180 and was surveying the damage to the oil field. Fully one half of the tank farm was now a sheet of flame. And, the B-47s had done a number on the railroad yards. The huge napalm bombs had splashed down upon the railroad cars and tracks. Thousands of Family troops below were instantly burnt to a crisp. Many secondary explosions were going off. The railroad yards were engulfed in the trademark greenish flame that napalm was known for. As the last of the Stratojets passed over, the intensity of the flames coming from the marshalling yard rivaled the ones blazing next door at the oil farm.

"That's what you fuckers get for attacking a stadium full of innocent people," Hunter cursed.

Now, the C-130s were just arriving over the city. The AA fire was still intense, but the C-130s were best suited of all to fight back. Many of the planes were carrying Gatlings or cannons, even a few small howitzers. As they were passing low over the downtown, the gunners—mostly Dozer's 7th Cavalrymen—shot at anything and everything that moved. At times, the planes were actually lower than the tops of the skyscrapers and their gunners blasted away at any building that looked like a target.

Less than two minutes later, four of the C-130s were through the smoke of the rail yard and depositing their TNT cannisters into the raging inferno of the oil yard. Their flight leader had steered them toward the north end of the facility, the only part of the tank farm that hadn't been ignited by Hunter's flight's bombing run. Taking the initiative, the C-130 flight leader had three of his ships hold their TNT bombs and fly on over a docking facility nearby. A large tanker was tied at the pier, as were hundreds of smaller boats. The C-130s came in, their rear doors wide open. With one kick, the TNT barrels started rolling out and landing with tremendous blasts on the docks. One hit the tanker amidships, which set off an even bigger blast, immediately sending the ship to the bottom of Lake Michigan.

Hunter had the B-24 right over the C-130s and really appreciated the flight leader's improvisation.

"I'll have to remember to buy that flyboy a drink when we get back," Hunter told his crew.

There were several other big ships at anchor in the

harbor. Hunter could tell they were troopships, and thereby worthy targets. Suddenly, the two F-4s of the Ace Wrecking Company flashed into view.

"Group Leader, Captain Crunch here," Hunter's radio crackled. "Do you see what I see?"

"Sure do, Phantom," Hunter replied. "Make Fitzie proud of you."

"Roger," came the reply.

Hunter watched as the two Phantoms dove at the troopships. Small arms fire erupted from the soldiers on board desperately trying to stop the attacking F-4s. Crunch fired his missile first, a Sidewinder he correctly assumed would home in on something—anything—on the ship emitting an infrared signal. The missile impacted *below* the waterline, exploding in the bowels of the ship and igniting its boilers. With a great geyser of water, the ship was raised off the water, cracked in two, then came back down again and sank.

"Good shouting, Captain," Hunter radioed to the lead F-4.

The second Phantom of the Ace Wrecking Crew took on the other warship. Someone on board had ordered the ship's assault guns to fire at the jet, foolishly as it turned out, because the shells were missing the fighter by an eighth of a mile and crashing into the dock facility on shore. Phantom Number Two made quick work of the ship, first blasting it with its cannons, then dropping two 500-pounders right down its stack. The impact of the bombs immediately capsized the ship, and causing it to turn hull up. A large cloud of steam rose as the explosions ignited under water.

"You guys make a great team," Hunter said, praising the Ace men.

"Our pleasure, Major," the pilot of Phantom Number Two replied.

Hunter circled around again and drew even. Down below, the B-29s were running the gauntlet of AA fire and approaching New Chicago. Per his orders, they spread out and proceeded to dump incendiary devices all over the city. Hunter could see fires starting up on block after block. More secondary explosions were going off. One B-29 took a SAM in the tail, partially severing it. As Hunter watched, the fatally-stricken plane continued its bombing run then plunged into the burning streets below.

Finally, the last of the B-29s had dropped its load and had turned for home. The F-20s, hardly scratched, had dropped down by this time, having shot down 28 MIGs and scared the rest away. They, along with the F-4s, would provide a more than adequate escort home.

Hunter couldn't resist taking a final pass over the city. He counted fourteen separate major fires rising above it. The oil farm continued to explode as did the stricken tanker. The railroad yards were now nothing more than flaming debris. He could also see four large columns of smoke rising from the direction of the airport, indicating the Hustler had done its work well. Back over the city, the fire itself were so intense, the heated air above it buffeted the B-24 as it made its flyover.

He brought the big bomber up to 50,000 feet, so high, the crew had to bundle up and go on oxygen masks.

The engines sprouting pure white contrails, he

389

swung the bomber back and forth high above the burning city, carving an enormous white "W" out of the clear blue sky.

Then, he switched to the Family's radio frequency and said: "Mrs. O'Malley's cow just kicked over another lantern, boys, courtesy of the Free Forces of Football City."

Then, he turned the B-24 south and headed for home.

CHAPTER TWENTY-SEVEN

Hunter nursed the lumbering B-24 back to a safe
landing at the Football City Airport. Its engines
straining and smoking, the plane's wings creaked and
groaned the entire return trip. It had taken more than
a few hits from groundfire, yet kept on flying, plug-
ging along. The old bomber had served them well.
But he doubted if the bird would ever fly again. As the
crew slid through the exit hatches, Hunter remained
behind to take one long last look at the plane. All
those years frozen in ice, just to be melted out for one
last mission. The B-24's official name was "Liberator." He ran his hand over the control cabin's wall,
"Perfect handle," he thought.

The airport was bustling with activity. On the way
back, he had taken advantage of a low cloud cover to
fly the B-24 over the Family's troop concentrations
waiting now just across the Mississippi River.

He wished he could bomb up again and strike at
the New Chicago army, but there was a more pressing
matter.

St. Louie was waiting for him and Dozer on the tarmac.

"Congratulations, Major, once again," the man said, shaking his hand.

"Thanks," Hunter said. "But there were a hundred guys up there with me." Then, changing the subject, he asked St. Louie what the situation was with the Family army.

"My agents tell me there are eighty thousand Family troops right across the river," St. Louie answered soberly. "They've got tanks and hundreds of artillery pieces. It's only a matter of time before they attack."

"Tonight," Dozer said. "They'll start throwing everything at us tonight."

Hunter looked at both of them. St. Louie's inner grief was so apparent, the man appeared to be aging right in front of him. Dozer looked like a man who hadn't slept in a year. At that moment, he realized these men were more than his comrades-in-arms. They were also his friends.

"Well, if they are going to attack us tonight," he said. "That means we only have a few hours to figure out how we're going to beat them, too."

They returned to the battle command center and took account of their forces. They still had enough men—almost 40,000—to fill three divisions. Thirty of the city's howitzers were operational and were in place along the river bank, and there was an odd assortment of mobile guns, rocket launchers and tanks.

All of the F-20s were still in flying condition, likewise the F-4s and the choppers. Hunter had previously ordered all of the B-29s, the B-25s, and the C-130s to be refueled, re-armed and made ready to stand by. Even the shitbox B-58 Hustler was gassed up and ready to go. But the surviving B-47 Stratojets would be practically useless to them now—they could neither bomb low nor provide ground support. Hunter ordered them stripped of usable parts, and their tanks drained. But even with that, the supplies would soon begin to dwindle. There was only so much JP-8 fuel to go around; the Texans had sent all they could spare and more. Now the pipeline was shut off. Hunter estimated he had enough left over to refuel the bombers once, the F-20s and the F-4s twice and the '16 three times. Then they would be dry.

And dry meant grounded.

St. Louie ordered all of the city's troops deployed to positions along the west bank of the Mississippi River. Across the muddy waters, the Football City forces could clearly see the Family troops bringing up artillery and digging in. Football City's ammunition supply was also low; if it hadn't been, St. Louie would have fired on anything that moved on the east bank of the river. But now, every commander in the Free Forces was under orders to "make every shot count."

On a suggestion from Hunter, Dozer sent his best explosives men to mine the seven bridges that spanned the Mississippi and led into Football City. He knew that eventually, every one of the bridges would be blown—by waiting, there was a good chance that they would catch some enemy troops or equipment on the bridges when they went down.

The Mississippi hugged the Football City border for 15 miles. By nightfall, St. Louie's intelligence corps reported as many as 2500 of the Family's large guns and tanks along that stretch. There were reports of gunboats and smaller ferries coming down the river from the interior of the Family's territory. Worse still, Football City airport radar had picked up many airborne blips on its screens shortly before nightfall.

Hunter wasn't surprised when the enemy aircraft report reached them in command center. He, St. Louie and Dozer were studying an enormous map of the city and its defenses at the time.

"One of two things has happened," he told them, reading the report. "Either they've hired on air pirates, or they've been supplied very quickly with more MIGs. Maybe both."

"Where the hell could they get MIGs so goddamn fast?" St. Louie asked, the exasperation coming through, loud and clear.

"If I had to guess," Hunter said. "I'd say the same people who own those East European ships we saw in the New Chicago harbor had something to do with it."

"The Russians?" St. Louie asked, his voice still containing a trace of disbelief.

"I'm convinced, without a doubt," Hunter said, adding, "Finally."

"Where does that leave us, Hawk?" Dozer asked,

wearily rubbing his eyes.

"Well, if they commit the MIGs to ground support or to bomb us, we can engage them with the F-20s," Hunter said. "But dogfights suck up fuel. We use the fuel to fight them and we lose the F-20s in the ground support role."

"And if we commit the F-20s to ground support too soon," Dozer continued the theory. "The MIGs can jump us once we've gone dry."

"That's the situation," Hunter agreed.

"What about the B-29s?" St. Louie asked.

"They've got full tanks, enough gas for two missions," Hunter answered. "I've ordered each of them to have as many guns as they can carry standing by. Machine guns, recoilless rifles, even RPGs if they can handle them. They'll stick them all out of one side, punch holes in the fuselage if they have to."

"To use as gunships?" Dozer asked.

"Right. First, we'll have them unload what we have left in bombs on the east side of the river, then come back, pick up their extra guns and turn them into Spookys. We'll assign at least one to each bridge. The rest will be vectored to where they are needed. Same with the C-130s and the B-25s. I don't know if they'll get the B-24s airborne, though."

"How about SAMs?" St. Louie asked.

"I'm sure we'll see a lot of them. Stingers, Blowpipes, the works," Hunter said grimly.

"Whew!" Dozer exclaimed. "It's gonna get crowded up there."

"We'll keep the choppers on this side of the river,"

Hunter continued. "They can help on ground support and recon, plus watch for the amphibious crossings."

St. Louie peered at the map of his dream city. "We just can't let any of those bastards get across the river," he said. "If we do, we're sunk."

"We'll blow the bridges," Dozer said, pointing at the huge map. "But I'm not so sure that will stop them. If they don't get across here, they could cross at any number of points north or south of the city. We know they've got boats they've floated down from Peoria. And, they've got pontoon bridges. If they do cross either north or south, we'll have to commit troops there, and leave our center and other flank open."

Hunter stared at the map and the markers indicating the Family's troop and gun concentrations. It was a matter of numbers. The Family's forces outnumbered Football City 2-to-1. They were better equipped. He couldn't imagine what their strength would be—materially and mentally—if his thrown-together air force hadn't bombed New Chicago. Nevertheless, what remained still added up against the Free Forces. It had all the makings of a last stand. Yet he was never one to give up hope.

"We'll have to take risks," he said finally. "Do the unpredictable. They won't be expecting us to launch all the bombers at once against them. It'll knock them for a loop, at least for a while. But then, we'll have to *keep* them off balance and . . ."

Dozer and St. Louie looked at him, both saying "And?"

"And," Hunter said. "Hope for a miracle."

The first shells from the Family's artillery started landing on the west side of the river at precisely midnight. The Free Forces' troops dug in along the river bank hunkered down as the artillery barrage intensified. Soon, Family guns all along the 15 mile stretch of river were firing into the city. The night sky was lit brighter than daytime. Streaks of red crisscrossed above the soldiers. It was at once fascinating and frightening.

Soon the shells were coming in so fast and loud, the Free Forces' troopers found their ears had started to bleed. They bravely held their fire. Most of the Family's shells were going over the troopers' heads anyway; the target of this opening barrage was Football City itself. Many of the beautiful buildings and casinos were reduced to rubble. Fires erupted everywhere. The massive Grand Stadium, a marshalling yard for the Free Forces, was taking an inordinate amount of pounding. Fortunately, the airport, located a few miles northwest of the stadium, was just out of range of the Family's gunners.

The nightmare continued for three hours. Slowly, the proud city, once a symbol of freedom, commerce and rebuilding, began to crumble. Small fires joined to create larger ones. Roads were damaged beyond repair, making the movement of emergency vehicles next to impossible. All the while, the Free Forces didn't fire a shot. In this, possibly last, battle, each bullet was worth its weight in gold.

Then the barrage stopped. The air, heavy with the smell of cordite, was suddenly silent, the only sounds being the crackling of the fires back in the city. An eerieness settled over the Free Forces lines. Many of the soldiers, without sleep, could see ghosts of shapes moving on the far side of the river 300 yards away. But they resisted all temptations to shoot at the spirits.

It was quiet for the next two hours.

The 10 B-29s, propellers whirring, their sides spiked with gun muzzles, lined up to take off. The sun was just peeking over the horizon, but the Football City airport was in the ninth hour of frantic activity. While the artillery barrage battered the helpless city, those gathered at the airport worked madly to get the remaining planes armed and loaded and airborne.

Hunter sat at the end of the runway, his F-16's souped-up engine turned off to save fuel, watching the parade of aircraft from different eras roll by. First the Superfortresses went up and formed a ring high above the airport. Next went the nine rugged C-130s. They took up a lower orbit north of the field. Ten F-20s sped off next, lifting into the air in pairs. Only after the Ace Wrecking Company's F-4s were airborne did he start his own engine and race down the runway. This would be Football City's last strategic bombing mission. Afterward, all the planes would be committed to tactical support, that was, helping the Free Forces' ground troops battle the Family. Just about all of the Vermont cache of weapons would soon be gone. The deployment of the big planes bordered on desperation. Whatever the outcome, the final act was underway.

The air armada formed up according to plan, then flew the short distance over the city to the battle area. Hunter, like many of the crew members, looked down on the devastated Football City. It was practically unidentifiable. Little remained except heaps of smoldering rubble. However, in the midst of the destruction, the Grand Stadium stood out. It *was* heavily damaged, yet not totally destroyed. It was a tough, solid structure and it had somehow made it through the terrible night's shelling. Flying on a staff above its highest point, someone had run up a shredded Football City flag.

Hunter had to laugh as he led the planes over the stadium. "All they wanted to do was play football," he thought. "What the hell was the matter with that?"

He unconsciously reached to his back pocket and felt the form of the folded flag he always kept there. For the first time in a while, he took it out, and felt it. His hand tingled at its touch. He remembered that terribly bleak day in New York City so long ago when he took it from the dead Saul Wackerman. Despite the dire situation, Hunter felt good inside. He had been true to his word, in any case. He hadn't forgotten. He was still fighting. The enemy was the same. The stakes were the same. The cause was the same. And it all came down to one word: *Freedom*. That's what Saul Wackerman died for. As did Jones. And the

399

millions killed in Europe. And the thousand defending Football City—those who would die that day. He thought of the enemy. Those who would repress them. Who would enslave them. The enemy may win the battles, but he knew they would never win the war. And the Free Forces may not win this fight. If not, it may take years . . . 20, 50, 80 . . . 100 years. But freedom-loving people would rise up again. The sons and daughters of these warriors would come back. And then the battles will be won. You can kill a man. But you can't kill his spirit.

He felt the flag once more, kissed it and then put it in his left breast pocket. "The bullet that takes me will have to go through you first," he said to himself.

The target of the bombing mission was the largest enemy troop concentration St. Louie's agents could pinpoint. It was located just across the Mississippi in the old city of East St. Louis. The Family was using the city as a makeshift forward headquarters, taking advantage of its railroad yards. Hunter hoped by bombing the city, he would further disrupt the lines of communications between the enemy commanders and their superiors sitting in the black, ultra-skyscraper once known as the Sears Tower back in New Chicago. He had briefly considered flying up to New Chicago and blasting the tower, but discounted the idea on two points. First, it would use up precious resources for less than tangible results—for all he knew the Family leaders might not be in the Black Tower when he arrived. Second, he was a pilot and every pilot was needed right here in Football City.

The bombing force arrived over the target area, led by Hunter and the F-4s. The F-20s cruised high above the airborne column, keeping an eye out for MIGs and conserving fuel. Luckily, no enemy jets were in the area. One by one, the airplanes unloaded their payloads—standard bombs, TNT barrels, odd napalm cannisters—then turned 180s for the 10 minute trip back to Football City. Only a handful of SAMs appeared, indicating the bombers had taken the Family by surprise. If they hadn't, the air would have been filled with the anti-aircraft missiles. This told Hunter something else: The Family either didn't have very good radar, or had turned it off as a precaution. Or maybe they were just lazy, sloppy, unconcerned about the airborne threat from Football City. Hunter entered all of the possibilities into his brain, to be recalled later when needed.

The bombers and escorts all landed safely back at Football City airport. As soon as the planes rolled into their stations, an army of monkeys appeared and started stripping everything connected with bombing from the planes. In their place, they installed guns of every size and shape. The B-29s were perforated with dozens of small gun ports, all on the starboard side and just large enough to stick the muzzle of a M61 machine gun or a similar weapon through. The C-130s, boasting powerful engines and thus being able to lift more, had cannons, RPGs, even small howitzers placed aboard, again, sticking out of freshly drilled gunports on the port side. The idea, familiar to those close to gunship tactics, was that, in action, the pilot would fly the plane in a continuous 360-degree turn to the starboard. The combined firepower of every available gun, matched with the slow, arching turn, presented a formidable airborne threat to enemy ground troops. Hunter estimated the gunships could stay flying for up to six hours if needed. By that time fuel would start to run out. No matter. Because he knew by that time, the battle would either have been won or lost.

He watched the feverish preparations, hoping the converted gunships could be flying within two hours. Still it was only just 7 AM. They had many hours to go in this, what would turn out to be, their longest day.

On the east bank of the Mississippi River, near the entrance to the Merrill Avenue Bridge, a battalion of the Family's crack sappers' regiment was waiting for its morning meal to be brought in. The unit's commanders knew they still had more than an hour to go before they would jump off and try to take the bridge leading into Football City. The soldiers were confident, even cocky. They were anxious to get the battle underway. Most had foregone sleep the night before simply to see the artillery barrage that had reduced Football City to near-rubble.

"How could anyone live through that?" they had asked themselves and each other. "We'll be playing football in their stadium by noon," others said.

Most of them were mercenaries, so there was a monetary reason to start the fighting. Their commanders were offering a piece of real silver for each enemy soldier they confirmed killed. A gold piece would be awarded for dead enemy officers. Plus, the first unit to reach the Grand Stadium would split a bag of gold. The sappers, being specialists, believed that gold was as good as in their pockets.

Their officers were confident too. The men were well-rested and in high, if not greedy, good spirits. They were all well-armed and looking proper in their jet-black with red trim uniforms. Now if only the morning meal would arrive, the unit would be fully prepared to go into action.

CHAPTER TWENTY-EIGHT

Suddenly, above them, the Family sappers heard the distinct sound of a helicopter.

"Here's the chow," one of the officers said.

"Finally," another, a major commented. "And, they're doing it in style—by chopper."

By this time, most of the unit was on its feet, lined up with mess kits in hand. The chopper circled, then came in, kicking up a good amount of dust as it approached the four-lane entrance to the bridge.

"The Family must be getting hard up," said one soldier as he watched the helicopter descend. "That chopper is a piece of crap!"

"That's straight shit, Jack," his buddy said, as the battered helicopter set down. "And what's that shit written on the side? What the fuck is the Down Maine Lumber Company?"

He never found out . . .

The side shutters on the Sea Stallion dropped down one second before the computer-fired GE Gatling guns inside opened up. Many of the 900 soldiers had no idea what was happening. The three Gatlings, each spewing 100 rounds *a second*, didn't sound like

404

ordinary guns. They had more of a mechanical, buzzing sound, one which was almost completely drowned out by the racket of the chopper blades. To many of the sappers, it just appeared like their comrades were falling for no reason at all. Even when they caught a burst of computer-controlled bullets in the guts, they died wondering what the hell was going on.

The carnage was quick, complete, almost surgical. More than 700 of the sappers lay dead or dying on the pavement. Those fortunate enough to find cover, lived, then bolted as soon as the deadly chopper lifted off. In less than a minute, the Stallion's guns had taken out one of the top units of the Family's army. No Free Forces' soldier even alighted from the chopper. The warriors were sitting behind video consoles, their triggers disguised as computer buttons. The enemy had never fired a shot.

"Serves you right, you fuckers," Dozer said, peering out one of the Stallion's windows as the pilots lifted the big helicopter away. "I hope they can fit you all in hell."

Back at the Family's forward headquarters in East St. Louis, the New Chicago commanders were in disarray. Their once-neatly pressed and clean black uniforms were now covered with dirt and dust. The early morning bombing raid had taken them completely by surprise, and had killed many of their top officers. The entire west side of the abandoned city was on fire. The commanders had been forced to move their HQ into the cellar of a partially-destroyed building, as protection against further air raids. Their biggest worry was communications with the front. It was spotty at best, giving them less and less control over the nearly 90,000 troops under their command. Now, to make matters worse, they had just received a report that their top sapper unit had been decimated by a helicopter posing as a supply chopper.

"The fools!" one of the commanders roared, pounding his fist on a map table that was illuminated by candles. The bombing had knocked out all of the headquarters' electrical power. "We've never delivered food to them in a helicopter before! What the hell make them think we would start now?"

"It's this guy Hunter who's behind it," another officer said, spitting the name out. "He's the guy who put the hurt on the 'Aks a couple of times at least. And he's been on our ass for months, we just didn't realize it."

"Look," a third officer said. "We've still got these guys almost 3-to-1. We blew the shit out of them last night. I say we jump off now. Get the thing over with!"

"What about the big boats?" another commander asked. "A lot of them got big firepower on them and we're supposed to use the others to get most of the troops across the river. Trouble is, they won't reach us until noon at the earliest."

"Let our guys use the bridges," the first officer roared. "There are seven of them, for Christ's sake. If they can't capture two or three of them, what the hell kind of army are they?"

"Right," another added. "And they've already got a bunch of smaller motorboats. So what if the first guys over get chopped up? If we can establish some beachheads now, when the big boats do come down-river, it'll be gravy."

"But most of the troops haven't eaten yet," one lone dissenter said. "We're having one hell of a supply problem ever since . . . well, you know, since those Football City flyboys iced the capital."

"Screw 'em!" the officer who liked pounding on the table screamed. "What the hell is this? A country club? We're paying these soldiers big bucks to kick ass on St. Louie. That don't mean they're entitled to grub every other God damn minute! I say send them off! Now!"

His suggestion was met with near-unanimous, if half-hearted, shouts of approval. Only the officer who was in favor of feeding the troops argued against it.

A quick vote was taken and the motion, as it was, passed. The officer who had protested was led out-side, forced to kneel down and shot twice in the back of the head. Soon after, the order to move out was flashed to the Family's front line units.

The shooting started a few minutes later . . .

The first shots fired by the Free Forces were from riflemen protecting one of the bridges leading into Football City. Just after 8 AM, a squad of sharp-shooters guarding the Alexis Avenue Crossway saw several figures splashing in the water under the span. They were Family skindivers trying to locate the charges the Free Forces had placed on the bridge. The sharpshooters peppered the water around the divers as Free Forces' frogmen entered the river from their side and swam out to meet the enemy. A fierce knife battle broke out under the bridge, with the Free Forces' divers eventually gaining the upper hand. By the time they had returned to land, shooting along the entire front had broken out.

There had once been a cohesive plan on the part of the Family to invade Football City: batter the city with artillery, send in sappers to take control of the bridges while waiting for the makeshift fleet of boats to get downriver. Now the front line officers learned the plans had been changed. The new orders were simply to "take the city." Every officer was on his own. Some of the units had the benefit of rafts and rubber boats, even some speedboats, with which to cross the Mississippi. Other units simply charged across the bridges. Still others decided to start their attack with a resumption of the artillery barrage and wait for the larger boats.

Back at the Free Forces' war command center in the basement of St. Louie's headquarters, the Football City commanders sifted through reports as they flooded in from the front and tried to come up with sensible defenses to meet every threat.

Meanwhile, at the airport, Hunter was ready to take off on the second mission of the day. The unpredictable side of war had already begun to take hold. The fighting was going full tilt along the river now, and the ground units were calling for air support. The B-29 gunships were first in line to take off.

Originally, he had planned to send the C-130s up with the Superfortresses. But that plan had to be scrapped earlier when he was forced to send the C-130s and the Cobra Brothers north to intercept a large flotilla of Family boats that was steaming down the Illinois River and soon to reach the Mississippi. His air cover over the river battle was cut in half.

Dozer was already out there somewhere, using the Sea Stallion to harass the Family lines of communication. The Ace Wrecking Company was also already in action; they had delivered an air strike minutes before on Family troops attempting to charge across the Gilean Boulevard Bridge in the south of the city, and were now strafing industrious Family amphibious soldiers trying to cross the river on rafts and in rubber boats.

Hunter finally took off, the F-16 loaded with three, 1000-pound anti-personnel bombs. He flew immediately to the Sullivan Square overpass, where Family divers had succeeded in dislodging explosives placed there by the Free Forces.

When he arrived over the concrete bridge, a Family tank column was attempting to cross. The B-29 gunship was already on station and attacking the half dozen tanks. He circled above and watched the fascinating engagement. The World War II-vintage B-29 Superfortress must have been carrying 20 gunners, firing everything from M-16s up to RPGs. Flying in a low, slow circle, the gunners aboard the big plane delivered a steady stream of fire on the tank column below. Many of them were firing with tracers in their ammunition, the long red streaks adding to the strangeness of the battle. Troops on the west side of the river also added to the lead shower. One by one, the tanks halted, unable to move in the withering hail of bullets. One tank—an M-1 Abrams—exploded. Then another. And another. The rear tank attempted to back off, but a gunner riding in the rear turret of the B-29 delivered a perfectly placed RPG right under the tank's fuel supply. It exploded with a loud *whump*! causing it to blow up and *over* the side of the bridge.

The remaining Family tank crewmen tried to abandon their machines, but the ever-circling B-29 stayed right on them, cutting down anyone who moved. In the course of five minutes, all of the tanks were reduced to burning hulks, and dozens of enemy tankers' bodies littered the overpass.

Hunter turned south and spotted a fleet of about 25 motorboats trying to cross a narrow part of the river, between the Sullivan Square Bridge and the Cardinal Avenue span. He brought the F-16 down almost level with the top of the water. The surprised Family troops saw him coming and vainly attempted to fire their rifles at him. It was no use. He opened up with his M61 cannon six-pack, riddling the boats, sinking a dozen instantly. Up ahead loomed the Cardinal Avenue bridge. Enemy boats were also trying to cross under the protection of the bridge supports as well as on the other side. Instead of pulling up, he booted the throttle and flew right under one of the spans. He never stopped firing. Those soldiers who survived were amazed that the streaking jet had actually come out from *underneath* the bridge.

He stayed low, angling over and above the enemy side of the river, dodging enemy flak as well as the hundreds of artillery shells that were being fired by both sides. The air was filled with bullets, rockets, surface-to-surface missiles, mortar shells, tank shells, and airplane exhaust. It seemed like both banks of the river were aflame. The smoke was blinding in some places. Through the smoke above him, he'd catch an occasionally glimpse of a B-29 or one of the F-4s or Cobras, each thick in the middle of action. His radio was filled with the excited chatter of war, cries of direct hits and calls for help. The battle was already more ferocious than anything he'd been in since World War III.

His cannons never stopped blazing. He shot at anything that moved. Jeeps, tanks, fuel trucks, troops, artillery guns. They all felt the wrath of the awesome power of the F-16's six guns. It seemed like hundreds of SAMs were fired at him, but he was much too low for most of the missiles to arm properly. In some cases, the missiles wandered around and sought out the nearest source of heat. One headed for an old commandeered Sunoco gasoline truck, that was serving as a mobile filling station for some Family vehicles. The missile impacted just behind the driver's cab, causing the full tank of gas to explode.

His body was vibrating with adrenaline as he continued his murderous, low-altitude run down the river. A barge full of Family troops was his next victim. He placed one of the anti-personnel bombs square on its deck, where it burst open in a ball of flame, ripping the 200 soldiers aboard with thousands

411

of pieces of hot, deadly shrapnel.

Another mile of strafing passed when his target acquisition computer started flashing. An aircraft was "hot," a half mile down the river. Looked like a chopper—a big one. He was there in a matter of seconds, just in time to see a heavily armed helicopter rising up from behind the trees on the bank. They had picked the wrong time to take off. In one motion, he armed and fired a Sidewinder which flew a spiraling course right into the chopper's exhaust pipe. The resulting explosion split the helicopter in two, the rotor continued to whip around and climb while the flaming body fell back to earth. He was by the wreck in a flash, but it was long enough for him to see the chopper was a Hind gunship—designed and built in the Soviet Union. He wasn't surprised to see that some Russians had joined the battle. That made it all the better. "*Sayonara*, comrades," he said bitterly as he continued to fly downriver.

He had reached the southern edge of the battle zone when he heard a call for help. Family troops were close to breaking across the James Street Bridge, the second span north of the city. He immediately put the F-16 on its tail and accelerated straight up. Attaining the height he needed, he put the jet over on its back, flipped over and cut the engine. Silently, he glided toward the James, saving precious fuel. Below him, smoke and flames were rising from the fighting up and down the river. He realized the Free Forces were taking a beating, yet holding up well. And, as far as he knew, no Family troops had yet crossed successfully.

412

He saw the James Street bridge below him and restarted the engine. The B-29 was on station, firing away at Family troops who had managed to drive many APCs more than halfway across the bridge. Suddenly, a SAM flashed up from the east bank and caught the B-29 on its left wing. The Superfortress shuddered once as the missile exploded. The big plane then turned over, flames engulfing its fuselage. Hunter could almost *feel* the pilot struggling with the controls. The doomed flyer managed to aim the bomber right at the span itself. With a tremendous explosion the B-29 crashed square into the top of the bridge, killing the Family troops and detonating the explosives put there previously by the Free Forces. The entire structure seem to lift out of the water then fall. A great gush of flaming, muddy water shot up as secondary explosions went off. By the time Hunter was in position, the bridge—and everyone on it—was gone.

More SAMs appeared from the east bank, so he turned in their direction. His target acquisition video screen showed him five SAM sites foolishly erected right in a row. Dozens of Family troops frantically moved about the missile launchers. It was a perfect target for his second anti-personnel bomb.

He came in low, popped his bomb release button, yanked on the side-stick controller and again, stood the '16 on its ass. The anti-personnel device exploded, perforating man and missile alike. Looking back through the bubble-top canopy, he saw the SAMs still on the launchers blow, causing a half dozen secondary explosions. "Someone should have told those boys how to deploy their missiles," he thought.

"Breakthrough on Alexis!"

It was the words Hunter had hoped he wouldn't hear, but at the same time, knew he would.

The call had come from Captain Crunch's weapons officer riding in the rear seat of the Ace Wrecking Company's F-4.

"Crunch, Hunter here," he called.

"We got you, Major," the reply came back. "We've got a breakthrough on Alexis. They must have disarmed the mines or they just didn't go off. They're pouring across right now, and our guys are going tooth and nail with them."

"Where's the gunship?"

"They iced it, Major," the reply came back through a haze of static. "Looks like a SAM got it. It's down and burning right next to the bridge."

"What's your weapons status?" Hunter asked, wheeling the F-16 around and heading for the scene.

"We got cannon enough for one more pass, but no ordnance. Wrecker Two is back at base getting reloaded."

"Roger, Crunch," he radioed back. "Let's do a one-two. I'll go in first. Just watch out for our troops."

"Roger, Hawk."

He arrived over the bridge to see hundreds of Family troops charging across the span. It was the only bridge that had not yet been blown and it seemed as if all of the enemy troops on the east side of the river had converged on it. Many, in fact, had reached the other side, where they were met by the Free Forces infantry. A sharp firefight was in progress around the approach to the bridge that once served as a toll island. The wreckage of the B-29 was burning a short distance away.

As planned, he went in first, dropping his last remaining anti-personnel bomb in the middle of the bridge, then opening up with the six-pack all the way to the east side. A couple of shoulder-launched SAMs flashed by him, but he virtually ignored them. The F-4 came in right behind him, chopping up more enemy troops, and momentarily stopping their flow across the bridge.

He was worried about this situation. The Alexis Bridge was two-tiered and had up and down spans, built in a time when the out-going used the upper span and the in-coming traffic the lower. The Family soldiers were flooding across both of them, with the troops on the lower span somewhat immune from the strafing attacks.

He had to gamble. The Family had either disconnected the explosives on the bridge supports, or, for whatever reason, the charges just didn't go off. He had to go with the second option. Neither he nor the Phantom had enough ammo to hold off the invading troops, and the rest of the Free Forces aircraft were tied up elsewhere.

He brought the '16 down low again, lowered the flaps and the landing gear, and prepared the air brakes. He had to get under the bridge to see if the explosives were still there. To do so, he'd have to slow the jet down to a crawl, almost stall it under the

415

bridge, just a split-second for him to give a look around. It was an old Thunderbirds' trick; no other pilot would even dream of trying such a maneuver under a bridge span. But he was looking forward to seeing if it could be done.

He approached the bridge and hit the air brakes. The jet's computer brain set as if the plane was coming in for a landing. The throttle went back automatically and the nose came up. The Family troops crossing the bridge saw him coming and started firing at him, a tempting target because he was going so slowly. He zig-zagged a little to deny them good aim. In a few seconds he was nearly under the bridge, wagging his wings to prevent the jet from plunging into the water just 30 feet below. The condition he had set up was as close as one could get to hovering in a jet, unless that jet was a VTOL Harrier.

He gave the underside of the bridge a quick scan, then hit his throttle. The engines kicked and a second later he was back up to speed. Mission accomplished. The explosive charges were still there.

Now all he had to do was ignite them. The wire controls leading to the detonator on the Free Forces' side were probably damaged in the fight, or, perhaps, the man with his hand on the plunger had been killed. Hunter would rely on the six-pack to finish the job.

He radioed the Free Forces' commander battling to stem the flood of Family troops coming across the bridge. He told him of his plan to shoot the explosives and ice the Alexis. All of the Free Forces' troops had to be prepared to get behind cover. He told their leader that when they saw him do a quick four-point maneuver, his soldiers should hit the deck. The ground commander, his troops outnumbered 6-to-1 and battling the attackers with bare hands, would have hung up on anyone else but Hunter. But knowing full well the reputation of the Wingman, he passed the word to his troops. "When the F-16 goes fancy, everyone duck!"

Hunter did a quick loop and approached the bridge again low over the water. The fire from the Family troops was much more intense this time. They were shooting at him from both levels of the bridge as well as the east side of the river. He kept the F-16 slow and steady as he approached the span, wheels down and air brakes engaged.

Slowly. Down a little. The cannon shot would have to find its way through the bridge's under structure to hit the TNT package. Up a hair. A little to the right. The Family was now starting to bring across tanks and APCs as the battle on the west side of the bridge turned into a simple holding action for the Free Forces' troops. Hunter figured there were probably a couple of hundred attackers on the west side already, and as many as a 1000 coming across the bridge's double decks.

Just 100 yards out. To the left. Steady. *Now!* He flipped the jet on its right wing, then its back, its left wing and upright again. That was the signal. The Free Forces' troops hit the dirt. Hunter pushed his weapons' trigger. A burst from the six-pack homed in on the explosive packages as if they were radar-guided. One package ignited, instantaneously blowing the 10 other charges.

He had pulled back on the '16's side-stick at the last possible instant and rode right up the side of the bridge, clearing it just as the TNT went off. There was an incredible explosion followed by a horrible creaking of bent metal so loud he could hear it in the cockpit above the noise of his engine and the non-stop radio chatter in his earphones.

When he flipped the jet over again, he saw the bridge had separated, the center span was gone and the two ends were twisting downward. The charging Family troops and vehicles that weren't blown up with the center span, couldn't stop their momentum in time and plunged into the water below. Those troops caught on the east side were now cut off. The Free Forces' troops re-emerged and began to slaughter them. In a matter of a minute, the attackers' flow across the Alexis bridge was severed and hundreds of enemy troops killed.

It was just about then that Hunter ran out of ammunition.

Football City airport was the scene of mass, if controlled, pandemonium. As Hunter was making his final approach for landing, he could see eight of the 12 F-20s preparing for take off. These were his reserves—his last two aces in the hole. Time was running out, he had to play them.

The battle, still only a few hours old, had already changed. The C-130s, sent north to meet the Family flotilla sailing toward the battle scene, had sunk nearly half the collection of heavily-armed tugboats, river barges and assorted yachts-turned-PT boats, before they ran out of ammunition and were forced to return. Trouble was, as many as 150 of the enemy craft made it through the air raid and had arrived at a critical part of the fighting. Football City commanders all along the front were frantically calling for air support against Family troops that were now in the boats and crossing the river en masse. Artillery fire from the east side had, if anything, increased, rivaling the intensity of the barrage the night before. The only difference was this time, the Free Forces' troops were the targets, not the once-glamorous buildings of Football City.

The F-20s, loaded up with the last of the 1000-pound bombs, would go after the Family gun emplacements. The returning C-130s, some with as many as 30 gunports drilled into their starboard side, would rearm, refuel and join the remaining B-29s, the choppers, the two B-25s and even the cranky B-58, and go after the enemy amphibious forces.

At this point, Hunter honestly had no idea which way the battle would go. The Free Forces' were outnumbered by at least 3-to-1, a disadvantage he had hoped to offset with the use of Football City's airpower. And the Family's energy crisis. The Free Forces were fighting valiantly, but, after all, they were made up almost two thirds of untrained volunteers. The New Chicago army was a well-trained band of thugs. Paid soldiers. They were fighting for money. The Free Forces were fighting for their lives and a way of life. Was he foolish enough to think that could make a difference?

But there was something more. He had a very strange feeling in his bones. It was very intense, so much so, his thinking was becoming blurred. The feeling hit him just as he was landing. By the time he was taxiing the '16, he was visibly shaking. *Something was wrong. Very wrong. Far off. Getting closer.*

He had just pulled up to his taxi station when he heard St. Louie's voice come over the radio. He was calling from the airport control tower.

"Hawk! Get up here now!"

Hunter climbed out of the '16 and sprinted over to the structure and up the stairs. In the control room, he found St. Louie and a group of Football City officers crowded around a radar screen. Their expressions ranged from extremely concerned to outright panic.

"Hawk," St. Louie said, the normally measured voice rising an octave with concern. "You'd better see this."

Hunter moved to the radar screen and took a look. The round, green video display had an arm of light sweeping 360-degrees every five seconds. At first, he saw nothing unusual—just blips of the Football City aircraft he knew were operating in the area. Then the light arm swept up to indicate the air traffic coming in from the northeast. He gasped.

"Holy shit!"

Now at least he knew what had caused the strange feeling that had come over him. He waited for the arm to sweep up to the northeast again. When it did, he knew he wasn't seeing things. There were at least 100 blips on the screen, heading south-southwest.

"They're coming this way," St. Louie said.

Hunter had *felt* them. As always, he knew, just by the feeling, seconds, even minutes before any radar. This time his special extrasensory perception almost overloaded and short-circuited.

"They're not just MIGs," he said, looking at the screen but actually *knowing* without its aid. "They're coming at us with everything. SU-14s, Mirages, Super Sabres, Starfighters."

"Christ!" one of the officers yelled. "What do we do?"

Hunter was still trembling, not with fear but with hate. Hate for the Family. Hate for the Russians. Hate for the people who killed Saul Wackerman. Hate for the people who killed Jones. Hate for the people who killed his country.

He felt a curious strength wash through him. He suddenly not only felt stronger, his mind became clearer. Clearer than it had ever been before. He knew what he had to do.

"Evacuate the airport!" he yelled. "Quick! They're heading this way to ice us! Right here! We've got to get everything off the ground!"

The officers went into action, grabbing radios and contacting the various crews of the planes waiting to launch. Within seconds, the take-off procedure was sped up. The half-minute between take-off protocol was dispensed with very quickly. Now the planes were rolling down the runway at the rate of one every 10 seconds. St. Louie got on another radio and started contacting the Football City aircraft already airborne. He was primarily concerned about the F-20s. They

421

wouldn't be able to come back and load up on missiles and ammo.

Hunter heard none of this. He was out of the control tower in a flash. Now, he was running. Running to the F-16. A band of monkeys was working on it. He didn't remember even talking to them. He was thinking of all the time he had put in back at the Aerodrome, working on modifications to the F-16. Now he was glad he did it. His mind was clear but racing fast. Next thing he knew, he was rolling down the runway, his cannons filled with ammunition, his wings weighted down by 20 Sidewinders, five times the number normally carried on a F-16.

"Got to give these boys a reception," he thought as he took off and turned toward the northeast.

At the same time, the battle at the Mississippi had again taken a dangerous turn. It was now obvious that another large enemy force had been held in reserve to see the outcome of the initial attack. When the Free Forces' held their own, the Family commanders, acting on orders from the top men in the Black Tower back in New Chicago, threw their reserves into the fray.

At the front, most of the Free Forces were getting their first look at what was left of the enemy flotilla. Most of the enemy craft were tugboats outfitted with heavy field cannons and RPGs. Others were actually small cargo ships and barges that once plied the Grand Lakes. The boats served two purposes for the Family. Some transported reserve troops from shore to shore while others used their firepower to keep the Free Forces' defenders occupied.

Every aircraft fighting for Football City had now joined in the battle. The rearmed Cobra Brothers were braving the violently choppy, shrapnel-filled air above the river to fly low and scorch enemy landing craft with their special flame-throwing weapons. The Stallion, with Dozer aboard and operating on the hit-and-run, attacked several key targets in the enemy rear. The Marine captain had also toyed with the idea of bolting up to New Chicago and blasting away at the Black Tower, just to take out the brains of the new Family attack. But like Hunter, he knew the situation at Football City was desperate, and that the Free Forces needed every gun they could get.

CHAPTER TWENTY-NINE

Hunter could feel the weight of the 20 Sidewinders cause the wings of the F-16 to bounce. No matter. He had reinforced the jet's body and wings long ago and was confident that the airplane could handle the strain.

Whether the pilot could or not was another matter . . .

He was boiling with hate. Too much hate. It was affecting his reflexes, his logical way of thinking and his inner vision. He couldn't wait to intercept the incoming Family air armada, although he was outnumbered 100-to-1. This could be it, he kept thinking. This could be the end of the line. But *he didn't care*. And that's what was bothering him.

He knew that none of the other Football City aircraft would be able to leave the river battle to help him. With the arrival of the enemy boats and reserves, that situation was beyond desperate. Anything short of divine intervention wouldn't be enough to turn the tide.

Tangling with the force of enemy planes coming his way would be no different. He was good. The best, in fact. But one jet against 100? Even he doubted it. But he vowed long ago to go down fighting, and if this was to be his fate, so be it. He realized he felt just as Jones did when he launched his one-man war against the Mid-Aks. Some things *are* worth dying for. He remembered his rebirth on the mountain in Vermont the day Jones died. He had worked and sacrificed and almost without feeling it, had changed since then as a man and a pilot. The innocence was lost. He hoped something was gained. For the first time ever, he felt ready to meet his destiny.

Suddenly, his target acquisition system started to go crazy. The Family aircraft were just over the horizon. There were so many of them that even the '16's sophisticated radar system couldn't handle them all. In fact, the number of blips showing up on his radar screen was only serving to confuse his on-board computers. If he set the Sidewinders on computer-command fire, they too would become confused and possibly detonate prematurely, it would all be too much for the machines.

So he had to take a chance. First, he armed all the missiles at once. Then, he flipped the weapons release switch from "Automatic" to "Manual." Finally, he coolly shut his radar off completely. He closed his eyes, took a deep breath and let "the feeling" overwhelm him, blast through him, take him apart and make him whole again.

When he opened his eyes, he knew he could carry out this attack entirely on instinct.

Then he saw them. First, there were the MIGs. At least two dozen of them, all of them painted shiny black and riding out front, looking for any opposition.

Next came the Mirages—20 of the French-built fighter-bombers, each one armed to the teeth with Exocet missiles. Then came 32 SU-17 Fitters—the Russian-built fighter-bomber he and his squadron faced in the battle over Europe. He was certain that no Family pilot had enough smarts to fly such a hot-shit jet. That led him to the only other conclusion. There were Soviet pilots behind the controls. The rats had come out of their holes.

The remaining 30 or so planes were made up of rogues—F-104 Starfighters, F-100 Super Sabres, some A-4s, a few A-7s, even some ancient F-94s. The planes in this rogue group had one thing in common: they were all types of aircraft favored by the air pirates. The circle was thus closed, he thought. The Family and the Soviets had finally openly teamed up with the aerial bandits.

The enemy aircraft were flying in a tight formation, spread out over two miles. It was a tactic indicating they were expecting to be intercepted. He knew his plane was already showing up on their radar systems, but he could have cared less. He was willing to let them use their electronic eyes for this fight. He would use his own.

He was 15 miles from them and closing when he put the '16 into a steep dive. Within a half minute, the enemy formation was right above him, but no fighters had broken off from the main group to chase him. That was exactly what he wanted. It told him that a Soviet pilot was the group leader and he was using inflexible Soviet tactics. The crude Soviet military way of thinking discouraged individual shows of initiative. Junior officers, whether they were on the ground or in the air, had to adhere to the higher officers' plans, no matter how flawed or ill-conceived. The goose-stepping, group-think spoke of everything wrong with the Soviet mind, and it had infected their system ever since they staged their completely phony revolution back in 1917. In this case, the infection had turned into a disease—a deadly disease.

On the other hand, Hunter was an individual. He thought for himself. That was the very heart of his people. He was more than a number. He was a human being. He could act and react as his instincts and experience and his inner vision told him to. He was free in his actions. They were slaves to theirs. He knew the formation would stick together no matter what. It was their biggest mistake.

He let the attackers pass over him, then put the F-16 into a wicked climb. There were heavy cloud banks all the way back to Football City. He would use them to his advantage. His heart was pounding, his muscles flexed. His mind was crystal clear. He took a few deep gulps of oxygen from his face mask, then reached down to the breast pocket of his flight suit. It was still there—the bulge of the neatly-folded flag. He took it out. His hand tingled when he touched it. He felt himself drawing even more power from it. He felt filled up. He folded the flag and put it away. Then, he leveled the plane off and found himself directly behind the enemy formation.

He was ready. More ready than he had ever been in his life.

"Hey Jones," he said aloud as he booted the jet up to afterburner. "I hope you're watching this . . ."

The Soviet colonel leading the flight first knew something was wrong when he saw four of his planes at the rear of his flight suddenly disappear from his radar screen. He heard the static-filled cries for help and the telltale squeals of feedback which indicated a plane had been destroyed. The next thing he knew, a red-and-white-and-blue F-16 flashed by his left wing. He never saw it coming; it had never registered on his Su-17's radar screen.

The F-16 was twisting and turning like it was in the middle of an aerial demonstration. And it was moving incredibly fast. The Soviet flight leader watched in awe as the plane, which he saw was carrying an unbelievable number of Sidewinders, shot out ahead of his formation, wheeled a 180 and headed back toward him, all in a matter of seconds.

The Soviet began screaming into his radio, "Stay tight! Stay tight!" It was as if all the jets in the formation were frozen in place. And the '16 was moving fast. *Too* fast, the Russian thought. And, still, it refused to show up on his radar screen.

The F-16 unleashed a spread of four more Sidewinders, each missile finding its mark instantly. Four more jets—a MIG, a Mirage and two Su-17s—were sent plunging toward earth. The plane then looped and disappeared into a cloud at the formation's rear, only to emerge at the front of the column yet again.

"This is impossible!" the Soviet flight leader screamed in broken English into his radio. "Are there two of them?"

His radio was filled with static and the panicky chatter of the pilots in the formation. "Two of them?"

he heard a voice come back to him. "My radar doesn't show one of them!"

Four more Sidewinders rocketed off the F-16's wings. Four more enemy planes exploded and began to fall. But this time, the wreckage of one of the doomed planes smashed into two pirate planes flying toward the rear of the column.

"*Szechezva!*" the Soviet flight leader said into his microphone. "He gets six planes with four missiles!"

Still, the formation flew on. The Soviet leader, his radar screen still blank on the attacking jet, strained his neck looking for the F-16. "Where is he?" he shouted, getting no reply from his charges. Suddenly, the Soviet was aware of something flying directly above his plane. He looked straight up and into the underside of the F-16 which was no more than 10 feet away. The Soviet panicked and put his plane into a sharp dive.

"How can this be?" the Soviet said into his microphone but to no one in particular. He watched as the F-16, turning an eight-point aerobatic turn, fired four more Sidewinders, hitting four more MIGs even though they were twisting out of the way. Then the plane accelerated and did a reverse loop so quickly, the Soviet colonel knew no pilot could stand the g-force that would be generated by such a maneuver. Yet, the F-16 flew on.

"This is not possible," he said, his brain disbelieving what his eyes were plainly showing him. "This pilot. This plane. Are they a ghost?"

The formation was still 50 miles from the target, and already 15 of the planes had been shot down. Finally, the Soviet knew he had to give the order.

"MIGs. Break formation," he called into his radio. "Break formation and attack that F-16!"

The remaining MIGs obediently broke from the stiff, boxlike flight path, paired up and began searching the sky for the attacker. Suddenly, he was coming at two of them, head on. The pair of MIGs split, but not before the F-16 delivered a burst of cannon fire, hitting both of the jets and causing them to explode. Two more MIGs vectored toward the F-16, firing two air-to-air missiles apiece before entering a large cloud bank. When they emerged, not only was the F-16 behind them, so were their missiles! The MIG pilots were frozen at their controls. How was it possible? Did the F-16 pilot actually draw the heat-seekers to him then shake them off, all in the time it took to pass through the cloud? They never figured it out. Their own missiles impacted on their exhaust pipes instantaneously, blowing them to pieces and scattering their bodies to the winds.

Four MIGs ganged up and found themselves on the mystery plane's tail. "We are chasing him now," the Soviet colonel heard one of his junior Soviet pilots say. Another cloud bank rolled by. Upon reaching the other side, the MIG pilots were astonished to see the F-16 high above them and diving in *their* direction. *"Impossible!"* one pilot screamed in Russian. The flight leader heard the sound of cannon fire over the radio, then four snaps in succession. He knew that four more of his airplanes were gone.

The air pirates flying to the rear of the column took it upon themselves to break formation. One pirate, a bandit named Rocko, found himself alone in his F-100 Super Sabre, isolated from the rest of the group.

"Why did I ever get mixed up with these crooks and Russians," he asked himself, nervously searching the sky for the F-16. He passed through a small cloud bank. When he came out, the F-16 was riding right beside him.

He was stunned. He could clearly see the pilot of the ghost plane looking back at him. The man *looked* so strange! He had a helmet on, with the dark green visor pulled down, yet Rocko could *feel* the man's eyes burning through him. The pirate felt his mind go blurry. Suddenly, a vision flashed into his head. An airliner, full of people. It was over the Great Lakes. He had shot it down. It was just for sport. The Free Canadians had hunted him ever since, but they'd never caught up to him. Now he saw inside the fiery cabin of the plane as it had fallen to earth. The people were screaming. Women. Kids. Old people. On fire. Dying. Their blood-curdling screams were coming over his headphones. *He couldn't stand it!* It was as if the pilot in the F-16 knew what he had done. The man with the burning eyes was compelling him to have the haunting vision. The screams got louder. He shook away the vision but the screaming remained. He closed his eyes, looked to his left and prayed the F-16 would be gone. He opened his eyes. It was still there.

Rocko felt a blood vessel in his head go pop. Suddenly the sky and the clouds were on fire. His plane was on fire. The F-16 was on fire. Red filled his eyes. He began to cry. He popped the canopy release lever and the bubble glass top on his F-100 flew away. The dials and switches inside the jet's cockpit instantly froze up and began to crack and burst. The force of the wind struck him, disintegrating his oxygen mask and carrying away his flight helmet.

Unprotected, the wind began to rip the flesh from his face. He was paralyzed, completely unable to move. His eyes began to clog. He began to take blood into his lungs. The pain was excruciating. He knew he was dying. Dying a death even worse than the people on the airliner he'd shot down. Worse than any of the innocent people he had killed. It was as if the pilot in the ghost plane willed him to do it. He vomited a wad of blood. Blood poured from his nose. His plane was really on fire now; the flames were catching on to his flight suit. The jet started to take the final plunge. With one last effort, Rocko managed to look to his left.

The F-16 was gone.

One by one, the Soviet flight leader saw the jets in the formation disappear. Four Mirages had simply evaporated from his radar screen. Confused and shaking, the colonel considered calling off the bombing mission. He quickly reconsidered, knowing full well the wrath of his superiors he would face if he abandoned the attack. Especially when he reported only one jet had turned them back.

The Russian collected himself and called for every remaining plane in the formation to count off. He wasn't surprised to learn that all of the pirates that hadn't been shot down had scattered and fled. He was left with 40 planes in all, a mix of Mirages, MIGs and Su-14s. Still a formidable, if confused force.

Suddenly, he caught a glimpse of the F-16 as it

streaked by off to his right. If possible, he believed it was moving even faster than before. The plane still carried eight Sidewinders, clearly evident as the plane split off and away from the main formation. Was the crazy pilot breaking off the attack?

The answer was no. In a matter of seconds, the F-16 was right below him, twisting, turning, going through impossible gyrations. The Soviet saw four flashes. Four missiles streaked by him and struck a MIG and three Mirages riding above him. The colonel had to dodge the flying debris. How can the man shoot four missiles and have them fly right by me, yet hit planes above me? He had given up trying to figure things out. What he was witnessing was metaphysical, he believed. At this point he simply wanted to unleash some bombs—one bomb—on target just to please his superiors. Then, he planned to escape, land his plane and never take to the air again.

He wouldn't live that long. Although the F-16, after firing the missiles, had passed right off his left wing, a few seconds later, it was streaking toward him from the dead right. A Sidewinder flashed from underneath the wing, and in an instant the F-16 disappeared. The missile kept coming and crashed into the canopy of the Soviet Su-17. It actually lodged there for one, long terrifying second. The Soviet was face-to-face with the tip of the Sidewinder missile. He could hear it ticking. He knew it would soon explode. The last thing he remembered before becoming one with the cosmos was the writing printed on the side of the missile. It read: "MADE IN AMERICA."

Without its leader, the attacking formation began to break up for good. Hunter was able to pick the stragglers off one-by-one, using the remaining Sidewinders, and when they were gone, the M61 cannon six-pack. Some of the enemy pilots simply ejected when they saw him coming. Others would swear they saw two of their comrades go down at once, hit by missiles fired from opposite directions. The handful that survived were permanently scarred for life. They would never dream again without seeing the ghostly F-16.

Fifty miles before the Football City airport lay a trail of wreckage of more than 60 airplanes. Not one attacker reached the target. In the years that followed, and in the many retellings, the story of how Hunter had stopped the 100 planes would pass from fact to history to legend.

CHAPTER THIRTY

He brought the battle-weary jet in for a landing at the Football City airport, its fuel tanks running dry just as the wheels touched the runway. He rolled the plane toward the nearest fuel truck. The place was strangely deserted. No radios were working. All the aircraft were gone, except for the B-58 which stood by the edge of the runway, its engines stopped cold. Off to the east, he could see columns of smoke rising from the battle scene. Every once in a while, an aircraft would break through the smoke, its guns firing, dodging anti-aircraft fire, only to plunge back into the dark abyss seconds later.

He felt completely drained, and hard-pressed to explain his action against the attacking force. The "feeling"—100 times stronger than he'd ever felt it before—had completely taken him over. He had felt as if he were disembodied and watching someone else fly the F-16, while at the same time, knowing it was him at the controls. He had performed maneuvers he knew were impossible. He had hit targets he knew were unhittable, even with the help of radar systems. And he'd gone into the battle with his turned off. With the

F-16, he had always felt as if he became part of the airplane, another cog in its machinery. This time, he felt as though the airplane became part of him. Beyond that, he found it unexplainable.

He tried to put it all into his memory banks, to be called up later and reconsidered, but he even found this nearly impossible. He felt revitalized yet drained. Nothing he had ever done compared to this. It was exhilarating and spooky at the same time. He knew he was changed forever.

The sound of a loud explosion brought him back to earth. A building less than a mile away from the airport had blown up in a cloud of fire and dust. He heard gunfire, getting closer. He saw the F-20s streaking back and forth over the fighting, still strafing, still delivering their ordnance.

The F-16 had come to a halt and he climbed out. Banging on the side of the fuel truck he could feel it still had some JP-8 left inside. He quickly unhooked the hose and started to drain the gas out of the truck and into his plane's fuel tanks.

The explosions and gunfire were getting ever nearer. He saw that most of the action looked to be centered near the Grand Stadium. The Family troops had broken through and the Free Forces were falling back toward the huge structure. Within a minute, the sky was filled with what was left of the Football City aircraft—the B-29s, the C-130s, the F-20s, the Cobras, the Stallion, even the B-25s. He knew they all must be low on fuel and ammo, but they courageously kept on fighting. Incredible what some people will risk and give up when freedom is at stake.

He had to get airborne again. His tanks filled, he

jumped back into the cockpit and started the engine. Soon, he was rolling out toward the runway again. He passed the abandoned B-58, noting the two small pools of gas around its fuel tanks. Obviously, the plane had refused to take off, so the monkeys had purged its tanks of its precious fuel.

Suddenly, his body was reverberating once again. *More airplanes. Big ones. Not fighters. Bombers. Coming this way. From the north-northeast.*

Could it actually be happening again? His instincts told him so. He switched on the '16's radar and got an electronic confirmation. A large group of planes— looked like 35 in all—was approaching from the northeast.

He was out of Sidewinders and carrying less than half a full-load of cannon ammo. But he knew he had to intercept this force, too. Almost numb, he racked his brain as he took off. Who could this be? He turned out over the airport and headed in the direction of the mystery formation. They were big planes, no doubt about that. Soviet Bear bombers? A second Family bombing mission? Revitalized Mid-Aks?

He wearily shook his head. He flew over the Grand Stadium and the scene below confirmed his worst fears. The Free Forces were retreating back into the heart of the wrecked city. He could see a number of the aircraft had crashed, knowing full well they had run out of fuel and went down fighting. The battle would soon be lost, and thus the war. Even a miracle would be hard-pressed to turn the tide. He prayed the spirit of the cause would survive after they were all gone.

He turned again and passed low over the battle

scene. Wagging his wings one last time, climbed, went full throttle and streaked toward the north to meet the incoming force of bombers.

On the ground, St. Louie himself had taken up a rifle and joined his troops in the defense of the city. They had been battling the Family reserve troops block-by-block, building-by-building, since the attackers broke through an hour before. He was firing from behind an overturned truck in the middle of a main throughfare. The air was filled with bullets, mortar shells and hand grenades. Dozer was at his side, as was Captain Crunch and his weapons officer. The famous Ace Wrecking Company F-4 had been zapped by a SAM while napalming enemy troops, but the two flyers parachuted to safety and had been fighting on the ground ever since. Their counterpart, Ace Phantom Number 2 was still airborne, strafing the invaders and providing recon information.

St. Louie's plan was to make a last stand at the Grand Stadium. The Family troops were pressing on the defenders from three sides—more than half the Free Forces' soldiers had been killed. The Family had suffered worse in numbers killed. The muddy Mississippi now ran thick with blood. But, it had always been a question of numbers—men, ammo, gallons of fuel. The Family—despite the devastating air raid on their capital—always had the numbers in their favor. St. Louie, the Father of Football City and the consummate gambler, knew the odds had always been against the Free Forces. But sometimes, you have to fight the battle even though you knew it was impossible to win. You had to make a stand, and if you died doing it, well, so be it.

The battle was at its darkest when they had heard the familiar scream of the F-16. The red-white-and-blue fighter had flashed over them, tipped its wings and roared off. For Hunter, it was an action of last camaraderie. For the troops fighting on the ground, it was like a bolt of lighting.

"Jesus Christ!" St. Louie had yelled when he saw the F-16 streak over. "That boy is *still* alive!"

Even the defending troops paused a minute to look up when the F-16 appeared. "The son-of-a-bitch is still flying!" a cheer went up. "Hunter is still with us!"

"Where the hell are the Family airplanes?" Dozer asked St. Louie, as he reloaded his weapon. "I thought they would have iced the airport by now."

"There were at least a hundred of them," St. Louie told him, firing his M-16 at two Family troopers as they ran toward a doorway right across the street. "Even Hunter couldn't have shot them all down!"

"Don't be so sure," Crunch said, managing a smile. "The Wingman ain't exactly human when it comes to flying."

"Amen to that," Dozer agreed. "But we were expecting the guy to come up with one too many miracles."

"You're right," St. Louie said, firing another burst and pinning the Family soldiers in the doorway. "But no one can ever say he didn't give it all he had."

Hunter watched the blips on his radar screen get

439

bigger. These were heavy bombers, he knew. Three columns of 12 each, with three bombers in the lead. They were flying high—close to 50,000 feet—indicating they had traveled a long way. He checked his weapons reserve. Probably two minutes of cannon ammo left, then that would be it.

The sun was just passing its high mark. "High noon," he thought. "High noon on the longest day."

Then he saw them. Faint outlines at first, trailing thick, white contrails, getting larger by the second. He climbed to 52,000, so he could dive on attack on his first pass. The shapes of the bombers were getting clearer now, their outlines turning distinct. He could hear their rumbling. He could feel the disturbance in the airstream they were creating. They were about twenty miles away when he squinted his eyes and took a long look.

"Oh, God!" he yelled. *"They're B-52s!"*

The B-52 Stratofortress was the heaviest of heavy bombers. The huge jet airplanes—long thin fuselage with wide, swept back wings supporting eight engines—were the workhorses of the Americans from the 1950s, through Viet Nam and up to the advent of the sleek, sophisticated B-1s. The B-52s had fought in World War III, over Europe and against the Soviet Navy in the Pacific. Louie St. Louie had once been a pilot in a B-52.

And now here were 39 of them. Heading for Football City. They were all painted one color—off white with lettering and numbers on their tails and wings which he couldn't make out. He knew '52 was capable of carrying up to 50 10,000-pound bombs—that was a half-million pounds of bombs per plane. No wonder that back in 'Nam, a B-52 strike caused the equivalent of a minor earthquake. And now the Free Forces were going to have 20 million pounds of TNT dropped on their heads? Football City would become a crater.

Hunter knew he couldn't stop them all, so he would try to stop the leaders. He put the F-16 into a steep dive and lined up his cannon sights on the lead plane . . .

"This is Big Thunder Leader calling F-16 . . . "

Hunter's radio crackled with the words just as he began his dive to attack.

" '16! '16! Break off! Break-off!"

They had spotted him. He was still closing in fast. The voice on the radio sounded familiar.

" '16! WE ARE FRIENDLIES! BREAK OFF!"

Hunter's mind started to click. Friendlies? The voice is what did it. He broke off the attack before firing a shot.

He reached for his radio. "Go ahead, Big Thunder. ID yourself."

"Hawk! It's me. J.T.!" the voice came back.

By this time, Hunter had swept past the huge bombers, and was turning 180 to close in on them again.

"J.T.?" Hunter radioed. "J.T. *Toomey*?"

"The one and only, Hawk," was the answer.

Hunter pulled up and leveled off beside the big bomber leading the formation. For the first time he could read the lettering on the side of the B-52s. It read: "Northern Pacific & Southern California Strategic Air Company."

"J.T.," Hunter said cautiously. "If this is you,

441

when was the last time we saw each other?"

"Jonesville, Hawker my man," the voice came back. "We had just iced some rent-an-army seaborne troops. I went off to sortie up to Boston and ran into more choppers than a 100-year-old dentist."

Hunter had to admit that only J.T. spoke like that. And the voice was the same. If it was a trick, it was an elaborate one.

Still Hunter remained cautious.

"Let me put it this way," the voice came back on. "Where the hell have you been, Hunter, my boy? I thought we were all supposed to link up out on the Coast?"

Hunter was surprised. The voice was right. The remnants of ZAP *were* supposed to head for the West Coast and re-form. He just assumed no one had made it.

"Hawk?" another voice came on the radio. "This is Ben Wa. No jive, Hunter. Your reinforcements have arrived."

"Reinforcements?" was all Hunter could say.

"That's straight, Hawk," the voice claiming to be Wa answered. "Your little war here is the talk of the land. You've got more people pulling for you than you know about. We've been having troubles ourselves. Minor stuff, compared to you, but it took us a while to muster up enough of these big boys to come and help out."

The strange flight was approaching Football City. Hunter had to decide to trust the voices or start shooting. He opted to trust them.

"We're loaded for bear, Hawk," J.T.'s voice came back on. "Just tell us where to put it."

It was just beginning to sink in. The awesome firepower of the B-52 formation was on his side. His former ZAP mates had come through in the end. The miracle had arrived.

"Roger, Big Thunder," Hunter called back. "Follow me."

CHAPTER THIRTY-ONE

After several anxious minutes, Hunter finally got through to the Free Forces' troops on the ground.

"This is Major Hunter," he told the radio operator, one of Dozer's Marines who happened to be monitoring the frequency. "Pass the word. This is five-by-five. Air strike coming in. A big one. All friendlies have to get inside the Stadium now."

"This is Tango Red, I copy you, Major, five-by-five," the operator said. "Let me repeat. Confirm you say big strike coming against enemy troops?"

"That's a roger," Hunter replied. He had just arrived over the battle zone, having shot ahead of the B-52 formation. He was hoping he wasn't too late. "Strike is in ten minutes. Counting right now. Please advise of your situation. I need a right-on fix on enemy positions."

"I roger you, sir," the Marine replied. "And I have you in visual. I am passing your orders along, and opening up this channel for our receivers."

There was a half minute of silence. Hunter booted it and flew low over the smoking city flying fast enough to discourage the Family gunners from taking a shot at him. He did a quick 180 over the river and headed back toward the Stadium.

"Major? This is Tango Red," the radio crackled to life. "All ground stations now tuned to you. Enemy drive has stopped. Repeat, enemy has halted and is in place. Possible regrouping."

"Please repeat, Tango Red," Hunter called back. "Do I copy enemy in place? Not moving?"

"That's a roger," came the reply.

Odd, Hunter thought. The Family was right on the verge of completely overwhelming the defenders and winning the battle. Why stop?

But then again, Hunter thought, why fight it? He'd just got lucky.

"Okay, Tango Red," Hunter replied. He knew the kit with the radio was a good one. All of Dozer's guys were. "What are your present defense perimeters?"

" '16," the voice came back. "Our positions are completely surrounded. Our lines are static. We control area two blocks square around Stadium. And that's it. Understand fall back to that position. My officers copy."

"Tell them they have to move quickly," Hunter told him. "This is a B-52 strike. Coming in now less than seven."

"We copy, sir," the Marine replied, his voice going up a level in excitement. "B-52s sir? Perfect time, repeat, conditions A-OK for strike. Enemy still in place. We are pulling back."

Hunter came down low over the Grand Stadium. He saw the Marine was as good as his word. There was a lull in the battle. Thousands of Free Forces' troops were pouring into the huge arena, battered and burning as it was. Above the grandstands the tattered Football City flag was still flying. He could almost feel the excitement rising up from the troops below. He was sure most of them had given up the battle— and the cause—as lost. And now they had a shot. The enemy had surrounded them in the most protected structure around. What the hell, the place could once hold 250,000. If there were 10,000 friendly soldiers left, there would be room to spare.

Around the Stadium, outside the two-block buffer zone, he could see tens of thousands of Family troops. Some were hunkered down, waiting in foxholes, door-ways, wrecked buildings. Others were sitting in smok-ing, idle tanks or APCs waiting for the go-word. There were even more in the rear area—just milling around, waiting. Waiting for the word to close in, tighten the circle and massacre the last of the Football City defenders.

For Hunter, the situation was this: He would have to call in the air strike on top of the surrounding enemy troops, yet save the soldiers inside the stadium. He knew it could get tricky, but it was a gamble he had to take.

The B-52s were now less than five minutes away. Hunter had already radioed warning of the strike to the other friendly aircraft in the area and they grate-fully evacuated the airspace. Now, he contacted the B-52s and began transmitting target information to each one of them. This was the critical part. He had to quickly take into consideration everything from wind direction and speed to the rotation of the earth. A reading in error of just a few seconds to bomb release and the Grand Stadium would go up in smoke with the rest of the city.

Hunter bypassed using his on-board computer—he preferred to calculate the target coordinates in his head. People's lives hung in the balance of accurate numbers. Using his own brain was the only real way that he could have trust in them.

His mental calculations complete, he called the final coordinates for the B-52 pilots, along with exact positions, release points and fusing instructions for each bomber. They would strike at concentrations of Family troops surrounding the stadium, then walk their bombs all the way back and across the river to sweep the enemy positions on the east bank of the Mississippi. He was acting as the sole forward air controller. The B-52s' bombardiers would drop only on his command. It was as if he alone had his hand on the bomb release lever. Once pushed, 20 million pounds of bombs would rain down—and around—the Free Forces. He knew he had never make such a crucial call before.

His radio suddenly crackled. "Hunter! Come in!" Hunter recognized St. Louie's voice.

"Go ahead," Hunter radioed back.

"Hawk, we're just about all in the stadium. Few stragglers. I wish the damn dome was working so we could close it up, but it's been knocked out. Do we have two minutes?"

"Just about," he replied. "Then get 'em all down on the ground and covered up. And have them stay that way."

"Roger, Hawk," St. Louie called back. "And when you finally come down from up there, will you please

447

tell me how in hell you came up with a B-52 strike?"

"When it's over," Hunter answered. "I'll be glad to."

The B-52s arrived over Football City two minutes later. Hunter counted down to the very last second, re-checked each of the 39 bombers' individual coordinates, took a deep breath and radioed: "Bombs away? Now!"

High above, the bombardiers started unleashing the strings of 1000-pounders onto the enemy-occupied streets around the Grand Stadium. Those huddling on the playing field inside instantly felt the ground begin to shake violently. Shock waves filled the air. The wind above them became hot and like a hurricane. The noise of the explosions around them were so loud, many found their ears bleeding. Most were too nervous to care or notice. They were too busy praying that a stray string of bombs wouldn't come down on them.

The enemy troops on the receiving end of the tremendous bombing never knew what happened. The B-52s were so high, they were no more than glints of white in the sky, followed by miles of contrails. The Family's final drive was still inexplicably held up. At the moment the hundreds of 1000-pound bombs came crashing down on them, many of the Family troopers, smelling the bloody lust of victory, were griping that their commanders told them to halt their advance. The majority would never know why they were stopped just minutes away from total victory.

The bombs continued to fall for five frightening

minutes. The aftershocks of the strike were so powerful, portions of the stadium's walls threatened to crumble. But the huge arena stayed together. Bits of debris and sparks rained down on the huddled defenders, starting several small fires. Few of the soldiers had ever heard anything so loud, so violent. The thundering roar of the bombing *was* to all who heard it, the very sound of death. The Free Forces' soldiers just thanked the spirits that Hunter was above, watching over them.

Then it was over. The last of the 1000-pound bombs exploded across the river. The reverberations echoed and died. The low, rumbling noise of the departing B-52 formation slowly faded away and then were gone completely. The soldiers inside the stadium cautiously dared to look up. Had they really made it? They listened. Something was strange. For the first time in what seemed like a century, Football City was quiet.

One by one, the defenders rose to their feet. Was it really over? They wondered. Their officers told them to stay put for the moment. St. Louie, Dozer and several others headed for the massive gates which led into the Stadium and pushed them open.

They were horrified. The entire section of the city from the Stadium to river—more than a mile of what was once urban sprawl—was completely obliterated. Flattened. Leveled down to the curbstones. There were few fires, some smoke, a million tons of rubble and a layer of dust hanging over everything. But beyond that, there was nothing over four feet standing.

"My beautiful city. Now it's Dresden," St. Louie said, almost unconsciously recalling pictures of that battered German city after the Allied bombers had gotten through with it.

"Worse," Dozer said, taking in the massive destruction. "Hiroshima. Without the rads." Even the battle-hardened Marine choked at the utter devastation.

One by one, then in groups, the soldiers of the Free Forces wandered out of the Stadium, their mouths hanging in awe. There was no need to fear being shot at by the enemy. There simply was no more enemy. No one could have lived through the massive carpet bombing. Not unless they had a guardian angel.

"Only Hunter could have directed a strike on a dime like this," Dozer told St. Louie.

They looked up and saw the F-16 high above them. It started to move among the fading white contrails of the now-long gone B-52 bombers. Carefully, the F-16 began spouting its own contrail. As the victorious survivors watched, the tiny jet carved out a miles-long letter "W" in the sky above Football City.

The word flashed across the continent almost immediately: tiny Football City had actually defeated the once-powerful New Chicago Family. The free governments remaining on the continent—especially Texas—breathed a sigh of relief. Freedom-loving citizens everywhere had been rooting for Football City although the former super-resort city had definitely been tagged as the underdog.

But sometimes, the underdogs win.

No telling or retelling of the story would be complete without detailing the heroics of Hunter—"The Wingman"—who stole jets from the air pirates for

Football City's air force, then went on to bomb New Chicago, singlehandedly stop a 100-plane bombing raid against the Free Forces, then direct a B-52 strike to win the battle on the ground. It was the stuff of legends, and he had just become one. Soon, his name was on the lips of every fighter—friend and foe alike—across the land.

Only three B-52s of the Northern Pacific and Southern California Strategic Air Company landed at the Football City airport after the bombing mission. The others linked up with their KC-135 flying tankers, refueled in the air, and headed back to the West Coast.

Hunter was on hand at the airport when the three big jets came in. The lead jet pulled up and came to a rest. The first person to emerge from the escape hatch underneath the cockpit was no other than J.T. "Socket" Toomey. Sunglasses cemented to the bridge of his nose, not a hair out of place. Ben Wa climbed out next. The hula-hula boy was all smiles as usual. Hunter sprinted to the side of the plane to greet them.

"You really ought to get out to the Coast, Hunter, my man," J.T. told him, pumping his hand and surveying the battle-scarred conditions of the Football City airport. "I think you need a change of surroundings."

"Great shooting, Hawk," Ben Wa beamed. "Can't do tricks without the Wingman."

Hunter shook his head and grinned. "Well, you guys provided me with the biggest surprise of my life when I heard friendly voices coming from those B-

52s."

"Oh, you ain't got the biggest surprise yet," J.T. said, mysteriously. "Get a load of this."

He was pointing to a third figure emerging from the B-52's escape hatch. The man was of thin, wiry build. A familiar hair and face. Even more familiar smile and voice. He walked forward, his hand extended. "Major Hunter, I presume?"

Hunter almost dropped on the spot. It was the general.

"General Jones," the man said, shaking Hunter's hand. "*Davy* Jones."

Hunter came speeding back to reality. "The general's twin brother," he said finally.

"That's right," Jones said.

Hunter had never known such identical-looking twins. It was spooky to stand and talk to a man that looked *exactly* like the one he had buried months before.

"I've heard a lot about you, sir," Hunter told him.

"And I about you, Major," Jones returned. Then he leaned in and whispered to Hunter. "I know Seth is dead. Even though I was out on the Coast, I knew—I felt—the exact second he died."

"He died a hero, sir," Hunter said, a slight lump of emotion rising in his throat. "I was with him. He gave his life to ice a lot of Mid-Aks—Mid-Aks who would have been here, fighting us today—if it weren't for him."

"I know," Jones said sadly. "I just wanted to thank you, Major. My brother . . . he spoke of you highly and often."

The conversation could go no further. Both men

were filled up with the memories of the late, great General Seth Jones. It was almost unbearably sad.

St. Louie and Dozer saved the day. They arrived beside the big bomber, and Hunter broke the silence by introducing everyone around.

"You will stay for the victory celebration, won't you?" St. Louie asked the B-52 airmen.

"Wouldn't miss it for the world," the other general said, breaking into a wide, familiar grin.

The people began returning to Football City the next day. After weeks of hiding in the hills, they were glad to reclaim their city, utterly devastated as it was. Food, medicine and other supplies started coming in via planes from Texas and Free Canada. Appropriately enough, the first plane in the Texas airlift was the huge C-5 Hunter had used in the early stages of rescuing the ZAP pilots.

The next night they finally solved the mystery of why the Family commanders had halted their advance just as they were about to overwhelm the outnumbered Free Forces.

"If you can believe it," St. Louie told Hunter and Dozer over a round of drinks amidst the rubble that was once his government house and headquarters. "I still had two agents in New Chicago. They just got in. Took them two days to float down the river.

"They said that right about the time we were about to be overrun, someone delivered an air strike on old Chicago."

"What?" Hunter had to hear it again to make sure it wasn't the whiskey.

"There's more. Not only did they pull this in daylight. They managed to ice the Black Tower."

"Holy shit!" Dozer said. "The place must have been thick with SAMs."

"So that's what happened," Hunter said, the information starting to sink in. "They lost their central command. With the Black Tower knocked out, the front line commanders couldn't take the initiative and move themselves."

"That's a stupid way of doing things," St. Louie laughed.

"That's also the *Soviet* way of doing things," Hunter said. "No freedom of thought. No freedom of action. Feelings are repressed. Imagination stifled. The Family was foolish to listen to them."

"But," Dozer said. "Who the hell did the air strike?"

St. Louie smiled. "Can't be certain," he said with a wink. "But my guys said the attacking aircraft were F-105 Thunderchiefs."

"Fitzgerald!" Hunter yelled. "Why that old Irishman! Neutral, my ass. There's never been an Irishman born who was neutral about anything!"

Two hours later they were able to raise the Aerodrome on the Free Forces' only working long-range radio transmitter.

"We owe you one, Mike," Hunter told him in all sincerity.

"Don't be foolish, Hawker, me boy," Hunter heard

the solid Irish brogue come back. "It was business. If the Family had won, they would have been sitting right in the middle of one of my most lucrative air routes. I couldn't allow that, now could I?"

"Sure," Hunter said, going along with his friend. "And if you think I believe that, you can take my wings, too."

"I got some more news for you, Hawker," Fitzgerald continued. "You might like to know that the Mid-Aks have regrouped. What's left of them, that is. Some new people have taken over from the 'Ak old guard. They call themselves The Circle. Quite mysterious. Apparently they've got some allies, too. Pirates. A few Family members, those who were lucky enough not to be in Chicago. Possibly some Russians and even freaks from the Badlands. The whole bunch of them met for the first time a few days ago, my spies tell me. Somewhere in old Delaware. And the first thing they agreed on was to put a price on your head."

"How much?" Hunter had to ask. It wasn't often a man got to know his true worth.

"Are ye ready for this?" Fitz asked with a chuckle that could be heard through the crackle of the radio transmission. "One half *billion* dollars in gold!"

"A half *billion*?" Hunter was shocked. He knew he had made some enemies. But a half billion dollars worth?

"That's correct, Hawker," Fitz said back. "Five hundred million dollars. After you boys did a number on Boston, and with Baltimore gone, all the 'Aks have left is money—the gold from Knox. Now they're willing to part with it just to get your head on a platter."

"I guess I should be flattered," Hunter said.

"Aye, you should," Fitz said. "And you should also be keeping an eye out over your shoulder. There's a lot of bums out there who'd be kings with a half billion in gold in their pockets."

Hunter turned serious. "Any other . . . news?" he asked.

"About Dominique?" Fitz said. "No. Sorry. I sent three of my best men up to Montreal as you asked. They found nothing. The last time anyone saw her, she was getting off the Beechcraft Jones sent up. It's like she disappeared into thin air, Hawker. Don't worry, though. We'll keep looking."

There was a brief silence. "Thanks, Mike," Hunter finally said.

"Well," Fitzgerald radioed back. "I've always been a sucker for the good cause, be it blasting hoodlums or finding lost girlfriends."

The next day was the victory celebration. Those who survived gathered in and around the Grand Stadium. Huge barbecue pits were dug and tons of Texas beef cooked. The Canadians delivered a plane filled with cases of whiskey. The Coasters sent wine and fruit. Fitzgerald himself arrived with five 747s filled with more than 1000 of the best-looking B-girls the Aerodrome could offer. The day's events included aerial demonstrations by the ex-ZAP pilots performing in the F-20s, and fly-bys by the surviving aircraft of the Free Forces air corps. Most of the pilots and all of the planes were in Football City to stay. In a matter of a few months, St. Louis had gone from no air corps to having the best equipped and manned on the continent.

The party atmosphere enlivened throughout the day and carried over into the night. A huge makeshift stage had been set up and all the principals of the fight were seated there. The different groups of soldiers—from the Football City regulars to the Free Canadians and Texans to the volunteers—all stood in front of the stage. Citizens—nearly fifty thousand of them—filled out the rest of the crowd.

Hunter looked at the soldiers on the stage. Sitting near him were the four pilots of the Ace Wrecking Company, next to them sat the Cobra Brothers. The former POW ZAP pilots and mechanics came next, along with Fitzgerald and the ground crew from the Aerodrome. Dozer's officers were close by, their commander decked out in Marine dress blues and smiling from ear-to-ear.

The members of the Sea Stallion assault team were seated directly to his right; General Davy Jones, three of his B-52 pilots, plus T.J. and Ben Wa, sat to his left.

St. Louie was speaking to the crowd over a crude but effective public address system.

"We owe our very lives to the men sitting on this stage and to the armies that stand before it," he told the crowd, working the masses like a good politician. "It makes my heart feel good that there is still some humanity left on this continent."

The crowd greeted his words with thunderous applause. Many were holding candles or torches and many waved Football City flags.

And then suddenly, St. Louie was saying: "And

now I want you to meet a man who fought like a hundred—or even a thousand men. I'm sure there isn't one among us who would disagree that without this man, it wouldn't have worked out the way it did.

"Ladies and gentlemen . . . Major Hawk Hunter!"

The next thing Hunter knew, he was on. Standing before the microphones, looking out on the sea of faces and candles and flags. The applause and shouts of "Hunter! Hunter!" rivaled the racket of the B-52 strike.

Hunter began slowly. "I didn't do anything that any one of you out there wouldn't have done if you had the chance."

His voice was echoing throughout the Grand Stadium. The eerie glow of the thousands of candles gave the ceremony a religious look.

"People around the world—especially in occupied Europe—would like to think that we here have short memories," he went on. "They would like to think that we have already forgotten about what this country was like before they betrayed us.

"Well, I haven't forgotten. Have you?"

His answer came back, loud and strong, from the voices of nearly 70,000 patriots "No!"

"I haven't forgotten that once a man could walk just about anywhere in this country and be free. I haven't forgotten that once a person could see what they wanted, hear what they wanted, read what they wanted, think what they wanted.

"And I remember the time—and it wasn't so long ago—when it was NOT against some law to mention the name of your own country. When you could fly its colors proudly. When you didn't have to worry about

458

who was looking over your shoulder, ready to pull a trigger when your back was turned."

The cheers from the crowd grew louder.

"Well, I think this is as good a time as any to say that we just aren't going to put up with those conditions any more!"

More cheers.

"We can all break the law tonight! Break the New Order! Smash it! It was bogus anyway!"

More thunderous cheers.

"Tonight. We can throw off the chains! We can send a message to those who would enslave us that we aren't that easy. That we still pull together like the old days. Before the New Order. I say GODDAMN the New Order!"

Deafening cheers rocked the stadium.

"We can't be afraid any more to say it! We should all say it. Together. We can break the spell. Break it now! Forever!"

The cheering was monstrous, sustained.

He reached into his breast pocket. The familiar shape of the flag was still there. His mind raced as he took it out and carefully unfolded it. The Thunderbirds. The space shuttle. The War. The trip back across the ocean. New York. The mountain. Jonesville. The 'Aks. Baltimore. A mountain in Vermont. The Aerodrome. The Pitts. Football City. In the air over New Chicago. The final battle.

Three faces came into his mind. One was poor Saul Wackerman. One was the general. One was Dominique. Where was she now? Alive or dead? Would he ever know?

He held the unfolded flag and looked at its colors.

459

A rush ran through him as he stared at it. To think something as beautiful as this was once "illegal."

Never again!

"Never again!" he yelled into the microphone to the ear-splitting roar of the crowd. He slowly raised the flag above his head. "Never again shall we be afraid to hold this flag up proudly . . ."

He took a deep breath.

". . . Or say the words: I am a citizen of the UNITED STATES OF AMERICA!"

The cheering turned into a chant. "USA! USA! USA! USA!" It echoed throughout the battered stadium and out across the countryside.

It would be a long time before Football City was quiet again.

THE SURVIVALIST SERIES
by Jerry Ahern